PARALLEL MYTHS

Parallel Myths

J. F. Bierlein

BALLANTINE BOOKS • NEW YORK

Copyright © 1994 by J. F. Bierlein

All rights reserved under International and Pan-American Copyright Conventions. Published in the United States by Ballantine Books, a division of Random House, Inc., New York, and simultaneously in Canada by Random House of Canada Limited, Toronto.

Permissions acknowledgments appear on page 338, which constitutes an extension of the copyright page.

Library of Congress Cataloging-in-Publication Data

Bierlein, J. F.
    Parallel myths / John Francis Bierlein.
        p.   cm.
    Includes bibliographical references and index.
    ISBN 0-345-38146-7
    1. Mythology—Comparative studies.   I. Title.
BL311.B54   1993   93-22128
291.1'3—dc20   CIP

Cover design by Judy Herbstman

Manufactured in the United States of America

First Edition: November 1994

10 9 8 7 6 5 4 3 2 1

To my mother,
Veronica LaFleur Parrent Bierlein
(1931–1992),
and
Robert G. Hirschfeld

Contents

Acknowledgments

My sincere thanks to:

My parents, John and Veronica Bierlein, for endless hours of dedicated editing, reading, moral support, and friendship above and beyond the call of parental duty;

My mother in her own right, as she died during the production of this book, for her gift to me of the love of reading and the life of the mind;

Robert G. Hirschfeld, for his consistent friendship and encouragement;

My wife, Heather C. Diehl;

Iris Bass and Lesley Malin Helm, my editors at Ballantine Books, for their assistance, advice, and consistently good humor;

My sister, Cheryl Bierlein Fowler;

Renee, for her encouragement and assistance;

My friends at the Hoyt Library, Saginaw, Michigan: Vi, Fay, Ernestine, Pat, and Kate, among others;

My high school English teachers: Kathy Hughes, John Kiley, Erik Swanson, and Art Loesel, for their introduction to the love of literature;

Many other friends, including Maggie Rossiter of the *Saginaw News*, Sam and Ilona Hirschfeld Koonce, Dr. Steven Hirschfeld, Dr. Bill and Darlene Underhill, and many others.

Preface

Myth is an eternal mirror in which we see ourselves. Myth has something to say to everyone, as it has something to say about everyone: it is everywhere and we only need to recognize it.

This book is for the person who would not normally think about mythology, let alone read a book on the subject. Based on the premise that to understand myths is an important step toward understanding ourselves, it was written as an invitation to the reading of myths and recognizing the mythic in our daily lives.

Throughout the 1980s and into the present decade, popular interest in mythology has been continually on the rise. It is being discovered by a new generation, in the way it has spoken to countless generations past. The popularity of the books of Joseph Campbell, the televised Peter Brook dramatization of the Indian epic *The Mahabharata*, and the prominence of myth in such radio and television programs as "Northern Exposure" are all evidence of this current fascination.

There have been numerous studies of myth and mythology. However, many of them, though fascinating, scholarly, and comprehensive, are written in language not readily accessible to the average thinking reader. They are not presented in a way that speaks directly to the person who is only just discovering the subject. I have felt that a "reader-friendly" approach to the subject is necessary, though it is my hope that my book will not be the last stop in the reader's exploration of myth, but a first step.

I have been intrigued by mythology since childhood. It began many years ago when my teacher read to us from Thomas Bulfinch's *Mythology*, and it grew through my high school and university years, and as I became acquainted with the writings of Joseph Campbell, Mircea Eliade, Paul Ricoeur, and others. This enjoyment has been complemented by a delight in opera; seeing the great myths presented in operatic form has made them more alive and given me new insights.

For most people, "mythology" means Greek or Norse mythology. However, this book goes beyond these sources to include myths from Africa, the Americas, Asia, and Oceania. Exposure limited to European literature does not allow the reader to see the fascinating parallels that exist among the myths of widely separated cultures.

Such parallels demonstrate that human beings everywhere have much in common; the "primitive" and the "modern" are not all that different as we might think. In reading these myths, the gaps between cultures narrow to reveal what is constant and universal in human experience.

I hope that you discover this fascinating bond of humanity while being thoroughly entertained.

—J. F. Bierlein

*Hamilton, Ontario, Canada, 1989 and
Frankenmuth, Michigan, 1993*

PART ONE

AN INVITATION TO MYTH

Life is a narrow vale between the cold
And barren peaks of two eternities.
We strive in vain to look beyond the heights,
We cry aloud; the only answer
Is the echo of our wailing cry.
From the voiceless lips of the unreplying dead
There comes no word; but in the night of death
Hope sees a star, and listening love can hear
The rustle of a wing.
These myths were born of hopes, and fears and tears,
And smiles; and they were touched and colored
By all there is of joy and grief between
The rosy dawn of birth and death's sad night;
They clothed even the stars with passion,
And gave to gods the faults and frailties
Of the sons of men. In them the winds
And waves were music, and all the lakes and streams,
Springs, mountains, woods, and perfumed dells,
Were haunted by a thousand fairy forms.
                              —Robert G. Ingersoll (1833–1899)

1. An Introduction

Was unterschiedet
  Götter von Menschen?
Dass viele Wellen
  Vor jenen wandeln
Ein ewiger Strom
  Uns hebt die Welle
Verschlingt die Welle
  Und wir versinken.

What is the difference
  Between gods and humans?
That many waves before each
  from an eternal stream
The waves lift us up;
  the waves overcome us,
and we are swept away.
                    —Goethe

WHAT IS MYTH?

What is myth? Let's begin by telling one.

Centuries ago in China, a young boy asked his grandfather how the world was created. The grandfather responded in the same way that his own grandfather had many years before:

> Once there was only a great chaos, Hundun. There were two emperors: Hu, the Emperor of the Northern Sea, and Shu, the Emperor of the Southern Sea. When they found Hundun, he was an incomplete being, lacking the seven orifices necessary for sight, hearing, eating and speech, breathing, smell, reproduction, and

3

elimination. So, zapping him with thunderbolts, they bored one
of these orifices every day for seven days. Finally, Hundun died
in the process. The names Hu and Shu combine to form the
word *Hu-shu*, or "lightning." Thus the work of creation began
when lightning pierced chaos.

Within our own century a strikingly similar view of the creation was
presented as a scientific theory. Harold S. Urey, the 1934 Nobel
Prize winner in Chemistry, speculated that the origins of life might
have been in the action of some kind of energy, perhaps lightning, on
the primordial atmosphere of the earth. Whether or not Urey was familiar with this Chinese myth we do not know, yet his explanation
echoed the one told by the Chinese grandfather.

In 1953, a graduate student of Urey named Stanley L. Miller put this
theory to the test in an experiment. He prepared two glass globes, one
of which contained the gases believed to have composed the early atmosphere of the earth, and the other to collect gases formed as a result
of his experiment. He activated the gases with "lightning" in the form
of 60,000 volts of electricity. To his surprise, some of the materials that
gathered in the second globe included nucleotides, organic components
of the amino acids that join together to make DNA, which is the basic
building block of all life. This was the first time that nucleotides had
been produced in any manner independent of a living organism.

On first reading, the Chinese myth sounds quite primitive. It is
anthropomorphic; that is to say, the characters are natural forces personified. The two elements that form lightning are referred to as "emperors," and chaos is portrayed in human form. This "primitive"
myth, however, converges with advanced and sophisticated speculations on the origins of life. This becomes our first clue as to what
myth is. It is the earliest form of science: speculation on how the
world came into being.

To the man on the street, however, the word *myth* brings to mind
lies, fables, or widely believed falsehoods. On the nightly news, a
health expert speaks of the need to "eliminate commonly held myths
about AIDS." In this context, *myth* is used to mean "a misconception"—in this case, even a dangerous misconception. But
myth, in the sense that we use it in this book, often stands for truth.

A myth is often something that only begins to work where our own five senses end.

If myth were only a collection of stories, of falsehoods, why then does it continue to fascinate us? Why has myth persisted for centuries? As we shall see, a single definition of *myth* is never adequate, for it is many things operating at many levels.

As we have seen, myth is the first fumbling attempt to explain *how* things happen, the ancestor of science. It is also the attempt to explain *why* things happen, the sphere of religion and philosophy. It is a history of *pre*history, telling us what might have happened before written history. It is the earliest form of literature, often an oral literature. It told ancient people who they were and the right way to live. Myth was and still is the basis of morality, governments, and national identity.

Myth is hardly the sole property of the "primitive, prescientific" mind. Our lives today are saturated with myth, its symbols, language, and content, all of which are part of our common heritage as human beings. Fables, fairy tales, literature, epics, tales told around campfires, and the scriptures of great religions are all packages of myth that transcend time, place, and culture. Individual myths themselves are strikingly similar between cultures vastly separated by geography. This commonality helps us to recognize the beauty of the unity in human diversity: We share something with all other peoples in all other times.

Now we can begin to make some very general statements about myth.

- Myth is a constant among all human beings in all times. The patterns, stories, even details contained in myth are found everywhere and among everyone. This is because myth is a shared heritage of ancestral memories, related consciously from generation to generation. Myth may even be part of the structure of our unconscious mind, possibly encoded in our genes.
- Myth is a telling of events that happened before written history, and of a sense of what is to come. Myth is the thread that holds past, present, and future together.

- Myth is a unique use of language that describes the realities beyond our five senses. It fills the gap between the images of the unconscious and the language of conscious logic.
- Myth is the "glue" that holds societies together; it is the basis of identity for communities, tribes, and nations.
- Myth is an essential ingredient in all codes of moral conduct. The rules for living have always derived their legitimacy from their origins in myth and religion.
- Myth is a pattern of beliefs that give meaning to life. Myth enables individuals and societies to adapt to their respective environments with dignity and value.

LANGUAGE AND MYTH

Our language is permeated with terms taken from the myths, especially Greek and Roman myths, that we use daily without ever thinking of their origins. To drive into the city, you may have to deal with the *chaos* (from the Greek myth describing the primordial state of things before creation) of traffic, while listening to the top-40 song "I'm Your *Venus*" (from the name of the Roman goddess of beauty) or thinking about buying *Nike* (named for the Greek goddess of victory) athletic shoes or perhaps a *Mars* bar (named for the Roman god of war). No doubt the tires on your car are made of *vulcanized* rubber (from Vulcan, the Roman patron god of metalworking). On your journey, you may pass a *museum* (named in honor of the Muses, patroness spirits of culture in Greek mythology); perhaps next *Saturday* (named for Saturn, the Roman god of agriculture) you will find some time to stop in.

The news comes over the radio. In *Europe* (named for Europa, a mortal woman who had a liaison with the Greek god Zeus), preparations are being made for the *Olympics* (a modern revival of the games held at Olympus, the home of the Greek gods), even as diplomats in *London* (named for Lugh, a Celtic sun-god) are discussing what will happen to all those *Thor* (the Norse thunder god), *Titan* (named for Greek giants), and *Jupiter* (the Roman name for Zeus) missiles.

When you are at the office, a moody co-worker may be described as *mercurial* (from Mercury, the Roman messenger of the gods). You may have *erotic* (from Eros, the Greek god of sexual love) thoughts about someone with whom you work. However, in these harassment-sensitive times, making an amorous advance to a colleague might prove the *Achilles' heel** to your otherwise honorable career. You may even be concerned about *venereal* disease (from Venus, the Roman love goddess). Oh, what the *hell* (from Hel, the guardian of the dead in Germanic mythology).

Modern technology allows almost instant communication around the world via fax, phone, and modem. But, whether you live in *Lyons*, France (named for the Celtic sun-god Lugh); *Athens*, Georgia; or *Gimli*, Manitoba (for Gimli, the highest heaven in Norse mythology), you are also linked to centuries past by myth.

Myth itself demonstrates a unique use of language. It uses objective words depicting concrete things to describe concepts that transcend our five senses, things even beyond our comprehension.

In many cultures, there is a generic term for the forces that are greater than ourselves or unseen, for the spiritual power of things that surpass our understanding, such as the Sioux *wakanda*, the Iroquois *orenda*, the Bantu *mulungu*, and the Latin word *numen*. In modern times, it is something along the lines of the "higher power" spoken of in Alcoholics Anonymous. We may not feel that we are directly able to relate to this power.

Ancient Romans, when dealing with an unknown deity, a "numen," addressed this force *si deus si dea* ("whether you be god or goddess"). Interestingly enough, in a quantum leap from culture to culture, the general term for a usually nonpersonified greater power was translated by missionaries as referring to God. For instance, the

---

*"Achilles' heel" comes from the Homeric epic. The gods had advised Achilles' mother that he would be impervious to injury if bathed in a sacred pool. His entire body was invulnerable to spears and arrows, except for his heel, which is the spot where his mother held him as she dipped him in the water. Needless to say, only a wound to the heel could kill him. Achilles' tendon is likewise named for him.

name of the Finnish sky deity, Jumala, is also the modern Finnish word for God, as is the case with *mulungu* in Bantu and *Manitou* in Chippewa. "The powers that be" became a term for a monotheistic deity.

Anthropomorphism is the projection of human features or qualities on the divine. It may be properly called "making a god in man's image." The king of the Greek gods, Zeus, was depicted as a henpecked husband, and for good reason, as he was constantly involved in affairs with both goddesses and mortal women. The sun was not merely the heavenly body but was personified as a god with a definite humanlike life history. In Greek mythology, the sun was at first the god Helios (Greek for "sun") and later was the chariot driven by the god Apollo. As we shall see, in many mythologies the marriage of "Father" sky and "Mother" earth produces all life.

In many of the myths contained in this book, the anthropomorphic element is obvious.* Human beings prayed to gods who looked like them; acted like them (sometimes with very poor morals); and had the very human traits of vanity, jealousy, hatred, and passion. The Jewish prohibition on making graven images had its origin in the need to separate its deity, beyond all human description, from the anthropomorphic gods of Semitic and Egyptian neighbors. The story of the Golden Calf in the biblical Book of Exodus is very likely an expression of "thieromorphism," the depiction of a god in animal form,

---

*An interesting insight into anthropomorphism is given by the German-born American theologian Paul Tillich in volume I of his *Systematic Theology*:

> The gods are subpersonal and suprapersonal at one and the same time. Animal-gods are not deified brutes; they are expressions of man's ultimate concern symbolized in various forms of animal vitality. This animal vitality stands for a transhuman, divine-demonic vitality. The stars as gods are not deified astral bodies; they are expressions of man's ultimate concern symbolized in the order of the stars and in their creative and destructive power. The subhuman-superhuman character of the mythological gods is a protest against the reduction of divine power to human measure. In the moment when this protest loses its effectiveness, the gods become glorified men rather than gods. . . . Therefore religion imagines divine personalities whose qualities disrupt and transcend their personal form in every respect. They are subpersonal or transpersonal personalities, a paradoxical combination which mirrors the tension between the concrete and the ultimate in man's ultimate concern and in every type of the idea of God.

in this case the Egyptian sacred bull Apis, or perhaps the goddess Hathor, who was depicted as a cow.

The personification of abstract concepts as gods was also common. Nike, the name of the Greek goddess of victory, also means "victory" in Greek. Eris was the Greek goddess of discord, and *eris* means "discord" in Greek. Iris, the name of the Greek goddess of the rainbow, means "rainbow" in Greek—as well as in modern Spanish (*arco iris*). This word is also the source of our word *iris* for both the flower and the colored portion of the eye, and the word *iridescent*. In French, the verb *iriser* means "to give off colors as through a prism." The Greek Uranus (*ouranos*) meant both the "Father" sky deity and the word *sky*, as did its Sanskrit (Indian) cousin, *Varuna*.

The names of the gods make a great deal more sense when one understands their linguistic derivations. Wotan, the German form of the name of the god known as Odin in Norse mythology, is reminiscent of the modern German word *wüten*, meaning "to rage." One of the names of the Greek god Apollo, Phoebus, means "the shining one," a reference to his role as sun-god.

Such gods were personifications, and yet they were viewed as real spiritual forces that had to be worshiped, implored, and appeased. This use of personification tells a great deal about the cultures in which it was common.

The Greek myth of Cupid and Psyche is, on the surface, a charming love story with a moral. But it makes a great deal more sense when it is understood that the names of the characters have meanings. Cupid is the Roman name for the Greek god of love, Eros; *eros* means "sexual love" in Greek. *Psyche* means both "soul" and "butterfly" in Greek. Therefore, this myth is a statement on the relationship between physical love and soul love, wherein the soul, like a butterfly, undergoes a metamorphosis.

Throughout the myths given here, we shall see many examples of this use of language. Often I have seen myths presented without an explanation of the meanings of the names. Although entertaining, such tellings of the myth give the reader a one-dimensional view.

Language is everything to myth. The spoken word has great power. It is through the spoken word that God creates the world in Genesis.

In the Talmudic story of Creation, the letters of the Hebrew alphabet compete to be the first letter of the first word spoken by God in the Creation. In Persian mythology, it is the utterance of only one word by Ahura Mazda (the Good God) that casts Ahriman (the Bad God) into hell. The name of God is still so sacred to the Jews that to pronounce it is to profane it.

The use of sacred languages is also a means to separate what is sacred from that which is profane (*profane* is used here to mean "common," "ordinary," "everyday"). The Latin mass, persisting in places to the present day, signified the unity of the Roman Catholic church in that the same words were spoken at every mass throughout the world, in a sacred language separate from the vernacular. The Orthodox Christian churches in many Eastern European countries use a language called "Old Church Slavonic," a now obsolete tongue, as the language of the liturgy. Modern Jews who speak Russian or English or French still pray in Hebrew, *ha loshen ha kodesh*,* the "sacred" language. Muslims in England and Indonesia recite the Koran in Arabic, believed to be the language in which God spoke to Muhammad; few of these people may otherwise speak Arabic.

The German scholar Ernst Cassirer, in his book *Language and Myth*, sees language as an indication of religious development. In the earliest phases of religion, the so-called primitive stage, there is the undifferentiated concept of "powers that be" that must be reckoned with or appeased. At a later stage, the stage of polytheism (from the Greek for "many gods"), there is personification of the gods by function, or an object such as the sun is personified. In this stage, the corn goddess must be well treated to ensure a good crop.

Cassirer then points out that reflection upon religious questions, and the earliest phases of philosophical speculation, brings a sense of monotheism (Greek for "one god"), a single deity that is behind all phenomena. This deity at first may be appeased as were the earlier gods. However, even this gives way as the relationship with the god

---

*Ha loshen ha kodesh: Hebrew, "the holy tongue." Yiddish, the German-derived "secular" language of the Central and Eastern European Jews, is *mama loshen*, or "the mother tongue."

or God becomes subjective and self-contained, rather than one in which forces are external, discrete dispensers of cosmic good or ill. It is at this stage that one seeks a "union" or "personal relationship" with God, internally communicating more easily with one God than with many. The Hindus speak of Brahman, the Supreme Being, as "the Great Self." The Christian speaks of the "heart" as the dwelling place of the Holy Spirit of God. In this stage, the deity is a subject that dwells *within* the individual.

TIME AND MYTH

Have you ever wondered why there are 365 days in a year? Of course, the obvious answer is that this is the time that it takes for the earth to revolve around the sun—the solar year. However, why is our calendar based on the solar, and not the lunar, year?

We received our calendar pretty much intact from the ancient Romans, who, in turn, believed that the Egyptians were the best astronomers in the world. According to Sir James G. Frazer, author of *The Golden Bough*, one of the pioneer works analyzing myth, the 365-day year has its origins in an Egyptian myth.

The Egyptian god Osiris, later the god of the dead, was the offspring of the illicit union of the earth god Geb and the sky goddess Nut (the ubiquitous Egyptian obelisks, such as London's Cleopatra's Needle, are phallic representations of Geb touching Nut). Nut was technically the wife of Ra, the sun-god, who was not at all amused to learn of his wife's pregnancy by another god.

To express his displeasure, Ra ordained that the child of this affair would be born in "no month and no year." Now, the promiscuous goddess Nut had yet another lover, Thoth, the god of wisdom. Nut explained her predicament to Thoth, who always had an answer for everything. Thoth challenged the moon to a game of backgammon. Because the moon was then the regulator of time, the Egyptian year consisted of thirteen lunar months of thirty days each, or 360 days. Thoth won one seventy-second part of every day from the moon, which together made five whole days. These days fell between the end of the last month and the beginning of the first month of the lunar year. Thus, these five days were in "no month and no year." Osiris was born during this five-day period, fulfilling the prophecy of Ra, the jealous husband, and reconciling the lunar year of 360 days with the solar year of 365.

The days of the week in the Germanic, Celtic, Indian, and Romance languages (with the exception of Portuguese) are based on mythology.

English	Dutch	German	Norwegian	Gaelic	French
Monday	Maandag	Montag	Mandag	De Luain	lundi
Tuesday	Dinsdag	Dienstag	Tirsdag	De Mairt	mardi
Wednesday	Woensdag	Mittwoch	Onsdag	De Ceadoin	mercredi
Thursday	Dondersdag	Donnerstag	Torsdag	Deardoin	jeudi
Friday	Vrijdag	Freitag	Fredag	De hAoine	vendredi
Saturday	Zaterdag	Samstag	Lørdag	De Sathairn	samedi
Sunday	Zondag	Sonntag	Sondag	De Domhnaig	dimanche

Italian	Spanish	Romanian	Hindi	Sanskrit
lunedi	lunes	luni	Ravivaar	Bhanuvaasarah
martedi	martes	marti	Somvaar	Induvaasarah
mercoledi	miércoles	miercuri	Mangalvaar	Bhaumavaasarah
giovedi	jueves	joi	Budhvaar	Saumyavaasarah
venerdi	viernes	vineri	Brihispativaar	Guruvaasarah
sabato	sábado	simbata	Shukravaar	Shukravaasarah
domenica	domingo	duminica	Shanivar	Shanivaasarah

Derivations

MONDAY—The moon's day.

TUESDAY—The day sacred to the Germanic war god Tir or Tiw; the day sacred to the Roman war god Mars.

WEDNESDAY—The day sacred to the Germanic chief god Wotan or Odin; the day sacred to Mercury, as in the unmistakable Romanian word *miercuri*.

THURSDAY—The day sacred to the god who dispenses thunderbolts, the Germanic Thor and the Roman Jupiter or Jove.

FRIDAY—The day sacred to the goddess of beauty, the Germanic Frigga or Freya.

SATURDAY—From the god Saturn, a predecessor of the Olympian gods. Sábado, etc., come from the Hebrew *Shabbat*, the English *sabbath*.

SUNDAY—The day sacred to the sun. In the Romance languages and Gaelic, it comes from the Latin *dominus*, meaning "Lord," hence "the Lord's day."

As if that weren't easy enough, the days of the week are all named in honor of a heavenly body identified with a god, a lineage that can be traced back to ancient Babylonia*:

Planet/Body	Babylonian	Latin	Old German	Old English
Sun	Samas	Sol	Sonne	Sun
Moon	Sin	Luna	Mond	Moon
Mars	Nergal	Mars	Zivis	Tiw
Mercury	Nabu	Mercurius	Wotan	Wotan
Jupiter	Marduk	Jupiter	Donner, Thor	Thor
Venus	Ishtar	Venus	Freia	Frigga
Saturn	Ninib	Saturnus	Saturn	Saturn

It is interesting to see the consistent parallel: Ishtar, Venus, and Frigga were all goddesses of beauty in their respective cultures. Mar-

---

*From Robert Graves, *The White Goddess.*

In India, the same pattern holds true and appears to be influenced by ancient Babylonia:

Hindi

MANGALVAAR—Mangal, the planet Mars.

BUDHVAAR—Budh, the planet Neptune.

BRIHISPATIVAAR—Brihispati, the planet Jupiter, the priest of the gods (devas).

SHUKRAVAAR—Shukra, the planet Venus
  (*Sanskrit*: Shukravaasarah).

SHANIVAAR—Shani, the planet Saturn
  (*Sanskrit*: Shanivaasarah).

Sanskrit

INDUVAASARAH—Indra, the sky god.

GURUHVAASARAH—Guruh, the planet Jupiter.

duk, Thor, and Jupiter were representatives of a younger generation of gods, as well as the dispensers of thunderbolts. Interestingly, both Marduk and Jupiter became chief gods by overthrowing an earlier deity.

The months, likewise, have a largely classical origin. Months, of course, are reckoned by the moon. The "many moons" of the American Indians in Westerns is actually the same as "many months," as our English word *month* is derived from *moon*.

Derivations

JANUARY—From Janus, the two-faced Roman god of the gates who faced backward and forward.

FEBRUARY—From the Latin *februare*, meaning "to purify."

MARCH—From Mars, the Roman god of war.

APRIL—From the Latin *aprire*, meaning "to open"; this is the month that flower buds begin to open.

MAY—From the Latin month sacred to older men or *maiores*. It was also sacred to the Roman goddess Flora, whose name means "flower." The custom of the maypole is certainly the continuance of a fertility ceremony, complete with phallic symbol.

JUNE—Either from Juno, goddess of childbirth and wife of Jupiter, or from the month sacred to young men, *juniores*.

JULY—From the deified Roman Julius Caesar.

AUGUST—From the deified Emperor Augustus.

SEPTEMBER—From *septem*, or "seven."

OCTOBER—From *octo*, or "eight."

NOVEMBER—From *novem*, or "nine."

DECEMBER—From *decem*, or "ten."

The very manner in which we reckon years, keeping track of our history, is based on myth and religion. Let's take a random year, 1993. This may well be read as "In the year of Our Lord (Jesus Christ) 1993."* Non-Christians use the term C.E., or Common Era, a concession to the Christian system of dating. This mythological or-

---

*A.D., Anno Domini—Latin: "The Year of the Lord"; B.C.—"Before Christ."

igin of dating is common throughout the world. In Japan, the traditional calendar begins with the mythical beginning of the reign of the first emperor, Jimmu, descendant of the sun-goddess Amaterasu. The Romans began their dates with the mythical founding of Rome by the twins Romulus and Remus in 754 B.C. (by our system of dating), and further subdivided dates according to the reigns of emperors. The Islamic world begins its calendar with the Hegira, the flight of Muhammad and his followers from Mecca to Medina in A.D. 622.

Myth paints the milestones by which we reckon time.

Sacred Time

> This is the authentic content of the Doctrine of Eternal Recurrence: that eternity is the Now, that the moment is not just the futile now, which is only for the onlooker, but the clash of a past and a future.
>
> —Martin Heidegger (1889–1976)

> The heterogeneousness of time, its division into "sacred" and "profane," does not merely mean periodic "incisions" made in the profane duration to allow of the insertion of sacred time; it implies further that these insertions of sacred time are linked together so that one might see them as constituting another duration with its own continuity. . . . A ritual does not merely repeat the ritual that came before it . . . but is linked to it and continues it, whether at fixed periods or otherwise.
>
> —Mircea Eliade (1907–1986)

Sacred time is a separate time for a separate reality that transcends clock, watch, and calendar, for it marks our appointments with the Eternal.

In reading myths and in practicing our religions, we make an almost unconscious distinction that separates time into "sacred" and "profane." "Profane" time is wristwatch and calendar time. Sacred time, however, is exemplified by the Christian Eucharist, the taking of consecrated bread and wine; when Christians observe it, it is a direct connection with the original Seder meal celebrated by Jesus and his disciples. For Catholic, Lutheran, Anglican, and Orthodox Christians, Jesus is believed to be present at each Eucharist. For most Protestant Christians, it is the continuation of a memorial of that meal. Each celebration of the mass on any given Sunday in Christendom is connected with the mass before it, all the way back to that Passover meal in Palestine two thousand years ago. That connection, the sense of timelessness within time, is an illustration of sacred time.

The Jewish Sabbath is perhaps the demonstration of sacred time that is most familiar to us. The Sabbath recalls the "time before time" and was instituted when God rested from the work of creation. The first humans lived in Paradise (*Gan Eden*, in Hebrew) and there was neither sin, work, nor fear. The devout Jew speaks of the righteous spending the afterlife in *Gan Eden*. A very famous Jew, Jesus Christ, told the thief on the cross next to his, "Today you will be with me in Paradise." The Messianic age, when the Jewish people will see the arrival of a Messiah, is spoken of as a re-creation of *Gan Eden* at the end of history. From the earliest past, one has a sense of what Paradise was like and the hope that it will return; the Sabbath is a little taste of *Gan Eden* in the here and now.

The sacred time of the Sabbath must be carefully separated for its duration from profane time through scrupulous ritual. The profane world of anxiety, work, and care must be left behind. Traditionally, Jews prepared special meals in advance of the Sabbath, as work would "profane" it. People wore special clothes for the Sabbath. The Sabbath was personified as "Queen Sabbath" and greeted as a beautiful bride in the hymn "Lekhah Dodi."

> *Lekhah dodi, likrat kallah*
> *P'nai Shabbat, nekabalah.*

> Come, dear friend, to meet the bride
> The Sabbath presence, let us welcome.

Like a bride, the Sabbath is something that is yearned for and met with joy. The day itself is an important part of Jewish identity; celebration of the Sabbath separates the Jew from his non-Jewish neighbors. The sacred time of the Sabbath is so clearly delineated that precise hours are given for the lighting of the traditional candles at its beginning. At its end, there is the ceremony of *Habdalah*, literally "separation." The *Habdalah* includes opening a box of aromatic spices as prayers are recited, allowing one to savor the last sweet moments of the Sabbath. With the closing of the *Habdalah* box, profane time returns.

HISTORY AND MYTH

History is not an objective empirical datum; it is a myth. Myth is no fiction, but a reality; it is, however, one of a different order from that of so-called empirical fact. Myth is the story preserved in the popular memory of a past event and transcends the limits of the external objective world, revealing an ideal world, a subject-object world of facts.

Historical myths have a profound significance for the act of remembrance. A myth contains the story that is preserved in popular memory and that helps to bring to life some deep stratum buried in the depths of the human spirit. The divorce of the subject from the object as the result of enlightened criticism may provide material for historical knowledge; but insofar as it destroys the myth and dissociates the depths of time from those of man, it only serves to divorce man from history. For the historical tradition which criticism had thought to discredit makes possible a great and occult act of remembrance. It represents, indeed, no external or externally imposed fact alien to man, but one that is a manifestation of the inner mysterious life, in which he can attain to the knowledge of himself and feel himself to be an inalienable participant.
                    —Nikolai Berdyayev, Russian Christian Existentialist
                    philosopher, *The Meaning of History*

I am not far from believing that, in our own societies, history has replaced mythology and fulfils the same function, that for societies without writing and without archives the aim of mythology is to ensure that as closely as possible the future will remain faithful to the past. For us, however, the future should always be different, and ever more different, from the present. . . . But nevertheless the gap which exists in our mind ... between mythology and history can probably be breached by studying histories which are conceived as not at all separated from [,] but a continuation of mythology.

—Claude Lévi-Strauss, French anthropologist,
Myth and Meaning

In short, it would be necessary to confront "historical" man (modern man), who consciously and voluntarily creates history, with that of the man of the traditional civilizations ... who has a negative attitude toward history. Whether he abolishes it periodically, whether he devaluates it by perpetually finding transhistorical models and archetypes for it ... the man of the traditional civilizations accorded the historical event no value in itself; in other words, he did not regard it as a specific category of his own mode of existence.

—Mircea Eliade

To so-called primitive man, myth is history. To modern people, myth and history are considered two distinct and very different things. Despite the fact that our own secular history is reckoned in terms that come directly from myth and religion, we do not, as a rule, see history as integral with our religious life in the same sense that earlier peoples did. One reason the mythic bases of dates and years exist is that it is only relatively recently that Western culture separated history and myth.

To a person living in a traditional culture, there is no such distinction, and myth is the only history that really matters. For the traditional culture, all that we do in our lifetimes is merely a replay of events that took place in the myths. History in our sense of the word, as specific and unique actions of persons living and dead, can be abolished and the time of beginning can be reestablished (this is the origin of our modern New Year's Eve revelry). All human experience in the past derived its value from myth, which was perceived as infinitely more significant than the life of an individual. Even today it is not uncommon for a person living in a traditional culture to not know his or her chronological age; it simply doesn't matter.

The rituals required by traditional cultures are a return to *in illo tempore* (Latin for "in that time"), the undated "once upon a time" period of myths providing the blueprint for all forms of human experiences and behavior.

In order to make sense of the myths as we read them, it is necessary to understand two very different views of history, the linear and the cyclical. We live in a generally linear conception of history: It begins at a fixed point and progresses in a straight line toward the present day. In Christianity, Judaism, and Marxism, time moves toward an end of history, whether an apocalypse or the establishment of a utopia. There is a past point of beginning and a future point of ending.

Viewed cyclically, however, history is merely a procession of identical cycles. There are eternal, endlessly repeating principles. Hindu myths do not speak of "the age of Kali" but say "in every age of Kali." The world, in Hindu thought, has been created, destroyed, and re-created many times, abolishing what the Western mind might think of as "history." Only Brahman* is eternal, and he takes on various avatars, or roles, to fit the stage of the cycle, whether as Brahma the Creator, Vishnu the Preserver, or Shiva the Destroyer. In such a worldview, linear history and chronologies mean very little, as they are dwarfed by the eternal principles manifested in the cycles.

The Aztecs of Mexico also viewed history in a cyclical way, in which they knew just enough about the earlier worlds to understand the redemptive principles and appropriate behaviors necessary in their present one. They really didn't need to know details of earlier eras. The only eternal factor was Onteotl, the Supreme Being; even the other gods passed away.

THE CIVIC MYTH

The destiny of the state was closely bound up with the fate of the gods worshipped at its altars. If a State suffered reverses, then the

---

*In India, "Brahman" is the eternal, absolute; "Brahma" is the form "Brahman" takes as Creator.

prestige of its gods declined in the same measure—and vice versa.
Public religion and morals were fused: they were but different aspects of the same reality. To bring glory to the City was the same
as enhancing the glory of the gods of the City; it worked both
ways.

> —Émile Durkheim (1858–1917), French sociologist
> and philosopher, on the civic religion of the
> Greek city-states

What gives nations their cohesiveness? Certainly it may be common
ethnicity or a common language; but in all states, and especially in
ethnically diverse states, myth acts as a social "glue." National
identity is based on a shared history and shared symbols of nationhood. The basis of the founding and legitimacy of governments, the
civic myths of countries unite their citizens by an acceptance of common symbols.

American civic myth consists of many symbols such as the flag,
the Statue of Liberty, and others. The best symbols of our civic myth,
appropriately enough, can be found on our money, where we share
the history of Washington, Jefferson, and Lincoln, as well as recognize the American eagle.

On British money and stamps, we find portraits of the Queen, the
symbol of national unity. In a Canadian wallet, we find her portrait
as "Queen of Canada" on bank notes printed in English and French,
the two national languages. The coat of arms of Canada contains both
the British Union Jack and the French fleur-de-lis.

In the former Soviet Union, the founding myth that held the nation
together has crumbled. The symbols of the Soviet state, Lenin and
the hammer and sickle, were the first things attacked as the Soviet
government fell. A majority of the population rejected the Soviet
civic myth* and sought to replace it.

The Jews and the early Christians were persecuted in ancient
Rome as "atheists." Now, they were hardly atheists in our modern
sense of the word. Rather, they refused to worship the emperor as a

---

*Or perhaps they never accepted it, their own national myths (i.e., Russian, Ukrainian,
Uzbek) being stronger.

god, a requirement of the Roman civic myth, part of what identified the Roman citizen. In Rome, religion and the state were entirely fused.

The Bible contains an excellent illustration of the binding power of civic myth, as well as what happens when the myth breaks down. To be a Jew in ancient Israel meant to accept the king and the Torah as the moral, civic, and religious authorities. One had to identify with the sacred history of the Jewish people and accept that nationhood was defined by a covenant with God. The Old Testament sets forth that Israel prospered when the nation was faithful to the covenant; when that covenant was abandoned and the people worshiped the gods of neighboring peoples, society broke down and the Jews were sent into exile. This is the power of myth in action.

MORALITY AND MYTH

For centuries morals and religion have been intimately linked and completely fused. Even today, one is bound to recognize this close association in the majority of minds. It is apparent that moral life has not been, and never will be, able to shed all the characteristics that it holds in common with religion. When the two orders of facts have been so closely linked, when there have been between them so close a relationship for so long a time, it is impossible for them to be dissociated and become distinct. For this to happen they would have to undergo complete transformation. There must, then, be morality in religion and religion in morality.

—Émile Durkheim

With their old taboos discredited, they immediately go to pieces, disintegrate and become resorts of vice and diseases. . . . Today [1961] the same thing is happening to us. With our old mythologically founded taboos unsettled by our own modern sciences, there is everywhere in the civilized world a rapidly rising incidence of vice and crime, mental disorders, suicides and dope addictions, shattered homes, impudent children, violence, murder and despair. These are facts, I am not inventing them. They

give point to the cries of the preachers for repentance, conversion and a return to the old religion.
—Joseph Campbell, *Myths to Live By*

Myth, especially as codified in religion, has always been the basis for the morality of a society. With a mythic basis—a revelation from God or the gods—the legitimacy of a system of ethics was absolute and unquestioned. There were no shades of gray, for to question the validity of the moral code was to question the validity of the myth and the legitimacy of the society itself.

To return to the example of Old Testament Israel, the state was defined by the Torah, which in turn established an absolute standard of morality in the Ten Commandments. In this case, the civic myth and the absolute standard of morality were inseparable. In many premodern cultures, the price of violating a taboo is not death but something far worse from the standpoint of traditional culture: banishment from the group.

The wholesale devaluation of life in our culture through violence, crime, and addictions, as well as the decline in public and private ethics, is an indication of the weakening of our respect for myth. The establishment and maintenance of a widely held moral code are the most important functions of myth.

As we read the myths of numerous cultures, we will see a number of moral lessons presented. Of particular interest are "dualist" myths, such as the Persian and Chippewa stories of Creation. In these, there are two deities, one good and one evil, and good always prevails. Such tales were moral object lessons for the people, a means of conforming the behavior of the individual to that of the group.

THE SENSE OF THE SACRED

From Rudolf Otto, *The Idea of the Holy*; quoted by Victor Gollancz in *From Darkness to Light*.

Max Eyth recounts in his story "Berufs-Tragik"* the building of the mighty bridge over the estuary of the Ennobucht.† The most profound and thorough labor of the intellect, the most assiduous and devoted professional toil, had gone into the construction of the great edifice, making it in all its significance and purposefulness a marvel of human achievement. In spite of endless difficulties and gigantic obstacles, the bridge is at length finished, and stands defying water and waves. Then there comes a raging cyclone, and building and builder are swept into the deep. Utter meaninglessness seems to triumph over richest significance, blind "destiny" seems to stride on its way over prostrate virtues and merit. The narrator tells how he visits the scene of the tragedy and returns again:

"When we got to the end of the bridge, there was hardly a breath of wind; high above, the sky showed blue-green, and with an eerie brightness. Behind us, like an open grave, lay the Ennobucht. The Lord of life and death hovered over the waters in silent majesty. We felt his presence, as one feels one's own hand. And the old man and I knelt down before the open grave and before Him."

Why did they kneel? Why did they feel constrained to do so? One does not kneel before a cyclone or the blind forces of nature, nor even before Omnipotence merely as such. But one does kneel before the wholly uncomprehended Mystery, revealed yet unrevealed, and one's soul is stilled by feeling the way of its working, and therein its justification.

---

*German: "Vocation Tragedy."
†The Ennobucht is an estuary on the Baltic Sea in northern Germany.

2. The Cast of Characters

The word *pantheon* comes from the Greek *pan*, meaning "all," and *theon*, meaning "gods." A pantheon is thus a collection of gods, the cast of characters of the myths.

THE GREEK AND ROMAN PANTHEON

Greek myth has many minor gods and goddesses, but the chief gods were the Olympian twelve, said to live at the summit of Mount Olympus in Greece, and the two gods of earth. The Latin (Roman) names of these gods are given in parentheses.

The Olympian Twelve

Zeus (Jupiter, Jove)

His name means "bright sky" in archaic Greek. He is the thunderbolt-wielding King of the Gods who overcame the Titans, an earlier race of giants, to establish his authority over the universe. His name is akin to the Latin *deus*, meaning "god" and the Sanskrit (Indian) *Dyaus*, the name of an early Indian sky-god.

Zeus cast lots with his two brothers over the domains. His brother Poseidon won mastery of the sea, and the other brother, Hades, became lord of the Underworld. Zeus is master of both the skies and the land surface of the earth.

Hera (Juno)

The wife and twin sister of Zeus, she is frequently angered by her husband's adultery, but at no time does she leave him. However, she has no fear of him and often scolds him.

Her name means "protectress" in Greek, and she is worshiped as the patroness of brides on their wedding night, of mothers in childbirth, and of nurses. She can renew her virginity periodically by bathing in a sacred spring. Wives appeal to her for revenge against their erring husbands.

Aphrodite (Venus)

Her name means "born of foam," as she is said to have risen naked from the foam of the sea, a fully mature woman, riding on a scallop shell.

She is the goddess of beauty and sexual desire. She is analogous to the Middle Eastern fertility goddesses Ishtar, Ashtaroth, and Astarte.

Her son is Eros (Cupid), the god of love, whose irresistible arrows cause mortals to fall hopelessly in love.

Zeus gave Aphrodite in marriage to Hephaestus, the crippled god of the forge, but she bore children fathered through an adulterous union with Ares (Mars), the god of war.

Her Latin name, Venus, is the root of *venereal disease.*

Hermes (Mercury)

His name means "pillar" or "phallus."

The son of Zeus by a nymph named Maia, he is the god of the crossroads and of commerce, a patron of travel and thieves, and is the messenger of the gods. He is pictured as having winged feet, and is a clever trickster.

Apollo

His name, which is the same in Latin, means either "apple man" or "destroyer." The son of Zeus by Leto, Apollo is a sun-god, driving the chariot of the sun across the heavens. He is the patron of both athletic contests and the arts. He speaks through the oracle at Delphi, called "the Pythoness." His twin sister is Artemis.

Apollo supplanted an earlier Greek sun-god, Helios (Sol), who was a personification of the heavenly body. One of his names is Phoebus, meaning "the shining one."

Artemis (Diana)

Twin sister of Apollo, a moon goddess, patroness of small children and hunters, she is a perpetual virgin. Among her names is Phoebe, the feminine version of Phoebus. Sacred to the people of Ephesus, she is prominently mentioned in the account of Saint Paul's mission to the Ephesians in the biblical Book of Acts.

Ares (Mars)

His name means "warrior." He is the bloodthirsty, hard-drinking, dishonest, and temperamental god of war, thoroughly unpopular among the other Olympian gods. His sister is Eris, meaning "discord." He is said to be a brother of Zeus and Hera.

Hestia (Vesta)

Her name means "hearth," and she is the patroness of the home and hearth. She is as gentle and kind as Ares is cruel. She never causes strife and is said to have invented the arts of home building.

Poseidon (Neptune)

Robert Graves claims that Poseidon's name is a derivative of *potidan*, or "he who gives to drink." Poseidon is the god of the sea, brother of Hades and Zeus.

Hades (Pluto)

His name means "blind." A brother of Zeus, he is the lord of the Underworld, the home of the dead. His Latin name, Pluto, means "rich" in Greek, reflecting that all the wealth of the mines under the earth is his. He is also therefore the god of wealth. His wife is Persephone or Kore, Proserpina in Latin.

Athena (Minerva)

According to Graves, her name comes from the Sumerian *anatha*, or "queen of heaven." Another of her names, Pallas, means "maiden" in Greek. She was said to have been born in a curious way: Zeus was suffering from a terrible headache and Athena emerged from his head, fully grown, wearing a suit of armor.

The patroness of the city of Athens, she is the goddess of wisdom and the inventor of the flute, the trumpet, the plow, the rake, the ox yoke, the horse bridle, the chariot, and the ship. She created numbers and mathematics, as well as cooking, weaving, and spinning. She is also the goddess of justice, and is the only Olympian to have ever defeated Ares in battle. She is a perpetual virgin, and the owl, still considered "wise," is her symbol.

Hephaestus (Vulcan)

His name may be a contraction of *hemero-phaestos*, or "he who shines by day." He is the son of Zeus and the husband of Aphrodite.

Depicted as ugly, he is the lame god of the forge, inventor of metalworking, and patron of smiths. He is the force behind the *volcano*, which comes from his Latin name, Vulcan. Today, the process of making rubber durable, stable, and strong by heat treating is called "vulcanization."

The Two Earth Gods

Demeter (Ceres)

Her name means "barley mother." She is the goddess of agriculture and may well be a survival of an ancient mother goddess. The
word *cereal* comes from her Latin name, Ceres, as does the modern
Spanish word *cerveza*, meaning "beer." It is she who makes the seeds
grow.

Dionysus (Bacchus)

His name means "lame deity." He is the god of the vine, grapes,
and wine, as well as the god of theater. His temple at Eleusis was the
site of the Eleusinian Mysteries. Drunken revelries are still called
"Bacchanalia," recalling an ancient Roman celebration in his honor.
Dionysus is a root of the common man's name Dennis or Denis.

The inclusion of Demeter and Dionysus in any list of important deities tells us much about the Greek way of life.

Bread and wine were staples of the Greek and Roman diets. In the
myths, one reads of someone becoming drunk by drinking "unmixed"
wine, as wine was customarily cut with water to reduce its potency
for ordinary household use, as is still common in France and Spain
today.

A Modern Pantheon?

> . . . though the West is nominally Christian, we have come to be
> governed, in practice, by the unholy triumdivate* of Pluto god of
> wealth, Apollo god of science, and Mercury god of thieves. To
> make matters worse, dissension and jealousy rage openly be-
> tween these three, with Mercury and Pluto blackguarding each
> other, while Apollo wields the atomic bomb as if it were a thun-

---

Triumdivate, triumdival: A collection of three separate gods of three separate essences. This is in contrast to the Christian "Trinity" or the Hindu "Trimurti" of three per-
sonages that are in essence one God.

derbolt; for since the Age of Reason was heralded by his eighteenth-century philosophers, he has seated himself on the vacant throne of Zeus (temporarily indisposed) as Triumdival Regent.

—Robert Graves, *The White Goddess*

THE NORSE PANTHEON

Odin (in German, Wotan)

Odin is the one-eyed ruler of the gods. He has one eye after bartering the other for a drink at Mimir's well of wisdom. Two ravens fly around the world gathering information for him. He is portrayed as wise and generally just.

Frey

The German and Scandinavian god of agriculture, trade, and peace. The modern German words *frei* and *Freiheit*—and their English counterparts, *free* and *freedom*—are related to his name.

Freya, Freja

The sister of Frey, a goddess of beauty and love.

Frigga

A German and Old English version of Freya or Freja, who may have been a separate goddess at one time. The Norse Frigga is the wife of Odin, a separate deity from Freya.

Tyr, Tiw

The god of war. He was more popular among the Germans and Anglo-Saxons, as he seldom appears in Scandinavian mythology.

Loki (in German, Loge)

A trickster, the source of deception and harm to the gods.

Hel

Odin's sister, who oversees the Underworld, where the dead dwell. She is the source of the German word *Hölle* and its English counterpart, *hell*.

THE GODS OF INDIA

The great absolute and eternal God is Brahman, called the Divine Self. However, Hinduism may take monotheistic forms, in that Brahman is ultimately considered by most Hindus as God, or even the "great force" behind God and the gods, and polytheistic, in that Brahman is manifested through many avatars, or incarnations, that are worshipped by the masses.

The Trimurti ("threefold statue"), or "trinity," of the Hindu godhead consists of Brahma the Creator, Vishnu the Preserver, and Shiva the Destroyer. All three of these are but mere incarnations of Brahman, the Eternal and Absolute, and all are male deities who have female counterparts, or "shaktis." The shakti of Shiva is Mahadevi (The Great Goddess), who is also called Jagan-Mata ("Mother of the World"). The Great Goddess is worshiped as the Supreme Being by certain sects in India. The shakti of Brahma is Sarasvati, while that of Vishnu is Lakshmi. All of these shaktis are worshiped by their own small sects.

The two great Hindu epics are *The Ramayana* and *The Mahabharata*, the latter made famous by a modern dramatization by Peter Brook. In both epics, Vishnu has taken human form to preserve mankind, as Rama in the first one, and as Krishna in *The Mahabharata*.

There are other Hindu deities:

• Brihaspati, the planet Jupiter, priest of the gods.
• Indra, the sky-god.

- Varuna, a Sanskrit name closely related to the Greek Uranus, and the chief of the early Hindu pantheon; also called "Father Heaven."
- Kubera, a god of wealth.
- Rudra, the storm-god, also an avatar of Shiva that destroys the world.
- Pushan, the guardian of the flocks.
- the three sons of Shiva and his shakti, Parvati (or Mahadevi):
  - Ganesha, the very popular elephant-headed god of wisdom (in India, when a statue of Ganesha is turned upside down, it means that a shop has gone bankrupt).
  - Skanda (or Kumara), a god of war.
  - Kamadeva, a god of love, and his wife, Rati ("sexual desire"); Kamadeva literally means "love god," and the ancient Indian sex manual, The Kamasutra, means "love chapters."

How Many Gods Are There?

From the *Brihadaranyaka Upanishad*, translated by F. Max Müller.

Then Vidagdha Saklaya asked him: "How many gods are there, O Yajnavalkya?" He replied with this very Nivid (Sanskrit: "saying"): "As many as are mentioned in the Nivid of the hymn of praise addressed to the Visvedevas, ... three and three hundred, three and three thousand."

"Yes," he said and asked again: "How many gods are there really, O Yajnavalkya?"

"Thirty-three," he said.

"Yes," he said and asked again: "How many gods are there really, O Yajnavalkya?"

"Six," he said.

"Yes," he said and asked again: "How many gods are there really, O Yajnavalkya?"

"Three," he said.

"Yes," he said and asked again: "How many gods are there really, O Yajnavalkya?"

"Two," he said.

"Yes," he said and asked again: "How many gods are there really, O Yajnavalkya?"

"One," he said.

THE EGYPTIAN PANTHEON

The Ennead

The word *ennea* means "nine" in Greek, and the principal Egyptian gods are nine in number. Ra, the ruler of the gods and the sun-god, emerged from the Watery Abyss to create the world. His children are Shu, the god of the air, a life spirit; and Tefnut, or moisture, the goddess of the world order. Their children are Geb, the earth god, and his wife, Nut, the sky-goddess, who in turn produced Osiris and Isis, who are husband and wife; and Set and Nephthys, who are also husband and wife.

Osiris, whose story is given later in this book, is the god of the dead. Isis is a goddess of wisdom and beauty. Set is the evil god of the desert, while Nephthys is the goddess of dusk. Osiris and Isis are the parents of Horus, the patron of the reigning pharoah.

Other Egyptian gods are:

- Bast, the cat goddess who is the patroness of love and "feminine" things.
- Hathor, the goddess of vengeance, the "eye" of Ra.
- Maat, the goddess of justice.
- Ernutet, patroness of women in childbirth.

THE HAWAIIAN PANTHEON

The Polynesians, including the Hawaiians, Tahitians, Maori, and others, divide all forces in the universe into "Ao" (the masculine force, day, and the sky) and "Po" (the feminine principle, night, and the earth). The Ao god is Ku, whose name means "rising upright," an allusion to both the sun and the phallus. The Po goddess is Hina, whose name means "leaning down," an allusion to the setting sun.

Prayers to Ku are thus said facing east, and those to Hina are said facing west.

Ku is the god of agriculture, and is also invoked by fishermen for an abundant catch. Hina is the queen of the Underworld, patroness of women. Ku and Hina are the primordial parents of the gods:

- Pele is the volcano goddess.
- Kanaloa is the sea god, a squid god, who is invoked for healing and by travelers.
- Maui is the trickster, the son of Kanaloa.
- Lono is an agricultural deity.

THE AZTEC PANTHEON

- Onteotl, the eternal and supreme god behind and above all gods.
- Tlaloc, the rain god, leader of the rain spirits, the Tlaloques, who live on mountaintops.
- Ehecatl, god of the winds, a form taken by Quetzalcoatl, the plumed serpent hero-god of the Aztecs.
- Xipe Totec, god of the spring.
- Xochipilli, god of flowers.
- Tlatzoteotl, goddess of sexual desire and, curiously, the goddess to whom the confession of sins is addressed.
- Huitzipochtli, the sun-god and patron of the Aztecs at war.

The Lesser Aztec Gods

- Teteoinnan, mother of the gods; Coatlicue, "she who wears the snake-skirt"; Cihuacoatl, "snake-woman"; and Itzpapalotl, "obsidian butterfly," are all goddesses of fertility and childbirth.
- Huehueteotl, the fire god.
- Centeotl, the god of maize.
- Ometochtli, the god of drunkenness.
- Chalchiuhtilicue, "the one who wears the jade skirt," the goddess of fresh water, and her sister, Huixtochihuatl, the goddess of salt water and the ocean.

PART TWO

THE MYTHS

3. Beginnings—
The Creation Myths

When Science from Creation's face
Enchantment's veil withdraws
What lovely visions yield their place
To cold material laws.
        —Thomas Campbell,
            Scottish Romantic poet,
            "To a Rainbow"

CREATION MYTHS OF INDIA

THERE WAS NOTHING

NOTE: This is the classic Nasadiya, or "There Was Not," hymn contained in the ancient Hindu scriptures, the Rig Veda. The source for this is *Textual Sources for the Study of Hinduism.*

There was neither non-existence nor existence then; there was neither the realm of space nor the sky which is beyond. What stirred? Where? In whose protection? Was there water bottomlessly deep? There was neither death nor immortality then. There was no distinguishing sign of night, nor of day. That One breathed, windless, by its own impulse. Other than that there was nothing beyond. Darkness was hidden by darkness in the beginning; with no distinguishing sign, all this was water. The life force that was covered with emptiness, that One arose through the power of heat.

Desire came upon that One in the beginning; that was the first seed of mind. Poets seeking in their heart with wisdom found the bond of existence in non-existence. Their cord was extended across. Was there below? Was there above? There were seed-placers; there were powers. There was impulse beneath; there was giving-forth above.

Who really knows? Who will here proclaim it? Whence was it produced? Whence is this creation? The gods came afterwards, with the creation of the universe. Who then knows whence it has arisen? Whence this creation has arisen—perhaps it formed itself, or perhaps it did not—the one who looks down on it, in the highest heaven, only he knows—or perhaps he does not know. ♦

THE THOUGHTS OF BRAHMA

NOTE: The source of this story is the Brahamanda Purana, one of the earliest Hindu scriptures. In this myth, Brahma, the Creator, assumes various kinds of bodies made from the three elemental substances: darkness *(tamas)*, energy *(rajas)*, and goodness *(satva)*.

Brahma has created and re-created the world many, many times. No one knows how many worlds there have been before this one or how many will come after it. There are four ages or *yugas* that together make one *kalpa* or eon. At the end of each *kalpa*, the creation is destroyed and returned to its transition state as a watery chaos.

As Brahma meditated, beings were born from his mind. He assumed a body made of darkness, and out of his rectum came a wind—thus were the demons born. Then Brahma discarded this body of darkness and the discarded body became night.

He then assumed a new body that was made mostly of goodness and light. Out of his mouth now came the shining gods or *devas*. He cast off this body, which became day. Even today, it is during the daytime that people visit the temples and worship the gods.

He took a third body that was all *satva* [goodness]. Brahma happened to be thinking fond thoughts of fathers and sons, mothers and daughters, and thus the "ancestor spirits" were born. These spirits appear in the dusk and the dawn, where day and night meet.

Brahma then cast off his third body and assumed a fourth that was made of the energy that emitted from his mind. With these thoughts, human beings, the thinking creatures, were created. Then he discarded this body and it became the moon. To this day human beings love the moonlight for dancing, singing, and making love.

Brahma now had a rather strange thought as he assumed a fifth body made of both energy and darkness, which caused him to emit horrible creatures that wanted to devour the primordial sea of chaos; these were the ogres.

Brahma was so disturbed by this last creation that all the hairs on his head fell out. These hairs became all the creatures that crawl around on their bellies, the snakes and other reptiles. They recall their origins by hiding in swamps, brush piles, under rocks, and other dark places.

Brahma was still troubled about creating the ogres and, thinking dark thoughts, he created the horrible Gandharvas, or ghouls.

By this time Brahma had again regained his composure and began thinking pleasant thoughts. His mind went back to the peaceful and happy time of his youth. In this state of happiness, the birds were created. Now from the body of Brahma, much more sprang forth: mammals, plants, and other forms of life.

The qualities that all living things have today are the products of what Brahma's thoughts were when they were born, and these features remain constant as long as the present world lasts. ◆

BRAHMA IS LONELY

NOTE: This very ancient myth comes from the *Brihadaranyaka Upanishad*, which may date from 1500 B.C., and the telling of this myth is based on the translation by F. Max Müller.

In the beginning, there was nothing but the Great Self, Brahman. That is to say, nothing but Brahman existed. When you sacrifice to this god or that goddess, it is really only Brahman that you are worshiping. He is behind all things.

Now Brahman looked around himself and saw nothing. He felt fear. Fear of what? Nothing but Brahman yet existed. He was all alone, and in order to fear, there must have been something else to fear. But Brahman was lonely. Even today lonely people often have fear as their only companion, whether or not there is an object to fear.

Brahman took the form of Brahma, the Creator. Brahma felt no delight; lonely people never do. He yearned for someone to keep him company and his thoughts split the temporary body he was using into two parts, like the halves of a clamshell coming apart. One of the two parts was male and the other female. They looked on each other as husband and wife. To this day, a happily married couple are like two parts of one being with Brahma in both of them. Now Brahma knew that these first humans would need fire to prosper. So he created fire out of his own mouth. In so doing, he singed the hairs off of the inside of his mouth. To this day, hair grows on the cheek, but not on the inside.

The male and female looked at each other and, recognizing that they were two halves of the same being, they united, making love in the usual way. Humankind was thus conceived.

But the female thought, "How can he make love to me if we are part of the same being?" So she now tried to elude the male by changing into a cow. But he then changed into a bull and they conceived the race of cattle. She then tried to elude him by becoming a mare; he became a stallion and horses were conceived. So it continued down to the tiniest of creatures. Why did she elude him? Women are still that way; they are often coy and will play hard to get. Men must sometimes change themselves in order to win a woman.

And so the creatures of the earth were developed by Brahma calling them forth by name and the action of the male and female. Thus, Brahma is inside of every living thing, for they came forth from him. ◆

THE CREATION MYTH OF IRAN

NOTE: The religion of Iran before the coming of Islam was Zoroastrianism, a faith based on the teachings of the prophet Zoroaster. There are about 100,000 Zoroastrians in the world, mainly in India and in Great Britain's Parsi community, as well as in Iran, where they have been cruelly persecuted.

The distinguishing characteristic of Zoroastrianism is its duality: the good god Ormazd is in a constant war against the evil Ahriman. Good will eventually triumph, but only after a fierce battle, reflected in this Creation story.

Ormazd is the Wise Lord, the eternal and omniscient source of all that is good. His opposite and the enemy of all creation is Ahriman, the source of all suffering, sin, and death. Ormazd, being omniscient, knew of the existence of Ahriman before the creation of the world. Yet the evil one was then unaware of the Wise Lord; evil ones are basically ignorant.

Ormazd began his work of creation by casting some of his pure light into the vast abyss of the cosmos that separated him from Ahriman. Ahriman was so shocked that he declared war on creation at the first glimpse of this light. Ormazd told Ahriman that there was no need for conflict; if Ahriman would only bless the creation and leave it alone, all would be well. Like most evil ones, Ahriman is suspicious; he thought that the Wise Lord was negotiating out of weakness. Thus, Ahriman continued his war against creation.

At this time Ormazd began to recite a sacred verse. Just one word of it so stunned Ahriman that he fell backward into hell, where he remained for three thousand years, allowing Ormazd to continue the act of creation unhindered—for a time.

Ormazd began by creating his Eternal Attendants, the Immortals, the Amesha Spentas. They are the personifications of the principles of good at work in the world. They include Vohu Mana (Good Mind),

Asha (Truth), Sraosha (Obedience), Armaiti (Devotion), and the twins Haurvetat (Integrity) and Ameritat (Immortality). They are collectively called "the children of God."

Next the Wise Lord created the beautiful worshipful ones, the Yazatas or angels. They serve Ormazd as messengers and warriors who defend all that is good. In times of danger and difficulty, the Yazatas are willing to help humankind when called upon. (After Ahriman was released from hell, he created a corresponding group of evil angels, inferior to the Yazatas. These demons exist for the sole purpose of making humans miserable.)

Ormazd is a spirit without a body. However, he has a male and a female aspect. In creating our physical bodies, he is our Father. In creating our spiritual being, he is our Mother.

Ormazd created all living things and, since he is light, all creatures need light to survive. Ormazd's last creations were Gayomart, the first man, and his ox. As they came directly out of the hand of the Wise Lord, Gayomart shone like the sun, and the ox, like the moon. Gayomart and his ox lived in peace for thirty years, at the end of which time the evil one was released from hell. Ahriman immediately went to work creating demons, flies, germs, disease, vermin, and every other vile thing. Ahriman is sometimes called the "lord of flies," because they buzz around filth, manure, and decaying things.

One of Ahriman's wicked attendants, a demoness named Johi, volunteered to make Gayomart and his ox suffer and die. Johi is the personification of all feminine evil. She is the source of prostitution, vanity, gossip, nagging, and other forms of evil seen in women. Not that women per se are evil, as they are the creation of Ormazd and are even possibly morally better than men.

Johi succeeded in making the ox sick and then turned her efforts to Gayomart. Since Gayomart had no sexual desire for her to prey on, he ignored her at first, which made her even more virulent. She then unleashed horrible diseases on the ox, who began to die. The Wise Lord gave the ox marijuana to chew, in order to ease its pain. Then the ox died.

Gayomart himself became mortally ill. When he died, his shining body decomposed, depositing gold and silver in the earth. From his sperm, a tiny plant with a male and a female shoot sprang from the ground and grew into a great tree that bore as its fruit the ten races of mankind. The tree separated, and the male part became a man named Mashya, and the female became his wife, Mashyane.

The Wise Lord loved Mashya and Mashyane, supplying them with every need without any work or effort. Ormazd spoke to them directly and told them the story of Gayomart, their father. They learned of Gayomart's faithfulness to the Wise Lord through many difficulties. Ahriman hated the two humans and sought to deceive them.

One day, the couple, hitherto unaware of evil, began saying to each other that it was Ahriman and not the Wise Lord that had created them. This was the first sin, a lie. And as it always is with lies, more were sure to follow. This first lie was the first of the many sins of mankind. At that instant Ormazd came to earth and told Mashya and Mashyane that they would have to henceforth work for a living. They would have to offer their praises and sacrifices only to the Wise Lord, or they would have no protection and be destroyed by Ahriman. He also instructed them how to have sexual intercourse in order to perpetuate their kind.

But Ahriman and Johi were determined to confound creation, and they took away the human couple's sexual desire for fifty years. When Mashya and Mashyane were able to produce children, the demons ate them. So the Wise Lord saved humankind by taking away a little of the sweetness of the children, and they became like the children of today.

Ormazd loves the human race and wants it to survive. He needs our help to defeat Ahriman. Likewise, without the help of the Wise Lord, Ahriman would destroy us. But the triumph of good is inevitable. ◆

*   *   *

Today it is everywhere self-evident that WE are on the side of light. THEY on the side of Darkness. And being on the side of Darkness, THEY deserve to be punished and must be liquidated (since OUR divinity justifies everything) by the most fiendish means at our disposal. By idolatrously worshipping our-

selves as Ormazd, and by regarding the other fellow as Ahriman, the Principle of Evil, we of the twentieth century are doing our best to guarantee the triumph of diabolism in our time.
—Aldous Huxley, *The Devils of Loudun*

THE NORSE CREATION MYTH

NOTE: The Germanic myths were held by peoples that included the ancestors of the modern Germans, Scandinavians, Dutch, and English. Since the Norse of Scandinavia were the last of these nations to be converted to Christianity, the Norse myths survived later than others. They survived latest of all in Iceland, whence comes this myth from the epic *The Elder Edda*.

Long ago there was no heaven above nor an earth beneath, only a vast bottomless deep shrouded in an atmosphere of mist. Somewhere in the middle of the abyss was a fountain from which twelve rivers flowed out like the spokes of a wheel. As the rivers traveled far from their source, they froze.

South of the world of mist, there was a world of light. Once a warm breeze blew out from the south and began to melt the ice. The contact of the warm air and the cold created clouds. These clouds congealed to form the frost giant, Ymir, and his cow, Audhumbla, whose milk nourished the giant. As the ice melted, salt was exposed, which Audhumbla licked. As she licked and licked, she exposed a man buried in the ice. On the first day, his hair was exposed; on the second day, one could see his whole head and shoulders. By the third day, his whole body was free of the ice. This was the first god, the father of Odin, Vili, and Ve.

These three young gods slew Ymir and his salty blood flowed out to make the seas (you will remember that Ymir had been nourished by the cow, who had licked salt out of the ice). The bones of Ymir formed the mountains and his flesh formed the earth. From his hair sprang up all manner of plants. Among these were Aske, the ash tree, and Embla, the elm. From the ash tree, Odin fashioned a man and from the elm, a woman. From Odin himself, the humans received life and a soul. Vili gave them reason and motion, while Ve gave them speech and motion.

Odin organized the world, separating the darkness from the light, creating night and day. Odin fashioned Midgard, or Middle Earth,* for mankind to dwell in. He also fashioned Asgard, home of the gods. The universe is supported by Yggdrasil, a mighty ash tree. One of her roots touches Asgard, another Midgard, and a third lies underground, where the souls of the dead dwell under the eye of Odin's sister, Hel.

Ymir the giant was not completely killed, part of his body is still alive and sleeps at the foot of the great ash tree Yggdrasil. When his body stirs, the earth quakes. ◆

The Norse Myth of the Creation of Man from an Ash Tree and Its American Indian Parallel

The Norse story of the creation of human beings from an ash tree is often linked to similar stories in North America. Many writers have sought to find Viking influences in the myths of the Algonquin Indians.

Lewis Spencer (1874–1955) writes in *The Myths of the North American Indians* about Norse-like spirits:

> But although Malsum [in the Algonquin myth] was slain he subsequently appears in Algonquin myth as Lox, or Loki, the chief of the wolves, a mischievous and restless spirit. In his account of the Algonquin mythology Charles Godfrey Leland appears to think that the entire [North American] system has been sophisticated by Norse mythology filtering through the Eskimo. Although the probabilities are against such a theory, there are many points in common between the two systems, as we shall see later, and among them few more striking than the fact that

---

*"Middle Earth"—See J.R.R. Tolkien's *The Lord of the Rings*.

the Scandinavian and Algonquin evil influences possess one and
the same name [Loki].

When Glooskap had completed the world he made man and
formed the smaller human beings, such as fairies and dwarfs.
He formed man from the trunk of an ash-tree, and the elves from
its bark. Like Odin, he trained two birds to bring to him the
news of the world. . . .

GREEK CREATION MYTHS

Matriarchal Creation Myths

EURYNOME AND OPHION

In the beginning was Chaos and darkness. Chaos was a great vast
sea in which all elements were mixed together without form. Out
of this sea rose Eurynome ("of the good name"), the Great Goddess
of all things. She emerged from the waves naked and began to dance
on the sea, as there was nothing firm for her to stand on. Suddenly,
the south wind blew and spun her around.

It is said that the north wind has miraculous fertility powers and,
when she spun around, Eurynome grasped at the north wind. The
great serpent of the waters, Ophion, saw Eurynome dancing and was
filled with desire. He made love to her immediately. She then assumed the form of a lovely bird and gave birth to the great universal
egg. Ophion coiled his tail around this egg until it cracked, spilling
out creatures all over the newly formed earth. Eurynome loved
Ophion for a time and they went to live on Mount Olympus, home of
the gods.

However, Ophion became obnoxious and tiresome, bragging how
he had fathered all living things. Eurynome grew weary of him and
"bruised his head with her heel" [compare this with the same phrase
in the Genesis story of Creation]. He was then cast down to the dark
regions of the earth. ♦

GEIA AND URANUS

Geia, Mother Earth, emerged out of Chaos and then bore her son, Uranus (which means "heaven" or "sky") while she was sleeping. When Uranus ascended to his place in the heavens, he showered his gratitude on his mother in the form of rain, which fertilized the earth, and all the dormant seeds within her came to life. ♦

An Oedipal, Patriarchal Creation Myth

THE BIRTH OF THE GODS

In the beginning there was only Geia (the Earth) and a great sea of Chaos. Out of Chaos came night and Erebus (darkness). From the night came the "ethers," or upper atmosphere, and day. The earth produced the sea, then the great ocean, and other children including the Titans, Hyperion (the sun, "he who flies over"),* Rhea, Mnesmosyne ("memory"), Phoebe (the moon, "the shining one"), and at last Cronus. The children of Geia, the earth, were fathered by Uranus, the sky.

Uranus became jealous of the affection that Geia had for her children and sought to destroy them. First, he hid them deep inside her in a cavern. She was tired of Uranus' jealousy; and, as her children grew, they caused her great pain. The youngest of these children, Cronus, decided to take revenge on his cruel father. Earth took Cronus into her bed with a sickle in his hand. When Uranus came to sleep with Geia, Cronus castrated his father and flung the parts into the sea, where they sired Aphrodite, the goddess of love, who emerged from the fertile sea foam.

---

*Hyperion was replaced by Helios ("sun"); later the sun was depicted as the chariot of Apollo.

The blood poured out over the earth, giving life to the Furies, the avengers who mete out justice.

Cronus was now master of the gods and he married Rhea. Their children were Hestia (goddess of the hearth), Demeter (goddess of agriculture), Hera (goddess of childbirth), Ares (god of war), and lastly, Zeus. Cronus, jealous of the attention Rhea gave her children, swallowed them all whole, except Zeus whom Rhea sent to Crete for safekeeping. She deceived Cronus into swallowing a stone that he believed to be Zeus. Like her mother, Rhea conspired with her son to take revenge upon her cruel husband. For Rhea knew that it would be Zeus who would overthrow his father and become king of the gods.

Zeus remained in a cave where he was nourished by the goat Amalthea and fed by the honey of wild bees. He grew to manhood in just a few short years, at which time Cronus vomited up all of his swallowed children, as well as the stone. The stone was placed by Zeus at Delphi, where the Oracle of the god Apollo is located. Cronus was killed. For ten years Zeus and his brothers battled against their uncles, the Titans, for mastery of the universe. Finally, with the Titans vanquished, Zeus set up his court on Mount Olympus as the uncontested master of the gods. ♦

CREATION MYTHS OF AFRICA

The Yoruba (West Africa)

In the beginning the world was a watery, formless Chaos that was neither sea nor land, but a marshy waste. Above it, in the sky, lived the Supreme Being, Olorun, attended by other gods, including Orisha Nla, called the Great God. Olorun called Orisha Nla into his presence and ordered him to make a world. It was time to make solid land and Orisha Nla was given a snail shell full of magic earth, a pigeon, and a five-toed hen to accomplish this assignment. Orisha Nla came down to the Chaos and set to work organizing it. He threw the magic earth into a small patch. The pigeon and the hen began to scratch in the magic earth, and they scratched until land and sea were entirely separated.

When Orisha Nla returned to the Supreme Being to report on his work, a chameleon was sent with him to inspect the job. The chameleon reported good things and Olorun, satisfied with the good report, dispatched Orisha Nla to finish. The first place on earth was known as *Ifé* which means "wide" in the Yoruba language. Later, the word *Ilé*, meaning "house," was added. Today the city of Ifé-Ilé is the most sacred to the Yoruba people.

The making of earth took four days. On the fifth, Orisha Nla rested from his work. The Yoruba traditionally have a four-day work week and rest on the fifth in memory of the creation.

Orisha Nla was sent back to earth to plant trees, including the first oil palm. Olorum made rain fall from heaven to water the seeds, which grew into a great forest.

In heaven, Olorun began to make the first people. They were fashioned from earth by Orisha Nla, but only Olorun, the Supreme Being, could give them life. Orisha Nla hid in Olorun's workshop to watch. However, Olorun knew that Orisha Nla was hiding there and put him into a deep sleep, and so only Olorun knows the secret of how to bring a body to life. To this day Orisha Nla, through the agency of parents, makes the body, but only the Supreme Being can give it life. ♦

Madagascar

THE THREE PEOPLE AND THE STATUE

The Creator made two men and a woman, each of whom wandered the earth alone unaware that the others existed. The first man was lonely and carved a statue of a beautiful girl out of wood. The second man happened to pass by and fell in love with the statue. However, the second man was shocked by its nakedness and clothed it, covering the statue with beautiful flowers. Later, the woman happened to be passing by and she too was lonely. She took the statue home with her and asked the Creator to give it life. The statue slept in bed with her, and by morning, it was transformed into a living girl.

The two men searched for the statue and when the three people met for the first time, they argued. The woman would not turn the girl over to the two men. Then the Creator intervened.

He ordained that the first man, who had made the statue, was the father of the girl. The woman who had taken it home was the mother. The man who had clothed the statue and fallen in love with it was to be the girl's husband. All human beings are descended from these two couples. ♦

Madagascar

MOTHER EARTH AND THE CREATOR

The Creator was watching his daughter, Mother Earth, making little dolls out of clay and he became interested. He spoke to his daughter about them and breathed life into them, creating living human beings.

As time passed, however, the humans multiplied and prospered. They gave thanks to Mother Earth but forgot all about the Creator. He told his daughter that it was wrong for her to accept all of the sacrifices of the humans without sharing them. Thenceforth, he would take the souls of half the humans as tribute and leave the other half alive. The reason most of the souls he takes are from old people is that he is patient. As the Creator gave humans their souls, that is all that he can take; Mother Earth made their bodies and that is the part of humans that goes to her at their death. ♦

CREATION MYTHS OF EGYPT

THE WATERY ABYSS

B efore the existence of Great Ra, the sun-god, was his father, the Watery Abyss. Ra emerged from the Watery Abyss and then all things came into being out of the words of his mouth. First, he blew out the first air (Shu), then he spat out the first moisture (Tefnut). These became the god of the air, Shu, who is the life force, and his wife, Tefnut, the organizing world order. Also out of the air and moisture, Ra created the Eye of Ra, the goddess Hathor, in order to see what he was making. When he had his eye, Ra began to weep. Human beings were created from his tears.

Hathor, the Eye of Ra, was angered that she was not attached to his body. So Ra found a spot for her on his forehead. Then Ra created the serpents, and other creatures came from them. ♦

The Memphite Theology of Creation

THE ENNEAD

NOTE: Memphis was the religious and theological center of ancient Egypt. The following myth is a product of the discourse that took place there. This text has been dated to about 2700 B.C. and is a translation by John A. Wilson in *The Ancient Near East*.

T here came into being as the heart and there came into being as the tongue [something] as the form of Atum. The mighty one is Ptah, who transmitted [life to all the gods] as well as to their kas [souls], through the heart, by which Horus became Ptah, and through the tongue by which Thoth [god of wisdom] became Ptah.

Thus it happened that the heart and tongue gained control over [every other] member of the body, by teaching that he is in every body and in every mouth of all gods, all men, cattle, all creeping things, and [everything] that lives, by thinking and commanding everything that he wishes.

His Ennead [the nine chief gods] is before him [in the form of] teeth and lips. That is [the equivalent of] the semen and hands of Atum. Whereas the Ennead of Ptah, however, is in the teeth and lips in this mouth, which pronounced the name of everything, from which Shu and Tefnut came forth, and which was the fashioner of the Ennead.

The sight of the eyes, the hearing of the ears, and the smelling the air by the nose, they report to the heart. It is this which causes every completed [concept] to come forth, and it is the tongue which announces what the heart thinks.

Thus all the gods were formed and his Ennead was completed. Indeed, all the divine order really came into being through what the heart thought and the tongue commanded. Thus the ka-spirits were made and the hemsut-spirits were appointed, they who make all provisions and all nourishment, by this speech. [Thus justice was given to] him who does what is liked, [and injustice to] him who does what is disliked. Thus life was given to him who has peace and death was given to him who has sin. Thus were made all work and all crafts, the action of the arms, the movement of the legs, and the activity of every member, in conformance with [this] command which the heart thought, which came forth through the tongue, and which gives value to everything.

Thus it happened that it was said of Ptah: "He who made all and brought the gods into being." He is indeed Ta-tanen, who brought forth all the gods, for everything came from him, nourishment and provisions, the offerings of the gods, and every good thing. Thus it was discovered and understood that his strength is greater than [that of the other] gods. And so Ptah was satisfied, after he had made everything, as well as all the divine order. He had formed the gods, he had made cities . . . he had put the gods in their shrines, he had established their offerings . . . he had made their bodies like that [with which] their hearts were satisfied. So the gods entered into their bodies of every [kind of] wood, of every [kind of] stone, of every [kind of] clay, or anything which might grow upon him, in which they had taken form. So all gods, as well as their kas gathered themselves to him, content and associated with the Lord of the Two Lands [Upper and Lower Egypt]. ◆

THE CREATION MYTH OF FINLAND

NOTE: The source of this story is the Kalevala, the Finnish national epic.

Ilma was the goddess of the air. She had a virgin daughter named Luonnatar who lived in the stars. Luonnatar became lonely and came down to the great primordial sea, where she found no place to rest, floating for seven hundred years.

Then she met a male duck who flew about looking for a place to nest.* Finding nothing on the great sea, he landed on Luonnatar's knee and built a nest. The male duck laid eggs in the nest and sat on them for three days.

Luonnatar was in great pain; the duck's nest burned the skin on her knee, so she turned over and the eggs fell into the sea. However, in the fertile primordial sea the eggs changed form. The yolk of the egg became the sun, and the white, the moon. The spots on the shell became the stars and the black flecks became clouds. ◆

THE CHINESE CREATION MYTH

Chaos was like a hen's egg. The parts of the egg separated into the Yin and the Yang, the male and female essences of all living things. The lighter parts rose to the top, becoming sky and heaven,

---

*As we read the Creation myths of the American Indians, we will again see the motif of the duck and the primordial sea.

while the heavier parts sank to become the earth and sea. Out of this egg also came the giant Pangu.

Pangu grew at the rate of ten feet per day for eighteen thousand years until his height spanned the distance between earth and heaven. Then Pangu died.

Upon his death, his body decomposed and his stomach formed the central mountains; his eyes, the sun and the moon; his tears, rivers; his breath, the wind; and his bones, metals and stones. His semen became pearls, and his bone marrow, jade. ♦

THE CREATION MYTH OF JAPAN

NOTE: The source of this story is the Kojiki, the mythical history of Japan and the genealogy of the first emperors.

In the beginning there was nothing but a vast oily sea of Chaos that contained a mix of all the elements. There were three spirits or "kami" in heaven who looked out over this sea and decided that a world ought to be created. The spirits produced many gods and goddesses, including Izanagi ("male who invites") and Izanami ("female who invites"). Izanagi was entrusted with a magic jeweled spear for this work.

Izanagi and Izanami descended from heaven and Izanagi stirred the spear around in the sea. When he pulled it out of the Chaos, some drops congealed on the tip of the spear. Then the drops fell back into the sea, where they formed an island.

Izanagi then asked Izanami what her body was like. She replied that it was very beautiful, but that there was a curious spot between her legs where the skin had not grown together. Izanagi found that interesting, as there was a place between his legs where the flesh protruded. They decided to join these parts together and when they did Izanami began to conceive many wonderful things.

The first thing they conceived was a disappointment—the leech. They placed it in a reed basket and cast it adrift. To this day, the leech still likes to live among the reeds. Then Izanami gave birth to an island—the Foam Island, which was useless. But, with a little practice, the couple produced the islands of Japan, waterfalls, mountains, and other natural wonders. Then Izanami gave birth to the Fire Spirit, which burned her body very badly, causing her to become seriously ill. While she was ill, her vomit became the Metal Mountain prince and princess, the source of all mines. Her feces became the clay, and her urine, the Fresh Water spirit.

But Izanami was dying. Izanagi wept bitter tears as she descended into the Land of Night. He begged her not to stay there, but she replied that she could not leave as she had eaten some of the food there. Izanagi then went into the Land of Night to fetch his wife. But when he arrived, he was horrified—she had begun to decay. When Izanagi finally took a good look at her, he was so horrified that he began to run away. Izanami sent the Ugly Night Spirit to retrieve him.

Izanagi continued to run in terror and disgust, leaving the horrible Land of Night behind him. As he was running away, he cast down the comb from the right side of his hair, and the comb miraculously became grapevines. Then he cast down the comb from the left side of his hair, and it became bamboo shoots. When the Ugly Night Spirit stopped to eat the grapes and bamboo shoots, Izanagi was able to escape toward the upper world.

Izanami was now more determined than ever to get her husband back. She now sent eight thunder-spirits and all the warriors of the Land of Night after him. But Izanagi outran them all. Out of breath, he stopped to rest beneath a peach tree at the border between the Land of Night and the upper world. When the forces sent by Izanami approached, Izanagi threw peaches at them. To his amazement, they ran in terror; to this day it is known that peaches dispel evil spirits.

Izanami was now furious. She called to her husband, "If you continue to flee, I will strangle one thousand of the people of earth every day." Izanagi replied that if she did that, he would cause one thousand new people to be born every day. Thus, death entered the world but the human race still survives. Izanagi then took a great rock and sealed off the Land of Night. Izanami's spirit remains there, ruling over the dead.

Izanagi was tired after his flight from the terrible land and refreshed himself by bathing in a stream. He needed to wash away the defilements of the terrible land of the dead and, as he did, gods and goddesses were produced. As he washed his left eye, Amaterasu Omikami, the sun-goddess and ancestress of the emperor, was born. As he washed his right eye, it became Tsukiyomi-no-Mikoto, the moon. When he washed his nose, Susano-O, the storm god, was born. ♦

THE POLYNESIAN CREATION MYTHS

NOTE: The Polynesian cultural area extends from Easter Island, off the coast of Chile, to New Zealand, Tahiti, and Hawaii.

AO AND PO

The entire universe is dual in nature. There is Ao: light, day, sky, the male principle. Its opposite is Po: darkness, night, the earth, the female principle. The darkness of Po should not be confused with the use of the word *darkness* to mean "evil." The darkness of Po is warm and nurturing like the earth or the womb.

In the Hawaiian Creation story, the Kumulipo, or "Genealogy of All Things," there was only a great watery Chaos at the beginning until Ku, the Creator, began to chant, separating Ao from Po.

> *Hanau ke po i ke po no*
> *Hanau mai a puka i ke ao malamalama.*
>
> Things born from po are po;
> things born from ao are ao.

Of course this could be translated a number of ways, such as "things of darkness give birth to darkness" and "things of light give birth to light." But the great act of Creation was the work of separating Ao from Po, making the world possible and separating day from night.

Ku drew out Kanaloa, the squid, later the god of the sea. Then Ku drew out Kane (Tane, in New Zealand). Perhaps Kane was born out of the union of Ku, as Father Sky, with Hina, as Mother Earth. *Kane* means "man." Kane had intercourse with a number of beings and thus produced grass, streams, and reptiles. But he wanted a child in his own image. So he took some soft red clay from Hawaiki, the mythical homeland of the Polynesians, and fashioned Hine-hau-ona, or "earth-formed woman." Their first child was Hine-titama, or "dawn woman," since dawn is the point when night meets day. But Kane became wicked and took Hine-titama, his own daughter, as a wife, concealing from her that he was her father.

This was a basic violation of the laws of nature, the great *kapu*, or taboo, against incest. Hina knew that Kane's desires were wrong. When Hine-titama learned that Kane was also her father, she ran screaming into her mother's domain, the Po world of the dead. Hine-titama cried, "You have broken the umbilical cord of the world!" So it was decreed that Kane could not touch his daughter. Hine-titama and her mother became co-rulers of the dead in the Po world beneath the earth. Kane was thenceforth confined to the Ao world above ground.

Because of Kane's crime, his children reside here on earth during their lifetimes. But when they die, they go to live with their mother, who as Mother Earth forms a protective barrier between the wicked Kane and his children below ground in the Po world. We also know Po in life as the creative world of night, a place of dreams, lovemaking, and the appearance of spirits. ♦

New Zealand

MOTHER EARTH AND FATHER SKY

The gods were born of the union of Rangi (Father Sky) and Papa-tuanuku, Mother Earth. Rangi is Ao, Papa is Po. Earth and sky made love and they produced seventy children, the gods. But there was no space for these children to grow up, as the earth and sky were still pressed together.

One of the gods, Tu-matauenga, father of discord and war, horrified his siblings by suggesting that the gods slay their father. But Tu-matauenga is no different than any other violent being who believes that killing is the answer to everything.

Tane-mahuta, the gentle god of the forests, had a more sensible idea, as befits one who has the patience to watch tiny seeds grow into great trees that touch the sky. He suggested that the younger gods merely make space for themselves by pushing up Father Rangi away from Mother Papa. The other gods thought this idea very sensible, with the exception of Ta-whiri-matea, the wind god, who roared his disapproval. Rongo-matane,* the god of agriculture, tried to separate earth and sky, but he could only make a space as high as a taro plant, not enough room. Tangaroa (Kanaloa, in Hawaiian), the sea god, tried, but only could separate them the space of a high wave, not enough room. Humia-tikitiki, god of the wild food plants, also tried, making a space only as great as a banana tree.

Patient Tane-mahuta observed the futile attempts of his brothers. This time, he decided to push the earth and sky apart by standing on his head and pushing up with his legs, something like the way that a tree grows. His shoulders touched Papa and his feet touched Rangi, and slowly he pushed them apart. Trees still separate the earth and sky in the same way.

The parents of the gods screamed and groaned as they were pushed apart. But as the space between them enlarged, light and dark were separated. Now there was room for the gods, for tall trees to grow, and for humans and animals to flourish.

Rangi is still saddened to be separated from Papa, and his tears form the dew every morning and sometimes even take the form of rain. ◆

---

*The Hawaiian god Lono.

CREATION MYTHS OF THE AMERICAS

Sioux

NOTE: The following is taken from *Letters and Notes on the Manners, Customs and Conditions of the North American Indians*, written by George Catlin, early explorer, painter, and writer.

Before the creation of man, the Great Spirit (whose tracks are yet to be seen on the stones, at the Red Pipe, in the form of a large bird) used to slay buffaloes and eat them on the ledge of the Red Rocks, on top of the Coteau des Prairies, and their blood running on to the rocks, turned them red. One day when a large snake had crawled into the nest of the bird to eat his eggs, one of the eggs hatched out in a clap of thunder, and the Great Spirit, catching hold of a piece of the pipestone to throw at the snake, moulded [sic] into a man. This man's feet grew fast in the ground where he stood for many ages, like a great tree, and therefore he grew very old; he was older than a hundred men at the present day; and at last another tree grew up by the side of him, when a large snake ate them both off at the roots, and they wandered off together; from these have sprung all the people that now inhabit the earth. ♦

Pawnee

Tirawa Atius (*atius* means "lord") is the great eternal God who created all things and supplies the needs of all creatures. He created the Path of the Departing Spirits, known to the White Man as the Milky Way. East of the Path is the Male Principle—the Morning Star, and to the west is the Female Principle—the Evening Star. All that has happened and will happen has been ordained by Tirawa, and the stars are his servants. From the east the Morning Star began to pursue Evening Star in order to make love to her, but she continued to elude him. She put hindrances in his path, but continued to beckon him all the while. Why? Because it was not yet time to make living things on the earth; and females always tease and flirt with males, as well as demand tests to prove men's character.

The number ten has always had significance for human beings, and this is because Evening Star placed ten obstacles in the way of her suitor. One of the hindrances was in the chaos beneath them. There was an endless sheet of water presided over by the Great Serpent. The Morning Star threw a ball of fire at the serpent, which caused the serpent to flee beneath the waves. As the fire hit the water, enough of the water dried up to reveal earth and rocks. From these materials, Morning Star threw a pebble into the sea of chaos and it became the earth.

When the earth was in its proper place, Tirawa appointed four lesser gods to administer it. They were East, West, North, and South. They joined hands at the edge of the great sea on earth and a land mass emerged.

Eventually, Morning Star caught up with Evening Star and made love with her. Soon Evening Star conceived a little daughter. When she gave birth to the little girl, she placed the child on a cloud and sent her to earth. High above the earth, Evening Star asked Morning Star to water her celestial garden and, as a love gift, he made the first rain.

In the celestian gardens of Evening Star, there grew a great many plants, including Mother Maize, the greatest of food plants. Evening Star gave maize to her daughter as a gift to plant on the newly emerged earth. Soon the Sun and the Moon produced a son, who married the daughter of Evening Star and Morning Star. Daughter-of-Evening-and-Morning-Star and Son-of-Sun-and-Moon are the parents of all living human beings, as well as the first beings to cultivate maize. ◆

Arikara

The Great Sky Spirit, Nesaru, sometimes called the Great Mystery, was the master of all creation. Below the sky was an endless body of water where two ducks eternally swam. Nesaru made two brothers, Wolf-man and Lucky-man, who commanded the ducks to swim to the bottom of the great water and bring up some earth. With this earth, Wolf-man made the Great Plains and Lucky-Man made the hills and mountains.

The two brothers went down beneath the earth and found two spiders. They explained to the spiders how to reproduce. The two spiders produced many kinds of animals and plants, including human beings. However, they also produced a race of evil giants.

These giants were so evil that Nesaru eventually had to destroy them with a great flood. However, Nesaru loved human beings and saved them from destruction. ◆

Chippewa/Algonquin

NOTE: Versions of this myth can be found throughout the Algonquin linguistic area, which extends from the Atlantic coast to the Mississippi River, and from North Carolina in the south to the Subarctic.

GLOOSKAP AND MALSUM

The great Earth Mother had two sons, Glooskap and Malsum. Glooskap was good, wise, and creative; Malsum was evil, selfish, and destructive. When their mother died, Glooskap went to work creating plants, animals, and humans from her body. Malsum, in contrast, made poisonous plants and snakes. As Glooskap continued to create wonderful things, Malsum grew tired of his good brother and plotted to kill him.

In jest, Malsum bragged that he was invincible, although there was one thing that could kill him: the roots of the fern plant. He badgered Glooskap for days to find the good brother's vulnerability. Finally, as Glooskap could tell no lies, he confided that he could be killed only by an owl feather. Knowing this, Malsum made a dart from an owl feather and killed Glooskap. The power of good is so strong, however, that Glooskap rose from the dead, ready to avenge himself. Alive again, Glooskap also knew that Malsum would continue to plot against him.

Glooskap realized that he had no choice but to destroy Malsum in order that good would survive and his creatures would continue to live. So he went to a stream and attracted his evil brother by loudly saying that a certain flowering reed could also kill him. Glooskap then pulled a fern plant out by the roots and flung it at Malsum, who fell to the ground dead. Malsum's spirit went underground and became a wicked wolf-spirit that still occasionally torments humans and animals, but fears the light of day. ♦

Iroquois

The first humans lived up beyond the sky as there was no earth beneath. One day, a great chief's daughter became ill and no cure could be found. A wise old man recommended that they dig up the roots of a certain tree in order to cure her. The people all worked together and dug a great hole around the base of the tree. In time, however, both the chief's daughter and the tree fell through the hole into the world below.

Below there was only a vast sea where two swans continuously swam. When the tree and the girl fell into the water, there was a clap of thunder. The swans heard this and came to see what had happened. They saw that the girl had fallen from the sky and went to save her. As this was all very strange to the swans, they went to the Great Turtle, wisest of all creatures, for advice.

The Great Turtle told them that the tree and the girl were a good omen. He then commanded all the creatures to find the tree and bring up the magic soil that was attached to its roots. The swans were assigned to take this magic earth and build an island for the girl to live on. All of the animals were involved in the search for the tree, but only an old toad was successful in bringing up any of the soil. She swam to the bottom, returned to spit out a mouthful of the dirt, and then died. The mouthful of earth then turned into a vast land mass.

But the earth was still dark at this time. The girl told the Great Turtle that there was light in the world above. So the Great Turtle instructed the burrowing animals to bore holes in the sky for light to shine through.

The girl is the mother of all living things. There are a number of theories of how she conceived the first humans on earth. One is that she was impregnated when she fell into the sea. Another is that the action of the magic earth with the sea caused her to conceive. In any case, the human race is the result of the union of the land and sea, as well as having origins in the sky above. ♦

Yuma

In the very beginning, there was nothing but water and darkness. The water sloshed around, splashing foam and spray. Some of the spray congealed and formed the sky. Kokomaht, the Creator, lived underneath the water and was two beings in one. He rose up out of the water and said his own name, Kokomaht, the Father and Creator of all.

But out of himself came another being called Bakotahl. When the other being called to Kokomaht out of the water, he asked, "Did you rise up from the water with your eyes open or shut?" Kokomaht knew that this other was evil, and decided to deceive Bakotahl, answering that his eyes had been open. So Bakotahl emerged from the water with his eyes open and became blind. Evil ones to this very day are still blind: *bakotahl* means "the blind one." All things made by

Kokomaht were good, while all things that Bakotahl produced were evil.

The two stood on the waters as there was no firm land created yet. Kokomaht asked his blind brother, "Where is the north?" But, being blind, Bakotahl pointed toward the south.

Then Kokomaht responded, "That is not the north," and then he created the four directions. He faced west and said, "This shall be the west." Then he faced east and said, "This shall be the east," and so on. He took four steps to the south and the south came into being; he took four steps north to create the north.

Then Kokomaht told his blind brother, "I will scatter the waters and make earth." So Kokomaht turned to face the north, creating a whirlwind that blew away enough water to create dry land. And Kokomaht then seated himself on the land. Bakotahl came to join him. Wishing to outdo his good brother, Bakotahl then said that he would make human beings.

Feeling around in the wet clay, Bakotahl took clay and water and began to make human beings, but they did not have fingers and toes. When the creatures were finished, Bakotahl showed them to Kokomaht, who knew that they were not right.

So Kokomaht decided to make humans. Taking clay, he formed a male with complete hands and feet. Kokomaht took the male and swung it four times to the north and then four times to the south, and it came to life. Then he made a female and did the same thing.

In the time that Kokomaht was busy making humans, Bakotahl had created seven beings. Kokomaht asked his brother what he was doing. Bakotahl responded that he was making humans, too. Kokomaht told his evil brother to examine the proper humans, perfectly made. Unlike the creatures made by Bakotahl, Kokomaht's humans had fingers that enabled them to make things and create works of art. Bakotahl was jealous and didn't like these perfect humans at all. Kokomaht stamped his feet and Bakotahl's creatures fell into the water and became ducks and geese.

This angered Bakotahl, who made a whirlwind that created all the enemies of humankind: disease, bad intentions, and plagues.

Kokomaht was now alone on the land with only a man and a

woman. So Kokomaht went to work creating more people—a male and a female of each race—the Cocopahs, the Mojaves, and the ancestral parents of all other peoples on earth. The last group he created were the white people. Kokomaht taught all these couples how to have intercourse and propagate the race.

As the people scattered to their own places on the earth, Kokomaht saw that his work of creation was done. But among the people was the Frog (Hanyi), who rebelled against Kokomaht and wished to destroy him through her powerful magic. Hanyi burrowed into the ground underneath the feet of Kokomaht and pulled out his breath until his throat became dry and he began to die. As he died, he taught the people the road of death.

Kokomaht had made himself a son, Komashtam'ho, who took up the post of the Creator. It was Komashtam'ho who made the sun that shines during the day by spitting into his hand, making a ball, and casting it into the sky. He threw it into the east, where the sun still rises. He spat into his hand and cast it into the heavens, where it became the stars.

The death of Kokomaht caused the people to despair. Komashtam'ho decided to burn the body of his father, the Creator, teaching the people the funeral rites. But there were no trees to burn in the fire. So, with a word, Komashtam'ho called trees out of the north and built a funeral pyre.

Before his death, Kokomaht had told the Coyote, "Take my heart; be good to all my creatures." But Coyote misunderstood the command. What Kokomaht had meant was "Be as I was"; Coyote thought that this command was to steal and eat the heart of Kokomaht. So the Coyote prowled around the funeral pyre waiting for just the right moment to climb up and eat the Creator's heart.

Komashtam'ho knew of Coyote's intentions and he dispatched the Coyote to travel to the east as the sun was rising, to fetch fire. Komashtam'ho knew very well that the humans would need fire in order to survive. When Coyote returned with the fire, he again plotted how to steal the heart of Kokomaht. However, the badger jumped up on the funeral pyre and succeeded in stealing the heart. All of the other animals tried to catch the badger, but none succeeded.

Komashtam'ho told the Coyote, "You will always be a thief, living by stealing. Men will despise you and kill you to defend their flocks." And all the people heard this.

Then Komashtam'ho spoke to all the people as the flames consumed the body of Kokomaht. He told them, "You will never again see Kokomaht in the flesh; he is dead. All of you will die someday as well. If Kokomaht had been allowed to live, then all of you would be immortal and the world would be overpopulated. But Kokomaht's spirit lives on and so will your spirits." The fire was so hot that it dried up the land, turning it into the desert where the Yuma people live today.

Just then a whirlwind formed around the ashes of Kokomaht and the people asked what it was. Komashtam'ho replied that the wind was the mighty spirit of Kokomaht. Although the body dies, the spirit lasts forever. Each man's spirit, at death, leaves the body and goes off to live with the spirits of those whom it loved in life.

The spirit of Kokomaht lives on to protect all that is good. Bakotahl lives under the earth and turns around, causing earthquakes. Bakotahl still causes suffering and evil among men. But the good spirit of Kokomaht can overcome any evil. ♦

Pima

CHUHWUHT: THE SONG OF THE WORLD

In the beginning there was only darkness and water. The darkness congealed in certain places and it is from this that the Creator was made. He wandered aimlessly above the water [compare this to the Genesis story] and began to think. He became fully conscious of who he was and what he was to do. He then reached into his heart and pulled out a magic creation stick.

He used this as a walking stick and when some resin formed on the tip [compare this to the Japanese Creation myth], he made it into ants. He took more of this resin and rolled it with his feet into a perfect ball while chanting

Chuhwuht tuh maka-i
Chuhwuht tuh nato
Chuhwuht tuh maka-i
Chuhwuht tuh nato
Himalo, Himalo
Himalo, Himicho!

I make the world, and see,
the world is finished.
I make the world, and see,
the world is finished.
Let it go, let it go
Let it go, start it forth!

As he chanted, the ball grew larger and larger until it became the present size of the earth; thus was the earth created. Then the Creator took a great rock, broke it, and threw it into the heavens, where the pieces became the stars. Then he made the moon in a similar fashion, but neither the moon nor the stars furnished enough light.

So the Creator then took two bowls of water from out of his flesh and he thought thoughts of light. The sun appeared in the sky as he pulled the bowls apart. But the sun did not yet move. So the Creator bounced it like a ball to the east and it bounced back to the west, even as it does today. ♦

Zuni

NOTE: Compare the spread of the green algae in this myth with the theory of scientific evolution.

In the beginning, there was only moisture, which became clouds. The Great Father Sun, the Creator Awonawilona, thickened the clouds into water that then formed a great sea. With his own flesh Awonawilona fertilized the sea and green algae grew over it. The green algae produced the earth and sky. The marriage of earth and sky and the action of the sun on the green algae produced all living things.

From the lowest of the four caves of the earth, the seeds of men and animals were incubated as eggs. The Creator provided enough warmth that the eggs were hatched and all living creatures were produced. ◆

The Playanos* of Southern California

An invisible, all-powerful being named Nocuma made the world. He rolled it into a ball with his hands. But it did not sit in its appointed place so he inserted a great black rock called Tosaut as ballast.

In the beginning the sea was a series of small streams choked with fish. It was so crowded that some of the fish tried to colonize the land, but they failed and died in the hot sun. Then some of the larger fish attacked Tosaut, releasing salt and more water; thus was the ocean produced.

With the sea and land completed, Nocuma took some soil and seawater and made a man, calling him Ejoni. Then he made a woman whom he called Ae. They were the parents of all human beings. ◆

Maya

NOTE: The Mayas were an advanced people who lived in the area now known as Guatemala, Honduras, Belize, and the Mexican state of Yucatán, where their descendants now live. This story is from the Popol Vuh, the Mayan epic. It is both a Creation myth and a beautiful morality tale.

Playanos is a Spanish word meaning "beach people."

There were four gods in heaven and each of them sat on his chair, observing the world below. Then the yellow lord suggested that they make a man to enjoy the earth and offer praise to the gods. The other three agreed.

So the yellow god took a lump of yellow clay and made a man from it. But his creation was weak; it dissolved in water and could not stand upright.

Then the red god suggested that they make a man out of wood, and the others agreed. So the red god took a branch from a tree and carved it into a human shape. When they tested it in water, it floated; it stood upright without any problem whatsoever. However, when they tested it with fire, it burned.

The four lords decided to try again. This time the black god suggested making a man out of gold. The gold man was beautiful and shone like the sun. He survived the tests of fire and water, looking even more handsome after these tests. However, the gold man was cold to the touch; he was unable to speak, feel, move, or worship the gods. But they left him on earth anyway.

The fourth god, the colorless lord, decided to make humans out of his own flesh. He cut the fingers off his left hand and they jumped and fell to earth. The four gods could hardly see what the men of flesh looked like as they were so far away. From the seat of the four lords, they looked like busy little ants.

But the men of flesh worshiped the gods and made offerings to them. They filled the hearts of the four lords with joy. One day the men of flesh found the man of gold. When they touched him, he was as cold as a stone. When they spoke to him, he was silent. But the kindness of the men of flesh warmed the heart of the man of gold and he came to life, offering praise to the gods for the kindness of the men of flesh.

The word of praise from the previously silent creature woke the four gods from their sleep and they looked down on earth in delight. They called the man of gold "rich" and the men of flesh "poor," ordaining that the rich should look after the poor. The rich man will be judged at his death on the basis of how he cared for the poor. From that day onward, no rich man can enter heaven unless he is brought there by a poor man. ♦

Inca

NOTE: The Inca empire covered the Andean region, including Peru, Ecuador, and Bolivia. The language of the empire, Quechua, is still spoken extensively in Peru and Bolivia. Please take note that the god in this myth is named Con Tiqui (or Kon Tiki) Viracocha. Thor Heyerdahl's voyage from Peru to Polynesia on the balsa raft *Kon Tiki* was intended to demonstrate commerce between the two cultures, as *tiki* is a term used by both the Polynesians and the Peruvians for "god."

In the most ancient of times the earth was covered in darkness. Then, out of a lake called Collasuyu, the god Con Tiqui Viracocha emerged, bringing some human beings with him. Then Con Tiqui created the sun (Inti), the moon and the stars to light the world. It is from Inti that the Inca, emperor of Tahuantisuyo,* is descended. Out of great rocks Con Tiqui fashioned more human beings, including women who were already pregnant. Then he sent these people off into every corner of the world. He kept a male and female with him at Cuzco, the "navel of the world."

Another story is that Con, the Creator, was in the form of a man without bones. He filled the earth with good things to supply the needs of the first humans. The people, however, forgot Con's goodness to them and rebelled. So he punished them by stopping the rainfall. The miserable people were forced to work hard, drawing what little water they could find from stinking, drying riverbeds. Then a new god, Pachachamac, came and drove Con out, changing his people into monkeys. Pachachamac then took earth and made the ancestors of human beings. ♦

---

*"The Four Corners of the World," the name for the Inca empire; "Inca" is properly the name of the emperor.

THE BABYLONIAN CREATION MYTH

NOTE: In the account of Creation in Genesis, God makes the world for humankind; in the Babylonian story, the gods make humankind to work for them.

In the beginning there was Apsu, the sky god, and Tiamat, the chaos goddess. From their union came all gods. These younger gods grew restless and chose Marduk as their champion. It is he who finished the work of creation by slaying Tiamat, his mother, and Kingu, her lover.

Then joined issue Tiamat and Marduk, wisest of gods
   They strove in single combat, locked in battle.
The lord spread out his net to enfold her
   The Evil Wind, which followed behind, he let loose in
      her face.
When Tiamat opened her mouth to consume him,
   He drove in the Evil Wind that she close not her lips.
As the fierce winds charged her belly,
   Her body was distended and her mouth was wide open.
He released the arrow, it tore her belly,
   It cut through her insides, splitting her heart.
Having thus subdued her, he extinguished her life.
   He cast down her carcass to stand upon it.
After he had slain Tiamat the leader,
   Her band was shattered, her troupe broken up;
And the gods, her helpers who marched at her side,
   Trembling with terror turned their backs about,
In order to save their lives.
   Tightly encircled, they could not escape;
He made them captives and he smashed their weapons.
   Thrown into the net, they found themselves ensnared;
Placed in cells, they were filled with wailing;
   Bearing his wrath, they were held imprisoned. . . .

The lord trod on the legs of Tiamat,
  With his unsparing mace he crushed her skull.
When the arteries of her blood he had severed,
  The north wind bore it to places undisclosed.
They brought him gifts of homage, they to him.
  Then the lord paused to view her dead body
That he might divide the monster and do artful works.
  He split her like a shellfish into two parts:
Half of her he set up and ceiled as sky,
  Pulled down the bar and posted guards,
He bade them to allow not her waters to escape.

. . . He constructed stations for the great gods,
  Fixing their astral likenesses as constellations.
He determined the year by designating the zones:
  He set up three constellations for each of the twelve
    months.

. . . When Marduk hears the words of the gods,
  His heart prompts him to do artful works.
Opening his mouth, he addresses Ea, god of waters,
  "Blood I will mass and cause bones to be.
I will establish a savage, 'man' shall be his name;
  Truly savage man I will create.
He shall be charged with the service of the gods
  That they might be at ease!"

. . . It was Kingu who contrived the uprising,
  And made Tiamat rebel, and joined battle.
They bound him [Kingu], holding him before Ea.
They imposed on him his guilt and severed his blood
    vessels.
Out of his blood they fashioned mankind.
  He [Ea] imposed the service and let free the gods.
After Ea, the wise had created mankind,
  Had imposed upon it the service of the gods. ♦

THE BIBLICAL CREATION STORIES

NOTE: The first Creation story is referred to as the "Elohist" version of the Creation, as God is referred to as Elohim (a plural form) in the original Hebrew. The second story is referred to as the "Yahwist" version, as God is referred to by the sacred name YHVH, transliterated as "Yahweh." It is believed by some Bible scholars that the two versions were integrated into the Torah at the time of its compilation. The authorship of Genesis, and the whole Torah, is traditionally attributed to Moses.

The First Account of Creation (Genesis 1:1–2:4)

In the beginning God created the heavens and the earth. Now the earth was a formless void, there was darkness over the deep, and God's spirit hovered over the water.

God said, "Let there be light," and there was light. God saw that the light was good, and God divided light from darkness. God called light "day," and the darkness he called "night." Evening came and morning came: the first day.

God said, "Let there be a vault in the waters to divide the waters in two." And so it was. God made the vault, and it divided the waters above the vault from the waters under the vault. God called the vault "heaven." Evening came and morning came: the second day.

God said, "Let the waters under heaven come together into a single mass, and let dry land appear." And so it was. God called the dry land "earth" and the mass of waters "seas," and God saw that it was good.

God said, "Let the earth produce vegetation; seed-bearing plants, and fruit-bearing trees bearing fruits with their seeds inside, on the earth." And so it was. The earth produced vegetation: plants bearing seeds in their several kinds, and trees bearing fruit with their seeds inside in their several kinds. God saw that it was good. Evening came and then morning came: the third day.

God said, "Let there be lights in the vault of heaven to divide day from night, and let them indicate festivals, days and years. Let them be lights in the vault of heaven to shine on the earth." And so it was. God made the two great lights: the greater light to govern the day, the smaller light to govern the night and to divide light from darkness. God saw that it was good. Evening came and morning came: the fourth day.

God said, "Let the waters teem with living creatures, and let birds fly above the earth within the vault of heaven." And so it was. God created great sea-serpents and every kind of living creature with which the waters teem, and every kind of winged creature. God saw that it was good. God blessed them, saying, "Be fruitful, multiply and fill the waters of the seas; and let the birds multiply upon the earth." Evening came and morning came: the fifth day.

God said, "Let the earth produce every kind of living creature: cattle, reptiles, and every kind of wild beast." And so it was. God made every kind of beast, every kind of cattle, and every kind of land reptile. God saw that it was good.

God said, "Let us make man in our own image, in the likeness of ourselves [*Elohim* is a plural word in Hebrew], and let them be masters of the fish of the sea, the birds of heaven, the cattle, all the wild beasts and all the reptiles that crawl upon the earth."

God created man in the image of Himself; in the image of God He created them; male and female he created them.

God blessed them, saying to them, "Be fruitful, multiply, fill the earth and conquer it. Be masters of the fish of the sea, the birds of heaven and all living animals on the earth." God said, "See, I give you all the seed-bearing plants that are upon the whole earth, and all the trees with seed-bearing fruit; this shall be your food. To all wild beasts, all birds of heaven and all living reptiles on the earth I give all the foliage of plants for food." And so it was. God saw all that he had made, and indeed it was very good. Evening came and morning came: the sixth day.

Thus heaven and earth were completed in all their array. On the seventh day God completed the work he had been doing. He rested on the seventh day and made it holy, because on that day he rested after all his work of creating.

Such were the origins of heaven and earth when they were created. ♦

Second Account of Creation (Genesis 2:5–25)

At the time when Yahweh God made earth and heaven there was as yet no wild bush on the earth nor had any wild plant yet sprung up, for Yahweh God had not sent rain on the earth, nor was there any man to till the soil. However, a flood was rising from the earth and watering all the surface of the soil. Yahweh fashioned a man out of the dust from the soil. Then he breathed into his nostrils a breath of life and thus man became a living being.

Yahweh God planted a garden in Eden, which is in the east, and there he put the man he had fashioned. Yahweh God caused to spring up from the soil every kind of tree, enticing to look at and good to eat, with the tree of life and the tree of the knowledge of good and evil in the middle of the garden. A river flowed from Eden to water the garden, and from there it divided to make four streams. The first is named the Pishon, and this encircles the whole land of Havilah where there is gold. The gold of this land is pure; bdellum [an aromatic resin] and onyx stone are found there. The second river is the Gihon, and this encircles the whole land of Cush. The third river is named the Tigris, and this flows to the east of Ashur [Assyria]. The fourth river is the Euphrates.

Yahweh God took the man and settled him in the garden of Eden to cultivate it and take care of it. Then Yahweh God gave the man this admonition, "You may eat indeed of all the trees in the garden. Nevertheless of the tree of the knowledge of good and evil, you are not to eat, for on the day you eat of it you shall most surely die."

Yahweh God said, "It is not good that the man should be alone. I will make him a helpmate." So from the soil Yahweh God fashioned all the wild beasts and all the birds of heaven. These he brought to the man to see what he could call them; each one was to bear the name the man would give it. The man gave names to all the cattle, all the birds of heaven and all the wild beasts. But no helpmate suitable for man was found for him. So Yahweh God made the man fall into a deep sleep. And while he slept, he took one of the ribs and enclosed it in flesh. Yahweh God built the rib he had taken from the man into a woman, and brought her to the man. The man exclaimed:

> This at last is bone from my bones
> and flesh from my flesh;
> This is to be called woman
> for this was taken from man.*

This is why a man leaves his father and mother and joins himself to his wife and they become one body. ♦

THE TALMUDIC CREATION STORY

NOTE: During the postbiblical period, Jewish rabbis debated and analyzed the fine points of the Old Testament, trying to clear up difficulties. The result of this process was the Talmud, the vast repository of commentary, wisdom, theology, and folklore that remains a priceless heritage of Judaism.

When God decided to create the world, the twenty-two letters of the [Hebrew] alphabet came into His divine presence; each one of them wanted to be the first letter of the first word spoken by God in the creation of the world. But it was the letter Beth that was chosen, as the first word out of the mouth of God was *baruch*, meaning "blessed." It was with a blessing that God began his work.

On the first day, God made the heavens and the earth, light and darkness, day and night. He took a stone and threw it into the great void, where it became the core of the earth. On the second day, God created the angels; on the third day he made the plants, including the giant cedars of Lebanon. That day he also created iron in the

---

*In Hebrew, this is a play on words; *ish* meaning "man," and *isha* meaning "woman."

earth for axes to cut the cedars down, lest they grow too tall and arrogant. The Lord created Gan Eden, the Paradise where Adam and
Eve would dwell, and which the righteous enjoy when they die. The
fourth day, the sun, moon, and stars were created. On the fifth day,
the sea creatures were made including Leviathan, as well as the
birds, including the legendary Zinn.

It was on the sixth day that God created the beasts, including the
giant Behemoth. It was also on the sixth day that God made human
beings. God had discussed the creation of humans with the angels,
who weren't too sure that it was a good idea. Some of the angels re-
sented the idea that God would create another sentient being and
they complained. God, tired of their impudence, pointed his finger at
these angels and they were consumed by fire. God then ordered the
angel Gabriel to go and bring soil from the four corners of the world,
with which to make man.

When Gabriel began his task, he learned that the earth was reluctant to give up any soil for the creation of humans. The earth knew
that mankind would someday ruin the earth and spoil its beauty.
Upon hearing this, God himself scooped up the earth and fashioned
Adam, the first man.

When God created the body of man, He prepared to join it with
the soul, which had been created on the first day. The angels were
again concerned that another creature with a soul would exist.
Among the most contentious of these angels was Samael [meaning
"venom of God"], who was also called Satan. He told God: "You created us, the angels, from your Shekhinah ["Divine Presence"] and
now you would place us over a lowly thing made of dirt? You would
waste a soul on a piece of mud? You would create a thinking being
out of dust?"

God was tired of Samael's incessant complaining and his arrogance
in questioning Him. He then cast Samael and his followers out of
heaven into hell.

Out of the dust of the ground gathered from the four corners of the
earth, God fashioned Adam [Hebrew: *adamah*], and into his nostrils
breathed the breath of life. Some say that this Adam was like a
twenty-year-old man.

Other Rabbis say that Adam looked out over the many animals on earth and noticed that they were all male or female, yet he had no female. So God first created a woman named Lillith out of dust. But Lillith set herself over Adam and balked at the way that he wished to make love, with the man on top. "Why?" She scowled. "Who are you to lord over me? We are both made of dust!" In her arrogance she recited the sacred, unspeakable name of God and disappeared from sight.

After this miserable creature went to live among the demons, God felt sorry for Adam and decided to make him a good woman, Eve. Adam ruled over all the plants and male animals in the east and north of the Garden of Eden, while Eve ruled the female animals in the south and west. Adam and Eve went about naked, except for a band over their shoulders that was inscribed with the sacred name of God.

And Adam and Eve lived in perfect innocence at this time. But Samael and Lillith were busy plotting how to confound these good people. ♦

THE CREATION

And God stepped out on space
And he looked around and said:
I'm lonely—
I'll make me a world.

As far as the eye of God could see
Darkness covered everything,
Blacker than a hundred midnights
Down in a cypress swamp.

Then God smiled,
And the light broke,
And the darkness rolled up on one side,
And the light stood shining on the other
And God said: That's good!

Then God himself stepped down—
And the sun was in his right hand,
And the moon was in his left;
And the stars were clustered about his head,
And the earth was under his feet.
And God walked, and where he trod
His footsteps hollowed the valleys out
And bulged the mountains up.

Then he stopped and looked and saw
That the earth was hot and barren.
So God stepped over the edge of the world
And he spat out the seven seas—
He batted his eyes, and the lightning flashed;
He clapped his hands and the thunder rolled—
And the waters came down,
The cooling waters came down.

Then the green grass sprouted,
And the little red flowers blossomed,
The pine tree pointed his finger to the sky,
And the oak spread out his arms,
The lakes cuddled down in the hollows of the ground,
And the rivers ran down to the sea;
And God smiled again
And the rainbow appeared,
And curled itself around his shoulder.

Then God raised his arm and he waved his hand
Over the sea and over the land
And he said: Bring forth! Bring forth!
And quicker than God could drop his hand,
Fishes and fowls
And beasts and birds
Swam the rivers and the seas,
Roamed the forests and the woods,
And split the air with their wings,
And God said: That's good!

Then God walked around
And God looked around
On all that he had made.

He looked at the sun,
And he looked at the moon,
And he looked at the little stars;
He looked on his world
With all its living things,
And God said: I'm lonely still.

Then God sat down—
On the side of a hill where he could think;
By a deep wide river he sat down;
With his head in his hands,
God thought and thought,
Till he thought: I'll make me a man!

Up from the bed of a river
God scooped the clay;
And by the bank of the river
He kneeled him down;
And there the great God Almighty
Who lit the sun and fixed it in the sky,
Who flung the stars to the most far corner of the night,
Who rounded the earth in the middle of his hand;
This great God,
Like a mammy bending over his baby
Kneeled down in the dust
Toiling over a lump of clay
Till he shaped it in his own image;
Then into it he blew the breath of life
And man became a living soul.
Amen. Amen.

             —James Weldon Johnson (1871–1938),
             African-American poet

SOME NOTES ON THE CREATION MYTHS

The Serpent

The serpent is common in many Creation stories and has been interpreted in a number of interesting ways. The most common, and ob-

vious, is as a phallic symbol, but this is only one facet of a complex image.

On the theme of the serpent in mythology, Joseph Campbell writes in *The Masks of God: Occidental Mythology:*

> The wonderful ability of the serpent to slough its skin and so renew its youth has earned for it throughout the world the character of the master of the mystery of rebirth—of which the moon, waxing and waning, sloughing its shadow and again waxing, is the celestial sign. The moon is the lord and measure of the life-creating cycle of the womb, and therewith of birth and equally of death—which two, in sum, are aspects of one state of being. The moon is the lord of tides and of the dew that falls at night to refresh the verdure on which cattle graze. But the serpent, too, is the lord of waters. Dwelling in the earth, among the roots of trees, frequenting springs, marshes and watercourses, it glides with a motion of waves; or it ascends like a liana into branches, there to hang like some fruit of death. The phallic suggestion is immediate, and as swallower, the female organ is also suggested; so that a dual image is rendered, which works implicitly on the sentiments. Likewise a dual association of fire and water attaches to the lightning of its strike, the forced darting of its active tongue, and the lethal burning of its strike. When imagined biting its tail, as the mythological "uroburos," it suggests the waters that in all archaic cosmologies surround—as well as lie beneath and permeate—the floating circlar island earth.

Isaac Asimov, in his book, *In the Beginning* . . . , notes that there is a connection between the serpent in the book of Genesis and the dragon in the Babylonian Creation myth.

> The serpent contradicts God [when he tells Eve that 'Ye shall not surely die if she eats of the fruit of the tree of knowledge']. Why?
>
> It seems motiveless, but the mere fact that the serpent does this gives us cause to suspect that it may be the principle of Chaos. In the Babylonian Creation-myth, Tiamat, the personification of Chaos, is described as a dragon, but a dragon is essentially a huge serpent, sometimes shown with wings (indicating perhaps the smoothness with which the serpent can slither here and there) and with fiery breath (indicating the serpent's poison).

Isaiah refers to all the terms used for Chaos when he promises the victory of God over the destructive forces: "In that day the Lord with his sore and great and strong sword shall punish leviathan the piercing serpent, even leviathan that crooked serpent; and he shall slay the dragon that is in the sea" (Isaiah 27:1).

In later times, when Judea was a province of the Persian Empire, the Jews picked up the notions of the eternal conflict between the principles of Good and Evil and abandoned the notions of a once-and-for-all victory of Good at the start.

Satan came into existence in Jewish thought as an eternal anti-God, striving constantly to undo the work of Creation and restore Chaos; eternal vigilance was required to prevent that. The thought then arose that the serpent was really the embodiment of Satan, a thought presented with unparalleled magnificence in Milton's "Paradise Lost."

There is, however, nothing in the Biblical story of the Garden of Eden to indicate that. The notion of Satan seems to have been entirely an afterthought.

From the Jungian psychological perspective, Dr. M. L. von Franz, writing in *Man and His Symbols*, edited by Jung himself, takes the following psychological view of the significance not only of the serpent motif but also of that of ducks and swans swimming on the primordial sea in the Finnish and North American Indian myths:

Other transcendent symbols of the depths are rodents, lizards, snakes and sometimes, fish. These are intermediate creatures that combine underwater activity and the birdflight with an intermediate terrestrial life. The wild duck or the swan are cases in point. Perhaps the commonest [sic] dream symbol of transcendence is the snake, as represented by the therapeutic symbol of the Roman god of medicine Aesculapius, which has survived in modern times as a sign of the medical profession. This was originally a non-poisonous tree-snake; as we see it, coiled around the staff of the healing god, it seems to embody a kind of mediation between heaven and earth.

A still more important and widespread symbol of chthonic (underworld) transcendence is the motif of the two entwined serpents. These are the famous Naga serpents of ancient India; and we also find them in Greece on the end of the staff belonging to the god Hermes. An early Grecian herm (altar to Hermes) is a stone pillar with a bust of the god above. On one side are the entwined serpents and on the other an erect phallus. As the serpents are represented in the act of sexual union and the erect phallus is unequivocally sexual, we can draw certain conclusions about the herm as a symbol of fertility.

But we are mistaken if we think this only refers to biological fertility. Hermes is Trickster in a different role as messenger [of the gods], a god of the crossroads and finally the leader of souls to and from the underworld.

The universal symbol of the serpent has a number of aspects, only a few of which were discussed above. However, people have always been intrigued by the reference to the serpent in the Old and New Testaments as "wise." Certainly this would seem to point to its seemingly miraculous quality of shedding its skin and regeneration. However, it also brings to bear thoughts of ancestral memory. The theory of scientific evolution and, certainly, the Genesis account, place the appearance of the serpent chronologically earlier than that of humans. Perhaps there is an ancestral memory of a time when reptiles, and not humans, were the dominant species on earth.

Another mythic theme is found in both the Greek myth of Eurynome and Ophion and the Genesis account of the Fall. This is the bruising of the serpent's head with the woman's heel. This may be seen in a variety of ways as well. One is that there was an early struggle between men and women as a matriarchy gave way to a patriarchy. If one accepts the serpent as phallic symbol, the fact that the woman bruises the serpent's head may be an early memory of the matriarchy defeating males. In Christian terms, this is considered the first Messianic prophecy: The son of a woman (Christ) eventually defeats the serpent (Satan).

Water

The ancient peoples were aware, as we are today, that water is a necessary precondition for life as we know it. During the Mariner probes of the planet Mars in the 1970s, the search for life was largely a search for water. Water is certainly an important part of us: Our bodies are two-thirds water by weight. Blood plasma is 90 percent water, and even "solid" muscle tissue is at least 80 percent water. It takes one thousand pounds of water to produce one pound of vegetable food. Thus, it is only natural that water is the perfect place to start in any story of the Creation.

In Jungian psychology, water is a dream symbol manifest in the myths and the unconscious mind and the wisdom contained therein. Thus, our dreams of bathing in or drinking water may be interpreted as symbolic of the quest for wisdom or for communication between the conscious and unconscious mind. Another possible Jungian approach to the water motif in the Creation myths is the dawn of human consciousness.

Judaism and Christianity are rich with metaphors of water. The Bible refers to "drinking of the living waters" of God's word. Baptism washes away sin and creates a "new being." The divinity of Christ in the New Testament was revealed as he was baptized by John the Baptist. Converts to Judaism are baptized, and ritual bathing in the *mikvah*, or purification pool, is a ritual requirement for women after menstruation.

Modern scientific theories also begin in the water. A watery chaos is considered the earliest home of life on this planet. Modern scientists speak of life as evolving in a primordial soup that constituted about 10 percent of the world's waters at one time. This "soup" contained the necessary materials for the creation of life, particularly the carbon compounds and hydrogen, which combine and recombine to form DNA, the basic "building block" of life.

Scientific theory has some fascinating parallels with the myths, including the Genesis account.

The Precambrian Period

The earth is about 4.7 billion years old, according to this theory, and the first life appeared in shallow pools about 2.7 billion years ago. The first fossil evidence of photosynthetic plant life has been dated to about 2.5 billion years ago.

The Cambrian Period

Louis Pasteur hypothesized that the first life on earth was anaerobic (not dependent upon oxygen), and that the first major shift in
the development of life took place when the world's oxygen level
reached one one-hundredths of its present state. This level is referred to as the first critical level for the development of life, and it
is at this point that the basic life forms shifted from being anaerobic
in nature to aerobic (requiring oxygen). This period is believed to
have taken place about 600 million years ago and is characterized by
a virtual explosion of life-forms in the seas. As per many Creation
stories, the land was not yet entirely separate from the water.

The Ordovician Period

About 500 million years ago. Vertebrate life-forms appeared and
the land was slowly emerging from the sea.

The Silurian Period

About 425 million years ago. The level of oxygen present in the
earth's atmosphere, due to the action of photosynthetic plants producing oxygen, reached the second critical level of one tenth of today's level. The continents were increasingly drier—the land was
"separated from the waters"—and the first terrestrial plants and animals appeared.

The Devonian Period

About 405 million years ago. The seed plants, bony fishes, and
amphibians appeared; the land was still a bit drier and there was glaciation on the earth.

The Mississippian Period

About 355 million years ago. The sharks and amphibians were greatly developed, as were large-scale trees and seed ferns. The climate was warm and humid.

The Pennsylvanian Period

About 310 million years ago. Reptiles appeared, but amphibians were the dominant animal life-form. The appearance of gymnosperm plants, vast forests, and swamps was characteristic of this period. This was also the period of the great formations of coal and petroleum deposits.

The Permian Period

This is the period, some 280 million years before the present, when the earth cooled and the land became much drier. With this change in temperature, many species became extinct.

The Triassic Period

Some 220 million years ago. The dinosaurs and gymnosperm plants became the dominant life-forms on earth. There was also a large-scale extinction of the tree ferns.

The Jurassic Period

Some 181 million years ago. The birds and mammals first appeared. The great period of the dinosaurs.

The Cretaceous Period

Some 135 million years ago. The monocotyledonous plants appeared, as did the first modern mammals. At the end of this period there was a widespread extinction of the dinosaurs.

The Paleocene Epoch

Some 65 million years ago. The first placental mammals appeared.

The Eocene Epoch

About 54 million years ago. The hoofed animals and the carnivores appeared.

The Oligocene Epoch

Some 36 million years ago. The climate became warmer and most modern species of animals appeared.

The Miocene Epoch

About 25 million years ago. The anthropoid (humanlike) apes were established; most mammals took forms that would be recognizable today.

The Pliocene Epoch

Man was evolving, some 11 million years ago, forests giving way to spreading grasslands.

The Pleistocene Epoch

About 1 million years ago. The first distinctly human social life appeared amid glaciation and significant extinction of many forms of life.

The Recent Epoch

The earth witnessed the dawn of the first truly "civilized" human societies about eleven thousand years ago. This is an interesting number, considering that the Hindu and Persian myths believe the present world to have begun at about that time.

* * *

My purpose here is not to participate in the Evolution-versus-Creationism battle, but rather to show that science and the great myths share striking similarities and demonstrate very similar speculations on the origin of life that cannot be ignored. The "how" of science and the "why" of myth converge at this point.

The Tree

The tree naturally lends itself to rich mythological symbolism. Its roots reach deep into the earth, the "mother" of many myths; its branches reach high to touch "father" sky. Unlike any other living thing, the tree continues to grow throughout its lifetime and has a life span of hundreds and even thousands of years. This makes the tree a potent symbol of immortality.

So it is little wonder that we find the tree so commonly in the myths. To the Norse, Sioux, Algonquins, and Persians, it is from the tree that man is created. As these trees become human beings, there is a powerful metaphor of "the Fall" in that, prior to becoming human, the trees were rooted and could touch the sky; as humans, they are rootless and cannot reach heaven.

The tree is a symbol of wisdom as well. Ancient poets must have looked at great trees and reflected on how many individual lives had passed during the life of the tree. It is beneath such a tree, the bo or bodhi tree, that Buddha was said to have achieved enlightenment. In Christianity, the tree is the vehicle by which sin came into the world and also represents redemption, as Jesus was crucified on a cross made from a tree, the cross actually referred to as a tree by Saint Paul.

Carl Sagan reflects on the crucial role that trees may have played in the development of human intelligence, and speculates on how their place in our ancestors' lives may continue to affect our own lives:

> For their surface area, insects weigh very little. A beetle, falling
> from a high altitude, quickly achieves terminal velocity; air re-

sistance prevents it from falling very fast, and, after alighting on the ground it will walk away, apparently none the worse for the experience. The same is true of small mammals—squirrels, say. A mouse can be dropped down a thousand-foot mine shaft and, if the ground is soft, will arrive dazed but essentially unhurt. In contrast, human beings are characteristically maimed or killed by any fall of more than a few dozen feet: because of our size, we weigh too much for our surface area. Therefore our arboreal ancestors had to pay attention. Any error in brachiating from branch to branch could be fatal. Every leap was an opportunity for evolution. Powerful selective forces were at work to evolve organisms with grace and agility, accurate binocular vision, versatile manipulative abilities, superb hand-eye coordination, and an intuitive grasp of Newtonian gravitation. But each of these skills required significant advances in the evolution of the brains and particularly the neo-cortices of our ancestors. Human intelligence is fundamentally indebted to the millions of years our ancestors spent in the trees.

And after we returned to the savannahs and abandoned the trees, did one long for those great graceful leaps and ecstatic moments of weightlessness in the shafts of sunlight of the forest roof? Is the startle reflex of human infants today to prevent falling from the treetops? Are our nighttime dreams of flying and our daytime passion for flight as exemplified in the lives of Leonardo da Vinci and Konstantin Tsiolkovski, nostalgic reminiscences of those days gone by in the branches of the high forest?

In the Jungian school of psychology, the prominence of the tree in both dreams and myths is attributed to the continuous growth of the tree, serving as a model for the positive process of human spiritual growth through experience:

Gradually a wider and more mature personality emerges and by degrees becomes effective and even visible to others. The fact that we often speak of "arrested development" shows that we assume that such a process of growth and maturation is possible with every individual. Since this psychic growth cannot be brought about by a conscious effort of will power, but happens involuntarily and naturally, it is in dreams frequently symbolized by the tree, whose slow, powerful involuntary growth fulfills a definite pattern.

Joseph Campbell recognizes the tree as part of the powerful collection of symbols of immortality:

> So that again, we recognize the usual symbols of the mythic garden of life, where the serpent, the tree, the world axis, sun eternal, and ever living waters radiate grace to all quarters—and toward which the mortal individual is guided, by one divine manifestation, or another, to the knowledge of his own immortality.

Herein lies the spiritual beauty of the Christmas tree. While it may be true that the Christmas tree is a vestige of an earlier Teutonic pagan custom, the evergreen tree, alive in the dead of winter, remains a symbol of immortality. The message attached is that, through the birth of Christ—heaven touching earth, as a tree appears to do— immortality comes to human beings.

4. The Earliest Times

I often wonder where lie hidden the boundaries of recognition between man and the beast whose heart knows no spoken language. Through what primal paradise in a remote morning of creation ran the simple path by which their hearts visited each other? Those marks of their constant tread have not been effaced though their kinship has long been forgotten. Yet suddenly in some wordless music the dim memory wakes up and the beast gazes into the man's face with a tender trust, and the man looks down into its eyes with amused affection. It seems that the two friends meet masked, and vaguely know each other through the disguise.

—Rabindranath Tagore (1861–1941),
Indian poet, "The Gardener"

THE BIBLICAL FALL
(*Genesis 3:1–24*)

The serpent was the most subtle of all the wild beasts that Yahweh God had made. It asked the woman, "Did God really say you were not to eat from any of the trees in the garden?" The woman answered the serpent, "We may eat the fruit of the trees in the garden. But of the fruit of the tree in the middle of the garden God said 'You must not eat it, nor touch it, under pain of death.' " Then the serpent said to the woman, "No! You will not die! God knows in fact that on the day you eat it your eyes will be opened and you will be like gods, knowing good and

evil." The woman saw that the tree was good to eat and pleasing
to the eye, and that it was desirable for the knowledge that it
could give. So she took some of its fruit and ate it. Then the eyes
of both of them were opened and they realized that they were
naked. So they sewed fig leaves together to make themselves
loincloths.

The man and his wife heard the sound of Yahweh God walking in the garden in the cool of the day, and they hid from Yahweh God among the trees of the garden. But Yahweh God called
to the man. "Where are you?" he asked. "I heard the sound of
you in the garden," he replied. "I was afraid because I was naked, so I hid." "Who told you that you were naked?" he asked.
"Have you been eating of the tree I forbade you to eat?" The
man replied, "It was the woman you put with me; she gave me
the fruit and I ate it." Then Yahweh God asked the woman,
"What is this you have done?" The woman replied, "The serpent tempted me and I ate."

Then Yahweh God said to the serpent, "Because you have
done this,

> Be accursed beyond all cattle,
> all wild beasts.
> You shall crawl on your belly and eat dust
> every day of your life.
> I will make you enemies of each other;
> you and the woman,
> your offspring and her offspring.
> It will crush your head
> and you will strike its heel."

To the woman he said: "I will multiply your pains in child-
bearing, you shall give birth to your children in pain. Your
yearning shall be for your husband yet he will lord it over you."

To the man he said, "Because you have listened to the voice of
your wife and ate from the tree which I had forbidden you to eat,

> Accursed be the soil because of you.
> With suffering shall you get your food from it
> every day of your life.
> It shall yield you brambles and thistles
> and you shall eat wild plants

With sweat on your brow
shall you eat your bread
until you return to the soil
as you were taken from it.
For dust you are
and to dust you shall return."

The man named his wife "Eve" because she was the mother of
all those who live. Yahweh God made clothes out of skins for the
man and his wife, and they put them on. Then Yahweh God said,
"See the man has become like one of us, with his knowledge of
good and evil. He must not be allowed to stretch his hand out next
and pick from the tree of life also, and eat some and live forever."
So Yahweh God expelled him from the garden of Eden, to till the
soil from which he had been taken. He banished the man, and in
front of the garden of Eden he posted the cherubs, and the flame
of a flashing sword, to guard the way to the tree of life. ♦

A Modern Theologian's Interpretation of the Fall

The story of Genesis, chapters 1–3, if taken as a myth, can
guide our description of the transition from essential to existential being. It is the profoundest and richest expression of man's
awareness of his existential estrangement and provides the
scheme in which the transition from essence to existence can be
treated. It points, first, to the possibility of the Fall; second to
its motives; third to the event itself; and fourth, to its consequences . . .

. . . If the transition from essence to existence is expressed
mythologically—as it must be in the language of religion—it is
seen as an event of the past, although it happens in all three
modes of time. The event of the past to which traditional theology refers is the story of the Fall as told in the Book of Genesis.
Perhaps no text in literature has received so many interpretations as the third chapter of Genesis. This is partly due to its
uniqueness—even in biblical literature—partly to its psychological profundity, and partly due to its religious power. In mythological language it describes the transition from essence to
existence as a unique event which happened long ago in a spe-

cial place to individual persons—first to Eve, then to Adam. God himself appears as an individual person in time and space as a typical "father figure." The whole description has a psychological-ethical character and is derived from the daily experiences of people under special cultural and social conditions. Nevertheless, it has a claim to universal validity. The predominance of psychological and ethical aspects does not exclude other factors in the biblical story. The serpent represents the dynamic trends of nature; there is the magical character of the two trees, the rise of sexual consciousness, the curse over the heredity of Adam, the body of the woman, the animals and the land.

These traits show that a cosmic myth is hidden behind the psychological-ethical form of the story and that the prophetic "demythologization" of this myth has not removed, but rather subordinated, the mythical elements to the ethical point of view. The cosmic myth reappears in the Bible in the form of the struggle of the divine with demonic powers and the powers of chaos and darkness. It reappears also in the myth of the Fall of the angels and in the interpretation of the serpent as the embodiment of a fallen angel. These examples all point to the cosmic presuppositions and implications of the Fall of Adam ...

—Paul Tillich, *Systematic Theology*

The Pain of Childbirth

So far as I know, childbirth is generally painful in only one of the millions of species on Earth: human beings. This must be a consequence of the recent and continued increase in cranial volume. Modern man and woman have brain cases twice the volume of *Homo habilis*. Childbirth is painful because the evolution of the human skull has been spectacularly fast and recent. The American anatomist C. Judson Herrick described the development of the neocortex in the following terms: "Its explosive growth late in philogeny is one of the most dramatic cases of evolutionary transformation known to comparative anatomy." The incomplete closure of the skull at birth, the fontanelle, is very likely an imperfect accommodation to this recent brain evolution.

—Carl Sagan, *The Dragons of Eden*

Death Enters the World

> One of the earliest consequences of the anticipatory skills that accompanied the evolution of the prefrontal lobes must have been the awareness of death. Humans are probably the only organism on earth with a relatively clear view of the inevitability of his own end. Burial ceremonies that include the interment of food and artifacts along with the deceased go back at least to the times of our Neanderthal cousins, suggesting not only a widespread awareness of death but also an already developed ritual ceremony to sustain the deceased in the afterlife. It is not that death was absent before the spectacular growth of the neocortex, before the exile fom Eden; it is only that, until then, no one had ever noticed that death would be his destiny.
>
> —Carl Sagan, *The Dragons of Eden*

THE TALMUDIC FALL

Satan, or Samael, entered the Garden of Eden (*Gan Eden*) riding on the back of a serpent. When the animals saw the serpent approach, they smelled the presence of evil and fled in terror.

Satan remembered the angelic songs he had learned while in heaven and began singing them in a sweet voice. Eve, totally innocent, stopped to listen to this beautiful music and became completely mesmerized. Hearing the praises of the Most High God, she listened intently and could hardly move. The serpent climbed up a tree and bit the fruit, releasing the venom of evil intention. While Eve was caught up in his musical spell, Satan urged her to eat this fruit, which she did. She then called to Adam to take a bite, and he did. With this action, the venom of evil intention coursed through their veins and became part of their very flesh and nature for, according to the Rabbis, the blood is where life resides. As soon as Adam and Eve finished eating, their eyes became dimmed to the Shekhinah, the "countenance" of God. For prior to this, they were able to look at God directly in the face and converse with him—but no longer.

With evil intention came desire, and nakedness fuels desire. The band around their shoulder that bore the name of God fell off their bodies. They were entirely naked, felt shame for the first time, and went to hide in the bushes.

The Most High God then cast Adam and Eve out of *Gan Eden* and posted the Cherubim,* armed with swords of fire, at the entrance.

The earth, you will recall, was reluctant to give up any of her soil for the creation of humans, as she knew that someday Adam would cause the earth to be cursed. As she had predicted, every manner of poisonous plant and noxious weed sprang from her body. Her beautiful fruits were now eaten by worms and insects. Rain was now necessary to keep her alive.

The righteous angels in heaven grieved over the fall of humankind. The cruel Lillith, who especially hated Eve, laughed bitterly to see humankind so stupidly separate itself from God. Of all the things God created, only the moon laughed. As a punishment, God dimmed its light so that it shines in the way it does today. ♦

Adam, Eve, and Lillith

The Talmudic commentators noted a number of interesting linguistic connections with the name of Adam. *Adam* means "man" in Hebrew, while *adamah* means "soil." *Adam* sounds like the word *edom* or *adom*, meaning "red," the color of a newborn child emerging from the womb. Adam's name, which is spelled with the Hebrew letters aleph, daleth, and mem, recalls the elements of the human body in traditional Hebrew medicine: *apher* ("dust"), *dam* ("blood"), and *marah* ("bitter," also the word for "bile"). The Jews of postbiblical times believed that these three elements had to be in their proper proportion or the human body would sicken and die (Graves and Patai, *Hebrew Myth*).

Scholars Robert Graves and Raphael Patai also trace the origin of

---

*Cherubim: a particular order of angels, often represented as winged children.

Lillith to a Babylonian and Assyrian evil female wind spirit *(Hebrew Myth)*.

Compare Lillith to Johi in the Persian Creation story.

THE STORY OF POIA
(Blackfoot Indian)

NOTE: This myth, from the Blackfoot Indians of the Great Plains of North America, contains many interesting parallels with the biblical story of the Fall.

Once during the summer in the earliest times, when it was too hot to sleep indoors, a beautiful maiden named Feather-woman slept outside in the tall prairie grass. She opened her eyes just as the Morning Star came into view, and she began to look on it with wonder. She mused in her heart how beautiful it was, and she fell in love with it. When her sisters got up, she told them that she had fallen in love with the Morning Star. They told her that she was insane! Feather-woman told everyone in her village about the Morning Star and soon she was an object of ridicule among her people.

One day she left the village to draw some water out of a creek. There she saw the most handsome young man she had ever imagined. At first she thought that he was a young man of her own tribe who had been hunting, and she coyly avoided him. But he then identified himself as the Morning Star. He said, "I know that you were watching me and fell in love with me. Even as you were looking up at the sky, I was looking down at you. I watched you in the tall prairie grass and knew that it was only you that I wanted for my wife. Come with me to my home in the sky."

Feather-woman was stricken with awe and paralyzed with fear. She knew that this was a god standing before her. She told Morning Star that she would need time to say good-bye to her parents and sisters. However, he told her that there was no time for this. He then gave her a magic yellow feather in one hand and a juniper branch in the

other. Then he told her to close her eyes. When she opened them
again, she was in the Sky-Country, standing before the lodge of
Morning Star, home of his parents, the Sun and the Moon, where they
were married. As it was daytime, the Sun was out doing his work, but
the mother, the Moon, was at home doing chores. She immediately
took a liking to the girl and gave her fine robes to wear.

Feather-woman loved her husband and his parents, and in time
she gave birth to a little boy whom they named Star Boy. But
Feather-woman needed to find things to do in her new home. So the
Moon gave her a root-digging stick to work with, carefully instructing
her not to dig up the Great Turnip that grew near the home of the
Spider Man, warning that terrible ills would be unleashed if she
did so.

Feather-woman was fascinated by the Great Turnip and wondered
why it was feared. After all, it looked like any other turnip, only
much larger. She walked closely around it, being careful not to touch
it. She took Star Boy off her back and placed him on the ground. As
she was digging, two great cranes flew overhead. She asked the
cranes to help her and they obliged her, singing a secret magic song
that made light work of digging the Great Turnip.

Now, the Moon had been very wise in warning Feather-woman not
to dig around the Great Turnip, for it plugged the hole through which
Morning Star had brought Feather-woman into the Sky-Country. With
a loud *plop* she pulled the Great Turnip out. Looking down through
the hole, she saw a camp of the Blackfoot Indians, perhaps her own
village, far below her. As she saw the mortals doing their daily
chores below, she became homesick and began to weep. In order to
conceal what she had done, she rolled the turnip loosely into place
and returned to the lodge where she lived with her husband and son.

When Morning Star returned to the lodge, he was very sad. He
said nothing, then, "How could you have been disobedient and dug
up the Great Turnip?" Moon and Sun were also sad and asked her
the same question.

At first Feather-woman did not answer, then she admitted her disobedience. Her in-laws had known that she would dig up the Great
Turnip, despite their warnings. The reason for the sadness was that

they knew that she had disobeyed them and must now be banished forever from the Sky-Country.

The next day, Morning Star took his wife to Spider Man, who built a web from the hole of the Great Turnip down to earth. When Feather-woman descended down the web, it looked to the people below like a star falling from the sky.

When Feather-woman arrived on earth with her child, she was welcomed by her parents and the people of their village. But she was never happy. Early in the morning, she looked up at the sky to speak with Morning Star, but he didn't answer her.

After many months had passed, Morning Star finally did speak to her. "You can never return to the Sky-Country," he warned. "You have committed a great sin and brought unhappiness and death into the world." Hearing this was too much for Feather-woman to bear; soon she died of her unhappiness.

The orphaned Star Boy lived with his human grandparents until they died. He was a shy boy who ran as soon as he heard the approach of a stranger's footsteps. The most notable thing about him was a scar on his face, which led to his nickname, Poia, meaning "scarface." As he grew into manhood, people cruelly ridiculed him because of his scar and his pretension to be the son of the Morning Star.

Thus maltreated, Poia was heartbroken by the further indignity of being rejected by the daughter of a chief. His life growing unbearable, Poia consulted with an old medicine woman. She told him that there was only one way for the scar to be removed: He would have to return to the Sky-Country and have his grandfather, the Sun, take it off. Knowing that his mother had been banished from the Sky-Country, this was bad news to Poia. How could he return to the land of his birth? The old woman said that there was a way back to the Sky-Country, but that Poia must find it himself. Feeling sorry for the boy, she gave him some food for the journey.

Poia traveled for days and days, over mountains, through forests, through snow, and across deserts, until he reached the Great Water that the white man calls the Pacific Ocean, for this is the farthest west, where the sun goes at night. For three days, Poia fasted and prayed. On the third day, he saw rays reflecting on the Great Water, forming a path to the Sun. He followed the path and arrived at the home of his grandparents, the Sun and the Moon.

Upon finding Poia asleep on their doorstep, the Sun was at first prepared to kill the mortal, as no earth-dweller could enter the Sky-Country. But the Moon persuaded him not to do so; she recognized the scar and told the Sun that it was their grandson. Soon, Moon, Sun, and Morning Star all welcomed Poia. At the request of his grandson, the Sun removed the scar.

The Sun also taught Poia great magic and the truths of the world. Poia's grandfather explained that the people on earth were suffering as a result of Feather-woman's disobedience. The Sun had a message for the Blackfoot people: If they would honor him but once a year by doing the Sun dance, all the sick would be healed. Poia himself learned the Sun dance quickly, and his grandfather grew to love him very much. His grandparents gave him a magic flute to charm women into falling in love with him. But, because of his mother's disobedience, Poia had to return to earth, which he did by walking down the Milky Way.

When Poia returned to the Blackfoot people, they honored him. He taught them the wisdom he had learned from the Sun and, most important, he taught them how to do the Sun dance, which indeed healed the sick. Because of Poia's great deeds, the Sun and Moon allowed him to bring his new wife, the chief's daughter who had once rejected him, to the Sky-Country, where they remained forever. Now Poia himself is a star that rises with the Morning Star. ♦

THE FOUR AGES OF MAN
(India)

As we know, the world has been created and destroyed many, many times. Only Brahma the Creator knows how many times this has happened. In each of these cycles of creation there are four ages, each characterized by an essential element. First, there is the golden age, an age of *Satva*, or "goodness." Next comes the age of *Rajas*, or "energy," followed by a third age that is a mixture of the two. Finally comes the fourth age, an age of *Tamas*, or "darkness," completing the cycle.

The golden age lasts four thousand years and is followed by a "twilight" or transition period that lasts four hundred years. During the golden age, people are born in pairs. They enjoy life fully, free of care, not having to work, eating whatever food is around them. They do not hate or become tired. They don't even need homes for shelter as the climate is perfect. There is no sadness.

The second age works on the principle that, when fulfillment is lost, another form of fulfillment is sought. When water reaches its subtle state, steam or vapor, it forms clouds. During the second age, these clouds give forth rain, and trees spring from the ground. The trees are the livelihood of the people, serving as homes and providing abundant fruit and wild honey for food. Sacrifices to the gods are characteristic of the second age, even as peaceful meditation was the nature of the golden age. The second age lasts three thousand years and is followed by a twilight of three hundred years.

Idyllic as life is even during the second age, the people begin to change. Their emotions of passion, greed, hatred, and anger emerge and ruin the peaceful environment. They begin to find their fulfillment in having more trees than their neighbor. Living in the trees, the first form of fixed dwelling, people grow possessive, wanting more and more of everything. They covet and eventually learn to steal and kill. They finally denude the world of trees and take so much from the earth that it can no longer supply their needs.

At this point, the people of the second age contemplate their fulfillment, causing the trees to again spring from the earth. But do the people learn from their earlier miserable experience? Hardly. Now they begin to rob and kill each other freely. Then Brahma, in every second age, creates the warrior caste, the Kshatriyas, to keep the people from butchering each other. Thus, the second age ends as a time of misery and anarchy.

Then comes the third age, which lasts for two thousand years, followed by a twilight of two hundred years. Because of the need to instruct people on morality, a sage named Vyasa appears in every third age to write the scriptures, the Vedas, and divide them into four parts. During this age, death, drought, and disease are the sufferings born of speech, mind, and action. As a result of this suffering, people become completely numb.

While in this state, human beings begin to contemplate a release from their sufferings. In their intellectual detachment from the world, people can begin to know themselves and see their faults. As meditation was characteristic of the golden age, and sacrifice of the second age, knowledge is characteristic of the third age.

Now, Dharma, the eternal principle of truth on which the universe itself rests, is like a four-legged stool. After the golden age, one leg of the stool of Dharma disappears; then at the close of the second age, a second leg disappears. The third leg is gone after the third; and by the coming of the fourth age, Dharma is very weak. By the fourth age, a dark age, there is little truth left in humankind and nothing for the universe to stand on.

In the fourth age, people walk around in darkness, completely ignorant and blind to the truth. Their senses are clouded in darkness and illusion *(maya)*. They are unable to separate what is true from what is false, and they really don't care about the difference. They are filled with jealousy and hate, even killing holy men who try to show them the truth and lead them out of darkness. Countries are always at war with each other for reasons that are trivial and even forgotten after the war has begun. Scripture has no more authority for people.

Things just continue to deteriorate throughout this dark age and in the end people are reduced to scavenging for their food, taking whatever roots, meat, or fruit they can find or steal. Even when they have gathered such meager things, someone else will try to steal them. They eventually have few, if any, possessions, and perform no rituals.

However, for those few wise people who survive the dark age, there will be opportunities to penetrate the illusions and find rare insights. Thus they will achieve a kind of mental peace. The few survivors of the dark age and the hundred years of twilight after it may live to see the golden age return and the four-legged stool of Dharma reestablished. Or they may find themselves at the end of the world cycle, witnessing the periodic destruction of the universe. ♦

THE FIVE AGES OF MAN
(*Greece*)

The first age of humankind was the golden age, when humans actually conversed directly with the gods and ate with them, and mortal woman had children by them. No one needed to work as people lived on the milk and honey abundant everywhere around them. There was no sadness. Some say that this golden age ended when humans became overly familiar with the gods, demonstrating arrogance and contempt. Some of the mortals even complained that they were as strong or as wise as the gods.

Next came the silver age, in which people first tilled the soil to earn a living and ate bread for the first time. Even though men lived to be a hundred years old, they were effeminate and utterly dependent upon their mothers [*Ed.'s note:* a matriarchy?]. They constantly complained about everything and were quarrelsome. The great god Zeus grew tired of their whining and destroyed them all.

Then came the first bronze age, when the first people fell like seeds from ash trees. People then ate both bread and meat, and were vastly more useful than the people of the silver age. But they delighted in wars and eventually killed each other off entirely.

The second bronze age was a glorious age of heroes. These people were fathered by the gods on human mothers. This was the age of Hercules and the heroes of the siege of Troy. These men fought gloriously, lived virtuous and honest lives, and went to the glorious Elysian Fields when they died.

We are presently in the iron age. You will note that the value of the metals decreases with each passing age. So it is with the character of humankind. It is worse in the iron age than it has been at any previous time. Men no longer converse with the gods; in fact, they ignore piety altogether. And who could blame the gods for being indifferent to the mortals? The people of the iron age are materialistic, treacherous, arrogant, sexually out of control, and violent. The only reason the gods have not destroyed humanity is that there are still a few decent people left. ♦

THE FIVE SUNS
(*Aztec*)

We are presently in the period of the fifth sun, but what were the earlier periods like?

The first of the five suns was the Sun of the Ocelot. At that time, the world was shrouded in darkness and humans lived by animal instinct alone, without the benefit of reason. Lacking thought, they were eventually all eaten by ocelots. The second sun was the Sun of Air, a world of spirits and transparent beings that may return someday. But the humans of this time did not understand the necessary principles to be redeemed from their sins and the gods changed them all into monkeys.

The third was the Sun of Fire. During this period, people again were ignorant of the gods. All the rivers dried up and all creatures were killed by roaring flames, with the exception of the birds, who flew to safety. The fourth sun was the Sun of Water, Tlaloc, the rain god, who destroyed all the people in a flood.

The fifth is our own period. This is the sun where the other four principles, animal energy, air, fire, and water, are combined and in balance. We cannot take it for granted that this sun will last forever; our continued existence is dependent upon following the "ladder of redemption" that is contained in the Aztec calendar and observing rituals. If the gods are again ignored, then this sun too will die and all of us with it. ♦

THE FIVE WORLDS
(*Navajo*)

The present world is the fifth world. In the first world, there were
three beings living in the darkness: First Man, First Woman, and
Coyote. The first world was too small and dark for them to live happily, so they climbed into the second world, which contained the sun
and the moon. In the east, there was blackness; in the west, yellow-
ness; in the south, blueness; and in the north, whiteness. Sometimes
the blackness would roll from the east and overshadow the entire
world. When the three beings arrived in the second world, the sun
tried to make love to First Woman. When she refused, there was discord. Coyote, who understood such things, called the other people of
the four directions together.

He advised them to climb up into the third world, a wide and
peaceful land. Upon their ascent, they found that Coyote had been
right; the new land was beautiful. They were greeted there by the
mountain people, who warned that they would all live in peace as
long as they did not disturb the water serpent, Tieholtsodi.

Telling Coyote not to do something was a guarantee that he would
do it. His natural curiosity got the better of him and he wandered
down to the sea. There he saw the water serpent Tieholtsodi's children playing and found them so attractive that he ran off with them
under his arms. Tieholtsodi became very angry and searched the
world for his children, but to no avail. Then he decided to flood the
world and flush out the thief.

As the waters rose, the people discussed how to escape the flood
and, through magic, they piled the four mountains of the four directions up, one atop the other. Still, the waters continued to rise, covering the first mountain, then the second, then the third, until the
people were huddled atop the fourth mountain wondering what to do.
So they planted a giant reed that grew high into the sky. Just as the
waters were lapping around them, they climbed up into the fourth

world. The last to leave was the turkey; to this day his tail feathers are white where the floodwater washed out the colors.

The fourth world was even larger than the third. However, it was dim and misty. There was a great river flowing through the fourth world. Human beings lived north of the river and human souls in animal form lived to its south.

About this time, humans grew quarrelsome. The men constantly argued with the women about stupid things. Each sex claimed to be the more important. The women argued that, were it not for them, everyone would die—after all, they planted the corn and harvested it, they made clothing and bore children. The men disagreed, saying they were the more important: Men did the rituals that guaranteed a good corn crop, plowed, hunted, built homes, and fathered children. In addition, they protected the villages from attack. The women countered that they made baskets, cooked the food, and tended the fires. The arguments could not be resolved, so the men decided to leave for four years.

But neither the men nor the women were happy during those four years. Men and women were meant to be together, despite their differences, and with separation came appreciation. Because the women did not know the proper corn rituals nor how to plow, the corn did not grow properly and there was not enough food to go around. With the failure of the crops, there was little that the women could do, as they did not know how to hunt.

The men weren't any better off than the women. Four years on their own made them irritable. Not knowing how to process cotton, the men found their clothing deteriorating into rags, and so their skin burned in the hot sun and froze in the cold weather. Although they knew the rituals and how to plow, they had no corn, as they didn't know the right procedures for cultivation and harvest. Although they knew how to hunt, they grew sick and their teeth fell out from chewing raw meat, as they knew nothing of cooking. Worst of all, they missed the delight of having little children around.

Thus the two sexes realized that each was incomplete without the other; neither was the more important. The women decided to overlook what they considered the men's "faults," and the men "forgave" the women for theirs. When they finally did get back together, it was a period of peace and happiness—and many, many children were born in that first year together.

Their peace was short-lived, however, for Coyote still had the children of Tieholtsodi with him. Tieholtsodi's flooding of the third world had been so complete that the waters rose up into the fourth, making the ground soft. A new flood threatened the people and they again stacked the four mountains on top of each other, planted the giant reed, and escaped to the fifth world, where we now live.

The beaver was the first to enter the fifth world and he returned with very discouraging news: From what he could see, all that was above them in the fifth world was the bottom of a vast lake. So the people then sent the locust, who went up to the surface of the lake.

On the surface there were two swans, the guardians of the fifth world. They told the locust that no one could enter the fifth world without passing a test. The newcomers had to take an arrow, swallow it, pass it out by the anus, then put the arrow back up the anus and spit it out by the mouth. The locust knew very well that most of the animals would never survive such a test. But, being a locust, he tricked the swans; he knew that he could pass an arrow through his own thorax and survive. Moreover, it was apparent that the swans had never seen a locust before.

So the locust amazed the swans by passing an arrow through his own thorax and he challenged the swans to do likewise, which, of course, would have been fatal to them. The swans knew that it would be suicide to pass an arrow through their chests, and they were impressed by the locust's courage and "magic." So they gave their permission for the people of the fourth world to enter the fifth.

Having endured two floods because of Coyote's theft of Tieholtsodi's children, the people wanted to avoid the same problem in the fifth world. So they ordered Coyote to give the children back. He did so and Tieholtsodi was pacified.

Upon their entry into the fifth world, the people found themselves on an island in the middle of this vast lake. They prayed to the Darkness Spirit, who cut a ditch to drain away much of the water; this ditch is today the Colorado River. Then they prayed to the four winds to blow day and night to dry up the soil on their island until more land was available. The sun and the moon were thrown up into the sky, and for four days the people watched the sun ascend up to its proper place in the sky.

However, when the sun reached that spot, it stopped, ceasing to move at all. Everything was in danger of being burned up. A great chief's wife came forward and told the people that she had recently dreamt that the sun would not move unless a human being died. She offered herself. The people wondered sadly where her spirit had gone until, one day, a man looked down a hole and saw the woman inside it, contentedly combing her hair. Since that time, one human being has had to die each day in order to make the sun move. ♦

NORTH AMERICAN INDIAN MYTHS OF EMERGENCE

NOTE: As in the Navajo myth of the five worlds, emergence from an underground world is a theme in the myths of a number of North American peoples. Here is the myth of the Mojave Apache, who lived in the southwestern deserts not far from the Navajo, and the Mandan Sioux, which comes to us from the Dakotas, thousands of miles from the home of the Mojave.*

What is the significance of such myths? Are they representative of successive stages of cultural development or consciousness? Are they evolutionary?

---

*The Mojave Apache myth is virtually identical to the Mandan myth—with only one difference. In the Mojave version, a hummingbird is first sent to the world above as a guide.

Mandan

The earliest people lived under the ground near a beautiful lake. Once, a great grapevine grew above their home. A root from the grapevine poked down into the village of the underground people. A few of the most courageous then climbed the vine into the world above.

When these explorers returned, they reported that the world above was more beautiful than anything they had imagined, teeming with fish and game, full of light and beautiful flowers. Soon large numbers of people began climbing the vine into the new world above.

One day, however, an obese woman began to climb and the root broke, leaving half of the people underground, where they remain to this day. When we die, we rejoin our cousins under the earth. ♦

Abanaki

NOTE: The character Kloskurbeh is identified with Glooskap of the Algonquin myths. The Abanaki, or Wabanaki, are an Algonquin people of Maine and New Brunswick.

First Manitou, the Great Spirit, made Kloskurbeh, the great teacher. One day when the sun was directly overhead, a young boy appeared to Kloskurbeh. He explained that he had been born when the sea had churned up a great foam, which was then heated by the sun, congealed, and came alive as a human boy.

The next day, again at noon, the teacher and the boy greeted a girl. She explained that she had come from the earth, which had produced a green plant which bore her as fruit. And so Kloskurbeh, the wise teacher, knew that human beings came forth from the union of sea and land. The teacher gave thanks to Manitou and instructed the boy and girl in everything they needed to know. Then Kloskurbeh went north into the forest to meditate.

The man and the woman had many, many children. Unfortunately, they had so many children that they were unable to feed them all by hunting and picking wild foods. The mother was filled with grief to see her children hungry, and the father despaired. One day the mother went down to a stream, entering it sadly. As she reached the middle of the stream, her mood changed completely and she was filled with joy. A long green shoot had come out of her body, between her legs. As the mother left the stream, she once again looked unhappy.

Later, the father asked her what had happened during the day while he was out trying to gather food. The mother told the whole story. She then instructed the father to kill her and plant her bones in two piles. The father, understandably, was upset by this command and he questioned the mother many times about it. Naturally, it was shocking and disturbing to think that he had to kill his wife in order to save his children. But she was insistent.

The father immediately went to Kloskurbeh for advice. Kloskurbeh thought the story very strange, but then he prayed to Manitou for guidance. Kloskurbeh then told the father that the mother was right; this was the will of Manitou. So, the father killed his wife and buried her bones in two piles as he was commanded to do.

For seven moons, the father stood over the piles of bones and wept. Then one morning, he noticed that from one pile had sprouted tobacco and, from the other, maize. Kloskurbeh explained to the man that his wife had really never died, but that she would live forever in these two crops.

To this day, a mother would rather die than see her children starve, and all children are still fed today by that original mother. Men like to plant in the cornfields extra fish they catch as a gift of thanks to the first mother and a remembrance that we are all children of the union of sea and land. ◆

THREE STORIES OF MAUI THE TRICKSTER (POLYNESIA)

NOTE: Maui, for whom the Hawaiian island was named, is the great trickster of Polynesian mythology, appearing throughout Polynesia from Hawaii to New Zealand.

MAUI PUSHES UP THE SKY

Maui as a trickster, the son of Tangaroa [Kanaloa, in Hawaiian] and a mortal woman. It was his nature to test the limits and patience of the gods, and he wasn't exactly the most honest of beings. By the time he was a young man, he was very handsome and charming, and also prone to bragging about his strength.

One day, at the time when the sky was still low enough to touch the earth, Maui happened to be walking along and saw a girl trying to push up the sky. "I have chores to do," she said, "but the sky keeps falling down on me, keeping me from getting where I need to be." As she was a very beautiful girl, Maui began bragging about his strength, that he was the son of Tangaroa and that he could certainly solve this problem. However, the girl giggled and said, "Whoever you are, you are a braggart!" Maui then began picking up big rocks and the girl became quite impressed with him.

Then Maui told the girl that he would be more than happy to push up the sky if she would sleep with him [in the original: "if he might have a drink from her gourd"]. Maui was so strong, handsome, and charming that she could not resist his advances. To keep his side of the bargain, Maui closed his eyes and pushed up the sky.

However, this feat made Maui so egotistical that it was the beginning of his undoing. ♦

MAUI STEALS FIRE

Maui was warned by his mother not to irritate Mahui-Ike, his great-great-grandmother, who was the keeper of the fire in the underworld. Maui thought of how powerful he would be if only he had fire. So he found the opening in the earth that leads to the underworld and went to see Mahui-Ike. The old woman was thoroughly charmed by her handsome descendant and asked what she could do for him. Maui asked for some fire to take home with him. So Mahui-Ike plucked out one of her fingernails, which was a blazing fire, and Maui returned with it to the world above.

Safely out of the sight of the old woman, Maui extinguished the fire in a stream. He then went back to Mahui-Ike and explained that the fire had gone out on his way home. The old lady responded that such things happen sometimes and she plucked out another fingernail and gave it to him. Again, he extinguished it as soon as he was in the upper world.

He did this over and over again until Mahui-Ike had only one toenail left. She had been patient with Maui until now, but it had become clear to her that her great-great-grandson was a trickster who had been toying with her. So she plucked out this toenail and chased Maui into the upper world with a great flame. She threw it to the ground, crying, "If it's fire you want, here it is!" At that the entire world was set afire. Maui changed himself into an eagle to escape the blaze. Then, consulting his father, Tangaroa, he made it rain, extinguishing the flames in all but one place from which all of today's fires have their origin.

Maui noticed that wood burns best, and to this day people burn wood for fuel. ♦

MAUI TRIES TO CHEAT DEATH

Hina, the first woman, is the keeper of the underworld of the dead. It is she who decides who dies and who lives. No one ever questioned this but Maui.

Maui had become annoyed with his brother-in-law, and he turned him into a dog. This distressed his sister so much that she tried to drown herself, but was saved at the last possible minute. Everyone agreed that what Maui had done to his brother-in-law was a horrible thing and that he would have to die for it. Maui then went to his father, Tangaroa, and asked what could be done to save his life. Tangaroa told him to go to Hina and ask her to be lenient with him, as he was the son of a god. Maui might have succeeded, but his arrogance made him believe that he could trick and mock death.

When Maui arrived in the underworld, the great Hina was sleeping. Maui asked all the animals to be quiet in order not to disturb her. Maui then crawled up between her legs and then came back out through her mouth. No one ever dared even think of doing such a thing. Maui knew that if he succeeded in doing this a second time, he would be immortal.

Beyond the gods, there is a justice which cannot be tampered with. For all of his powers, Maui was stupid in not realizing this. So he crawled back up between her thighs. The animals were so amazed at his audacity that a little bird broke out laughing aloud, waking Hina. Maui was then crushed to death.

Since that time, no mortal has ever attained immortality, and Hina never sleeps anymore. In the old times, people only died during the night, when Hina was awake, never during the daytime when she was sleeping. Since Maui's disturbance, people can die at any time of night or day. ◆

PROMETHEUS AND EPIMETHEUS
(*Greece*)

There was once a time when the Titans, powerful giants,* walked the earth. During the battle between the Titans and the Olympian gods, led by Zeus, there were two Titan brothers who fought on the side of Zeus. One was Prometheus, the creator of humankind, who fashioned people from clay, and the other was Epimetheus.†

Although allies of Zeus, the two brothers were still Titans, and the Olympian gods did not entirely trust them. Once there was a discussion over what parts of the sacrificial bull should be offered to the gods. Of course, the gods expected the best parts, the fat and the good meat. But Prometheus deceived Zeus. He divided the bull into two sacks. In the one sack he placed the good meat, but put the entrails on top so that Zeus would think the sack useless and give it back to Prometheus. In the other sack, Prometheus put the bones, but placed the fat on top. When Prometheus offered the two sacks to Zeus, the god naturally chose the one with the fat on top. However, when Zeus learned that he had been deceived, he said, "Let Prometheus and the humans eat their meat raw—I will never let them have fire!"

Prometheus knew that mortals would need fire in order for civilization to develop: Cooking, pottery, and metalwork all require fire. So Prometheus went to Athena, the goddess of wisdom, ostensibly to plead his case. However, he never spoke to Athena. He snuck into the palace of the gods through the back door, and when he came to the chariot of the sun, he stole some of the fire, concealing it in

---

*The Titans were the giants of Greek mythology, comparable to the Nefiliim in the book of Genesis in the Bible, the "sons of God" who married human women. They are analogous to the Jotunheim giants of Norse myth and the giants prominent in Peruvian and American Indian myths.

†Prometheus means "forethought;" Epimetheus means "afterthought."

a hollow fennel stalk. He then returned and gave the fire to human-kind in direct violation of Zeus's command.

When Zeus discovered the theft he was furious. Prior to the robbery, there had been only males among the humans. So Zeus ordered Hephaestus, the smith of the gods, to make a female human from clay. He made a beautiful woman, and Aphrodite gave her still more beauty and taught her charm. Athena gave her skills in cooking, weaving, and spinning, and other gods and goddess gave her still more gifts. Thus, she was called Pandora, meaning "all-gifted."

It was Zeus's intention to give Pandora to Prometheus as a "gift." As a further gift, the gods sent a sealed clay jar with her. Prometheus advised his brother, Epimetheus, not to accept these gifts. But Epimetheus ignored him. Zeus punished Prometheus for warning his brother by having Prometheus chained to a rock in the Caucasus Mountains, where a vulture perpetually tore at his liver.

Alarmed by the horrible vengeance of Zeus, Epimetheus took Pandora as his wife. Pandora had been warned by Prometheus not to open the clay jar, but her curiosity got the better of her. Finally, she could bear it no longer; she opened the jar. Out flew every plague that has since oppressed mankind—greed, lust, sickness, old age, famine, and a host of others. Yet, there was one commodity left in the jar—hope. And as long as hope remains, we can bear all of the other ills that may befall us. ♦

THE ORIGIN OF MEDICINE
(Cherokee)

There was once a time, not long after the creation of the world, when humans and animals freely communicated. However, they did not remain on good terms for very long. The humans began to kill the animals for their furs and for food. It was easy to do at this time, as the animals were completely unprepared to be hunted and they walked up to human beings, trusting them. Then the animals became angry.

The tribe of the bear met in council, led by old White Bear. After several of the bears had voiced their complaints against the human beings, the entire tribe declared war on the humans. Once the angry crowd calmed down, White Bear told them that the human beings had a decided advantage—the spear, and the bow and arrow. So the bears decided to make their own weapons.

However, the bears had a problem: Their claws made it impossible to throw a spear. They couldn't shoot arrows either, as their claws made it impossible to properly draw back on a bow. Some of the younger bears thought of cutting their claws, but White Bear told them that bears needed claws to climb trees and subdue their food.

Meanwhile, the deer were also angry and they too met, presided over by Little Deer. The deer, of course, are less violent creatures than are bears, so they did not consider making war on human beings. However, they resolved to use their magic: Thenceforth if a hunter wished to kill a deer, he must first ask permission of the spirit of Little Deer or else seek his pardon afterward. Any human hunter failing to do so would be stricken with rheumatism.

The fish and reptiles also met to discuss their future relationship with the humans. They decided to haunt mankind with terrible dreams of serpents. Only the Cherokee can banish such dreams with the help of a medicine man.

The birds and insects met in council; each of them named a disease they could spread among the humans.

The plants, however, thought that all of this was getting out of hand, pointing out that, since many of the animals themselves killed for food, they were wrong to be so sharp in their judgment. Since the plants are everywhere, they had overheard the councils of the bears, deer, fish and reptiles, birds and insects, and knew what diseases would be inflicted on humans. So each plant decided to act as a remedy for one of the diseases, and thus was medicine born. ♦

MURILÉ AND THE MOONCHIEF
(*Kenya*)

Once there was a youth named Murilé, whose mother incessantly nagged at him, criticizing him over every little thing. Nothing he did was ever right; even his best efforts brought snide remarks from her. Growing tired of this, Murilé borrowed his father's stool, which had been in the family for countless generations. He sat on the stool and recited every magic incantation he knew. Suddenly the stool began to fly up off the earth in the direction of the moon.

When he landed on the moon, he came to a village and asked for directions to the home of the Moonchief. The villagers asked Murilé to work for them in exchange for the information. They came to like him and then told him how to get to his destination, and he went on his way.

When Murilé arrived at the village of the Moonchief, he was appalled at how backward the people there were. They knew nothing of fire; they ate their meat raw, had no pottery, and shivered at night from the cold. So Murilé took sticks and built a fire, which made him a great hero to the moon people and a favorite of the Moonchief. He was hailed as the greatest magician the people had ever known.

In recognition of his services, Murilé was showered with gifts and honors. The Moonchief and his subjects could not give Murilé enough cattle and wives. Every father wanted Murilé to marry his daughters.

Soon a very rich man with many cattle and wives, Murilé prepared to return to earth in triumph: Now his mother would see that her son had amounted to something. So he sent his friend, the mockingbird, to announce his imminent return to earth. However, Murilé's family did not even believe their son was alive; they had given him up for dead long ago. When the mockingbird flew back to the moon with this report, Murilé could not believe that the mockingbird had spoken to his family. So the mockingbird went back to Murilé's earthly village and brought back his father's walking stick as proof of the visit.

Finally convinced, Murilé prepared to return to earth. He dressed his wives and many children in their finest clothing and covered them with jewels. He had so much wealth to show off that his mother was sure to be impressed. With this great entourage to bring with him, Murilé could hardly travel back on the magic stool, so the entire party left on foot. Murilé became exhausted. One of his finest bulls told Murilé that he (the bull) would carry his master back to earth in exchange for a promise: that Murilé would never kill him and eat him. Murilé gladly consented.

The family of Murilé on earth were thrilled to see him and marveled at his wealth and fine new family. Even his mother rejoiced to have him home. Consistent with her character, she went about bragging to everyone of her rich and powerful son. Murilé made his parents swear never to harm the bull that had brought him home, and they agreed.

However, as time passed, the parents forgot their promise. After all, Murilé had so many cattle that they probably forgot which bull was which. So his parents killed the bull and Murilé's mother prepared a dish seasoned with its fat and broth. As Murilé sat down to eat, the meat spoke to him, reminding him of the promise. As Murilé took the first taste of the bull's meat, the earth swallowed him up. ♦

THE HUMAN RACE IS SAVED
(Iroquois)

There was once a great warrior named Nekumonta who was married to the beautiful Shanewis. During the winter when the snow was deep and food was scarce, a terrible plague struck the earliest people, and many died. Nekumonta watched as, one by one, all of his brothers and sisters and both of his parents perished. The plague continued until Nekumonta, Shanewis, and a handful of villagers were the only ones left. But it looked as if the race of humans was going to die out, for Shanewis fell ill and lay near death, and many of the villagers complained of symptoms. Nekumonta could not bear to think that he would lose his wife and knew that, if he could save her, the human race could be preserved.

So Nekumonta prayed to the Great Spirit asking for guidance in finding the right herbs to save Shanewis's life. Covering her with furs to keep her warm, Nekumonta set out to find a cure. He searched and searched for herbs in the deep snow, but found nothing. Exhausted, he fell asleep.

When he awoke, he continued for three more days, wandering over frozen lakes, through forests, and over hills without success. Then a little snowshoe rabbit appeared to him.

He asked the rabbit, "Where can I find the herbs planted by the Great Spirit, to save my wife and my people?" But the little rabbit just twitched his nose and hopped away.

Nekumonta then came to the den of a hibernating black bear and asked the bear for help. The sleepy bear just grunted and rolled over.

On the third night of his journey, Nekumonta himself began to feel ill and he fell to the ground in a deep sleep. All the birds and animals remembered his many kindnesses. Nekumonta had never killed an animal unless he really needed it for food and clothing. They remembered how he had honored the trees and flowers. As they looked on him, their hearts were overcome with compassion and they resolved to help him. The animals, trees, birds, and plants all cried to the Great Spirit on his behalf.

As Nekumonta slept, a message came to him from the Great Spirit. In his dream he saw the beautiful Shanewis, still ill, but singing a strange and beautiful song. Then he heard the sound of a waterfall. The waters now sang the same song, but the words were clearer: "Find us, Nekumonta, and your Shanewis will live!"

At this, the young warrior awoke with a start, the words still clear in his mind. He looked in all directions, but found no waterfall. Yet the singing of the waters continued.

Nekumonta frantically dug in the snow to find the waters. He be-

gan to take sticks and rocks and dig into the frozen earth. He continued digging until he had dug a very large hole in the ground.
Suddenly, a tiny stream began to bubble up into the hole. Soon the
waters began to fill the hole, and waves of health and happiness overtook him. Moments after bathing in the waters, Nekumonta was refreshed, stronger than ever.

After raising his hands in thanks to the Great Spirit, he went back
to the hole and took some clay to make a jar to carry the water back
to his village. When Nekumonta returned to the village, he could see
that he was just in time. The last remaining people were all very
sick, and Shanewis herself was almost entering the land of shadows.

Shanewis was too weak to drink, so Nekumonta forced the healing
waters between her lips. She then rose up, healthy and more beautiful than ever. The few remaining people also drank and were instantly healed. The plague was now gone and the people forever
remembered Nekumonta as the one who saved the human race. ♦

5. The Flood Myths

The animals marched in two by two
Hurrah! Hurrah!
The animals marched in two by two
Hurrah! Hurrah!
The animals marched in two by two,
the cat, the dog, and the kangaroo
and they all marched into the ark
just to get out of the rain!
   —Old Sunday school song, sung
    to the tune of "When Johnny
    Comes Marching Home Again"

THE STORY OF NOAH
(Genesis 6:5–9:17)

Yahweh saw that the wickedness of man was great on the earth, and that the thoughts in his heart fashioned nothing but wickedness all day long. Yahweh regretted having made man on the earth, and his heart grieved. "I will rid the earth's face of Man, my own creation," Yahweh said, "and of animals also, reptiles too, and the birds of heaven; for I regret having made them." But Noah had found favor with Yahweh.

This is the story of Noah:

Noah was a good man, a man of integrity among his contemporaries, and he walked with God. Noah became the father of three sons, Shem, Ham, and Japheth. The earth grew corrupt in God's sight, and filled with violence. God contemplated the

121

earth; it was corrupt, for corrupt were the ways of all flesh upon the earth.

God said to Noah, "The end has come for all things of flesh; I have decided this, because the earth is full of violence of man's making, and I will efface them from the earth. Make yourself an ark out of resinous wood. Make it with reeds and line it with pitch inside and out. This is how to make it: the length of the ark is to be three hundred cubits; its breadth, fifty cubits; and its height, thirty cubits. Make a roof for the ark . . . put the door of the ark high in the side, and make a first, second, and third deck.

"For my part I mean to bring a flood, and send the waters over the earth, to destroy all flesh on it, every living creature under heaven; everything on the earth shall perish. But I will establish my Covenant with you, and you must go on board the ark, yourself, your sons, your wife, and your sons' wives along with you. From all living creatures, from all flesh, you must take two of each kind aboard the ark, to save their lives with yours; they must be a male and a female. Of every kind of bird, of every kind of animal, and of every kind of reptile on the ground, two must go with you so that their lives may be saved. For your part provide yourself with eatables of all kinds, and lay in a store of them, to serve as food for yourselves and them." Noah did this; he did all that God had ordered him.

Yahweh said to Noah, "Go aboard the ark, you and all your household, for you alone among this generation do I see as a good man in my judgment. Of all the clean animals you must take seven of each kind, both male and female; of the unclean animals you must take two, a male and a female (and of the birds of heaven also, seven of each kind, both male and female), to propagate their kind over the whole earth. For in seven days' time I will mean to make it rain on the earth for forty days and nights, and I will rid the earth of every living thing that I made." Noah did all that Yahweh ordered.

Noah was six hundred years old when the flood of waters appeared on the earth.

Noah and his sons, his wife, and his sons' wives boarded the ark to escape the waters of the flood. (Of the clean animals and the animals that are not clean, of the birds and all that crawls on the ground, two of each kind boarded the ark with Noah, a male and a female, according to the order God gave Noah.) Seven days later the waters of the flood appeared on earth.

In the six hundredth year of Noah's life, in the second month and on the seventeenth day of that month, that very day all the springs of the great deep broke through, and the sluices of heaven opened. It rained on the earth for forty days and forty nights.

That very day Noah and his sons Shem, Ham, and Japheth boarded the ark, with Noah's wife and the three wives of his sons, and with them wild beasts of every kind, cattle of every kind, reptiles of every kind that crawls on the earth, birds of every kind, all that flies, everything with wings. One pair of all that is flesh and has the breath of life boarded the ark with Noah; and so there went in a male and a female of every creature that is flesh, just as God had ordered him.

And Yahweh closed the door behind Noah.

The flood lasted forty days on the earth. The waters swelled greatly on the earth, and the ark sailed on the waters. The waters rose more and more on the earth so that all the highest mountains under the whole of heaven were submerged. The waters rose fifteen cubits higher, submerging the mountains. And so all things of flesh perished that moved on the earth, birds, cattle, wild beasts, everything that swarms on the earth, and every man. Everything with the breath of life in its nostrils died, everything on dry land. Yahweh destroyed every living thing on the face of the earth, man and animals, reptiles, and the birds of heaven. He rid the earth of them, so that only Noah was left and those with him in the ark. The waters rose on the earth for a hundred and fifty days.

But God had Noah in mind, and all the wild beasts and all the cattle that were with him in the ark. God sent a wind across the earth and the waters subsided. The springs of the deep and the sluices of heaven were stopped. Rain ceased to fall from heaven; the waters gradually ebbed from the earth. After a hundred and fifty days, the waters fell, and in the seventh month, on the seventeenth day of that month, the ark came to rest on the mountain of Ararat. The waters gradually fell until the tenth month, when on the first day of the tenth month, the mountain peaks appeared.

At the end of forty days Noah opened the porthole he had

made in the ark and he sent out the raven. This went off, and flew back and forth until the waters dried up from the earth. Then he sent out the dove, to see whether the waters were receding from the surface of the earth. The dove, finding nowhere to perch, returned to him in the ark, for there was water over the whole surface of the earth; putting out his hand he took hold of it and brought it back into the ark with him. After waiting seven more days, again he sent out the dove from the ark. In the evening, the dove came back to him and there it was with a new olive branch in its beak. So Noah realized that the waters were receding from the earth. After waiting seven more days he sent out the dove, and now it returned to him no more.

It was in the six hundred and first year of Noah's life, in the first month and on the first of the month, that the water dried up from the earth. Noah lifted back the hatch of the ark and looked out. The surface of the ground was dry!

In the second month and on the twenty-seventh day of the month, the earth was dry.

Then God said to Noah, "Come out of the ark, you, yourself, your wife, your sons, and your sons' wives with you. As for all the animals with you, all things of flesh, whether birds or animals or reptiles that crawl on the earth; let them be fruitful and multiply on the earth." So Noah went out with his sons, his wife, and his sons' wives. And all the wild beasts, all the cattle, all the birds and all the reptiles that crawl on the earth went out from the ark, one kind after another.

Noah built an altar for Yahweh, and choosing from all the clean animals and all the clean birds he offered burnt offerings on the altar. Yahweh smelled the pleasing fragrance and said to himself, "Never again will I strike down every living thing as I have done."*

> As long as earth lasts
> sowing and reaping
> cold and heat
> summer and winter
> day and night
> shall cease no more. ◆

---

*Geza Roheim, a Hungarian disciple of Sigmund Freud, attributed the universality of flood myths to dreams that occurred while the sleeper had a full bladder.

MANU AND THE FISH
(*India*)

Once very long ago a man named Manu was washing himself. When he reached into the water jar to wash his hands, he pulled up a small fish.

The fish spoke to him, saying, "If you take care of me and protect me until I am full grown, I will save you from the terrible things to come." Manu asked the fish, "What do you mean? What terrible things?" The fish told Manu that there would soon be a great flood that would destroy every human being on earth. The fish then instructed Manu to place him in a clay jar for safety, and Manu complied. As the fish grew, Manu kept placing it in a series of larger clay jars until the fish was full grown and could be placed safely in the sea. Soon the fish became a ghasha, one of the largest fishes in the world.

The fish instructed Manu to build a large ship, as the flood was now only months away. As the rains began, Manu tied a rope from his ship to the ghasha, which safely guided him as the waters rose. The waters grew so high that the entire earth was covered. As the waters subsided, the ghasha guided Manu to a mountaintop. ♦

UTNAPISHTIM
(*Babylonia*)

Gilgamesh, the hero of the great epic, met the old man Utnapishtim, who had become a god by virtue of his goodness and obedience to the gods in saving all humankind and animals from the great flood. Utnapishtim related his story to Gilgamesh.

The gods came to Utnapishtim to warn him of the coming of a horrible flood. They told him to stop his work, tear down his house, and begin work immediately on building a great ship that was ten dozen cubits high in length and ten dozen cubits wide. He was to hammer water plugs into the ship and cover it with pitch. He was to take animals of every kind, both male and female, as well as his family, provisions, gold, silver, and other fineries.

After he completed the ship, it began to rain in torrents. The flood was so terrible that even the gods were frightened. Ea, the god of the waters who had perpetrated the flood, saw that it was much worse than he had planned. Ishtar, the goddess of beauty, who had spoken evil in the assembly of the gods, causing the flood, wailed to see her children "turned to clay" as a result of her misdeeds.

For six days and nights a wind blew over the flood and the weather finally calmed. As the waters subsided, it was clear that the earth had been flattened and all living creatures annihilated. Utnapishtim bowed his head low and wept. The ship finally rested on the summit of Mount Nisir in the north. After the ship had rested there for seven days, Utnapishtim sent a dove free. As there was no land for the dove to rest on, she returned to the ship. He then sent a swallow, but she too returned. Finally, he sent out a raven and it never returned as it found land sufficient to rest on. Utnapishtim then knew he could leave the ship. ♦

THE FLOOD MYTH OF HAWAII

NOTE: It would appear that Hawaii had its own indigenous flood myth before the arrival of the missionaries. But there are two versions, one clearly influenced by the Bible story and one that preceded it. The following comes from Martha Beckwith, *Hawaiian Mythology*.

Twelve generations from the beginning of the race, in the genealogy of Kumuhonua, during the so-called Era of Overturning, occurs the name of Nu'u, called also Nana Nu'u . . . He is called "a great Kahuna" and in his time came the flood

known as Kai-a-ka-hina-li'i, which may be translated as "Sea
caused by Hahinali'i" or as "Sea that made the chiefs fall
down." Nu'u himself is called Kahinali'i from this catastrophe,
and after the flood he is known as Ku-kapuna, his wife as Ku-
kekoa, and their three sons have names of winds that bring rain.

The story of Nu'u as told to the missionaries shows a decided
tendency to strain after biblical analogy.

In the Fornander version, Nu'u builds "a large vessel and a
house on top of it . . ." In this he is saved from the flood and after its subsidence Kane, Ku, and Lono enter the house and send
him outside, where he finds himself on the summit of Mauna
Kea on Hawaii at a place where there is a cave named after his
wife Lili-noe. He worships the moon with offerings of awa (a
leaf), pig, and coconuts, thinking that this is the god who has
saved him. Kane descends (some say on a rainbow) and explains
his mistake and accepts his offerings. In this version, as told on
the island of Hawaii, he has three sons and his wife is named
Lili-noe. . . .

Although Hawaiian tradition knows of the flood of Kahinali'i
and the term Wa'a-halau-ali'i-o-ka-moku is familiar to old Hawaiians and may be translated "Canoe like a chief's house," the
idea of a houseboat such as the legend describes is not a native
tradition. Old people on Hawaii [have said] that "they were informed by their fathers that all the land had been overflowed by
the sea except a small peak on Mauna Kea where two human
beings were preserved from the destruction that overtook the
rest, but that they had never heard of a ship of Noah, having always been accustomed to call it the Kai-akinali'i. ◆

TATA AND NENA
(*Aztec*)

NOTE: In contrast to the Hawaiians, the Aztecs did have a flood myth that was clearly indigenous and preceded the arrival of Europeans. Note the similarities with the American Indian myths given later.

During the era of the fourth sun, the Sun of Water, the people grew very wicked and ignored the worship of the gods. The gods became angry and Tlaloc, the god of rains, announced that he was going to destroy the world with a flood. However, Tlaloc was fond of a devout couple, Tata and Nena, and he warned them of the flood. He instructed them to hollow out a great log and take two ears of corn— one for each of them—and eat nothing more.

So Tata and Nena entered the tree trunk with the two ears of corn, and it began to rain. When the rains subsided and Tata and Nena's log landed on dry land, they were so happy that they caught a fish and ate it, contrary to the orders of Tlaloc. It was only after their stomachs were full that they remembered Tlaloc's command.

Tlaloc then appeared to them and said, "This is how I am repaid for saving your lives?" They were then changed into dogs. It was at this point, where even the most righteous people were disobedient, that the gods destroyed the world, ushering in the present era of the Fifth Sun. ◆

DEUCALION
(*Greece*)

At a very early point in history, perhaps even before the end of the golden age, humankind grew very wicked and arrogant. They grew more tiresome by the day until Zeus finally decided to destroy them all. Prometheus, Titan creator of mankind, was warned of this coming flood and he in turn warned his human son, Deucalion, and Deucalion's wife, Pyrrha. Prometheus placed the two of them in a large wooden chest. And it rained for nine days and nine nights until the entire world was flooded except for two mountain peaks in Greece, Mount Parnassus and Mount Olympus, the latter being the home of the gods.

Finally the wooden chest landed on Mount Parnassus, and Deucalion and Pyrrha got out of it only to see that the entire world around them had been destroyed. From the trunk, they took out enough provisions to feed themselves until the waters subsided. Then when they came down from the mountain, they were horrified. Everywhere around them were dead bodies of humans and animals; everything was covered with silt, slime, and algae. The couple was grateful to be saved and they gave thanks to the gods for their deliverance.

Zeus spoke to them out of the sky, saying, "Veil your heads and cast behind you the bones of your mother." Pyrrha responded, "We have no mother with us, only my husband and I were in the chest." But Deucalion knew what Zeus meant and threw some rocks behind him. For rocks are the bones of Mother Earth, the mother of all. These rocks were transformed into people who repopulated the earth.* ♦

NORTH AMERICAN FLOOD MYTHS

Mandan

NOTE: This account comes from George Catlin's nineteenth-century book, *Manners, Customs and Conditions of North American Indians.*

In the middle of the ground, which is trodden like a hard pavement, is a curb (somewhat like a large hogshead [barrel] stand-

---

*In Greek this is the result of a play on words: *laos* means "people" (the source of our English word *laity*) and *laas* means "stones."

Deucalion was the son of Prometheus, whose name means "forethought," and the father lived up to his name by warning of the flood.

ing on its end) made of planks (and bound up with hoops) some eight or nine feet high, which they religiously preserve and protect from year to year, free from mark or scratch, and which they call "the big canoe"; it is undoubtedly a symbolic representation of their traditional history of the flood.

Knisteneaux

NOTE: This story was also reported by Catlin.

Many centuries ago a great flood covered the earth, destroying all the nations. At that time, all of the tribes of the Coteau des Prairies climbed up the Coteau, a ridge emerging out of the prairie, in order to escape the rising waters. After the tribes had gathered, the water rose to cover them all, turning their bodies into a mass of red pipestone rock. From that day on, the Coteau has been considered neutral ground to all the tribes, and there they could meet in safety to smoke the peace pipe.

While the people were all drowning, a young virgin named K-waptah-w grabbed the foot of a very large bird who was flying over the Coteau. The bird carried her up to a high cliff, safely above the flood waters. Here the girl had twins fathered by the war-eagle. From those twins the world was repopulated. ♦

Choctaw

NOTE: This story was told to Catlin by the Choctaw Peter Pinchlin.

Our people have always had a tradition of the Deluge, which happened in this way: There was total darkness for a great time over the whole of the earth; the Choctaw doctors or mystery-men looked out for daylight for a long time, until at last they despaired of ever seeing it, and the whole nation was very unhappy. At last a light was discovered in the North, and there was great rejoicing, until it was found to be great mountains of water rolling on, which destroyed them all, except a few families who had expected it and built a great raft, on which they were saved. ◆

Creek-Natchez

The dog warned his master to build a raft because all things were about to be destroyed by a flood. The waters rose, lifting man and dog above the clouds into a wonderful land of trees. The dog told the man that the only way he could ever return to his homeland was if he, the dog, were thrown into the water. The man was loyal to his friend and was reluctant to do this. The dog also told the man not to leave the raft for seven days after the waters had subsided. With pain in his heart, the man threw the dog overboard.

As the dog had predicted, the waters did subside and the man waited seven days as he was instructed. At the end of the seven days, multitudes of people approached the raft, some wet and dressed in rags, and others were dressed in finery. When they arrived at the raft it was clear that they were not humans, but spirits of the many killed in the flood. ◆

Mojave-Apache

NOTE: Do you remember the emergence myths in the last chapter? This myth is both an emergence myth and a flood story.

Many years ago, people lived under the ground. There came a time when there was no food, when the people sent a hummingbird up to see what he could find for them to eat. He saw the deep roots of a grapevine, which he followed up to the surface of the earth. The people went up through the hole and began living above ground.

One day a man looked down into the hole made by the vine,

through which the people had entered the upper world, and saw that water was rising up through it. The wise ones knew that a great flood was coming and that something had to be done to save humankind.

They then cut down a great tree and hollowed it out to make a canoe, placing a young girl in it. The tree-trunk canoe floated high on the waters until nothing but water could be seen in any direction. The wise ones had warned the girl not to leave the vessel until it touched land, even if she heard the waters going down.

Finally, the tree-trunk canoe touched ground. When the girl emerged, all the world had been drowned. She wondered whether she would always be alone. She went up to the mountains to rest. As she lay down, the sun shone on her, warming water that dripped down on her body from the rocks. This magic water impregnated her and she later gave birth to a daughter who conceived in the same way. All of us are descended from her. ♦

Cree

Wisagatcak the Trickster built a dam across a stream in an attempt to capture the Great Beaver as it left its lodge. He waited all day until finally, at dusk, the huge creature swam toward him. Now, the Great Beaver possesses powerful magic and, as Wisagatcak prepared to spear it, created a spell that caused a muskrat to bite Wisagatcak in the behind, making him miss the target. Though spared, the Great Beaver was angry and wanted revenge.

The next morning Wisagatcak was dumfounded. After being bitten, he had dismantled his dam, but the water level had not gone down even though the stream was now flowing freely through the spot where the dam had been. Even more strange—the water level continued to rise higher and higher. The Great Beaver had worked powerful magic indeed; the entire world was flooding. For two weeks, the Great Beaver and the little beavers kept busy making all the waters of earth to rise until not one spot of dry land could be found. In great haste, Wisagatcak built a raft of logs and took many animals aboard with him.

The water continued to rise for yet another two weeks. At the end of the two weeks, the muskrat left the raft to search for land, but even the muskrat, who is accustomed to living between earth and water, drowned. Then a raven left the raft. He flew around the entire world, but found no land, only water. Then Wisagatcak made his own magic with the help of a wolf on his raft.

During the next two weeks on the raft, moss grew all over its surface. The wolf ran around and around on the raft, causing the moss to become magically expanding earth, until the raft was a vast land mass. However, to this very day, water springs up through holes in the ground—cracks in that original raft. ◆

Algonquin

NOTE: In the stories of Noah, Utnapishtim, Wisagatcak, and this one, a raven is sent out to find land.

The god Michabo was hunting with his pack of trained wolves one day when he saw the strangest sight—the wolves entered a lake and disappeared. He followed them into the water to fetch them and as he did so, the entire world flooded. Michabo then sent forth a raven to find some soil with which to make a new earth, but the bird returned unsuccessful in its quest. Then Michabo sent an otter to do the same thing, but again to no avail.

Finally he sent the muskrat and she brought him back enough earth to begin the reconstruction of the world. The trees had lost their branches in the flood, so Michabo shot magic arrows at them that immediately became new branches covered with leaves.

Then Michabo married the muskrat and they became the parents of the human race. ◆

THE FLOOD MYTH OF THE INCAS

Once there was a period called the Pachachama, when humankind was cruel, barbaric, and murderous. Human beings did whatever they pleased without any fear. They were so busy planning wars and stealing that they completely ignored the gods. The only part of the world that remained uncorrupted was the high Andes.

In the highlands of Peru there were two shepherd brothers who were of impeccable character. They became very concerned when their llamas acted strangely. The llamas stopped eating and spent the night gazing sadly up at the stars. When the brothers asked the llamas what was going on, they replied that the stars had told them that a great flood was coming that would destroy all creatures on earth.

The two brothers and their families decided to seek safety in the caves in the highest mountain. They took their flocks with them into a cave and then it began to rain. It rained for months without end. Looking down from the mountains, they saw that the llamas were right: The entire world was being destroyed. They could hear the cries of the miserable dying humans below. Miraculously, the mountain grew taller and taller as the waters rose. Even so, the waters began to lap at the door of their cave. Then the mountain grew still higher.

One day they saw that the rain had ceased and that the waters were subsiding. Inti, the sun-god, appeared once again and smiled, causing the waters to evaporate. Just as their provisions were running out, the brothers looked down to see that the earth was dry. The mountain then returned to its usual height, and the shepherds and their families repopulated the earth.

Human beings live everywhere; llamas, however, remember the flood and prefer to live only in the highlands. ♦

THE FLOOD MYTH OF EGYPT

The sun-god Ra, was warned by his father, the Watery Abyss, that humankind had grown too wicked and was on the verge of full rebellion against the gods. So Ra took his eye, the goddess Hathor, and sent her to investigate and punish the evildoers.

Hathor went to earth and began slaying thousands of humans, then millions. She was so terrible that the streets of the town of Chetenuten ran like a river with blood. So much blood poured into the Nile that it overflowed its banks, and the mixture of blood and water inundated the land, destroying everything in its path. The mixture even met the sea, which, in turn, overflowed its banks. Hathor had become literally bloodthirsty, drinking this gory liquid.

Ra's original intention was to punish, but not destroy, humankind. So he called Thoth, the wisest of the gods, for advice. Ra then sent the goddess Sektet and told her to grind a great volume of the dada [perhaps the date] fruit and mix it with barley to make strong beer. Then the beer would be mixed with the blood of hapless humans to attract Hathor.

Ra then instructed his servants to take the jugs of beer and pour them out near Hathor on whatever dry land remained. The beer formed a great sea. Hathor was drawn by the smell of the blood and began to drink the beer until she was so drunk that she could not even stand. Completely intoxicated, she could no longer identify the few humans left and she staggered off to sleep.

From that remnant, humankind repopulated the earth.

Ra was tired of dealing with human beings, Hathor, and the other problems on earth. So he went off to rest on the back of the great cow of heaven, appointing Thoth as his governor on earth. This was an excellent choice, as Thoth taught people how to write, compose poetry, and govern themselves. ♦

6. Tales of Love

We insist that life must have a meaning—but it can have no more meaning than we ourselves are able to give it. Because individuals can do this only imperfectly, the religions and philosophers have tried to supply a comforting answer to the question. The answers all amount to the same thing: love alone can give life meaning. In other words: the more capable we are of loving, and of giving ourselves, the more meaning there will be in our lives.

—Hermann Hesse (1877–1962), *Reflections*

Man can live his truth, his deepest truth, but cannot speak it. It is for this reason that love becomes the ultimate human answer to the ultimate human question. Love, in reason's terms, answers nothing—certainly not death—certainly not chance. What love does is to arm. It arms the worth of life in spite of it.

—Archibald MacLeish (1892–1982)

GREEK AND ROMAN LOVE MYTHS

NOTE: The Greek and Roman mythologies were full of tales of romances with object lessons. The Latin poet Ovid, in particular, retold many myths of love and is our source for most of these stories. Hence the names of the gods are in their Roman forms.

CUPID AND PSYCHE

There was once a king with three beautiful daughters, the fairest of whom was Psyche, the youngest. Her name means "soul" and "butterfly" in Greek. Her beauty was such that the entire world soon knew of her and men swooned at the very mention of her name. Not only was she physically beautiful, but she was a kind and innocent girl as well. Through no fault of her own, people began to compare her with Venus [Greek: Aphrodite], the goddess of beauty. In time, the temples of Venus were ignored; no one brought sacrifices or invoked the name of the goddess for help. For, as the people saw it, Venus was a distant goddess who lived on Mount Olympus, while the very picture of beauty, Psyche, lived in their midst.

Venus became very angry about the attention given this mere mortal girl and she called her son Cupid [Greek: Eros] to assist in solving this problem. The arrows of Cupid are irresistible and invincible; anyone they strike falls hopelessly in love. Venus asked Cupid to make the vilest, ugliest man on earth fall in love with Psyche.

Upon inspecting the situation, however, Cupid fell in love with the girl himself and forgot all about his mother's command. Venus merely took the silence of her son as his assent that he would do her bidding, certain that the matter would be taken care of promptly.

But as time went on, not only didn't a terrible man fall in love with Psyche; *no one* fell in love with Psyche. Men still looked at her and praised her beauty, but not a single one approached her. Her two sisters had married well, while this most beautiful of mortals appeared to be headed for a lonely spinsterhood. Her parents despaired and decided to seek the advice of the oracle of the god Apollo at Delphi.

Apollo himself was known for his taste for beautiful mortal women, but he was also the brother of Venus and did not wish to incur her wrath. So, speaking through the oracle, he did the diplomatic thing, telling the parents that Psyche would indeed have a lover—a horrible winged serpent. The parents were advised to take her up to a lonely rock to meet her lover, who was as strong as the gods and could not be resisted.

Sadly, her father obeyed this advice and left the beautiful Psyche on the mountaintop. Filled with sorrow, fear, and dread, she wept inconsolably until she fell asleep. The gentle southern wind, Zephyr, soothed her with gentle breezes.

When she awoke in the morning, she found herself in a palace more grand than any she had ever imagined. Dozens of beautiful servant girls attended her every whim. They placed her in the most comfortable bed she had ever slept in. During the night she was gently awakened by the loveliest voice she had ever heard—it was her lover. In the darkness, his skin and body felt like that of a beautiful youth, not a winged monster. She was certain that this was a youth of great beauty, perhaps even a god. After their first night together, she was resolved to see his face.

He was insistent, however, that she should never, under any circumstances whatsoever, look at his face. Once she had seen his face, he would have to leave her forever. So she endured this rule for a time, while still pleading to see his face. He consistently refused, which made her curiosity all the more powerful.

One day she coaxed him into allowing her sisters to visit the palace. He was reluctant to do this, but was so completely in love with her that he could not refuse. So, during the day, the gentle wind Zephyr whisked the sisters up to the palace for a visit. The sisters, though married to wealthy men, were unprepared for the splendor they saw and became insanely jealous of Psyche. The visiting sisters began to ask Psyche probing questions about her lover while they feasted on exquisite foods. As she had never seen his face, her answers were full of inconsistencies.

The sisters noted the holes in Psyche's stories and they began to taunt her by saying, "This is a splendid palace, but that is still too high a price to pay for having to sleep with a monster." When the sisters left, Psyche was filled with doubt. On the one hand, she was fairly certain that her lover was a handsome young man. On the other, maybe the sisters had a point; she had never seen his face. Perhaps he *was* a monster.

Psyche resolved that she would try to see his face by stealth. She stayed up waiting for him to return. When he finally walked into the dark bedroom and fell into a sound sleep, she slipped down the hall and grabbed an oil lamp, which she brought to the bedroom. Seeing him for the first time in the light, she could not believe her eyes: This was the most handsome youth in the world, perhaps even a god. She leaned over to kiss him. Then some of the hot oil spilled from the lamp onto his shoulder, waking him with a start.

He leaped up from the bed and shouted, "I told you *never* to look at my face!" Taking on the divine mantle of invisibility, he fled the room. She raced down the hall after him, but it was too late. As he ran, she heard him identify himself—he was Cupid, the god of love himself. And his final words to her that night were that love could not dwell where there is no trust.

Cupid went to the home of Venus, his mother. He had a painful burn on his shoulder where the hot oil had dripped, and he wanted her to tend to it. When he told his mother the story of Psyche, she became enraged. She now hated the beautiful mortal more than ever. Beauty is always least beautiful when threatened by a rival; nor is there any greater womanly spite than that of a mother against her son's lover when that love has gone sour. Venus was absolutely determined to destroy Psyche; the girl had not merely been a threat to the cult of Venus, she had had an affair with Venus's own son!

Likewise, Psyche knew that she was doomed. Not only was it clear enough that her affair with Cupid was over, but her very life was in danger. All that she could do was to throw herself on the mercy of Venus and vow to serve her all her days. She was hoping that the goddess had at least one ounce of compassion left.

Zephyr carried Psyche to the chambers of Venus, who was relishing the chance for revenge on her mortal rival. Psyche flung herself at the feet of the goddess, pleading for mercy. Venus decided to give Psyche an impossible task and then destroy her. So she handed Psyche a pile of the smallest of seeds—poppy, millet, and mustard seeds—and ordered her to have them separated by kind before nightfall. The task was impossible. Psyche began to cry. As her tears hit the floor, the ants took pity on her. The queen ant ordered her sub-

jects to help Psyche separate the seeds by kind. Soon, with thousands of busy little ants working, the job was done. When Venus returned and saw this, she was angrier than before. In fact, the ants
still live underground to avoid her wrath.

As night fell, Psyche became very hungry. But Venus gave her
only a morsel of dry bread and forced her to sleep on the cold stone
floor. Venus knew that nothing could destroy beauty like deprivation.

The next day Venus gave Psyche another impossible task, to gather
golden fleece. Down in a valley near a river, Venus kept a flock of
sacred sheep with golden fleece. However, these sheep had heads
like lions and had torn many a mortal to shreds. Psyche went down
to the riverbank and wept, resigned to her doom. Utterly despondent,
she contemplated drowning herself in the river. Just then she heard
a sweet little voice, like that of a child. Between her toes was a tiny
reed that advised her to pick the golden fleece from the thorny bram-
bles where the sheep had passed through. This way she could gather
plenty of the golden wool in safety. Soon Psyche had gathered as
much golden wool as she could carry. She had completed Venus's
second impossible assignment.

Venus was still prepared to destroy Psyche, so she gave the girl a
pitcher and ordered her to fill it with water from the falls on the
River Styx, the river that is the border between the lands of the living
and the dead. When she arrived, it again appeared that she was
doomed: In order to reach the waterfall, she had to climb up slippery
rocks alongside boiling rapids that could sweep her down to the land
of the dead. Left to her own devices, Psyche would have been finished.

But a great eagle—probably Jupiter [Greek: Zeus] in disguise, as
he is an incurable romantic—swept her safely up to the waterfall.
Psyche filled the pitcher to the brim and returned to Venus.

At this point you may well wonder how it could be that a goddess
would act so spitefully, stupidly, and cruelly. Remember that Venus
is the goddess of beauty. With beauty comes vanity; and vanity, when
threatened by a rival, causes beauty to become very ugly indeed.

Venus next sent Psyche directly into the land of the dead. Psyche
was to ask Proserpina [Greek: Persephone], queen of the Under-

world, for some of her beauty. All of the stress and strain of plotting revenge had taken its toll on Venus's looks.

Very few mortals have ever visited the Underworld and returned to tell about it. It is the abode of the dead, and the living cannot return unless they have the help of the gods. Psyche passed a magic tower, where a guide took compassion on her. The guide told her that she would need to pay a fare to Charon, the ferryman of the dead, to take her across the River Styx into the land of the dead. When Psyche responded that she had no money, the guide told her that Charon was especially partial to honey cakes and gave her a cake to give the ferryman. It is very likely that this "guide" was the god Mercury [Greek: Hermes], who directs the dead to the Underworld, protects travelers, and makes a point of helping lost causes.

Psyche entered the Underworld without incident. Charon, usually quite gruff, was charmed by her beauty—and the cake—taking her across the Styx without any thought of a fare. When she arrived at the throne of Proserpina, the goddess gladly put some of her beauty in a box and sent it with Psyche.

Now here is where Psyche failed miserably. For however wise and good a woman may be, she will do anything for the secret of eternal beauty. Psyche held it right in her hands, and her curiosity was killing her. As she walked along, she grew obsessed by the contents of the box. She opened it; it appeared empty. Then she fell into a deep sleep, more beautiful than ever.

Before Venus had time to wonder what was keeping Psyche, Cupid stepped in to save the mortal girl. Healed from his wounds, he escaped from the palace of Venus—for not even gods can imprison love. He immediately found Psyche, put some of the beauty back into the box, and kissed her. With the beauty returned to the box, Psyche awoke. Cupid told her to take the box immediately to Venus without fear.

As Psyche started on her way, Cupid went to Jupiter to proclaim his love for Psyche and ask the help of the master of all gods in uniting them forever.

Jupiter, as we have said, is a romantic. He listened sympathetically to Cupid's story and then told the young god: "Once physical love [*eros* in Greek] and the soul [*psyche* in Greek] are united, not even the gods can separate them. Therefore you and Psyche shall be husband and wife." Jupiter sent for Psyche and she drank the celestial ambrosia that transforms mortals into immortals. Psyche and Cupid lived happily among the gods. Venus was so pleased to have her mortal rival off the earth, out of sight of the human beings whose adoration Venus desired, that she actually turned into a rather nice mother-in-law. And so it was that physical love and the soul were united, but only after many difficult trials. ♦

PYRAMUS AND THISBE*

Pyramus and Thisbe were two very beautiful youths who lived in the city of Babylon. They grew up in adjacent houses, separated only by a thin wall, and grew to love each other very much. However, their parents did not allow them to see each other, and the two yearned with desire. They discovered a tiny hole in the wall just large enough for them to whisper through. It was still too small for them to kiss through, let alone see each other. However, the more that lovers are separated, the more resolved they are to be together.

So the two made plans to escape and be together. The plan was to slip just outside the city to the tomb of Nimus and meet underneath a mulberry tree there. It was widely known that a fierce lioness guarded the tomb, but the young lovers had no fear.

Thisbe came out and tiptoed around the side of the tomb, but Pyramus was nowhere to be found. Then, to her horror, she saw the lioness, whose jaws were dripping with blood. She thought the very worst—that Pyramus had been killed. Thisbe ran in terror from the lioness and in her haste she dropped her cloak.

Pyramus, very much alive, came on the scene only to see the fierce lioness standing on a girl's cloak. He too thought the worst—

*This myth is the basis of the play presented within Shakespeare's *A Midsummer Night's Dream*.

that his lover had been a victim of the lioness. Stricken with grief, he watched the lioness walk away. Then he took the bloodstained cloak in his arms and wept, saying, "It is I who killed you! You came here to meet me and didn't find me. I will join you, my love." With that Pyramus took his dagger and plunged it into his heart. His blood spurted upward and stained the berries of the mulberry tree.

Thisbe crept up from the side of the tomb and saw the dying Pryamus. She took him in her arms and said, "It is I who killed you, my love. I will join you!" Pyramus's eyes opened for the last time, only to see Thisbe plunging his dagger into her own heart.

Now the gods saw all this, and they are usually on the side of young lovers, regardless of how desperate the situation is. The gods then ordained that the berries of the mulberry tree remain red forever in memory of Pyramus and Thisbe. Some say that young lovers who die by suicide end up in a strange land on the edge of the land of the dead, wandering about for a century as miserable ghosts. But it is generally agreed that the gods allowed Pyramus and Thisbe to spend eternity together. ◆

BAUCIS AND PHILEMON

In former days it was common for the gods to venture out among mortals in disguise. This was their best method of "taking the pulse" of the world below. Jupiter [Zeus] and Mercury [Hermes] wanted to find out whether the inhabitants of Phrygia were friendly or not; they had heard complaints about the lack of Phrygian hospitality. Jupiter is the patron of travelers on the road; Hermes is the god of commerce and also a patron of wayfarers. The two gods traveled down in the guise of poor, ragged tramps, going from door to door throughout the length and breadth of Phrygia, among the rich and the poor. Not one door was opened to them.

Finally they came upon the humble little hovel of an elderly couple, Baucis and Philemon. The two old people occupied only one little room and they were very poor indeed. Yet they were the most hospitable people in all Phrygia. They gathered together the few vegetables and scraps of meat they had and offered them to the strangers. Philemon told the guests, "I have a little wine to refresh you," and he poured it out of a crude, cracked clay jar for his guests.

Poor as they were, neither Baucis nor Philemon uttered a single word of complaint. In fact, the gods were deeply moved when the old man told them, "We have very little to offer you, strangers, but what little we have is yours." The gods drank more and more of the wine, and still old Philemon's cracked jar remained full.

A miracle was taking place—not only did the wine jar remain full but, in place of the common table wine originally in the jar, it now held the finest of vintages. Likewise, when the food was brought to the table, still more food appeared out of nowhere. Baucis and Philemon were mystified. Finally, the gods revealed their true identities and the old couple fell to the ground in reverence.

The gods then told the old people how inhospitable the Phrygians had been to them, and how the kindness of Baucis and Philemon had made a deep impression on them both. Jupiter told them that he was aware that the neighbors had been rude and cruel to Baucis and Philemon, despite their kind hearts. As he finished speaking, Jupiter caused the fields around their tiny hut to flood, killing all the neighbors. Despite the wickedness of the Phrygians, Baucis and Philemon wept for their countrymen.

While the waters rose, so did the hut of Baucis and Philemon, which remained high and dry. Suddenly it was transformed into a shining temple of marble. Jupiter and Mercury appointed Baucis and Philemon priestess and priest of their temple. They faithfully tended the temple until they were well over one hundred years old.

When the couple became too frail to carry out their duties, a wonderful thing happened. Jupiter remembered that Philemon never wished to be separated from his beloved Baucis. Being a sentimental romantic, Jupiter caused them to grow into a beautiful oak tree with its two trunks entwined. Jupiter had kept his promise: Baucis and Philemon remained together forever. ♦

VERTUMNUS AND POMONA

The wood nymphs are beautiful creatures that love the forests and avoid the open fields as a rule. However, there was one wood nymph, Pomona, who loved the orchards best of all. Nothing gave her greater pleasure than playing among the grapevines and apple trees. She was so beautiful that many suitors came to see her, including even kings, but she was more interested in dressing vines than in loving.

Among the most ardent of her suitors was Vertumnus, who was partly immortal. It is believed that either his father or his mother was a god or goddess. He was very persistent, but Pomona ignored him. He brought her gifts of flowers and fruit, which she accepted without thanks.

Vertumnus took on the guise of a rude shepherd, and Pomona was even more scornful than before. She treated this country bumpkin with great scorn.

Then one day Vertumnus disguised himself as an old woman out picking fruit. When Pomona encountered this "old woman," she was friendly, even gracious. The "old woman" told Pomona that she was the most beautiful fruit in the orchard and the most lovely flower of the field. Pomona was flattered. Then the "old woman" kissed Pomona in a manner that no old woman would ever kiss a young girl. Pomona was aghast and disgusted.

To make his point, Vertumnus then pointed to grapes growing on a trellis, saying how lovely they were. Without the trellis, he pointed out, the grapes would be trod underfoot; without the grapes growing on it, the trellis would be useless. The two needed each other. Pomona knew exactly what point Vertumnus was trying to make and she prepared to flee.

Just then, Venus, the goddess of love, appeared and told Pomona, "This is your true husband; it is ordained that you marry him." Certainly Pomona had no choice after that; the two were married. And it so happened that she fell in love with him over time and they tended the orchards together.

And so it is: Lovers belong together like the trellis and the grape; each is incomplete without the other. ♦

APOLLO AND DAPHNE

Daphne [Greek for "laurel"] was a wood nymph, the daughter of the river god Peneus. She was one of those free-spirited women in mythology who was more interested in hunting and fishing than in men. Her father despaired that she would ever marry; he was more interested in grandchildren than in having still more game to eat.

The god Apollo saw Daphne one day and fell instantly in love with her. He was unable to think of anything but her and he pursued her to no avail. Daphne was absolutely indifferent to his attentions; it mattered not whether he was god or mortal. She also knew that relationships with gods were often complicated and even dangerous. She was, after all, half divine, yet mortal. Finally Apollo chased her through the forests until she was stricken with fear. There was no way that she could outrun him, so she cried to her father to save her with a miracle.

Suddenly, she felt her feet become rooted in the earth. She could not move. Leaves began to sprout from her arms—she had become a living laurel tree. The gods have a way of sorting things out of the most desperate situations, so they made the laurel tree the sacred tree of Apollo.

To this day, whether at poetry contests or athletic events, both within the purview of Apollo, the winner is crowned with laurels. ♦

NOTE: In some versions of this myth, Daphne is the daughter of Mother Earth, who saves her. The following is from Ernst Cassirer, *Language and Myth*.

> Or take the myth of Daphne, who is saved from Apollo's embraces by the fact that her mother, the Earth, transforms her into a laurel tree. Again it is only the history of language that can make this myth "comprehensible," and give it any sort of sense. Who was Daphne? In order to answer this question we must re-

sort to etymology, that is to say, we must investigate the history of the word. "Daphne" can be traced back to Sanskrit [the language of ancient India] "Ahana," and Ahana means in Sanskrit, "the redness of dawn." As soon as we know this, the whole matter becomes clear. The story of Phoebus [a name for Apollo—"the shining one"] and Daphne is nothing but a description of what one may observe every day: first the appearance of the dawnlight in the eastern sky, then the rising of the sun-god who hastens after his bride, then the gradual fading of the red dawn at the touch of his fiery rays, and finally its death and disappearance in Mother Earth. So the decisive condition for the development of the myth was not the natural phenomenon itself, but rather the circumstance that the Greek word for the laurel (daphne) and the Sanskrit word for the dawn are related. . . .

TWO PERUVIAN LOVE STORIES

CONIRAYA AND CAVILLACA

There was a very ancient *huaca** named Coniraya. Some call him Coniraya Viracocha, as he may have been a son, or even an incarnation, of Viracocha, the sun-god. In any case, he came to earth in the guise of a poor mountain shepherd, dressed in coarse llama wool. Anyone looking at him would have thought him to be a poor *campesino*† from the mountain highlands. But to those who saw through his guise, it was apparent that Coniraya Viracocha was a great and wise teacher who taught many useful arts to the people—irrigation, terrace farming, keeping records with the *quipu*,** and other important things. During his travels he saw and fell in love with

---

*This term (pronounced "WAH-cah") should not be directly translated as "god," but rather stands for a divine spirit that is associated with a certain place.

†Spanish for "peasant."

**Although the Incas did not have writing, they kept records through the use of color-coded knotted cords, which they called *quipu* (pronounced "KEE-poo").

a haughty female *huaca* named Cavillaca. As she was of the highest
lineage, she ignored Coniraya, whom she took for the most vulgar
peasant.

So Coniraya assumed the guise of a bird and sat in a lucma fruit
tree near the home of Cavillaca. He noticed that Cavillaca liked the
lucma best of all fruits. So he fashioned some of his sperm into the
form of a lucma fruit, which Cavillaca ate. She then conceived a
child.

When she gave birth to this son, she protested that she was a virgin, but no one believed her. She was outraged by the disgrace of
having a child out of wedlock and knew that only a *huaca* could do
such a thing. So she called all of the *huacas* together to learn who
was the father of her child. When the *huacas* arrived, they were all
dressed in their finest of clothing, each hoping that Cavillaca might
take him as a husband. However, not one of the *huacas* admitted to
being the father of the baby. Coniraya, still dressed in the clothing
of the poorest shepherd, sat silently in the assembly of the *huacas*.

Finally, Cavillaca placed the little boy on the ground and he immediately crawled to his true father—Coniraya. Seeing his shabby
appearance, she was so outraged that she stormed out of the assembly and fled toward the sea.

Coniraya, however, was still deeply in love with her and ran
through the countryside in pursuit. He asked the animals for assistance in finding her. First, he asked the mighty condor, who told the
truth. In thanks, Coniraya blessed the condor, assuring it that it
would fly and nest higher than any other bird, safe from all danger.
No other creature would be able to prey upon it or disturb its eggs.

Further along, Coniraya met a fox, which lied to him. The fox said
that Cavillaca had passed through many days before and there was
little hope of catching up to her. Knowing that this was a lie,
Coniraya cursed the fox and all its descendants. To this day, humans
hunt the fox and the people of the high Andes hate the animal, considering it a bad omen.

Then Coniraya asked the puma, who told the truth. The puma told
Coniraya to hurry as Cavillaca had just passed through. Then
Coniraya blessed the great cat. It would be the executioner of evildo-

ers and be free to eat the llamas unhindered. As a sign of respect, no hunter may remove the head of the puma from its body to this very day.

Coniraya next met an obnoxious group of parrots, who answered only by repeating his questions. He cursed the parrots, giving them loud voices that made it easy for hunters to find them. Since the parrots did not know the difference between truth and falsehood, they were forever condemned to only repeating what they heard.

Finally Coniraya arrived at the coast only to find that his beloved and their son had been turned to stone. Filled with grief, Coniraya met the daughters of the god Pachachamac, who served as the guardians of the sea. Their mother, Urpi-Huachac, was away visiting when Cavillaca arrived. Coniraya knew that Urpi-Huachac had changed Cavillaca and their son into rocks. Coniraya charmed the elder of the two daughters and had intercourse with her, as an insult to Urpi-Huachac. When the younger daughter refused his advances, she flew away in the form of a pigeon. He cursed her, and to this day pigeons are utterly dependent upon the scraps left by others in order to eat.

He saw the sacred fish pond that Urpi-Huachac tended. At that time, it contained all the fish in the world. In his wrath, he ripped a hole in the side of the pond, releasing all the fish into the sea, where they live today. ◆

OLLANTAY AND CUSICOLLUR

NOTE: This love story became the basis of a famous sixteenth-century Peruvian play that is still performed.

Ollantay was an honest, just, and brave warrior, faithful to the emperor, or Inca. However, he broke one of the most important laws of Tahuantisuyo (the Inca Empire) by falling in love with the beautiful Cusicollur, the Inca's daughter. Cusicollur loved Ollantay as well, and the two went secretly to a kindly old priest to be married.

The old priest listened to them sympathetically, but sadly replied that a commoner could never marry a daughter of the Inca, a descendant of Inti or Viracocha, the sun-god. In fact, were he to marry them, the old priest himself could lose his life. Cusicollur told the priest that it was not a sin for her to marry Ollantay; rather, it was a greater sin to keep them apart.

Sometime later, Cusicollur learned that she was pregnant. She told her father and he sent her away to live with the priestesses of the sun, where no man may ever go, not even the Inca himself. There she gave birth to a beautiful little daughter named Yma Sumac, which means "very beautiful." The child was taken from her to be raised in a separate part of the temple. Meanwhile, the great Inca pronounced a death sentence on Ollantay.

The Inca's troops pursued Ollantay and his men into a valley, where Ollantay's men soundly defeated the pursuers. However, the Inca's general, Rumanahui, waited for Ollantay's warriors to fall asleep. Then Rumanahui opened the gates and his warriors took Ollantay and all his men prisoner. Ollantay himself was bound with ropes to be taken to Cuzco, capital of the empire, for execution.

On the journey to Cuzco, a messenger ran to Rumanahui with the news that the old Inca had died and his son, Tupac Yupanqui,* Cusicollur's brother, was now ruler of Tahuantisuyo. Ollantay was a boyhood friend of the new emperor; perhaps there was still hope.

At Cuzco, Tupac Yupanqui awaited Ollantay and looked very sad. "My father, dear friend, the great Inca Pachacutec, ordered your execution and there is nothing I can do but carry it out. But, since you are my friend, I will allow you to speak."

Ollantay told the emperor that he understood the law and his friend's duty to carry it out. But he was not a traitor to the emperor; the law was a traitor to love. This law had kept apart two people who loved each other and even had a child together. He could never love anyone but Cusicollur. Then he told the emperor, "The gods, not

---

*Tupac Yupanqui, and probably Ollantay, were historical characters who lived roughly during the twelfth or thirteenth century A.D., some three or four centuries before the arrival of the Spanish conquistadores.

men, decide who falls in love with whom." Thus, it was the will of the gods that he and Cusicollur marry. Even though the new Inca was a god himself, he could not stop the power of love.

Tupac Yupanqui was deeply moved by these words. Today he is still remembered as one of the wisest and most compassionate of all the Incas. He revoked the death sentence on Ollantay, convinced that this was the will of the gods. Tupac Yupanqui then ordered Cusicollur and Yma Sumac brought to the palace. Ollantay and Cusicollur were married, and Ollantay became the Inca's chief general and adviser. ♦

ANGUS OG
(*Scotland and Ireland*)

Angus Og ["Angus the Young"] is the Gaelic god of love. And as love always makes people youthful, the name fits. Four bright birds hover about his head—the embodiment of his kisses. Anyone hearing the songs of these birds falls hopelessly in love. Angus is the son of the Dagda ("the Good God"), the Supreme Being. Angus himself is constantly in love.

Once Angus fell dangerously ill from "love sickness" for a young girl, and his mother, Boanna, searched all of Ireland to find her without success. Then the great Dagda was called in, but even he could not find her. The Dagda asked Bov the Red for assistance, as Bov knew all mysteries. Bov himself did not know where she was, but he eventually found her at the Lake of the Dragon's Mouth.

Angus then went to see Bov and they feasted together for three days. Eager to see his beloved, Angus begged Bov to take him to her. When they arrived at the Lake of the Dragon's Mouth, Angus saw a hundred and fifty beautiful maidens, the most beautiful in the world, walking in pairs, each pair linked by a chain of pure gold. One maiden was taller than the rest; this was the girl that Angus loved. Angus was seized with desire and wanted to carry her off. However,

Bov warned that she would not be separated from the others without difficulty. The girl's name was Caer, and she was the daughter of an unrelated semidivine prince of the province of Connacht.

Angus went to see the king and queen of Connacht to seek their assistance in winning the hand of Caer, but even the king and queen had no power to help. What irony! Angus, who made all lovers fall in love, was unable to win the hand of his own beloved without help. The king and queen, however, did agree to send a message to Caer's father asking for Caer's hand on Angus's behalf.

Angus approached Caer's father to ask her hand, but the older man refused to see the young suitor. The armies of the Dagda and the king of Connacht besieged the home of Caer's father and took him prisoner. However, Caer's father finally explained that he had no power to give his daughter in marriage; her magic was more powerful than his. He further explained that Caer lived six months out of every year in the form of a woman and the other six months in the form of a swan. On the feast of Samhain,* Caer would be found again at the lake with the other girls, all in the form of swans.†

Angus went to the lake on the feast of Samhain and begged Caer, now a swan, to be his bride. She asked who he was and he explained that he was Angus Og, the god of love. As he spoke his name, he himself was transformed into a swan, and he and Caer lived together forever after. Angus now often appears to lovers in the guise of the swan, and this is why lovers like to meet near lakes. ♦

---

*Samhain (pronounced "SOW-un") is the feast of Halloween, or the Christian All Saints' Eve. It was on this day that the Gaelic people believed the spirits came to visit the living, and they offered these spirits gifts and food.

†As we noted earlier, the swan is often, like the serpent, interpreted as one who inhabits two worlds. Compare the swans in the story of Angus Og with the swans that appear in Finnish and American Indian myths. Also, compare Cupid [Greek: "Eros"] with his irresistible arrows and Angus's birds. Cupid is often pictured as having wings, and Angus flies from place to place as a swan.

ALGON AND THE SKY-GIRL
(*Algonquin Indian*)

Algon was a great hunter who found a strange circle cut in the prairie grass. Hiding in the bushes nearby, he watched to see what might have caused it. Finally, a great willow basket descended from the sky bearing twelve beautiful maidens. The maidens got out of the basket and began singing celestial songs and doing circle dances. All of the girls were beautiful, but the most beautiful of all was the youngest, with whom Algon was immediately smitten.

He ran toward the circle in the hope of stealing her away, but just as he arrived, the girls were alarmed and left in the basket, which flew high into the sky. This happened again three more times, but Algon's resolve only grew. Then he devised a strategy.

He placed a hollow tree trunk near the circle. Inside the tree trunk lived a family of mice. He took some charms out of his medicine bag and transformed himself into a mouse. When the girls in the basket next arrived, he and the other mice ran among the girls. The girls stomped on the mice, killing all of them but Algon, who then resumed his human form and carried off his beloved.

He took her to his village and in time she fell in love with him. They had a son and the three lived very happily for a time. But as the years passed, the sky-girl grew very homesick. She spent the entire day gazing up at the sky, thinking of her sisters and parents. This homesickness continued until she could no longer bear it. So she built a magic willow basket, placed her son and some gifts for her people in it, climbed in, and headed for the sky. She remained there for years.

In her absence, Algon pined for his wife and son. Every day he went to sit in the magic circle, in the hope that they would return. He was now growing old.

Meanwhile, in the far-off sky-country, his son was growing into manhood. The lad asked questions about his father, which made the sky-girl miss Algon. She and her son spoke to her father, the chief of the sky-people. He told them to go back to the earth, but ordered them to return with Algon and the identifying feature of each of the earth animals.

Then the sky-girl and the son returned to earth. Algon was overjoyed to see them and was eager to gather the gifts the sky-chief wanted. From the bear, he took a claw; from the eagle, hawk, and falcon, a feather; from the raccoon, its teeth; and from the deer, its horns and hide. He placed all of these gifts in a special medicine bag, and ascended with his wife and son to the sky-country in their willow basket. His father-in-law divided the tokens among his people, offering tokens to Algon and the sky-girl; and they chose the falcon feather. The chief said that they should always be free to travel between the sky-country and the earth, and so Algon and his wife became falcons. Their descendants still fly high and swoop down over the forests and prairies. ♦

7. Morality Tales from the Myths

Listen to this law, my people,
Pay attention to what I say;
I am going to speak to you in parable
and expound the mysteries of our past.

What we have heard and known for ourselves,
And what our ancestors have told us,
must not be withheld from their descendants,
but be handed on by us to the next generation;

that is: the titles of the Lord, his power
and the miracles he has done.
When he issued the decrees for Jacob
and instituted a law for Israel,

he gave our ancestors strict orders
to teach it to their children;
the next generation was to learn it,
the children still to be born,

and these in turn were to tell their own children
so that they too would put their confidence in God,
never forgetting God's achievements,
and always keeping his commandments.

—Psalms 78:1–7

MORALITY TALES FROM THE MAHABHARATA
(*India*)

THE VIRTUE OF COMPASSION

There was once a hunter from the city of Varanasi [Benares], on the sacred Ganges River. He went out to shoot antelope with his bow and a full quiver of poison arrows. When he was far out into the forest, he spotted a herd of antelope and shot his arrows at them, missing every one. One of his arrows, however, did hit an ancient tree where a kindly old parrot lived. As soon as the arrow struck, the old tree began to wither and die. But the parrot, who had been born in that very tree and spent all of its life there, refused to abandon it.

The parrot remained in the tree, not even leaving to find new food to eat. As the tree withered, so did the parrot. The bird just remained in the very spot where it was born, motionless and mourning in silence. The sky god Indra looked down on the faithful parrot and decided to visit the bird, taking the human form of a noble Brahman.

Indra, in this guise, asked the bird, "Why don't you leave this tree? It is almost completely dead." But the parrot replied, "I cannot leave this tree. I was born here; for my entire life, this tree has given me a home, food to eat, and refuge from my enemies. How could I ever leave such a faithful friend?" But Indra replied, "It is you, O parrot, who is a faithful friend." Deeply moved by the parrot's loyalty, Indra touched the withered tree and it was restored to life.

Indra then told the parrot, "I have brought the tree back to life, but it is really you, the faithful parrot, that kept it alive."

With this story of friendship, faithfulness, and the virtue of compassion, everyone who hears it will be blessed; everyone who tells it will be blessed twice. ♦

THE KING, THE HAWK, AND THE PIGEON

There was once a beautiful pigeon who was being pursued by a fierce hawk. The pigeon asked King Vrishadarbha of Varanasi for protection. The kindly king said, "Why are you so afraid, little fellow?" The pigeon replied that the hawk was about to tear it to shreds. The king told the pigeon, "I will do all I can to defend and protect you, even if it costs me my own life. The gods have certainly sent you to me as a test."

Then the hawk came to the king and said, "Look, I understand that you are compassionate, and that you promised the pigeon that you would risk your own life to save its life. However, I am a hawk; hawks eat pigeons. If I don't have a pigeon to eat, I might starve to death. Now, if you are truly compassionate, you will hand the pigeon over and I can eat it. Then we can forget about all of this business."

Then the king said, "O hawk, you can fly anywhere—why don't you just eat something else? Why not a frog or a bull or any other animal?" The hawk replied that it was not its nature to eat beef or frog or anything but pigeons. At this point the hawk grew impatient and said, "If you feel so strongly about having to protect the pigeon, why don't you offer me some of your own flesh in an amount equal to the weight of the pigeon?" The king agreed to do this, to the amazement of all his court.

So the pigeon was weighed on a scale and the king actually cut pieces from his own flesh to try to equal its weight, but the little bird always weighed more! The king did this until he was merely a skeleton, and still the little bird weighed more.

Suddenly, the heavens opened and celestial music poured through the palace of the king. The gods had watched the entire proceeding and they were deeply moved by the king's great loyalty in keeping his vow to a humble pigeon. A shower of nectar fell from heaven and the king was restored to his healthy former condition. Indra himself rode down from heaven in a chariot and carried the king away alive to the highest heaven.

For Indra told all that were there: "It is one thing to make a promise and keep it. It is quite another to keep the promise so well that one sacrifices one's self. He who puts himself at risk to help another is truly a friend of the gods." And whoever hears this story will be blessed; whoever tells it will be blessed twice. ♦

GAUTAMA AND THE ELEPHANT

There was once a sage named Gautama who found a motherless baby elephant and took care of it. He grew to love this elephant and protected it until it became a mighty beast. Indra was watching all this from heaven, and came to earth in the form of King Dhitarashtra.

In this mortal guise, he tried to take the elephant away from Gautama, but Gautama implored him not to separate him from the elephant who was indispensable to him as a companion; it carried food and water. But "Dhitarashtra" replied that such a handsome animal should be the property of a king, not of some sage living in the forest.

Gautama replied that he did not consider the elephant "property" or a "possession" but, rather, his oldest and dearest friend.

"Dhitarashtra" then tried to buy the elephant, offering Gautama gold, silver, cattle, beautiful maidens, even a palace. Gautama told him, "Even if you go to the realm of Yama [death] and take me with you, you will not be able to take my elephant away from me."

Indra, as Dhitarashtra, replied, "Those who go down to the land of death ruled by Yama are sinful, and slaves of their desires." Gautama replied, "There is much truth to be found in the land of the dead; there the weak are equal to the powerful and can even overcome them." Then the "king" said, "I am too powerful and too holy to go to the land of Yama." Gautama said, "That may well be, but even if you go up to the highest heaven ruled by Indra, you shall never have my elephant." This persisted until the "king" said, "What if I go to the place of Brahma the Creator and he tells me that the elephant is mine?"

The sage laughed and said, "Brahma the Creator knows all things and loves all things; your power means nothing to him. But the power of love that I feel for my elephant is more powerful than wealth, weapons, or anything else in the universe. I know who you are—you are Indra, who tests the wise."

Indra was so delighted by the faithfulness of Gautama to his elephant that he offered the sage any request. Gautama could have asked for riches or property, but all he asked for was to remain with his elephant. Indra told him, "You need not ask for wisdom; you already have that. As for riches, you are the richest man on earth, he who knows the value of a good friend." Years later, when Gautama was ready to die, Indra took him and the elephant alive together to the highest heaven.

And he who hears this story will be blessed; he who tells it will be twice blessed. ♦

ANANSI THE SPIDER
(*West Africa*)

NOTE: These stories are of particular interest because they come from the Ashanti of Ghana and were brought to the Americas, where they survive—in the American South, the West Indies, and Brazil—as the "Annancy" stories.

They are wonderful lessons about the results of arrogance.

ANANSI AND THE EAR OF CORN

Anansi was one of God's chosen, and he lived in human form before he became a spider. One day he asked God for a simple ear of corn, promising that he would repay God with one hundred servants. God was always amused by the boastful and resourceful Anansi, and gave him the ear of corn. Anansi set out with the ear and came to a village to rest. He told the chief of the village that he

had a sacred ear of corn from God and needed both a place to sleep
for the night and a safe place to keep the treasure. The chief treated
Anansi as an honored guest and gave him a thatched-roof house to
stay in, showing him a hiding place in the roof.

During the night, while the entire village was fast asleep, Anansi
took the corn and fed it to the chickens. The next morning Anansi
woke the village with his cries. "What happened to the sacred corn?
Who stole it? Certainly God will bring great punishment on this village!" He made such a fuss that the villagers begged him to take a
whole bushel of corn as a demonstration of their apologies.

He then set down the road with the bushel of corn until it grew too
heavy for him to carry. He then met a man on the road who had a
chicken, and Anansi exchanged the corn for the chicken. When
Anansi arrived at the next village, he asked for a place to stay and
a safe place to keep the "sacred" chicken. In this new village,
Anansi was again treated as an honored guest, a great feast was held
in his honor, and he was shown a house to stay in and given a safe
place for the chicken.

During the night Anansi butchered the chicken and smeared its
blood and feathers on the door of the chief's house. In the morning
he woke everyone with his cries, "The sacred chicken has been
killed! Surely God will destroy this village for allowing this to happen!" The frightened villagers begged Anansi to take ten of their finest sheep as a token of their sincere apology.

Anansi drove the sheep down the road until he came to a group of
men carrying a corpse. He asked the men whose body they were
carrying. The men answered that a traveler had died in their village
and they were bearing the body home for a proper burial. Anansi
then exchanged the sheep for the corpse and set out down the road.

At the next village, Anansi told the people that the corpse was a
son of God who was sleeping. He told them to be very quiet in order
not to wake this important guest. The people in this village, too, held
a great feast and treated Anansi as royalty.

When morning came, Anansi told the villagers that he was having
a hard time waking the "son of God" from sleep, and he asked their
help. They started by beating drums, and the visitor remained

"asleep." Then they banged pots and pans, but he was still "asleep." Then the villagers pounded on the visitor's chest, and he still didn't stir.

All of a sudden, Anansi cried out, "You have killed him! You have killed a son of God! Oh, no! Certainly God will destroy this whole village, if not the entire world!" The terrified villagers then told Anansi that he could pick one hundred of their finest young men as slaves if only he would appeal to God to save them.

So Anansi returned to God, having turned one ear of corn into one hundred slaves. ♦

HOW ANANSI "TRICKED" GOD

Anansi was terribly conceited after the whole affair of the ear of corn. God found Anansi entertaining, but his bragging was growing tiresome. So God gave Anansi a sack and said, "I have something in mind; figure it out and bring it back to me in the sack." Anansi asked questions, but God would give no further clues as to what that "something" might be. God sent the mortal on his way, saying that if he were only half as clever as he boasted he was, then he should have no problem figuring out what "something" God wanted.

Anansi was puzzled. How was he to know what God wanted in the sack? He left heaven and had a meeting with the birds, explaining his predicament. The birds were sympathetic, but had no clues to offer. However, each agreed to give Anansi one feather, enabling Anansi to fly. Anansi made these feathers into a beautiful cloak, and then flew up to heaven, where he perched in a tree next to God's house.

Some of the people of heaven saw this strange "bird" and began talking about it. They asked each other what kind of bird this might be. God himself did not recall making any sort of creature that looked like that. One of those present suggested that, if Anansi were so clever, *he* might know what sort of bird this was.

Anansi, in the tree, heard all of this. God's attendants were speaking among themselves when one said, "Good luck finding Anansi—God sent him on an impossible mission. How was Anansi to know that God wanted the sun and the moon brought to him in a sack?"

Overhearing this, Anansi went out to fetch the sun and the moon. He went to the python, the wisest of all things, and asked how one might capture the sun and the moon. The python advised him to go to the west, where the sun rests at night. The moon could be found in the east around the same time. So Anansi gathered the sun and the moon, placed them in the sack, and took them to God.

God was so pleased with Anansi's ingenuity that he made Anansi his captain on earth. ◆

ANANSI AND THE CHAMELEON

As we have said, Anansi grew more and more conceited and arrogant. In fact, God became so annoyed by Anansi's boast that he had "tricked" God in the episode of the sun and the moon that he was seriously considering removing his patronage from Anansi.

Anansi lived in the same village as the Chameleon. Anansi was rich and owned the finest fields in the area, while the Chameleon was poor and worked hard in his meager fields to make ends meet. However, one year rain fell on Chameleon's fields, which were now abundant with beautiful crops. No rain fell on Anansi's land and the crops dried up and dust blew everywhere. Anansi then resolved to take Chameleon's fields for himself.

Anansi first tried to buy the fields, but Chameleon refused to sell. Anansi offered more and more in exchange, but Chameleon still held on to the land.

Early one morning, Anansi walked boldly down the road to Chameleon's fields and began harvesting the crops. When Chameleon saw this, he became very angry and chased Anansi away.

When a chameleon walks, it leaves no tracks; it is virtually impossible to tell where a chameleon has been. Knowing this, Anansi took Chameleon to court to sue for possession of the fields. The chief asked Chameleon to prove that the fields were his; Chameleon had no proof to offer. Anansi, on the other hand, took the chief to Chameleon's fields, showing the many footprints on the road. These were Anansi's footprints, and the chief awarded the fields to Anansi right then and there.

Although the court decision gave the land to Anansi, God has a higher justice than that which the courts mete out. Chameleon dug a deep, deep hole and put a roof on it. From the outside, the hole looked tiny. But, in fact, Chameleon had dug a vast cavern underground. Then the Chameleon took some vines and some flies and made a cloak. When the sun hits flies, they shine a variety of colors, but they are still flies. Chameleon went down the road wearing this cloak of flies when he encountered Anansi.

Anansi's first words to Chameleon were, "Hello, my friend. I hope that there are no hard feelings between us." Anansi saw what appeared to be a beautiful cloak and offered to buy it. Chameleon pretended to be magnanimous and told Anansi that the cloak would be his if only Anansi filled Chameleon's "little hole" with food. Anansi readily agreed, bragging that he would fill it twice over.

Anansi then took the cloak to the chief who had acted as judge in the lawsuit and gave it to the chief as a gift. The chief admired the cloak and thanked him profusely.

Anansi worked day and night to fill Chameleon's hole with food and still the hole was not full. He worked weeks and still the hole was not full. Anansi knew that Chameleon had tricked him.

In the meantime, the chief was walking down the road wearing the cloak of flies. One day the vines broke and the flies buzzed off in every direction, leaving the chief naked and livid with anger at Anansi. The chief grew angrier with each step he took. When the chief found Anansi, he ordered him not only to return Chameleon's property but to give Chameleon the best of his own fields as well. As soon as Chameleon took possession of Anansi's best field, it rained on that field for the first time in months, and now Chameleon was the richest in the village. ◆

HOW ANANSI BECAME A SPIDER

There was once a king who had the finest ram in the world. When this ram happened to be grazing on Anansi's crops one day, Anansi threw a rock at it, hitting it between the eyes and killing it. Anansi knew that the king would punish him for what he had done to the prize ram, and he immediately schemed how to get out of the situation. Needless to say, Anansi resorted to trickery.

Anansi sat under a tree to think of an escape when, all of a sudden, a nut fell and struck him on the head. Anansi immediately had an idea. First, he took the dead ram and tied it to the nut tree. Then he went to a spider and told it of a wonderful tree laden with nuts. The spider was delighted and immediately went to the tree.

Anansi then went to the king and told him that the spider had evidently killed the prize ram; the ram was hanging from a tree where the spider was spinning webs. The king flew into a rage and demanded the death penalty for the spider. The king thanked Anansi and offered him a great reward.

Anansi returned to the spider and warned it of the king's wrath, crying out to the whole world that the spider had killed the ram. The spider was very confused. Anansi told the spider to go to the king and plead for mercy, and perhaps the spider's life would be spared.

Meanwhile, the king had gone home for lunch and told his wife what happened. The wife laughed and said, "Have you lost your mind? How on earth could a little spider make a thread strong enough to hold a ram? How in the world could that little spider hoist the ram up there? Don't you know, Anansi obviously killed your ram!" The king was angry that he had been deceived and told his court to fetch Anansi immediately.

When the king's men came for him, Anansi assumed that it was to bring him to the palace for his reward for turning in the spider. So Anansi went along willingly. He walked into the palace as if he owned the place and then said to the king, "Well, what is my reward for the killer of your ram?"

This enraged the king so much that he kicked Anansi, splitting him into many pieces; he was no longer a man, but a spider with long legs. ♦

GREEK MORALITY TALES

ICARUS AND DAEDALUS

Daedalus [of whom we shall read again in a later chapter] was the greatest builder of all time. It is he who built the great Labyrinth in Crete at the orders of King Minos. Ariadne, the daughter of Minos, asked Daedalus for assistance in aiding the escape of the hero Theseus. For aiding the escape of Ariadne and Theseus, Minos had Daedalus locked in a tower, together with Icarus, Daedalus's son.

Daedalus spent his days devising a means for escape. He climbed up on the parapet of the tower and gathered the feathers of birds. He also gathered wax from a hive that some bees had built in the tower. The guards did not notice his work.

Over the space of several months, Daedalus had fashioned enormous wings out of the wax and feathers. The larger feathers were put in place, sewn along a light frame that Daedalus had made of wood that he bribed the guards for, and the smaller feathers were held together with the beeswax. Daedalus wanted to use these wings to escape from the tower. However, Icarus was lighter than he was, and thus was the perfect one to try out wings before the escape.

Daedalus instructed Icarus to watch the birds and see how they fly. Icarus needed to perfectly duplicate the motions of the birds with the wings his father had fashioned. Most important of all, Daedalus instructed his son not to fly too low or he would fall into the ocean and drown; he could not fly too high either—or the sun would melt the wax.

Icarus then leaped off the tower and began flying like a bird. To his amazement, this was great fun. He swooped out over the ocean, diving and rising again. He made a great circle around the tower. Then he tried flying a little higher, and he made circles so high in the sky that his father could barely see him. Exhilarated by his successes, rather than use common sense and return to the tower, Icarus tried to fly still higher and higher until, as his father had predicted, the wax melted and the lad plunged to his death in the ocean.

This is why the gods never allow human beings to fly: They cannot stay within their limits. If they communicate with the gods, they become overly familiar and forget their place. Humans were given reason and skill, but still they use their hands to make weapons to kill each other off. One is well-advised to heed Daedalus's warning and not fly too high or too low. ♦

ARACHNE

O f all the human sins that annoy the gods, the worst of all is hubris, or arrogant pride. This is the sort of attitude that leads human beings to contest the gods and defy them. Arachne was one such foolish mortal.

Arachne was a peasant girl who was famous throughout Greece for her skills as a weaver and spinner. No one could spin as well or as fast as Arachne—among mortals at least. The cloth that she produced was the finest ever seen.

It was Athena, the goddess of wisdom, who first invented the arts of spinning and weaving. Arachne began to boast that her patroness, Athena, was probably not able to make as fine a cloth as she. At first the goddess laughed and ignored the vain girl. But then people began to believe these boasts, ignoring the temples and festivals of Athena. The usually peaceful and patient goddess became very angry.

Athena came to earth and appeared to Arachne, challenging her to a spinning match. The girl and the goddess each began spinning with as much speed and skill as they could. Arachne's results were impressive, and Athena was surprised to find her a worthy contender. And if Arachne had been humble and silent during the contest, all might have been well. Instead, Arachne had loudly proclaimed her spinning to be superior to that of Athena, in the very presence of the goddess.

Athena looked at Arachne (which means "spider") and told her, "If it is spinning you do best, you may do it forever!" And with that, Arachne became a spider. And Arachne's children spin to this very day. ♦

MIDAS

When King Midas was an infant, a curious omen took place. While the baby was sleeping, ants gathered up grains of wheat and marched them up to his lips, presaging that Midas would be a wealthy man.

Dionysus, the god of the grapes, has a debauched son named Silenus,* who is very rarely sober and tends, when drunk, to forget where he is. This worries his father terribly. While sojourning in Midas's kingdom Silenus, per usual, got drunk and stumbled about confusedly. In that area there was a terrible whirlpool that had claimed the lives of even many sober men. Silenus stumbled into the waters and would have perished had Midas not saved him.

In gratitude, Dionysus offered the king whatever he wanted. Midas asked that the touch of his hand would turn everything to gold. Dionysus asked him. "Are you sure?" But Midas was insistent. At that, everything that the king touched turned to gold.

At first, Midas found this wonderful; he turned flowers, stones, trees, and other objects to gold. However, he became hungry. As he sat down to eat, his food turned to gold. His daughter came to embrace him; she also turned to gold. Midas was grieved and feared that he would starve to death. Dionysus had known that this would happen; the god hoped that Midas would learn the lesson of greed.

---

*Silenus is sometimes depicted as Bacchus's foster father.

Hearing the pitiful pleas of King Midas, Dionysus removed the golden touch.

As well-known as the story of Midas is, there is another tale that demonstrates the results of pride: Midas became reknowned for his wealth and for his wisdom as a ruler. Once the king attended a musical contest between Apollo and the mortal Marsyas that was judged by a river god named Tmolus. Tmolus, of course, awarded the prize to Apollo. However, the arrogant Midas dissented and argued with the river god, saying that Marsyas was a match for the god. At which point Apollo turned the king's ears into those of an ass.

For a long time after, Midas was able to hide this punishment by wearing a cap, and he extracted a promise from his barber never to reveal this secret under pain of death. It was virtually impossible for the barber to keep from laughing when he cut Midas's hair. When the barber could bear it no longer, he dug a hole in a riverbank and whispered into it, "Midas has the ears of an ass."

Sometime later, however, a tiny reed grew out of that very hole and whispered the secret to every passerby. Midas then had the barber killed. But the ass's ears remained. ♦

NARCISSUS

Narcissus may possibly be the most handsome male who ever lived. At his birth, the blind seer Teiresias prophesied that Narcissus would enjoy a long life only if he never knew himself or saw his own reflection. By the age of sixteen, Narcissus already had left a string of broken hearts, both male and female as he found no one good enough for him.

Among those who sought Narcissus's favors was the nymph Echo. Hera, the wife of Zeus, had punished Echo by not allowing her to speak but only to repeat what she heard. This was because Echo had detained Hera by telling long stories, allowing Zeus to carry on trysts with the nymphs while Hera was thus distracted.

Narcissus called out, "Is anyone here?" "Here! Here!" cried Echo.

Then Narcissus said, "Come over here." "Here! Here!" cried Echo. Narcissus walked in the direction that the voice seemed to come from and said, "Don't avoid me!" Echo answered "Don't avoid me!" Then Narcissus saw Echo run from her hiding place to meet him. When he saw her, she wasn't good enough. So Narcissus called out, "You'll never lie with me!" to which Echo responded, "Lie with me! Lie with me!" To no avail; Narcissus was not interested. Because of this misunderstanding, Echo was yet another rejected lover.

One male suitor of Narcissus was Ameinius, who was repeatedly shunned by him. Narcissus sent Ameinius a sword as a present, to placate him. Because he had been rejected, Ameinius used the gift to kill himself, calling on the gods to avenge his death. The gods were more than happy to oblige this request. They were thoroughly tired of Narcissus's egotism, cruelty to his suitors, and heartless attitude toward others.

This is how the death of Ameinius was avenged and the prophecy of Teiresias fulfilled: Narcissus went to sit by a riverbank and fell in love with his own reflection in the water. When he bent down to kiss his own reflection, he fell into the water and drowned.

Another version is that Narcissus fell in love with his reflection in the river, then he spent hours trying to make the image speak to him. When the man in the river, the first person he had ever fallen in love with, did not answer him, he plunged his own dagger into his heart, serving justice upon the youth who had caused so many suicides of rejected lovers.

From his blood came the white flower called the narcissus, which recalls his great beauty. ♦

TANTALUS

The story of Tantalus is a lesson for gluttons and social climbers. King Tantalus was of both mortal and divine parentage and may even have been, according to some versions, a son of Zeus himself, fathered on one of the god's many mortal lovers. In any case,

Tantalus was, for a time, a favorite of the gods. He was allowed to feast in the halls of Olympus on nectar and ambrosia, which were usually reserved only for the gods. When he was there, he gorged himself.

Tantalus decided that his neighbors would be most impressed if he invited the gods to his own home at Corinth for dinner. In checking his larder, he found that he did not have enough food to go around. Having once invited the gods, he could hardly retract his invitation, so he committed a terrible crime; he killed his own son and made him into stew.

As if that wasn't wicked enough, Tantalus stupidly thought that the gods would think the meat came from a young goat. But of course they knew better. And the punishment suited the crime.

Tantalus lost his kingdom and was killed by Zeus himself. In the Underworld, Tantalus spends all eternity hanging in a tree laden with fruit, but as soon as the fruit is close enough to pick, it moves out of reach. At his feet are the sweetest waters in the universe; they continually rise up to his chin but, as he bends down to take a drink, they subside. Thus, Tantalus is forever hungry and thirsty in the midst of plenty.

One good thing that Tantalus did, however, was give us the English word *tantalizing*. ♦

8. Four Parallel Stories

THE STORY OF TWO BROTHERS
(*Blackfoot Indian*)

There were once two brothers, Nopatsis, the elder, and Akaiyan, the younger. Nopatsis was married to a thoroughly evil woman, who lusted for Akaiyan and wanted to see the younger brother ruined. This shrew of a wife pestered Nopatsis day and night to send his brother away. At the same time, she made seductive advances toward Akaiyan. She then resorted to the most evil and wretched thing she could do.

One day when Nopatsis returned home, he found his wife with her clothing ripped and her hair in a mess. The wife told him that Akaiyan had tried to "have his way" with her. Nopatsis was livid and sickened by this report. He then resolved to do away with his brother.

Every summer, the waterfowl molt, leaving thousands of feathers on the surface of the lakes. The people gather the small feathers to make fletching for their arrows. It so happened that Nopatsis lived on the shores of such a lake, and it was only natural for the two brothers to gather the feathers together. Nopatsis and Akaiyan went out in a buffalo-hide boat to an island in the middle of the lake, far from shore, where the feathers were usually quite dense.

While Akaiyan was busy gathering feathers, Nopatsis left him to die on the island. This lake was deep, prone to sudden storms, and the island was too far from the mainland for a person to leave without a boat. Thus it was pointless for Akaiyan to try swimming home. As Akaiyan looked toward home, he saw Noptasis jeering and uttering curses at him. Nopatsis repeated the terrible lie that his wife had told him, shouting it across the lake. Akaiyan cried out that he was innocent, but it was now too late.

Deeply hurt, Akaiyan looked into the water and began to cry. He prayed to the nature spirits to help him. He called to the Sun and the Moon to vindicate him. Then he built himself a shelter made of branches and a bed made of feathers. He learned how to make clothing for himself from the skins of ducks and geese, taming some of them and feeding them in order to have food for the winter. He lived in this way for many months.

One day a little beaver came and invited Akaiyan to visit his family's den. Akaiyan was by now very lonely, and gladly accepted. When he entered the lodge, the Great Beaver, so old that his fur was white, treated Akaiyan as an honored guest, asking how he came to be living on the island. Akaiyan then told the story of his wicked sister-in-law. The Great Beaver was outraged by the injustice done to Akaiyan and vowed to do whatever he could on behalf of this innocent young man. At the gracious invitation of the beavers, Akaiyan spent the winter in the warmth of their lodge, learning all the medicine and magic of the beavers.

As summer returned, the Great Beaver asked Akaiyan what gift he would like to take with him. Akaiyan responded that he would like to take his host's youngest son as a companion. The Great Beaver was reluctant to grant this, as this son was his favorite. But, at last, the Great Beaver agreed, also giving Akaiyan instructions for building a sacred beaver lodge when he returned to his home village on the mainland. The knowledge of the Great Beaver had such powerful magic that Akaiyan now had supernatural powers on his side; there was nothing more for him to fear, whether on the island or at home on the mainland.

In several months, Nopatsis returned to the island, expecting to find the bones of Akaiyan, who had long been given up for dead. While Nopatsis was busy looking around, Akaiyan carried the little beaver in his arms and then got into Nopatsis's boat, which he took to the mainland. The roles were reversed; it was now Nopatsis who pleaded with his brother across the water.

On his return to the mainland, Akaiyan was well received by the people of the beaver lodge. As the Great Beaver had instructed, Akaiyan built a sacred beaver lodge and taught the people the dances and chants of the beavers.

After this had been accomplished, Akaiyan returned to the island to bring the little beaver back to his family. He also found the bones of Nopatsis and buried them. The Great Beaver was so pleased that Akaiyan had returned his son that he gave him the sacred peace pipe as a sign of his gratitude. ♦

THE STORY OF TWO BROTHERS
(*Egypt*)

NOTE: This story is from *The Ancient Near East*, volume I, edited by James B. Pritchard and translated by John Wilson.

There were two brothers, Anubis, the elder, and Bata, the younger. Anubis had a very wicked wife who was determined to destroy Bata. Bata, however, was a rare young man, handsome, wise, and good. The two brothers farmed together and tended a fine herd of cattle.

One day when they were out working in the fields, Anubis sent Bata back to the house to get some seed to plant. When Bata arrived there by himself, his sister-in-law said how strong and handsome he was, and she took his arm and pulled him toward her body. She told him that Anubis wouldn't miss him if he returned to the fields a few minutes late. She then asked Bata directly to make love to her.

Bata was horrified by this suggestion from his brother's wife. He told her, "You have been like my own mother, and Anubis, like my own father. How could you even think of such a wicked thing?" He then ran away, bringing the seed to Anubis in the fields.

When Anubis came home from the fields, he found his wife in disarray. She made herself look disheveled; she had eaten grease and fat to make herself vomit. She lay on the bed, sobbing. When Anubis asked what the matter was, she told him that Bata had raped her. She told Anubis, "If you let your brother live, I will kill myself."

Anubis was outraged and disgusted. He took his spear, hid behind the door of the stable, and waited for Bata to return.

Bata still had work to do in the fields, and had said nothing to his brother of what had happened at the house. He also knew that his wicked sister-in-law would tell lies, so he was very cautious as he returned home. As he approached the stable, he saw Anubis's feet under the door, waiting for him. Bata fled. The door of the stable burst open and Anubis chased after his brother with the spear, ready to hurl it.

As Bata was running, he prayed to Ra, asking the sun-god to preserve him from his brother, to punish the wicked, and to vindicate him. At that moment, just as Anubis was closing in on Bata, the god caused a river to flow between them. To ensure that Anubis would not be able to ford the river, Ra planted many crocodiles. So Anubis was on one side of this river, unable to cross, while Bata remained safely on the other.

Bata shouted to his brother, "Ra is my protector. Wait until he appears at sunrise. At that time, the gods will show you who is innocent and who is guilty." At sunrise, Bata told the story and this time Anubis listened. Then, to confirm his vow and make a sacrifice to Ra, Bata cut off his penis and threw it into the river, where it was swallowed by a fish sacred to Ra.

Bata bled to death. Anubis returned to his house, deeply grieved. He killed his wicked wife and fed her to the dogs. ♦

BELLEROPHON
(*Greece*)

Bellerophon was accused of killing both the wicked Bellerus (hence the name Bellerophon, which means "murderer of Bellerus"), as well as Bellerophon's own evil brother, Deliades. Bellerophon then fled to the palace of King Proeteus of Tiryns, seeking asylum. As Bellerophon was of royal blood, King Proeteus gladly granted asylum. Proeteus's wife, Anteia, was a wicked woman who fell in love with the young visitor and tried to seduce him many times. But Bellerophon chastely refused her advances. Anteia, however, told Proeteus that Bellerophon had tried to rape her. Proeteus now wanted to kill him.

But it would have violated protocol for the king to kill a guest of royal birth. So Proeteus sent Bellerophon to King Iobates in Lycia, accompanied by a sealed letter explaining that Bellerophon had tried to violate Anteia, Iobates's daughter. The letter asked for Iobates's assistance in killing Bellerophon.

However, Iobates also thought it bad protocol to kill a visitor of royal blood. So he decided to give Bellerophon a dangerous, possibly fatal, task. Iobates asked Bellerophon to kill the horrible monster the Chimera. This was a fire-breathing monster that had the head of a lion, the body of a goat, and a serpent's tail. But before taking up the task, Bellerophon spoke to a seer who told him that the job would be simple with the help of Pegasus, the flying horse.

So Bellerophon found and tamed Pegasus, and killed the Chimera with ease.

Iobates, still wishing to see Bellerophon dead, did not reward the young hero for this, but rather sent him to defeat two fierce armies, one of which was that of the Amazons, a race of women warriors. By flying over them, mounted on Pegasus, Bellerophon defeated both armies with ease.

Iobates continued to plot the demise of Bellerophon, and did not reward the young hero for his great deeds, and Bellerophon did not understand how the king could be so ungrateful. Offended, Bellerophon rode Pegasus to visit the sea god, Poseidon. Poseidon decided to punish Iobates by causing a great tidal wave to strike the kingdom of Lycia. When the waves were in sight, the people of Lycia begged Bellerophon to call them off. The promiscuous Lycian women stood along the shoreline and lifted up their skirts, offering themselves to Bellerophon in the hope that he would call off the tidal wave. But Bellerophon's high morals kept him from taking advantage of their offer. Flying high over Lycia on the back of Pegasus, Bellerophon asked Poseidon to call off the tidal wave.

After this brush with destruction, Iobates was certain that Bellerophon was innocent of the alleged seduction; the gods would not have defended the young man were he guilty. Iobates asked Bellerophon to see him, producing the letter and demanding a true account of what happened from his daughter. When it was apparent that Anteia had lied, Iobates offered Bellerophon an apology and the hand of another daughter, Philonoe, in marriage. With that, Bellerophon became the heir to the throne of Lycia.

However, it was pride, not sex, that proved Bellerophon's undoing. He tried to fly Pegasus to Mount Olympus, the home of the gods. As Bellerophon neared the palace of the gods, Zeus became angry. The king of the gods sent a fly to bite Pegasus. The flying horse threw Bellerophon, who plunged to the ground. Now Zeus is the owner of Pegasus.

Bellerophon, however, did not die of the fall. He landed in a mass of thorn bushes, thoroughly humiliated. He spent the rest of his days walking the earth as a beggar. ♦

JOSEPH AND POTIPHAR'S WIFE
(*Genesis 39*)

Now Joseph had been taken down to Egypt. Potiphar the Egyptian, one of Pharaoh's officials and commander of the guard, bought him from the Ishmaelites who had brought him down there. Yahweh was with Joseph, and everything went well with him. He lodged in the house of his Egyptian master, and when his master saw how Yahweh was with him and how Yahweh made everything succeed that he [Joseph] turned his hand to, he was pleased with Joseph and made him his personal attendant; and his master put him in charge of his household, entrusting everything to him. And from the time he put him in charge of his household and all his possessions, Yahweh blessed the Egyptian's household out of consideration for Joseph; Yahweh's blessing extended to all his possessions, both household and estate. So he left Joseph to handle all his possessions, and with him at hand, concerned himself with nothing beyond the food he ate.

Now Joseph was well-built and handsome, and it happened some time later that his master's wife looked desirously at him and said, "Sleep with me." But he refused and answered his master's wife, "Because of me, my master does not concern himself with what happens in the house; he has handed over all his possessions to me. He is no more master in this house than I am. He has withheld nothing from me except yourself, because you are his wife. How could I do anything so wicked, and sin against God?" Although she spoke to Joseph day after day he would not agree to sleep with her and surrender to her.

But one day Joseph in the course of his duties came to the house, and there was not a servant there indoors. The woman caught hold of him by his tunic and said, "Sleep with me." But he left the tunic in her hand and ran out of the house. Seeing he had left the tunic in her hand and left the house, she called her servants and said to them, "Look at this! He has brought us a Hebrew to insult us. He came to me to sleep with me, but I screamed, and when he heard me scream and shout he left his tunic beside me and ran out of the house."

She put the tunic down by her side until the master came home. Then she told him the same tale. "The Hebrew slave you brought us came to insult me. But when I screamed and called out he left his garment at my side and made his escape." When the master heard his wife say, "This is how your slave treated me," he was furious. Joseph's master had him arrested and committed to the jail where the king's prisoners were kept.

And there in jail he stayed. But Yahweh was with Joseph. He

was kind to him and made him popular with all the prisoners in the jail, making him responsible for everything done there. The chief jailer did not need to interfere with Joseph's administration, for Yahweh was with him, and Yahweh made everything he undertook successful. ♦

*   *   *

We have presented four parallel myths here, one from the Blackfoot Indians of the North American plains, one from Egypt, another from Greece, and the Bible story of Joseph and Potiphar's wife. All four have the same basic plot.

It is easy to argue that the Egyptian, Greek, and Hebrew stories may be examples of interborrowing; all three nations were on the shores of the Mediterranean and connected through trade. However, it is difficult to explain the parallel between these myths and the Blackfoot story.

9. Some Brief Myths of the Hero

THE STORY OF SIEGFRIED
(*Norse/Germany*)

The story of Siegfried is ancient and corresponds with hero myths in many other cultures, such as the myths of Herakles (Hercules), Perseus, and Theseus in Greece; Quetzalcoatl in Mexico; and others in virtually every culture. Siegfried is one of the best known mythical heroes, especially famous for his place in the "Ring" cycle of operas by Richard Wagner.

This myth, like all myths concerning heroes, presents an allegory of the trials all humans face. Siegfried's story is all the more poignant in that he defies the gods and heroically faces his own inevitable death. It is a good example of the hero myth because it contains all the key elements of that kind of tale.

The version of the Siegfried myth given here is based on several sources including the Norse *Volsungasaga*, in which Siegfried is called "Sigurd," as well as the German epic, the *Niebelungenlied*. The treatment of the story is derived from such German writers as Karl Goedeke (1814–1887) and August Tecklenburg (1863–1930), as well as the poet Johann Ludwig Uhland (1787–1862). This narrative resembles the story of the Wagnerian opera (whose libretto Wagner wrote himself) with some minor differences in detail. The Norse

Brynhild is the German Brünnhilde; the Norse Oithinn or Odin is the German Wotan; the Norse Gunnar is the German Gunther; and Krimhild or Kriemhild becomes Griemhild in German, as she is named in the Wagnerian opera. The Norse Gudrun is Gutrune in German.

Siegfried, whose name means "Victory-Peace," was the son of the warrior hero Siegmund ("Victory-Mouth") and his wife, Sieglinde ("Victory Linden Tree"). Siegmund was the great champion of the Niebelungen and their king, Alberich.

Alberich had a Ring in his possession which gave its owner mastery of the world. He had the potential power to defeat even Wotan, the king of the gods. As king of the Niebelungen (dwarves who lived beneath the earth, working as miners and metalworkers), Alberich was master of a vast treasure of underground gold.

A giant, Fafner, guarded the treasure of the Niebelungen, including the Ring, in the form of a fierce dragon. Wotan's interests were served by having the Ring in the hands of a giant and not in the hands of his opponents, the dwarves. Fafner and Wotan both knew that their days were numbered, that a hero would be born with a sacred mission to cause their downfall.

When Siegmund was killed in battle, the dying Sieglinde gave birth to her son, Siegfried, entrusting him to a dwarf named Mime. Mime raised the lad as his own son, knowing the prophecy that Siegfried would be the Walsung ("world") hero who would redeem the Niebelungen treasure and recover the Ring.

As young Siegfried grew to manhood, there were many questions about his true identity. Since his earliest days, Siegmund had called Mime "Father," but the tall young hero was certainly not a Niebelung. Mime had always hidden the truth from Siegfried in the hope that he, Mime, and neither Wotan nor Alberich, would be the possessor of the Ring and the treasure. Finally, Siegfried grew tired of the inconsistencies in Mime's story and threatened the dwarf's life in order to force a true account.

One day Wotan, the one-eyed king of the gods, was wandering on earth and came to the home of Siegfried and Mime. He wore a traveler's cloak to hide his missing eye and conceal his true identity. In his hand he carried a walking stick carved with sacred runes and made from a branch of the ash tree, Yggdrasil, that supported the entire universe. The runes were the laws that governed all who lived in the universe, whether man, dwarf, giant, or god.

Wotan had lost an eye by giving one of them up at Mimir's well of wisdom in exchange for a drink of the sacred waters. With his dearly bought wisdom, Wotan knew of the inevitability of the Twilight of the Gods, when his rule of the universe would be overthrown. Wotan also knew that the mission of the young Siegfried would only hasten the Twilight.

Mime asked Wotan many questions, as the traveler exuded wisdom: "Who lives on the surface of the earth?" Wotan answered, "Human beings." "Who lives beneath the earth?" Wotan responded, "The Niebelungen." "Who lives above, in the heavens?" Wotan replied, "The gods, who rule the universe, Wotan, Donner [Thor, the thunder god], Freja [Freya, the goddess of beauty], and the rest. They are attended by the Walküre [Norse: Valkyries] who carry slain heroes from the battlefield into the feasting hall of the gods at Walhalla ["the hall of the slain"]."

Wotan could speak only the truth, and Mime persisted in his questions: "Who are the greatest and most beloved among human beings?" Wotan replied, "The Walsungs, Siegmund and Sieglinde, and their son, the world hero who is to come. Only a Walsung can slay the dragon Fafner and win the Ring. It is said that Wotan himself broke the sword Nothung that is the only means to slay this dragon. Fate decrees that he who reforges this sword will be the world hero." Siegfried, listening carefully to the traveler's words, now realized his own identity and what mission he was ordained to fulfill. Then the stranger slipped quietly into the deep forest.

As Wotan disappeared, Siegfried ordered Mime to reforge Nothung so that he, Siegfried, might fulfill his mission. Mime protested that even his great skill could not reforge the magic sword. So, pushing Mime aside, Siegfried himself took the shattered fragments of the sword and began to reforge them at Mime's anvil. He accomplished this with little difficulty. With the last stroke of the hammer, the anvil disappeared deep within Erde, the goddess of the earth. Erde was a goddess and the sister of Wotan; she was quick to tell her brother of what she had witnessed.

The next day Siegfried set out into the forest on the first of his tasks—to slay Fafner and reclaim Alberich's treasure and the coveted Ring. He came to a glade where Fafner had coiled his tail around an ancient ash tree. Around the tree was a protective circle of fire. Fafner himself breathed flames and the blood of hapless victims dripped from his teeth. Siegfried fearlessly walked through the flames unharmed and Fafner then recognized who this brave mortal was. With one blow, Siegfried slew Fafner. As the dragon lay dying, he asked Siegfried who had reforged the magic sword, and was told, "It was I, Siegfried the Walsung."

The blood of Fafner had dripped down the sword onto Siegfried's hand, and he touched his lips to the blood. This enabled Siegfried to understand the prophetic language of the birds.

The birds told Siegfried that Alberich's treasure was in a nearby cave. He went into the cave and, having no interest in the treasure, took the Ring as a souvenir of his exploit. Siegfried did not understand the full significance of his possession of this Ring, which made him master of the universe. But the Ring also bore a curse: Alberich had ensured that any holder of the Ring other than himself would be doomed to die through the treachery of another. Now Siegfried had unwittingly sealed his own tragic fate.

As Siegfried was preparing to leave, Mime and Alberich arrived on the scene. Now able to read the motives of Mime's heart, he saw through his foster father completely. Mime's words of flattery were merely a cover for his own evil plans. Siegfried knew that Mime intended to kill him and take the treasure for himself. With a blow of Nothung, Siegfried slew Mime. Alberich laughed cruelly and regained the treasure Siegfried was leaving behind. Remembering the curse that he, Alberich, had placed on the holder of the Ring, he allowed Siegfried to continue wearing it, confident of the hero's impending destruction.

The birds then told Siegfried of another task. A beautiful maiden, not a mortal but a Walküre named Brünnhilde, had been put to sleep by her father, Wotan, for disobedience. She slept on a great rock, encircled by flames. Only a Walsung hero born without fear could rescue her, waking her with a kiss. Siegfried seized the opportunity for adventure.

What was Brünnhilde's crime? Before the birth of Siegfried, his parents, Siegmund and Sieglinde, fought bravely as the champions of the Niebelungen against Wotan. After Siegmund was slain in battle, the then-pregnant Sieglinde begged Brünnhilde for help. The Walküre had whisked her out of danger. Although Brünnhilde had acted out of compassion, she had given comfort to her father's enemies. Thus was Brünnhilde placed into a deep sleep. Wotan had ordered Loge, the trickster and god of fire, to make a circle of flames to detain mortals from rescuing her.

As we have said, the young hero did not grasp the full meaning of his possession of the Ring, nor the significance of rescuing Brünnhilde in defiance of Wotan. As he approached the rock, Wotan—still in the disguise of a traveler—dissuaded him from rescuing Brünnhilde. This time Wotan did not carry a walking stick but a spear. Siegfried now knew that this stranger was none but Wotan. This spear was the very one that had shattered Nothung in the hands of his father, Siegmund. Wotan, however, knew that Siegfried had possession of the Ring and therefore he did not engage the hero in combat. Words were now the only weapons in the arsenal of Wotan, and Siegfried continued on toward the rock.

Siegfried arrived at the great rock and passed through the wall of flames. He saw what appeared to be a sleeping warrior in battle armor. But as he drew closer, he saw that it was the beautiful Brünnhilde. He kissed her and she awoke. However, in removing her helmet, Siegfried had transformed her from a Walküre into a mere mortal woman. Siegfried placed the Ring on her finger as a token of his love, and vowed to return for her.

Siegfried then rode to the land of the Giuchungen [Norse: Giukungur], who were ruled by the cowardly and treacherous King Gunther with the aid of his wicked mother, Griemhild, a sorceress.

Siegfried's brave deeds were now well known throughout the world, and Griemhild knew who the young hero was. The sorceress wanted Siegfried to be the husband of her own daughter, Gutrune, and Brünnhilde would then be the bride of Gunther.

When Siegfried arrived, Gunther gave a great feast and swore an eternal oath of blood loyalty with Siegfried. Griemhild slipped a magic potion into Siegfried's drink that made him forget about Brünnhilde. Then the young hero married Gutrune, per Griemhild's plan. To complete her scheme, Griemhild enchanted Siegfried into assuming the appearance of Gunther, and sent him back for Brünnhilde. She thought that a new hero, and not Siegfried, had come to rescue her. Siegfried, as Gunther, spent three nights with the Walküre, his sword chastely separating them.

Siegfried brought Brünnhilde back to the palace of the Giuchungen, and he assumed his own appearance once again. Brünnhilde now believed that the cowardly Gunther had rescued her, not brave Siegfried, and she was bitter that Siegfried had "forgotten" his vow to her and married another.

In the course of a quarrel with Gutrune, however, Brünnhilde learned the truth: Gutrune let out that Siegfried had actually rescued her, but it was too late, as the hero was Gutrune's husband now and Brünnhilde could never have him.

To create discord, Brünnhilde went to Gunther and told him that Siegfried had, in fact, made love to her during their three nights together. Brünnhilde demanded that Gunther kill Siegfried and defend her honor. Gunther replied that he could not do this, as he had sworn the eternal blood oath with the hero. However, he dispatched his brother, Hagen, to kill Siegfried. During the night, as Siegfried slept with Gutrune, Hagen stabbed the hero to death.

Now Brünnhilde had made certain that her Siegfried would never live with another woman. She had fulfilled the curse of Alberich. Brünnhilde threw herself on Siegfried's funeral pyre to join him in eternity, and the flames engulfed the whole of Walhalla. ◆

THESEUS
(*Greece*)

The myth of Theseus is an example of the power of the myth as an allegory of human life. Theseus must pass many tests and endure many trials before he faces his most significant challenge: defeating the bull-man Minotaur in the middle of the Labyrinth, a vast maze. Our own lives at times seem like mazes going nowhere. However, by knowing where he has been Theseus finds an escape from the maze. For us, myth is one way for modern man to know where he has been, and to work through the "maze" of our perplexing existence.

There is an intriguing historical perspective to this myth. During the 1890s, Sir Arthur John Evans excavated the royal palace at Knossos, Crete. There was, in 2000 B.C., an enormous difference in the level of development on Crete in comparison to that in mainland Greece. Interestingly, Evans found flush toilets and advanced plumbing in the palace, advancements that would not come into common use in Western Europe until the end of the nineteenth century. More important to our investigations, the labyrinthine hallways of the palace, the many depictions of bullfights, and evidence of commerce with the mainland of Greece all add veracity to the story of Theseus, an early king of Athens.

To a simple visitor from Bronze Age Greece, the vast corridors of the palace must have seemed like a maze; the sight of men riding bulls would have easily given rise to the Minotaur—a half-man, half-bull monster.

One of the best sources for the story of Theseus is the account presented by the ancient biographer Plutarch in his *Lives of the Noble Greeks and Romans*. Another excellent treatment of the story, by a modern author, is André Gide's *Theseus*.

THE YOUTH OF THESEUS

King Aegeus of Athens had two wives, Melite and Chalciope, neither of whom gave him an heir. Aegeus traveled to Corinth, where he consulted with the sorceress Medea. She agreed to provide him with the magic necessary to sire a son in exchange for his promise that he would offer her protection and asylum in Athens, to which he readily agreed.

At the town of Troezen, en route back to Athens, Aegeus had an affair with Aethra, a woman of the blood of the royal house of Athens. He warned her that if this liaison were to produce a son, she must keep the child in Troezen and secretly raise him there. Aegeus then placed his sandals and sword under a rock sacred to Zeus: His future heir would prove himself by finding this "deposit" [the Greek word is *thesaurus*, basis for the English words *thesaurus* and *treasure*]. The true son of Aegeus would be able to lift the rock and bring the tokens to Athens as a demonstration of his claim to the throne.

Unknown to Aegeus, Aethra gave birth to a boy, naming him Theseus ["deposited"], recalling the tokens of kingship that her lover had deposited under the sacred rock. The child grew strong and wise, showing that he had the favor of the gods. With great ease he lifted the rock and removed the tokens of kingship. He then set out for Athens to make his claim to the throne. But the roads between Troezen and Athens were plagued by bandits, and thus Theseus had his first heroic task to perform.

The first bandit he met was Epidaurus the Lame, reknowned for killing hapless travelers with a brass club and taking their money. When Epidaurus tried to attack Theseus, he had met his match at last. Theseus seized the brass club and slew Epidaurus.

The second bandit was the wretched Sinis Pityocamtes ["Sinis the Pine-bender"]. This psychopath used to bend the tops of pine trees low with his great strength, then ask travelers to give him a hand in his work. When the traveler had a good grip on the tip of the pine tree, Sinis would let go. The traveler would then be flung through the air only to fall to his death. Theseus killed Sinis in the same manner that Sinis slew his victims.

Then there was Sciron ["parasol"], who forced his victims to wash his feet, then when they were bent down, he kicked them into a steep gorge into the sea, where they were eaten by turtles. Theseus meted Sciron the same fate.

Theseus was considered by the Athenians to be the father of Greek wrestling, after demonstrating his mastery of Cercydon, an evil bandit who challenged every traveler to a wrestling match that always concluded with Cercydon dashing his opponent's head against a rock. Cercydon met the same fate as his victims at the hand of Theseus. Just as Theseus neared the outskirts of Athens, he also killed a fierce wild boar that had claimed many human lives.

News of Theseus's exploits preceded him to Athens, where the people were thrilled to be rid of the bandits and the boar. ✦

THESEUS IN ATHENS

Many years had passed since King Aegeus had been in Troezen where Theseus was conceived. The king did not know that he had such a son. Meanwhile, Medea had been driven out of Corinth and fled to Athens, where Aegeus had assured her asylum. Aegeus took Medea as his third wife and they had a son, Medus, whom Aegeus erroneously considered the son and heir Medea had promised.

News of Theseus had spread to the palace. Aegeus had no idea that this hero might be his son, and he was afraid that Theseus would prove a rival to his rule. Medea knew exactly who Theseus was, and feared that the hero would take the throne away from her son. Aegeus and Medea knew that they had to welcome Theseus to Athens, but they also wanted to kill him. So Medea prepared some poison from the wolfbane plant and placed it in a cup of wine.

During the feasting, Theseus took his sword from the scabbard and used it to cut some meat; it was the sword that Aegeus had deposited under the rock many years before. Aegeus recognized the sword and knew that Theseus was his son and true heir. He immediately knocked the poisoned wine onto the floor and rejoiced, proclaiming Theseus as his heir. Moreover, as Aethra, Theseus's mother, was of the royal blood of Athens, there was no way that Theseus's claim to the throne could be contested. Medea was angry with this and was driven into exile for her treachery. ♦

THESEUS AND THE MINOTAUR

Crete is an island off the coast of Greece that was ruled by King Minos. Minos had sent his only son on a diplomatic delegation to Athens. The Cretans were known throughout the world for their skill with bulls, and King Aegeus asked the Cretan prince, Androgeus, for help in killing a particularly fierce bull that plagued the countryside near Athens. In the process, Androgeus was killed.

Minos demanded revenge. He invaded Athens and vowed to destroy the city unless the Athenians offered a tribute. The only tribute that could compensate for the loss of the Cretan heir to the throne was for the Athenians to send their seven finest young men and as many young women to Crete once every nine years. The young Athenians never returned; in Crete they were murdered by a horrible monster, the Minotaur.

The story of the Minotaur is yet another example of human stupidity toward the gods. King Minos had been given a beautiful white bull by the sea god, Poseidon, who expected it to be returned to him as a sacrifice. Instead, Minos prized the bull and refused to let go of it. Poseidon was angry and caused Pasiphae, Minos's wife, to fall in love with the bull. She later gave birth to the horrible Minotaur, who was half human, half bull, and the fiercest creature alive. Minos did not kill the Minotaur. Rather, the king asked Daedalus, the world's greatest builder, to construct a Labyrinth, a maze of corridors, in which the monster could be safely kept, and Minos would give the Minotaur human beings to eat. The young Athenians were placed in this hopeless maze and murdered by the fierce man-beast.

Theseus arrived in Athens during the ninth year of this human sacrifice. He stepped forward and offered to be one of the seven young people chosen to go to Crete. His father despaired of sending the heir to the throne on such a mission, but Theseus assured Aegeus that he would kill the Minotaur and end the slaughter of Athenian youth. So Theseus boarded the ship and left for Crete. It was understood by the Athenians that they should watch the sail: If the ship returned with a black sail, then the young Athenians had all perished. However, if the ship returned with a white sail, the young Athenians had been spared and were aboard this ship home.

Upon arriving in Crete, the Athenians were paraded through the streets. Ariadne, daughter of King Minos, fell instantly in love with Theseus and went to Daedalus for assistance in saving the handsome Athenian. She then gave Theseus a ball of string to unwind behind him: By knowing where he had been, Theseus could retrace his steps and escape the Labyrinth. Fortunately for the other thirteen young Athenians, Theseus was the first of their party to encounter the Minotaur, whom the hero easily killed with his bare hands.

Thus the fourteen young Athenians escaped unharmed. Ariadne had received a promise from Theseus that he would take her to Greece with him, where they would marry. On the way, however, she became violently ill and Theseus dropped her off on the island of Naxos.* Another version of the story is that she became tiresome and nagging during the voyage and was simply left there. In any case, the ship returned to Athens with all fourteen Athenians on board.

In their haste to return, however, someone forgot to replace the black sail that had graced the ship on its outward journey with the white one that indicated that the young Athenians were safe. For months, King Aegeus had watched the seas for a sign of this ship. When he saw the black sail as the ship returned, he thought that his son and heir had perished in Crete. In despair, he threw himself to his death in the sea, which is now called the Aegean Sea. Thus, upon the ship's return to Athens, Theseus found himself king.

The hero was acclaimed as the founder of Athenian democracy. In-

*The basis of Richard Strauss's opera *Ariadne Auf Naxos*.

stead of ruling the people himself, he allowed them to rule themselves. He was a wise and beloved king, the patron of culture. During his reign, skilled artisans and thinkers from throughout Greece moved to Athens to work under his patronage. Things in Athens were happy and prosperous; the Cretans no longer demanded tribute. With affairs in order in his realm, Theseus set out for more adventures.

He went on an expedition against the fierce female warriors, the Amazons,* and sailed with Jason in search of the Golden Fleece. Theseus's loyalty to his friends was well known. When Herakles [Hercules] went mad and killed his wife and children, Theseus alone defended him—possibly the world's first insanity defense. Theseus even gave asylum to the aged Oedipus.

His aid to Oedipus, however, brings to mind a sad irony in Theseus's own life. Theseus was married to Phaedra, Ariadne's sister; he also had a handsome son named Hippolytus by an earlier marriage. Phaedra fell hopelessly in love with Hippolytus and repeatedly tried to seduce him. This came about because Hippolytus's looks had attracted the affections of the goddess Aphrodite, but he was a devotee of the perpetually virgin hunt goddess Artemis and so he was not interested in sex. Hippolytus's appreciation of Artemis's patronage angered the jealous Aphrodite, who now vowed to destroy him. It is said that Aphrodite caused Phaedra to fall in love with Hippolytus.

As Phaedra continued to demand the affections of Hippolytus, the boy rebuffed her—it was not right to sleep with one's stepmother. In despair, Phaedra hanged herself, leaving a suicide note claiming that Hippolytus had caused her death. When Theseus found the note, he was grieved and disgusted. He prepared to send Hippolytus into exile. When the boy protested that he had done nothing to harm his stepmother, Theseus refused to believe him. In his anger, Theseus rashly called on Poseidon, god of the sea, to destroy Hippolytus. As the boy set out on his journey, a sea creature came out of the water

---

*In Greek, this means "without breasts." The Greeks believed that the Amazons removed one breast in order to enable them to draw their bows in battle. The Amazon River of South America is so named because early explorers saw women warriors on its banks.

in front of his chariot. The horses were frightened and Hippolytus was fatally thrown from the vehicle.

The dying boy was brought before his father. The goddess Artemis herself appeared to Theseus to tell him that Hippolytus was innocent of any wrongdoing with regard to Phaedra. Artemis explained that Aphrodite had been behind the plot, and that Phaedra had been bewitched; that the jealous goddess had planned to destroy Hippolytus for spurning her as well as all other women in his devotion to chastity. Distraught, Theseus begged the gods for mercy.

The gods were merciful to a point. But Theseus, as justice would have it, later died by the treachery of a friend, because he had believed the lies of Phaedra and cursed his own innocent son. ◆

HIAWATHA TARENYAWAGON
(*Iroquois*)

The actual Iroquois legend of Hiawatha bears no relation to the stories contained in Longfellow's *Song of Hiawatha*. Longfellow's work portrayed Hiawatha as a hero of the Algonquins, and not the Iroquois. Longfellow's work was set in the Lake Superior region, while the actual Iroquois homeland of Hiawatha was in central and western New York State. The myths retold by Longfellow were actually stories of the Algonquin deity Michabo.

The myth of Hiawatha is a wonderful example of the "civic myth," documenting the founding of a nation. In this case, the nation is the Five Nation Confederacy of the Iroquois, whose system of government was studied by the American founding fathers in their formulation of the U.S. Constitution.

Tarenyawagon, the upholder of the heavens, was awakened from his slumber by the horrible cries of anguish from earth. The humans were murdering each other, fighting against terrible giants, and falling into anarchy and deep despair. Taking the form of a mortal man, Tarenyawagon came to earth, taking a little girl by the hand, leading a miserable band of the human refugees to a cave where he told them to sleep, as hope had returned to humanity.

When the people had rested, Tarenyawagon again took a little girl by the hand and led the people toward the rising sun, where they built a great lodge house. There they lived happily. The former refugees prospered and had many children. Tarenyawagon called the people together and then told them to form five great nations and scatter. A few families were separated from the group; they were called Tehawroga, "those of different speech." From the moment that Tarenyawagon named them this, they began to speak a language different from the other people. To these "people of different speech," the Mohawk nation, Tarenyawagon gave tobacco, squash, corn, and beans, and also dogs to help them hunt. He taught them to be great farmers and hunters. Then he left, again taking a little girl by the hand.

Again, he separated some of the families and took them to a beautiful valley. He named them the Nehawretago, the "tall tree people," in honor of the fine forests in their new homeland. They also had their own separate language and became the Oneida nation.

Then, again taking a little girl by the hand, he led some families to a great mountain called Onondaga, which was the name of this new nation. They too began to speak their own language.

He separated more families, and taking another little girl by the hand, he took them to the lake called Goyoga, and the people became known as the Cayuga people.

There were now only a few families left, so Tarenyawagon took a little girl by the hand and led the families to another mountain called Canandaigua. This was to be the home of the people he named Tehonenoyent, the Seneca nation. Their name means "keepers of the door," as they are the sentinels of the five nations.

Now why did Tarenyawagon take a little girl by the hand as he founded these nations? The Iroquois people of the Five Nations are a matriarchal society, where the most respected leaders are the old women. These girls grew up to be the leaders of their nations. It is through the mother that one inherits among the people of the Five Nations.

Some of the people left the land of the Five Nations and went far to the west to the river called the Mississippi,* from where they never returned. Separated by the great river, none of the Five Nations ever saw them again. But the Five Nations who remained in their homeland prospered.

Tarenyawagon gave each of the Five Nations its own particular gift. To the Onondaga was given the knowledge of the universal laws and the ability to understand the great Creator. To the Oneidas was given skill in making baskets and weapons. To the Mohawks was given great ability in hunting. Then Tarenyawagon went to live among the Onondaga people, where he took the name Hiawatha.

In the laws of the universe it is written that for every joy there must be a sorrow, for every darkness a light, and for every death a life. Even as the Five Nations lived in peace, the Wild People [the Algonquin tribes] came and attacked them from the northwest, out of the Great Lakes region. These people were not as civilized as the Five Nations and were a threat to all the people of Tarenyawagon.

So the Five Nations met together for a common defense. The people waited for three days for Hiawatha to come to lead them. On the fourth day he appeared in his magic birch canoe, accompanied by his daughter Mnihaha [the "Minihaha" of Longfellow], who was his child by an Onondaga wife. Hiawatha met with all the leaders of the Five Nations, greeted them as his brothers, and spoke each of their languages.

Out of heaven came a great noise like rushing water and thunder. Out of the clouds appeared the Great Mystery Bird of Heaven who then carried away Hiawatha's daughter. He laid his hand on her head in blessing before he commended her to the Great Mystery Bird. Hiawatha was so saddened by her departure that he sat in silent mourning and meditation, wrapped in a panther skin, for three days. Hiawatha never explained this mystery to the people, but many old people say that the girl was given to God in exchange for peace.

After the mourning period had ended, Hiawatha purified himself in a clear lake and called the leaders of the Five Nations together. He told them that the Five Nations were to be as one nation forever.

Mississippi is an Algonquin, probably Chippewa, word meaning "great water."

Never again would they act separately. The downfall of one nation would be the downfall of all, as the victory of one nation would be the victory of all. He told the people to choose the wisest of their women to rule them.

The Onondagas were to be the warriors of the Iroquois. The Seneca were to speak on behalf of the Five Nations. The clever Cayuga were to be the guardians of the rivers, while the Mohawk would farm and hunt for all the tribes.

Then Hiawatha slipped into his magic birch canoe and rode into the sky. ♦

THE MYTH OF SISYPHUS
(*Greece*)

A Modern Hero?

The French existentialist writer Albert Camus (1913–1960) saw the myth of Sisyphus as a model for the futile striving of human existence. Camus, an atheist, was on an anguished philosophical search for meaning. Without God and a myth-based culture, Camus saw nothing to give human life meaning—until he saw in this myth that futile striving itself can give life meaning, defying the certainty of death and even the futility of the striving itself.

Sisyphus was a wealthy Corinthian who defied the gods and even death.

Once Zeus spied the beautiful Aegina, daughter of the river god Asopus, and carried her off through the streets of Corinth. When her father asked the Corinthian townspeople about the incident, not one would speak to him, out of fear of the wrath of Zeus. However, the clever Sisyphus saw this as his golden opportunity and seized it.

One of the chief problems of Corinth at that time was that there was no water source within the city walls. The Corinthians tired of having to haul water long distances into their town. Sisyphus approached the river god and offered information on Aegina in exchange for water. If Asopus would cause a spring to bubble up within the city walls of Corinth, then Sisyphus would gladly tell all he knew of the abduction. Asopus agreed, Sisyphus talked, and a spring of sweet, fresh water bubbled out of the ground.

When Asopus was thus able to confront Zeus and demand the return of his daughter, the king of the gods was furious—he knew which Corinthian had talked. Zeus spoke to his brother, Hades, the lord of the dead, and the latter dispatched Death to collect Sisyphus.

When Death arrived in the world of the living, she became light-hearted upon being in the world above ground. Usually accustomed to being met with dread, she was dismayed when Sisyphus jovially invited her to sit down with him for food and drink. The two talked and joked. Then Sisyphus offered to show her a pair of handcuffs of his own making. Being in a playful mood, Death put them on. When time passed and the joke had worn off, it was apparent that Death had become the prisoner of Sisyphus.

With that the entire character of the universe changed. Hades received no new subjects. Nothing, neither plant nor animal nor human, died. With Death thus captive, the gods began to complain; without Death the world would be overpopulated. Death was one of the few certain controls that the gods had over mortal humans. Most outraged of all was the usually unpopular Ares, god of war, who complained bitterly that without Death there was simply no point to war: Soldiers slain on the battlefield leaped up to fight again.

Meanwhile, on earth, the humans rejoiced. They had quickly noticed that no one died. Feeling that they would all live forever, they went on a spree. There was one very miserable side effect, however: The very ill just remained very ill, without Death to relieve their miseries. Watching this, Zeus grew angrier still and dispatched Ares to free Death and seize Sisyphus. Ares did so, taking the soul of Sisyphus down to Hades.

But Sisyphus had not yet run out of tricks. He had instructed his wife not to bury his corpse when the gods had plucked out his soul. On his arrival in the realm of the dead, Sisyphus complained that he could not possibly be allowed to remain there, as his corpse was not properly buried, nor were the correct rites performed. Hearing this,

Hades granted Sisyphus three days in which to set things in order. But after the three days had passed, it was clear that Sisyphus had no intention of returning to the land of the dead. The gods had been tricked again.

This time, Zeus wanted to see everything done properly, so he sent Hermes, the messenger of the gods, who was the usual guide of the dead to the Underworld. Hermes seized Sisyphus's soul, buried his body with all the necessary rituals, and took the soul down to the Underworld.

Having bound Death and mocked the gods, Sisyphus was sentenced to spend eternity rolling a great rock up a steep hill, only to have it roll back down for him to perpetually repeat the futile ascent. ♦

The following is taken from *The Myth of Sisyphus* by Albert Camus, translated by Justin O'Brien. It was written in 1943, during a desperate time, when Camus's native France was under Nazi occupation and things looked futile and dark.

> The gods had condemned Sisyphus to ceaselessly rolling a rock to the top of a mountain, whence the stone would fall back of its own weight. They had thought with some reason that there is no more dreadful punishment than futile and hopeless labor. . . .
>
> . . . If one believes [the Greek poet] Homer, Sisyphus was the wisest and most prudent of mortals. According to another tradition, however, he was disposed to practice the profession of highwayman. I see no contradiction in this. Opinions differ as to the reasons why he became the futile laborer of the underworld. To begin with, he is accused of a certain levity in regard to the gods. He stole their secrets. Aegina, the daughter of Aesopus [Asopus], was carried off by Jupiter [Zeus]. The father was shocked by that disappearance and complained to Sisyphus. He, who knew of the abduction, offered to tell about it on condition that Aesopus would give water to the citadel of Corinth. To the celestial thunderbolts* he preferred the benediction of water. He

---

*You will recall that Zeus was the wielder of thunderbolts.

was punished for this in the underworld. Homer tells us also that Sisyphus put Death in chains. Pluto [Hades] could not endure the sight of his deserted, silent empire. He dispatched the god of war, who liberated Death from the hands of her conqueror.

It is said that Sisyphus, being near to Death, rashly wanted to test his wife's love. He ordered her to cast his unburied body into the middle of the public square. Sisyphus woke up in the underworld. And there, annoyed by an obedience so contrary to human love, he obtained from Pluto permission to return to earth in order to chastise his wife. But when he had seen again the face of this world, enjoyed water and sun, warm stones and the sea, he no longer wanted to go back to the infernal darkness. Recalls, signs of anger, warnings were of no avail. Many more years he lived facing the curve of the gulf, the sparkling sea, and the smiles of earth. A decree of the gods was necessary. Mercury [Hermes] came and seized the impudent man by the collar, and snatching him from his joys, led him forcibly back to the underworld, where his rock was ready for him.

You have already grasped that Sisyphus is the absurd hero. He is, as much through his passions as through his torture. His scorn of the gods, his hatred of death, and his passion for life won him that unspeakable penalty in which the whole being is exerted toward accomplishing nothing. This is the price that must be paid for the passions of this earth. Nothing is told about Sisyphus in the underworld. Myths are made for the imagination to breathe life into them. As for this myth, one sees merely the whole effort of a body straining to raise the huge stone, to roll it and push it up a slope a hundred times over; one sees the face screwed up, the cheek tight against the stone, the shoulder bracing the clay-covered mass, the foot wedging it, the fresh start with arms outstretched, the wholly human security of two earth-clotted hands. At the very end of his long effort measured by skyless space and time without depth, the purpose is achieved. Then Sisyphus watches the stone rush down in a few moments toward that lower world whence he will have to push it up again toward the summit. He goes back down to the plain.

It is during that return, that pause, that Sisyphus interests me. A face that toils so close to stones is already stone itself! I see that man going back down with a heavy, yet measured, step toward the torment of which he will never know the end. That hour, like a breathing space which returns as surely as his suffering, that is the hour of consciousness. At each of those moments when he leaves the heights and gradually sinks toward the lairs of the gods, he is superior to his fate. He is stronger than his rock.

If this myth is tragic, that is because the hero is conscious. Where would his torture be, indeed, if at every step the hope of succeeding upheld him? The workman of today works every day in his life at the same tasks, and this fate is no less absurd. But it is tragic only at the rare moments when it becomes conscious. Sisyphus, proletarian of the gods, powerless and rebellious, knows the whole extent of his wretched condition; it is what he thinks of during the descent. The lucidity that was to constitute his torture at the same time crowns his victory. There is no fate that cannot be surmounted by scorn.

If the descent is thus sometimes performed in sorrow, it can also take place in joy. This word is not too much. Again I fancy Sisyphus returning toward his rock, and the sorrow was in the beginning. When the images of earth cling too tightly to memory, when the call of happiness becomes too insistent, it happens that melancholy rises in man's heart; this is the rock's victory, this is the rock itself. The boundless grief is too heavy to bear. These are our nights of Gethsemane.* But crushing truths perish from being acknowledged. Thus, Oedipus at the outset obeys fate without knowing it. But from the moment he knows, his tragedy begins. Yet at the same moment, blind and desperate, he realizes that the only bond linking him to the world is the cool hand of a girl [Antigone, Oedipus's daughter and sister]. Then a tremendous remark rings out: "Despite many ordeals, my advanced age and the nobility of my soul make me conclude that all is well."

. . . thus gives the recipe for the absurd victory. Ancient wisdom confirms modern heroism.

One does not discover the absurd without being tempted to write a manual of happiness. "What! by such narrow ways—" There is but one world, however. Happiness and the absurd are

*Gethsemane: A garden where Jesus Christ underwent a prayerful ordeal prior to his trial and crucifixion.

two sons of the same earth. They are inseparable. It would be a mistake to say that happiness necessarily springs from the absurd discovery. It happens as well that the feeling of the absurd springs from happiness. "I conclude that all is well," says Oedipus, and that remark is sacred. It echoes in the wild and limited universe of man. It teaches that all is not, has not been, exhausted. It drives out of this world a god who had come into it with dissatisfaction and a preference for futile sufferings. It makes of fate a human matter, which must be settled among men.

All Sisyphus' silent joy is contained therein. His fate belongs to him. His rock is his thing. Likewise the absurd man when he contemplates his torment, silences all the idols. In the universe suddenly restored to its silence, the myriad wondering little voices of the earth rise up. Unconscious, secret calls, invitations from all the faces, they are the necessary reverse and price of victory. There is no sun without shadow, and it is essential to know the night. The absurd man says yes and his effort will henceforth be unceasing. If there is a personal fate, there is no higher destiny, or at least there is but one which he concludes is inevitable and despicable. For the rest, he knows himself to be the master of his days. At that subtle moment when man glances backward over his life, Sisyphus returning toward his rock, in that slight pivoting he contemplates that series of unrelated actions which becomes his fate, created by him, combined under his memory's eye and soon sealed by his death. Thus convinced of the wholly human origin of all that is human, a blind man eager to see who knows that the night has no end, he is still on the go. The rock is still rolling.

I leave Sisyphus at the foot of the mountain! One always finds one's burden again. But Sisyphus teaches the higher fidelity that negates the gods and raises rocks. He too concludes that all is well. This universe henceforth without a master seems to him neither sterile nor futile. Each atom of that stone, each mineral flake of that night-filled mountain, in itself forms a world. The struggle itself toward the heights is enough to fill a man's heart. One must imagine Sisyphus happy.

10. The Journey to the Underworld and the Path of Death

The only religious way to think of death is as part
and parcel of life; to regard it, with the
understanding and the emotions, as the inviolable
condition of life.
> —Thomas Mann, *The Magic Mountain*

Now what is history? It is the centuries of
systematic explorations of the riddle of death, with
a view toward overcoming death. That's why people
discover mathematical infinity and electromagnetic
waves, that's why they write symphonies.
> —Boris Pasternak (1890–1960), *Doctor Zhivago*

ISHTAR IN THE UNDERWORLD
(*Babylonia*)

NOTE: In the most common version of this story, Ishtar, the goddess of love, beauty, and fertility, visits the Underworld in search of her lover, Tammuz. This is also an agricultural myth; while Ishtar is in the Underworld, no crops grow—a mythic depiction of the winter months.

Ishtar, the goddess of love, was restless. She had never visited the land of the dead, where her evil sister, Ereshkigal, ruled. She asked the permission of the other gods to go there and they consented only after the greatest reluctance. She started on the road to the Underworld.

She arrived at the first gate of the Underworld and said,

> O gatekeeper, open thy gate
> Open thy gate that I may enter
> If thou openest not the gate so that I cannot enter
> I will smash the gate down
> I will raise up the dead, eating the living
> So that the dead outnumber the living!

The gatekeeper went to his queen, Ereshkigal, to inform her that Ishtar was at the gate. Ereshkigal was not pleased to learn that her beautiful sister had arrived, and she turned pale, saying,

> Who drove her heart to me?
> What impelled her spirit here?
> Should I eat clay for bread?
> Shall I drink muddy water in place of beer?
> Should I mourn for the men who left their wives behind?
> Should I mourn for the girls who leave their lovers' laps?
> Should I mourn for the little ones who die before their
>   time?

Ereshkigal then told the gatekeeper that Ishtar would be permitted to enter only if she observed the laws of the Underworld. The dead must leave all signs of their earthly station, all wealth, and all privilege behind them, including their jewels and clothing; for in death all are equal. In the Underworld there is no light; the souls there must eat dust and clay.

At the first gate, in compliance with this law, Ishtar was obliged to remove her crown. At the second gate, she had to take off her earrings; at the third, her necklace; at the fourth, her breast ornaments; at the fifth, her belt; at the sixth, her hand and leg bracelets; and at the seventh, she removed her waistcloth, leaving her naked.

As soon as Ishtar had entered the last gate, Ereshkigal burst out at her, "What do you want here? Do you want to know what it is like for the dead?" Ereshkigal ordered her assistants to unleash sixty miseries on Ishtar, afflicting each part of the beautiful goddess's body with one of the pains that are used to punish the dead for their sins.

Meanwhile the other gods watched this from their thrones in the sky and became quite concerned. With Ishtar in the land of the dead, all reproduction on earth came to a halt. Men no longer made love to women, nor bulls to cows, nor stallions to mares; nothing. The plants stopped bearing fruit for the people to eat; famine threatened. Papsukkal, the god of agriculture, ran to Sin, the moon god, and reported that all creation would die if Ishtar remained in the Underworld much longer.

So Ishtar's brother, Ea, the god of water, created the eunuch Asushunamir, making him far more beautiful than any "male" on earth. Ea's plan was to send Asushunamir to the Underworld to divert Ereshkigal, allowing the beautiful Ishtar to leave. When Asushunamir arrived at the first gate into the Underworld, the gatekeeper reported to his queen that the most handsome man on earth was on his way to her. Ereshkigal was so excited that she forgot all about Ishtar.

As Ishtar left via the seventh gate, the first gate out of the Underworld, her waistcloth was returned to her; Asushunamir simultaneously entered the first gate into Ereshkigal's realm. As Ishtar passed through the sixth gate, her hand and leg bracelets were returned to her; the eunuch entered the second gate. At the fifth gate, Ishtar's magic belt was given back to her; Asushunamir came through the third gate. As Ishtar left through the fourth gate, her breast ornaments were returned; Asushunamir entered the fourth gate. At the third gate, Ishtar's necklace was returned to her; Asushanamir moved through the fifth gate. As Ishtar left the second gate, her earrings were returned to her; Asushunamir stepped through the sixth gate.

As Ishtar was leaving the first gate, the last gate out of the Underworld, she received her crown—and was free. Asushunamir was wearing only a waistcloth, and when he entered the seventh and last gate into the Underworld, and removed the cloth, Ereshikigal saw that he was not the lover she had hoped for—he was a eunuch! The queen of the Underworld was furious: Her brother and sister gods had tricked her.

When Ishtar returned to the world above the ground, all life began to flourish once again. ♦

MARWE IN THE UNDERWORLD
(Kenya)

There was once a girl named Marwe. She and her brother were responsible for keeping the monkeys from raiding the family bean fields. One day they had faithfully done their duty when both of them became very thirsty. They turned their backs on the fields and went to a pool to take a drink. When they returned to the fields, the monkeys had eaten all the beans. Marwe so feared the wrath of her parents that she drowned herself; her brother rushed home with the terrible news. Her parents were so shocked and grieved that they forgot about the bean field.

Marwe sank to the bottom of the pool until she entered the land of the dead. She first came to a house where an old woman lived with her children. The old woman identified herself as Marwe's guide in the land of the dead. For many years Marwe lived with the old woman and helped with the chores. After a time Marwe became very homesick and began to think of her parents and brother. The old woman was able to read the girl's heart, and she knew that Marwe wished to rejoin the living. So one day the old woman asked Marwe if she preferred the hot or the cold. Marwe didn't understand and the woman repeated the question. Finally Marwe answered that she preferred the cold, not knowing what this meant.

The old woman had Marwe dip her hands into a clay jar of cold water, and when she pulled her hands out, they were covered with jewels. She put her feet and legs into the jar, pulled them out, and they too were covered with jewels. Smiling, the old woman dressed Marwe in the finest robes and sent her home. The old woman also had the gift of prophecy, and told Marwe that she would soon marry the finest man in the world, a man named Sawoye.

When Marwe arrived home in her fine robes and jewels, her family was overjoyed. They had given her up for dead long before. They marveled at her fine clothing and their newfound wealth. Word spread quickly through the countryside that there was a rich, eligible young woman in the territory, and Marwe's home was visited by hundreds of suitors. Marwe ignored all of the men, including the most handsome, except for a man named Sawoye who suffered from a terrible skin disease that made him look ugly. But, having been to the land of the dead, Marwe was able to read the hearts of men and knew that Sawoye was best.

Sawoye and Marwe were married with great feasting, and after their wedding night, when the marriage was consummated, Sawoye's skin disease disappeared, showing his face to be the most handsome of all. As Marwe had plenty of fine jewels to spare, they bought a herd of cattle. Soon Marwe and Sawoye were the wealthiest people in the land.

One might expect that they would now live in happiness, but the many suitors of Marwe were envious of Sawoye. All of their friends and neighbors changed, resenting the wealthy young couple. The hostility grew more bitter with each day until a group of neighbors attacked Sawoye and killed him.

But Marwe had herself already died, and knew the secrets of the Underworld, including how to revive the dead. She took her husband's body inside their home and recited magic incantations that she had learned from the old woman in the land of the dead. Sawoye revived, stronger than ever. When their enemies returned to divide up the wealth, Sawoye slew them all. Marwe and Sawoye lived in prosperity and happiness for the rest of their lives, and since both had died, they met their ends without fear. ◆

SAVITRI
(India)

In ancient India there was a beautiful, pious, and uncommonly wise princess named Savitri. As she grew into a woman, her father, King Ashvapati, despaired that she would never marry and produce an heir. For Savitri was more interested in philosophical questions than in any of the young princes who visited her as suitors. Her interest was not in wealth, jewels, or power, but in spiritual things. At that time kings usually chose husbands for their daughters, but Savitri was so wise that the king decided to allow her to choose her own husband.

To her father's surprise Savitri asked to choose her husband from among the holy men, not the wealthy princes. Her father was at first very shocked. But then Savitri explained that her choice would be a holy man of princely rank. Ashvapati was so relieved that his daughter at last was interested in a husband that he readily gave his consent.

Savitri donned the costume of a holy hermit, a sadhu, and traveled throughout the land. Everywhere that she went people were moved by her beauty of face and soul, her charity, piety, and great wisdom. Indeed, she was absent so long that her father was growing worried about her. But the reports of Savitri's good deeds poured in from throughout the realm. Even the holy hermits were impressed by her wisdom for one so young.

When Savitri finally returned to her father's palace, she gave alms to the poor gathered at the gate. There was much excitement in the palace as Ashvapati and his adviser, the sage Narada, went to greet her at the gate. This was contrary to custom; the king never met any visitor at the gate.

Savitri announced that she had chosen a husband. There was a king who was completely blind and who had lost his kingdom, having been deposed by an evil usurper who took advantage of the king's blindness. This king had a son named Satyavant ("Truth-seeker") who had gone to live among the sadhus until the throne was restored. Savitri explained that only Satyavant, who had lived as a holy hermit, could rule wisely and understand the plight of the poor. Having lived a life of poverty, Satyavant alone could see through the illusions and judge the people fairly. But even as she spoke of Satyavant, Narada grew sad. The sage turned to her and said, "My child, all that you say is true, but you cannot marry him. It is ordained that Satyavant will die within a year of your wedding."

King Ashvapati, hitherto thrilled that Savitri was about to marry, was distraught. Satyavant certainly sounded like a perfect son-in-law, but he could not bear to see his beloved daughter widowed so young. Moreover, Satyavant might die before Savitri could produce an heir. With a deep sigh Ashvapati told Savitri that she must not marry her chosen prince.

But Savitri was wise and persuaded her father to give his blessing; it was better to be married for love even if just for one year. Whether or not Satyavant was to die, she was in love with him and no other. Savitri said that she was prepared for whatever the gods had ordained. Ashvapati granted her wish.

Ashvapati had just begun to plan a royal wedding with great feasts, but Savitri insisted that she marry in the style of the holy hermits, not of wealthy rulers. Luxury, she pointed out, was only an illusion. Again, Ashvapati granted her request.

Savitri went out into the forest among the sadhus and there she and Satyavant were married, clad in the robes of simple hermits. She shared her husband's contemplative life on the edge of the great forest, the deepest, darkest forest in the world. She never told Satyavant of his foretold death. As she gave alms to the poor, people would say, "May you never know widowhood," and the tears would stream down Savitri's face. As the first year of their marriage drew to a close, Savitri prayed to the gods to give her the strength to protect her husband.

On the very eve of their first anniversary, Satyavant asked Savitri to accompany him into the deep forest to cut wood. As they walked into the ever-thickening woods, the animals knew of Satyavant's imminent death, and fled. The little birds sang their best songs, thinking that this might be the last sound Satyavant heard. They proceeded farther and farther into the forest, where it was so thick that one could not see thc sunlight. They walked on, Satyavant with his ax over his shoulder and Savitri at his side.

Then Satyavant began to chop down a great tree. Suddenly he dropped his ax and turned white. He was in horrible pain and he told Savitri that it felt as if his head were being pierced by a thousand needles [a cerebral hemorrhage?]. Darkness clouded his eyes and he fell to the ground barely breathing.

At that moment Savitri heard the footsteps of a stranger approaching. This stranger had dark blue skin and red eyes—he was no stranger; it was Yama, the lord of the dead. Nonetheless Savitri asked the "stranger" to identify himself. "You know who I am," said Yama. "You also know why I am here." Yama took his cord and wrenched the soul of Satyavant from the body. As Yama turned around to take the soul to his kingdom, Savitri fell on the ground in his path.

Yama told her that it was useless; Satyavant's time had come as the gods had ordained. But Savitri pleaded with him, and Yama asked her politely to get out of his way. Then Savitri rose to her feet and began to follow Yama to the Underworld.

Yama told her to turn back; this was the land of the dead, not the living. It was now Savitri's duty to be a good wife and see to it that the funeral rites were properly performed, not to detain Yama from his mission. Yama, who is often thought of as heartless and cruel, can be compassionate. Often he will take the souls of very sick people to free them from their suffering. The lord of the dead was touched by Savitri's insistence.

Yama said, "Your love for your husband is very great and so is your courage; I will grant you one wish." Savitri replied, "Restore the kingdom to Satyavant's father." Yama told her, "It is done. Now return to the living, Savitri."

But Savitri would not turn back. She was so close to the gates of Yama's kingdom that the sky was now black and she could hear the snarling of the four-headed dog that guards the gate to the dead.* No mortal had ever come this close to the land of Yama.

"Please turn back now!" ordered Yama. "No living mortal can ever enter my kingdom!" Savitri told Yama that she would not leave her husband for any reason. Yama begged her once more to turn back, but she refused. Yama then said that no man had ever entered his kingdom; Savitri, always wise, responded that she was no man, but a woman. Yama was now as impressed by her wisdom as by her courage, and he offered her a second wish. "Restore the life of my husband." Yama granted this wish, saying, "It is already done—now go back and you will find Satyavant, not dead but sleeping."

Before Savitri turned back, Yama told her, "Just one more thing—my blessing goes with you always. You have learned the wisdom of the gods. No woman could ever have followed me alive to the very door of my kingdom if the gods were not on her side. Your wish and more will be granted you, for you know that love is stronger than death; love is the power that Yama cannot defy. Return to where you left Satyavant and live well."

She walked back to the glade where Satyavant lay, not dead, but sleeping as Yama had promised. She kissed him and his eyes opened. He told Savitri that he had a strange dream wherein Yama had carried his soul away, but Savitri's love had rescued it. Savitri laughed and told him to forget this silly dream. It was not until many years later that she told him that this story was no dream; it had actually happened.

As they left the deep forest, messengers came to Satyavant with wonderful news: His father was restored to the throne. In fact, the old king had regained his sight as soon as he sat on his rightful throne! The young couple ran to the palace and Satyavant's father was delighted to see his son for the first time in years, and to lay eyes on his beautiful daughter-in-law. Something inside the heart of the old king told him that Savitri had brought this reversal of fortune to pass.

---

*In Indian mythology a four-headed dog guards the gateway to the Underworld. As we shall soon see, the three-headed dog Cerberus performs the same function in Greek mythology.

Satyavant and Savitri passed many more years in the forest, living a simple life as hermits, raising their children in poverty, humility, honesty, and wisdom. Later, when Satyavant's father died at a goodly age, Satyavant and Savitri ruled the land of both Satyavant's father and Savitri's father, Ashvapati, with equity.

When it was time to die, Yama greeted them as old friends and told them that their souls were only with him for a visit, as they were to go to the highest heaven. When they left this earth, they had over one hundred descendants. ♦

PARE AND HUTU
(New Zealand)

Pare was a beautiful girl who flirted with a boy named Hutu, but then refused him her favors. Deeply hurt by the rejection, Hutu ran away in anger. Confused and guilty, Pare hanged herself and descended to Po, the land of night where the dead dwell, which is governed by Hina, the first woman. Hutu still longed for Pare and, with Hina's help, Hutu followed Pare to the Underworld. Why did Hina help him? You will recall that she too knows the pains of love.

There Hutu did all he could to attract Pare's attention and affections. But Pare was lost among the multitudes of the spirits of the dead and he still could not find her. Hutu finally got her attention by bending down a young tree and then swinging high into the air. Pare saw Hutu do this and joined him in the game. They swung higher and higher until they were able to grasp the roots of plants poking through from the Ao world above. Then they were able to pull themselves up out of the land of the dead.

No one can live in the Ao world of the living without a soul, except during twilight and dusk, when Ao meets Po. So Hutu forced Pare's soul up through the soles of her feet. With her body revived, Pare and Hutu married and became the ancestors of a great tribe. How did

Hutu have the magic to force Pare's soul into her body? Love is stronger than death. ♦

SAYADIO IN THE LAND OF THE DEAD
(*Iroquois*)

Sayadio was a warrior who had a younger sister who died. He grieved for her so much that he resolved to find her and bring her back to life from the land of the spirits. The search took him years, and just when he was about to give up he encountered a wise old man who knew the secrets of the spirit world. This old man gave him a magic gourd in which he might catch the spirit of his sister. Upon further conversation, Sayadio learned that this old man was the guide on the path to the part of the spirit world where his sister now was.

When Sayadio arrived in the land of the spirits, the spirits fled from him in fear. He recognized Tarenyawagon, who had lived on earth as Hiawatha, the great teacher of the Five Nations. Tarenyawagon now was the spirit master of ceremonies, and he was as compassionate as he was when he was on earth. Tarenyawagon told Sayadio that the spirits of the dead were about to have a great dance festival, in which his sister would take part. As soon as the spirits formed the dance line, Sayadio recognized the spirit of his sister. When he went to embrace her, however, she disappeared.

He turned again to Tarenyawagon for advice. The teacher gave him a magic rattle. His sister was so entranced by the dance music and the magic sound of the rattle that Sayadio captured her spirit with ease, placing it in the magic gourd.

Sayadio returned to the village with his sister's spirit in the gourd. Just when the ceremony to reunite the spirit with her body had begun, a foolish curious girl opened the gourd and the sister's spirit vanished. ♦

THE SPIRIT BRIDE
(*Algonquin*)

There was once a young warrior whose bride died on the eve of their wedding. Although he had distinguished himself by his bravery and goodness, the death left the young man inconsolable, unable to eat or sleep. Instead of hunting with the others, he just spent time at the grave of his bride, staring into the air.

However, one day he happened to overhear some elders speaking about the path to the spirit world. He listened intently and memorized the directions to the most minute detail. He had heard that the spirit world was far to the south. He immediately set out on his journey. After two weeks, he still saw no change in the landscape to indicate that the spirit world was near.

Then he emerged from the forest and saw the most beautiful plain he had ever seen. In the distance was a small hut where an ancient wise man lived. He asked the wise man for directions.

The old man knew exactly who the warrior was and whom he sought. He told the lad that the bride had passed by only a day before. In order to follow her, the warrior would have to leave his body behind and press on in his spirit. The spirit world itself is an island in a large lake that can be reached only by canoes waiting on this shore. However, the old man warned him not to speak to his bride until they were both safely on the island of the spirits.

Soon the old man recited some magic chants and the warrior felt his spirit leave his body. Now a spirit, he walked along the shore and saw a birchbark canoe. Not a stone's throw away was his bride, entering her own canoe. As he made his way across the water and looked at her, he saw that she duplicated his every stroke. Why didn't they travel together? One can only enter the spirit world alone and be judged only on one's individual merits.

Midway through the journey, a tempest arose. It was more terrible than any he had ever seen. Some of the spirits in canoes were swept away by the storm—these were those who had been evil in life. Since both the warrior and his bride were good, they made it through the tempest without incident and soon the water was as smooth as glass beneath a cloudless sky.

The island of the blessed was a beautiful place where it was always late spring, with blooming flowers and cloudless skies, never too warm or too cold. He met his bride on the shore and took her hand. They had not walked ten steps together when a soft sweet voice spoke to them—it was the Master of Life.

The Master told them that the young warrior must return as he came; it wasn't his time yet. He was to carefully trace his steps back to his body, put it on, and return home. He did this and became a great chief, happy in the assurance that he would see his bride once again. ◆

OSIRIS AND ISIS
(Egypt)

Osiris was a god who once ruled Egypt as a king during the time when death had not yet entered the world. In fact, the people knew nothing of sin; there was neither violence nor greed, envy, hatred, nor any other division among humans. People spoke sweetly to each other in poetry; they were always honest and gentle. Osiris himself loved the people and taught them the arts of raising crops, irrigation, wisdom, and the laws of the gods.

Geb (earth) and Nut (sky) were the parents of both Osiris and his wife, Isis. As they were gods, there was no sin in their being husband and wife as well as brother and sister. They ruled the land together in prosperity, causing the Nile to overflow its banks, leaving moist, rich silt that produced bread. Their faithful companion was the god of wisdom, Thoth, who invented writing and numbers, teaching these arts to the first people.

However, the gods also had a wicked brother, Set, who ruled the lifeless desert. Even as Osiris was the author of creativity and life, Set was destructive. He was so violent by nature that he ripped a hole in his mother's side when he was born. As the people reclaimed land through irrigation, he was angered that Osiris was diminishing his desert kingdom. He grew to envy his brother more day by day.

Set looked out over his kingdom and saw only dunes, scorpions, and rocks. He had plenty of time to think, as nothing ever happened in his realm. Once he measured Osiris by observing his brother's shadow, and then built a beautiful casket of fragrant wood for Osiris.

Before the arrival of the dry season (Set's favorite, of course), Set called a great feast of all the gods, placing the casket in the center of the entrance hall. All of the gods admired the box: It smelled of balsam, cedar, and incense woods. They played, taking turns lying in it. Osiris was late in arriving at the feast; all of the other gods were already in the dining hall. So Set and Osiris were alone in the entrance hall with the casket. Set persuaded his brother, who was honest and trusting, to try out the casket. As soon as Osiris was in the casket, Set's attendants came out, nailed the box shut, and sealed it with hot lead.

The sound of the hammers roused the other gods from their feasting. As they entered the entrance hall, Set and his minions had already fled with the casket into the desert night. The gods tried to pursue them, realizing that Osiris was inside the box, but it was too late. Finally, the evil ones flung the casket into the Nile, by which time Osiris had died of suffocation.

From the moment of the death of Osiris, Egypt suffered miseries hitherto unknown. Set's deserts encroached upon and parched fertile farmlands, causing famine. The people began to fight and steal for the meager remaining food. Mothers did not sleep at night, as the cries of their hungry children kept them awake. With the disruption of agriculture and irrigation, Set's kingdom of sand grew until it nearly reached the banks of the Nile. The despair was so great that the people envied the dead.

Isis, her sister Nephthys (who was Set's wife), and the wise god Thoth went in search of Osiris throughout the land of Egypt, following the course of the Nile. The casket had drifted down the river through the delta and into the Mediterranean Sea. Finally it arrived in the land of Byblos,* which was ruled by King Melkart and Queen Astarte.†

Meanwhile, a small tree had sprung up near the casket. Over time, it became a great tree that swallowed the casket in its trunk. The sweet-smelling woods it now enveloped caused the tree to give off a pleasant fragrance that made it famous throughout the world. Isis heard of this phenomenon and the description of the scent sounded like that of the casket.

While following the casket to Byblos, Isis had cut off a lock of her hair as a sign of mourning. Thoth advised her to regain her strength by resting on an island in the papyrus swamps of the Nile delta. Seven scorpions accompanied Isis on her journey. While she was resting at the home of a pious woman, one of the scorpions bit the woman's child, killing him. Moved by the cries of the mother, the goddess brought the child back to life.

Before Isis reached Byblos, King Melkart and Queen Astarte decided that the famous tree was one of the treasures of their kingdom and ordered it cut down. It was then fashioned into a pillar in their palace. Thus, when Isis arrived at Byblos, there was only a fragrant stump left. She remained seated on this stump for many months, saying nothing.

When Melkart and Astarte learned of the beautiful stranger, probably a goddess, they immediately sent for her. When Isis came to the palace, she placed her hand on the queen's head; immediately a sweet fragrance emanated from Astarte's body. Isis nursed the queen's child upon her finger as other women nurse by the breast. As the nurse of the royal child, Isis lived in the palace.

At night, by stealth, Isis chipped away at the pillar that contained Osiris, throwing the wood chips into the fire. The wood had been transformed magically by contact with her husband so that, when it burned, one could pass through the flames without harm. Isis placed

---

*Byblos is present-day Lebanon.

†Astarte is a form of the name Ishtar; Melkart means "king."

the royal child right into the flames to keep it warm, and the baby remained safe.

Queen Astarte walked into the hall and, terrified to see her child in the fire, pulled it out of the heat. Isis now took the form of a swallow and flew around the pillar. She spoke to the heart of Astarte, explaining that the child would have gained immortality by remaining in the flames just a little while longer; as it was, the baby was assured of a long life. Isis then reassumed human form and told Astarte the entire story of Osiris. In the morning, King Melkart ordered that the pillar be split and the casket removed.

Isis returned to Egypt with the casket. When she opened it, she found that Osiris had not decomposed; his body was perfectly preserved. She took the lifeless body of her husband into her arms and kissed him, breathing life into him, and he revived. Still afraid of his evil brother, they remained in hiding.

But Set had certainly found out that Osiris was alive once more, because the desert immediately retreated and began to produce crops again. People resumed living in peace with their neighbors. Of course, Set again began to plot the murder of his brother. One day, under the pretext of hunting gazelles, Set came upon the sleeping Osiris and cut his body into fourteen pieces, scattering them throughout the land. To this day, there are fourteen places in Egypt known as "tombs" of Osiris. With the death of Osiris, evil again swept the land, but to a lesser degree than before.

Isis traveled throughout Egypt to gather the fourteen dismembered pieces of Osiris's body. She reassembled her husband on an island in the Nile. When the pieces were all together, peace returned to Egypt. But a voice spoke to Isis, saying this peace would not last: Set had poisoned the hearts of men. Still, there would never again be a period completely devoid of goodness. Osiris's soul had now gone to the land of the dead, where he was King of the Dead and the Great Judge, and now mortal men and women could gain immortality of the soul at death, their bodies and souls to be reunited by resurrection. Although Set had brought sin into the world, Osiris brought hope.

Soon after Osiris went to the Underworld as king, to Isis was born his child, whom she named Horus. Nephthys and Thoth protected and instructed the boy. Horus was ordained to be the great avenger of his father, the champion of the gods and mankind against Set. With the birth of Horus, Set would never again rule uncontested. But Set caused a scorpion to bite Horus, killing him.

Isis prayed to Ra, the sun-god, who sent Thoth to teach her the incantations that would revive the boy. It was well, however, that Horus spent a little time in the land of the dead—it enabled him to meet his father, Osiris, and learn his wisdom: Horus is considered the patron of the reigning pharaoh and the guardian of the prosperity of Egypt. ♦

The Laws of Osiris

Osiris established the laws that govern the land of the dead. There are three parts to a human being—his body, his "ka" spirit, and his "ba" spirit. At death, it is the ka that continues to live, and the human body is preserved by mummification, as it is the property and home of the ka. When Osiris calls the dead to live in the resurrection, the ka can take full possession of the body.

At the moment of death, the ka leaves the body and proceeds to its judgment. The soul wanders through the halls of the palace of Osiris where forty-two assessors initially consider the evidence of the life of the soul. These assessors are entirely impartial; one's station in life makes no difference to their judgment in death. The ultimate judgment of the soul, however, is in the hands of the three judges of the dead in the Hall of the Two Truths.

These judges are the gods Horus, Anubis, and Thoth. Thoth, the god of wisdom, places a pure white feather symbolizing *Ma'at*, or "truth," on one side of a scale balanced against the evidence of the individual's life. If the soul honestly declares that it has not committed any of the forty-two sins, then Thoth takes the soul by the hand to the throne of Osiris, who then rules over the soul in everlasting bliss, and who will someday resurrect the body and reunite it with the soul.

If a person committed less than half of the forty-two sins, then Thoth makes the recommendation to Osiris that the soul be allowed to enjoy everlasting bliss. For such individuals, the crucial evidence is the evidence of the heart—the intentions. Some say that the hearts of the warmhearted and the coldhearted are even weighed on different scales.

On the other hand, if the soul has committed over half of the forty-two sins, and it is coldhearted, Osiris either orders it to be reincarnated and to pay for its sins through labor on earth, or he sends it to one of the hells to be purged of its sins and then retried.

In Egyptian tombs, one finds food and personal possessions interred along with the body. This is to provide for the sustenance of the ka spirit, which doesn't eat much, and also for the day when Osiris resurrects the body. The body is mummified in imitation of the preservation of the body of Osiris.

The Egyptian commonly referred to the recently deceased as "the Osiris ——" much as modern people say "the late ——." ♦

BLUE JAY IN THE LAND OF THE DEAD
(*Chinook*)

BLUE JAY FINDS A WIFE

Blue Jay was a trickster who enjoyed playing clever tricks on everyone, especially his sister Ioi. As she was the eldest sister, Blue Jay was supposed to obey her. But he deliberately misinterpreted what she said, excusing himself by saying, "Ioi always tells lies."

Ioi decided that it was high time for Blue Jay to quit his playful life of trickery and settle down with a wife. She told him that he must select a wife from the people of the land of the dead, who were called the "Supernatural People." Ioi recommended that Blue Jay choose an old woman for a wife and suggested the recently deceased wife of a chief. But Blue Jay balked; he wanted a young and attractive woman. He found the corpse of a beautiful young girl and took it to Ioi, who advised him to take the body to the land of the dead to be revived.

Blue Jay set out on this journey and arrived at the first village of the Supernatural People. They asked him, "How long has she been dead?" "Only a day," he answered. The Supernatural People of the first village then informed him that there was nothing they could do to help him; he must go on to the village where people who were dead for exactly one day were revived.

Blue Jay arrived at the second village the next day and asked the people to revive his wife. The people here too asked him how long she had been dead. "Two days now," he replied. "There is nothing we can do; we only revive those who were dead exactly one day." So Blue Jay went on.

He reached the third village on the day after that and asked the people to revive this wife. "How long has she been dead?" they asked. "Exactly three days now." "Most unfortunate," they replied. "We can only revive those who have been dead exactly two days." And so it went on from village to village until Blue Jay finally came to the fifth village, where the people could at last help him. The people of the fifth village liked Blue Jay and made him a chief. But the trickster tired of the Underworld and wanted to take his newly revived wife back to the land of the living.

When Blue Jay arrived at home with his wife, her brother saw she was alive once more and ran to tell their father, an old chief, who demanded that Blue Jay cut off all of his hair as a gift to his new in-laws. When there was no response from Blue Jay, the chief became angry and led a party of male relatives to find him. Just as they nearly caught him, Blue Jay assumed the form of a bird and flew off again to the land of the dead.

At this, his wife's body fell to the ground, lifeless. She went to meet her husband in the land where he was now an exile. ◆

IOI AND THE GHOST HUSBAND

The ghosts went in search of a wife and one of them fell in love with Blue Jay's sister Ioi. They brought animal teeth as gifts and the night after the wedding feast they disappeared, taking Ioi with them.

Blue Jay did not hear from Ioi for an entire year. He then decided to visit the land of ghosts in order to see her again. He went about the villages and among the animals asking for directions, but none would answer him. Finally, he found someone who would guide him there in return for payment.

In the land of ghosts, he found Ioi standing amid piles of bones that were introduced to him as Ioi's in-laws. At times the bones would leap into normal human form, but they would return to piles of bones when a loud noise was made.

Ioi asked Blue Jay to take her young brother-in-law fishing. The boats of the ghost people looked terrible; they were full of holes and covered with moss. Finding that a shout would turn his fishing companion into a pile of bones, Blue Jay had great fun. Among his many pranks, Blue Jay took the bones and mixed them up, placing the skull of a child on an adult torso, then laughing when the strange thing came to life.

The next time Blue Jay went fishing with Ioi's young brother-in-law, they kept what they caught, which looked to Blue Jay like branches but which were actually fine salmon in the ghost world. Another time the ghost people became very excited: A "whale" had been found beached. But to Blue Jay's eyes it did not look like a whale, but rather like a large log. The ghost people began stripping the bark off the log, praising it as the richest whale blubber they had ever had. Knowing that by shouting he could reduce them all to bones, he did so, and then took the blubber for himself—but in his hands it still looked like tree bark.

The ghost people tired of Blue Jay's pranks at their expense, and Ioi's husband begged her to send the trickster home. So Ioi sent her brother up to the world of the living to put out five prairie fires. She gave him five pots of water, but—as usual—he ignored his sister's instructions, claiming, "Ioi always tells lies." So he poured the water on the fires without taking care to see how much was needed for the job. By the time Blue Jay reached the fifth fire, there was no water left. The fire consumed him and he died. But the dead don't know that they are dead right away.

Upon arriving in the land of the dead, Blue Jay did not believe that he was dead. When Ioi sent her canoe to greet him—a canoe that had looked before to Blue Jay as miserable and full of holes—he said, "What a fine canoe! I have never seen one this fine." When the people brought him fine salmon—which had seemed before to Blue Jay to be mere tree branches—he said, "What excellent salmon; I have never seen any so fine."

The people in the land of the dead tried to convince Blue Jay that he was actually dead, but he refused to believe it, saying, "Ioi always tells lies." Remembering his tricks with the ghost people, Blue Jay shouted. However, now the ghosts did not reduce to piles of bones; in fact, nothing happened.

Still not convinced that he was actually dead, Blue Jay went to pester the medicine men in the land of the ghosts. They became annoyed with him and made him insane. When Ioi found him, he was dancing on his head.

Ioi told the people, "My brother is now very dead—he has lost his mind." ♦

THE GREEK AND ROMAN AFTERLIFE

At death, the soul leaves the body and travels to the Underworld, guided by the god Hermes. At first it arrives on the banks of the River Styx (meaning "hateful"). Mourners are well advised to place a coin in the mouth of the deceased in order to pay Charon, the ferryman, to take the soul across this river. Without the proper fare, the soul may wander for a hundred years as a ghost.

Once across the Styx, the soul is taken to the three judges of the dead—Rhadamanthus, Minos, and Aeacus. It is said that Rhadamanthus judges the Europeans, Aeacus the Asiatics, and Minos, who lived on the earth as king of Crete, takes only the hardest cases. Based on the decision of its appropriate judge, the soul may then proceed leftward to the Hades of punishment, where one is repaid one hundredfold for the misdeeds of life. A good person may be conducted toward the right, whence he or she proceeds to the Elysian Fields—a place of perpetual bliss covered with sacred purple light (purple is the color of nobility). Plato tells us that every good deed is repaid here one hundredfold. Any soul in the Elysian Fields can be reincarnated and return to the earth as many as three times. However, before leaving, the soul must drink the water of Lethe, or "forgetfulness."

ORPHEUS AND EURYDICE

Orpheus was the greatest musician who ever lived. He was the child of a mortal father and the Muse Calliope, patroness of music. His aptitude for music was noticed early in his childhood and the god Apollo himself gave the child a lyre to play. As he grew into manhood, Orpheus fell in love with Eurydice and married her.

While they were still newlyweds, Eurydice took a walk near the river. A man attempted to seize her by force and she accidentally trod on a poisonous viper while fleeing. Orpheus was so filled with grief that he begged the gods to allow him to enter the Underworld to bring her back. His songs of mourning were so moving that the gods agreed; Apollo was his patron for the journey.

Upon arriving on the banks of the River Styx, the border between the world of the living and the Underworld, the sky went from sunshine to dark shadow. Orpheus began to play his lyre; Charon was so charmed by the music that he took Orpheus across the river, forgetting about the fare. The snarling guard of the gate to the Underworld, the three-headed dog Cerberus, stopped barking and listened to the music. The three judges of the dead paused to listen as well, and the torments of the punished souls, including Sisyphus, ceased for a few moments.

Finally Orpheus met Hades, lord of the Underworld, and the music melted the heart of the king of the dead. He gladly granted Orpheus's request on one condition: Orpheus must not turn to look at the face of Eurydice until they were both safely out of the Underworld and stood once again in the land of the living. Were Orpheus to look back but once, Eurydice would have to stay in the Underworld forever.

Understanding this, Orpheus began his ascent to the land of the living, with Eurydice behind him. He kept his eyes fixed firmly in front of him. But as thoughts of her filled his head, he could not bear it; he turned back and lost his wife forever. ◆

AENEAS IN THE UNDERWORLD

Upon his arrival in Italy, Aeneas,* ancestor of the Caesars, consulted with the Italian oracle, the Sibyl, for advice. She knew very well that Aeneas missed his late father, Anchises, and that the best advice for Aeneas could only come from his father. The Sibyl then agreed to conduct Aeneas to the Underworld to see his father.

The path to the Underworld was a gloomy one, shrouded in darkness. They passed the foul-smelling Lake Avernus until they encountered the black poplar trees that mark the border between the land of the living and the Underworld. The Sibyl suggested that Aeneas sacrifice four black bulls to Hecate, the goddess of the night. As the smoke from the sacrifice rose high, thunder sounded and the earth quaked. The Sibyl then pointed to a tree with a golden bough, advising Aeneas to break off the bough for his journey.

Then the Sibyl faced Aeneas squarely and said, "Now you will

---

*The story of Aeneas is from the Latin epic the *Aeneid* by the Roman poet Virgil. The story recounts how Aeneas fled Troy after the Trojan War and traveled to Italy, where he was a founder of Rome. The *Aeneid* was the Roman founding myth; Roman nobles strived to trace their ancestry to Aeneas.

need all your courage." The two entered the mouth of the Underworld, walking past the horrible spirits of Discord, Disease, Hunger, and War, onto a field occupied by the hapless souls who had not been properly buried and must wander that shore for a century before entering the Underworld. The Sibyl and Aeneas came to the banks of the River Styx, where Charon, the ferryman, told them gruffly that the dead—and not the living—were his passengers. However, Aeneas showed Charon the golden bough; the ferryman then conducted them across the river.

The boat passed the field of mourning where tragic young lovers who had committed suicide wandered. They passed the seats of the three judges of the dead.

They now came to a fork in the river. From the left they heard the screams of the punished souls. To the right they saw the purple rays emanating from the Elysian Fields where the good and the great dwell in everlasting bliss. The Sibyl instructed Aeneas to place the golden bough in the rock wall opposite the fork in the river. Then Charon veered sharply to the right, toward the Elysian Fields. There Aeneas saw the great heroes, poets, sages, and others, including—at last—Anchises, his father.

Aeneas wept with joy at the sight of his father. When the ferry landed, father and son embraced. Anchises said that his son would be the founder of the greatest empire the world had ever known. As they parted, Anchises took Aeneas to the well of Lethe to drink of the waters of forgetfulness.

Then the Sibyl conducted Aeneas back to the land above the ground, where he fulfilled his fate. ♦

PERUVIAN DEATH MYTHS

There are two human souls, the Athun Ajayo and the Jukkui Ajayo. The Athun Ajayo is created by Pachamama [Mother Earth] and is the soul that provides consciousness, movement, and other signs of life. The Athun Ajayo survives after the death of the body.

The Jukkui Ajayo is the soul that provides the body with immunity from diseases as it maintains the proper equilibrium among the mind, the body, and the Athun Ajayo. It is the Jukkui Ajayo that wanders about during sleep, transmitting its impressions in the form of dreams. If the Jukkui Ajayo leaves the living body, there is no protection against disease. When a body dies, the Jukkui Ajayo leaves permanently within the first week of death.

Both Ajayos hover about the body of the deceased for three days. Bachelors and spinsters are well-advised to stay away from the corpse during this time, as the Athun may take a soul with it to be a spouse in the afterlife.

The Athun Ajayos return to earth to visit the living, especially during the Christian feast of All Saints' Day on the first of November. At that time one may speak with the Athuns of dead relatives and give them gifts.

SOCRATES ON THE GRECO-ROMAN AFTERLIFE

From Socrates's "Speech on His Condemnation to Death":*

Moreover, we may hence conclude that there is great hope that death is a blessing. For to die is one of two things: for either the dead may be annihilated and have no sensation of anything whatever; or, as it is said, there is a certain change and passage of the soul from one place to another. And if it is a privation of all sensation, as it were, a sleep in which the sleeper has no dream, death would be wonderful gain. For I think that if anyone, having selected a night in which he slept so soundly as not to have had a dream, and having compared this night with all the other nights and days of his life, should be required on consideration to say how many nights he had passed better and more pleasantly than this night throughout his life, I think that not only a private person, but even a great king himself would find them easy to number in comparison with other days and

*In *The World's Great Speeches*, edited by Lewis Copeland.

nights. If, therefore, death is a thing of this kind, I say it is a gain; for thus all futurity appears to be nothing more than one night.

But if, on the other hand, death is a removal from hence to another place, and what is said can be true, that all the dead are there, what greater blessing can there be than this, my judges? For if, on arriving at Hades, released from those who pretend to be judges, one shall find those who are true judges, and who are said to judge there, Minos and Rhadamanthus, Aeacus and Triptolemus, and such others of the demigods who were just during their own life, would this be a sad removal? At what price would you not estimate a conference with Orpheus and Musaeus, Hesiod and Homer? I indeed should be willing to die often, if this be true. For to me the soujourn there would be admirable, when I should meet with Palamedes, and Ajax, son of Telamon, and any other of the ancients who has died by an unjust sentence. The comparing my sufferings with theirs would, I think, be no unpleasant occupation.

But the greatest pleasure would be to spend my time in questioning and examining the people there as I have done those here, and discovering who among them is wise, and who fancies himself to be so but is not. At what price, my judges, would not any one estimate the opportunity of questioning him who led that mighty army against Troy, or Ulysses, or Sisyphus, or ten thousand others, whom one might mention, both men and women? With whom to converse and associate, and to question them, would be an inconceivable happiness. Surely for that the judges there do not condemn to death; for in other respects those who live there are more happy than those that are here, and are henceforth immortal, if at least what is said be true.

You, therefore, O my judges, ought to entertain good hopes with respect to death, and to meditate on this one truth, that to a good man nothing is evil, neither while living nor when dead, nor are his concerns neglected by the gods. And what has befallen me is not the effect of chance; but this is clear to me, that now to die, and be freed from my cares is better for me. On this account the warning in no way turned me aside; and I bear no resentment toward those who condemned me, or against my accusers, although they did not condemn and accuse me with this intention, but thinking to injure me: in this they deserve to be blamed.

. . . But it is now time to depart,—for me to die, for you to live. But which of us is going to a better state is unknown to everyone but God.

PERSIAN (ZOROASTRIAN) DEATH MYTHS

NOTE: Zoroastrianism, the ancient religion of Persia (now Iran), is a faith founded on the teachings of the prophet Zoroaster. There are now only 100,000 Zoroastrians in the world, principally in India, Iran, and Great Britain.

At death the soul hovers over the body for three nights. On the first night, the soul contemplates the words of its past life; on the second, it contemplates its thoughts; and on the third, it contemplates its deeds. Then the soul passes on to the three judges who are absolutely impartial and care nothing about the person's status in life. The three judges base their decision upon the person's deeds, which are recorded in the House of Song. The soul's merits are weighed on a scale. If the good outweighs the bad, then the soul proceeds on to heaven. If the good and bad are equal, the soul proceeds to Hamestagan, or Purgatory, where it is cleansed of its sin. If the bad outweighs the good, then the soul goes to hell.

As the souls leave the place of judgment they are met by a guide. For the good, this guide is a beautiful young woman; for the bad it is an ugly hag. Then the guide identifies herself—"I am your own conscience." All souls, good or bad, are conducted by their guides to the Chinvat bridge.

At this bridge the path into heaven widens for the good; for the evil it becomes razor thin and they plunge into hell. However, hell is not permanent; once the sins are expiated the soul may return to the seat of judgment for a review of their case. If sufficiently purged, the soul may proceed into heaven.

At the end of time, at the last judgment, all will be resurrected, and the body and soul reunited and judged as a whole. ♦

NACHIKETAS
(India)

There was once a Brahman herdsman named Vajashrava who earnestly desired to win the favor of the gods; he wanted to give them something to ensure prosperity. However, all of his cows were old and no longer gave milk. His crops were poor and he had barely enough to feed his family. Vajashrava spoke with his son, Nachiketas, about this predicament. Nachiketas replied, "Father, you have nothing to give to the gods but me. To which god would you offer me?" Vajashrava sadly said, "To Yama, lord of the dead."

Nachiketas was an unusually wise young man and thought about this. He knew that there was nothing to fear; he was neither the first nor the last person to be offered to Yama. Certainly the blessings that would derive from this offering would be great. So the young man agreed. Nachiketas made his way to the land of the dead, but Yama was out gathering souls. Nachiketas waited for Yama for three days.

When Yama returned, his servants told him that a noble Brahman named Nachiketas awaited him. Certainly, given the wait, the young man was entitled to some welcome hospitality. Moreover, Yama knew that great harm comes to those who have a Brahman guest and fail to feed and welcome him.

So Yama told Nachiketas that, as an honored guest who had patiently waited for three days, the young mortal was entitled to three wishes that could not be refused. Nachiketas first wished that his father would recognize him and welcome him when he returned from the land of the dead. The second request was to know where the sacred fire that leads directly to heaven might be found. Third, Nachiketas asked to know the secret of what is beyond death, beyond the reach of Yama in the Underworld.

Although Yama gladly granted the first two requests, he was most reluctant to grant this third wish. Yama told Nachiketas, "Even the gods of old were in doubt as to this mystery. Ask anything else, whether wealth, fame, sons, long life, or any other wish, but not this."

Nachiketas told Yama that wealth does not last forever, even a long life must come to an end, sons can be both a sorrow and a blessing, and all material things come to rust and rot; all these material blessings are but illusion. Yama then offered Nachiketas fine wives, the fairest maidens of Indra's heavens, and worldly power. Nachiketas replied that all these things are but pleasure, and pleasure is also an illusion. The youth said, "There is nothing but the mystery beyond death that interests me."

Yama smiled and responded, "You are very wise, Nachiketas. Duty is one path and delight is another. It is always best for one to choose duty, for delight can lead astray. The fool believes that only the life of this world is real and sets his heart on pleasures and wealth. Even the learned fall prey to illusion. But beyond death, I tell you, is the great and eternal One.* Many do not know the eternal One, nor do they seek him.

"To know the eternal One that is greater than all gods is to be deathless, O Nachiketas; the One never was born and never dies. Smaller than small and greater than great, the Self indwells in the human heart of those who seek Him. The human who knows the One knows no grief; there is nothing that can discourage him. This cannot be learned by mere explanation, nor even by knowing and reciting the Scriptures. When every knot in the human heart is loosened, then one can know the One."

This third wish granted, Nachiketas returned to the land of the living. In asking Death what is beyond Death, he assured his immortality. ◆

---

*Brahman.

JEWISH DEATH MYTH

THE RABBI'S DEAD VISITOR

Once, after his death, a prominent Jew in the congregation of the Tsaddik [holy man] Rabbi Yissochor of Velburz came to ask him for help; as his wife had died, said the man, he needed money to remarry.

"But you're dead yourself," said the Tsaddik. "What are you doing in the land of the living?"

The dead man refused to believe him until the rabbi made him lift up his coat and showed him that there were shrouds underneath it. After he had departed, the rabbi's son asked him, "Father, how do I know that I am not also a dead person who is haunting the land of the living?"

"If you know there's such a thing as death, you're not dead," said the rabbi. "The dead themselves know nothing of death." ♦
—Pinhas Seder, *Jewish Folktales*, translated by Hillel Halkin

TIBETAN DEATH MYTHS

At the exact moment of death the soul first experiences the colorless light of emptiness, which bathes it. If one merges with the light at this opportunity, one is saved. Most people, however, first fall unconscious and then are shocked back into consciousness by the terror of the recognition that they are dead. Often the recognition that one is dying is frightening and the soul tries to flee; this is futile. If one tries to maintain a separate identity by clinging to the illusion of the ego, it is also pointless. Very few people attain salvation or have the insight necessary to understand what is happening.

For those who miss salvation at this first opportunity, there comes a period of nightmares that expiate the sins of a life, as well as pleasant dreams about the best times on earth. A few days after death the "mental body" merges; it is really the essence of a person charged with the karma of the past. It can travel through time and space at will.

Three and a half days after the moment of death, Buddhas and Boddhisatvas [saints] will appear in all their radiant glory and goodness. Their light will be so bright that the soul will have a hard time facing them directly. If one understands this without being frightened, the soul merges into the very heart of God and salvation is won. If one fails to understand what is happening, then the soul proceeds on its journey. The majority of people never understand this holy vision.

If one doesn't understand what has just happened, then the next seven days will be horrifying. Angry deities will assail you, you will be asked why you failed to do good, why you didn't hear the call of religion during your life, why you ignored the needs of others. You will hear yourself condemned for having failed to heed the saving truths.

This is a crucial point in the journey of the soul: There is another opportunity for salvation. However, the majority just continue on, tormented, and become part of the great Wheel of Becoming, facing reincarnation. But beware: Your next encounter is with Yama, lord of the dead.

You will tell Yama of your life; it is stupid to try to conceal anything or to lie. Yama holds before you the shining mirror of karma in which all things come to light and you pronounce your own judgment. That mirror is your conscience.

At this stage you will see various lights shining in the distance; these are the paths of destiny. You may follow a red light, which will lead you to rebirth among the Asuras, who are warlike spirits; this happens to one who has had a violent nature in life—it is not a pleasant rebirth. A blue light indicates that your rebirth will be as a human being. A green light means that your ignorance will lead you to be reborn among plants or animals. White lights are good news— you will be reborn in one of the heavens.

At this point, should you be drawn to the green or blue light, you will see pairs of animals or humans, respectively, engaged in intercourse. This attracts you. If in the next life you are to be a female, you will be attracted to the male; if you are to be male, you will be attracted to the female.* At the moment that the egg and sperm unite, the new incarnation begins. ♦

BALDUR
(Norse)

NOTE: The myth of Baldur is of great interest for a number of reasons. It is given as a possible source of the superstition associated with the number thirteen—and especially Friday the thirteenth. It is also comparable in many ways to the Algonquin myth of Glooskap and Malsum, which is considered by some scholars to be an inter-borrowing from the Norse.

In any case, this is an excellent example of myths of the journey to the Underworld.

Baldur, a son of Odin and his wife Frigga, was the most beloved of the gods, but he was tormented by frightening dreams warning of his death. He told his parents of these dreams, and Frigga went about extracting promises from all living things not to harm Baldur, overlooking only the insignificant little mistletoe plant.

Odin was not satisfied with these steps and he went to see his sister Hel [the root of our word *hell*] in her realm, the land of the dead. He also spoke to Angerbode the Sorceress, who was dead and lived in the Underworld.

The inhabitants of Asgard, home of the gods, totaled twelve including Baldur. However, the evil giant Loki, a god of fire, had sworn a brotherhood oath with Odin and was not considered a thirteenth

---

*Shades of Freud's Oedipal theory.

god. On the day sacred to Frigga [Friday], all thirteen of these gods assembled. Now that Baldur was apparently invulnerable to any living thing, the gods had great fun flinging objects at him, watching them bounce off him without a scratch.

Loki took the form of a woman and went to Frigga for an explanation of this curious sport. Frigga explained about the oaths. Loki asked if there were any exceptions. Being a wife of Odin, Frigga was incapable of lying. So she said that she had indeed overlooked the mistletoe because it seemed so harmless. Not wasting a moment, Loki cut some sprigs of mistletoe and fashioned them into darts. Standing at the side of the other gods was the blind god Hodur. Loki asked him why he wasn't joining in the fun. Hodur explained that there was no point in his flinging things at Baldur if he couldn't see them bounce off him.

With Loki's cunning and assistance, however, Hodur flung a mistletoe dart at Baldur, who fell dead instantly. The other gods were horrified, knowing that Loki had perpetrated this terrible deed. Frigga, stricken with grief for her son, told the assembled gods that whoever would travel to Hel and ransom Baldur would become her favorite. Hermod, another of Odin's sons, volunteered and mounted Odin's eight-legged horse, Sleipnir, to travel to the Underworld. Hermod came to the bridge of Gyoll, which all must cross to enter the land of the dead. A beautiful maiden waits at this bridge to conduct the dead to their home.

She asked Hermod what the nature of his business was. When Hermod replied that he had come to ransom Baldur, she replied that she had seen him arrive. Hermod, on Odin's steed, leaped over the gates of the land of the dead and confronted Hel, who told him that she would release Baldur on one condition—if all living things would weep for the murdered god.

Hermod reported this back to the gods and soon all things, the mountains, rocks, trees, animals, and birds wept for Baldur. However, one creature refused to weep: an old witch named Thakkt. The heartless wretch said, "I will weep only dry tears for him; people die every day!" Thus Baldur remained in the land of the dead.

All Viking heroes had a ship of their own, and Baldur's ship was the finest. The gods prepared a great funeral pyre on Baldur's ship and placed the body on it, set it afire, and cast it out to sea.

Loki was now punished for his calumny. He fled the angry gods to hide in the mountains, building a hut with a door on each side to enable him to see any approaching danger. Odin, knowing all things, soon found Loki's hiding place, but with his knowledge of fishing, the evil god changed himself into a salmon to escape Odin. Thor, the thunder god, cast a net with which to capture Loki. When Loki leaped high as salmon do, Thor caught him by the tail and gripped it hard. To this day, the tail of the salmon is finer and thinner than the tails of other fish, and Loki is still remembered as the inventor of the fisherman's net.

Loki was then chained to a rock, where he will remain until the Twilight of the Gods. His wife Siguna is there with him. The gods placed a venomous serpent over his head; when the venom drips onto his face, the pain is horrible. Loki's cries cause the earth to quake. But as Odin knows, the day is coming when Loki will have his revenge on the gods. ♦

THE DEATH OF MOSES
(The Talmud)

When Moses reached the age of 120, Samael, now called Satan, asked the Almighty if he could serve as the angel of death and collect the soul of the lawgiver.

God responded, "What makes you think that you could take the soul of such a holy man, one beloved by me? And how would you approach this servant of Mine and take his soul? What do you think Moses would do when he saw you? Moses has seen My divine face on Mount Sinai—his hands have touched My law. Would you take his soul out by these hands? Or would you take his soul out by the ears—his ears have heard My voice. Would you take his soul from his feet? Those are feet that have stood on holy ground! You have my permission to *try* to take his soul."

Samael buckled on his sword and went to Moses just as the great leader of the Exodus was writing the Most Holy Name of God with a stick. As Moses wrote, his face became radiant and shone like the sun. The power of God's name caused Samael to flee in terror. Samael screwed up all of his courage and returned, squeaking out in a timid, wimpy voice, "Moses, give me your soul."

Moses laughed at the devil and said, "Never to you, O enemy of God and mankind. Don't you remember? I am the one chosen by Almighty God to lead his people out of Egypt, the one to whom He spoke from the burning bush, the one to whom He entrusted the Torah. Who do you think you are asking for my soul? Get out of here!" With this, Samael fled in terror.

Samael went back to God and told the Lord what had happened (as if He didn't already know?).

God laughed again at Samael. "You pitiful little ignorant one. I remember when you rebelled against me, when you tempted my children in the Garden of Eden. You thought yourself so clever! I gave you permission to try to collect the soul of Moses and you crawl back to me with your tail between your legs! Let's see if the 'glorious' fallen angel can collect the soul of Moses—for it is by your hand that death entered the world."

Samael was now angered by this laughing contempt with which both God and Moses treated him. He went to Moses with new resolve. But Moses made him flee once again, this time by only reciting a few words of the sacred Torah—the Law of God.

Then Moses spoke to God, saying:

> O Most High God—who created the world in love;
> O Most High God—whose first word was a blessing;
> Don't turn me over to our enemy!
> Treat me with love.
> I know that Samael only comes to collect my soul for
> you and not himself.
> But keep me out of his hands entirely;
> keep me from the hated foe of all humankind.

God then heard the words of Moses and sent three angels to collect the lawgiver's soul: Gabriel, Michael, and Zagzagel. Gabriel arranged for a place for Moses to lie down and die. Michael spread out the royal purple robe for Moses to lie on as Zagzagel positioned a pillow for the holy man's head. Then God spoke to the soul of Moses:

> My beautiful daughter, come home.
> For one hundred and twenty years, you have lived in a
>   righteous body.
> But now it is time to return to Me.
> This is my will,
> which you have followed all these years.

Moses heard God tell his soul, "Return to your rest as God commands." With that God took the soul from Moses' body with a kiss, sending it to a place beside His throne. The angels buried the body of Moses in a secret place, knowing that Samael was still searching for him.

Samael asked the sea, "Have you seen Moses?" The sea replied, "Not since the Exodus, when he parted the waters." Samael asked the people in the Promised Land of Canaan. They told him that Moses had never entered there. Samael asked the rocks; they replied that they had not seen Moses since he caused a spring of water to pour forth, or since he had carved the tables of the Law from rock. Samael asked the mountains; they told him that they had not seen Moses since he had received the Law on Sinai.

Samael then asked the angels, who responded—

> We have heard mourning on earth and rejoicing in heaven. But
> we haven't seen him.

What they said was actually true. Only Gabriel, Michael, and Zagzagel of their number had actually seen Moses; the other angels had seen his soul, which is invisible. Angels never lie, but neither are they stupid.

Finally Samael went among humankind and asked for Moses. Humans are the prey of Samael and they usually greet him with fear. But this time they rejoiced and delighted in telling the evil one—

You will never find him here.
You can never find him here.
You have nothing more to do with him—
The deceiver has been deceived!
His soul is in heaven in the presence of God,
where your corruption can never go!

And with a curse on his lips, Samael returned to hell, entirely con-
founded. ♦

11. The End—
Visions of the Apocalypse

When the end comes, Armageddon outta here . . . !
—J. F. Bierlein

HOW RUDRA DESTROYS THE UNIVERSE
(*India*)

The earth has been created, destroyed, and re-created many times—only the Eternal knows how many times this has taken place. Or perhaps he does not know. The laws of the universe are fixed: the Four Ages of man naturally occur and recur as Dharma—the four-legged stool of truth—is established and disintegrates, one leg at a time, until there is nothing for the world to stand on. However, the destruction of the universe is inevitable in every cycle.

At the beginning of each cycle, the world is created by Brahma; during the cycle, the world is sustained by Vishnu; then, it is destroyed by Shiva.

A cycle, or "Day of Brahma," lasts 12,000 years of the *devas*, or 4,320,000 human years. At the beginning of each such "Day," when the Eternal One wakes up, the world is re-created.

Every cycle is divided into fourteen *manvantaras*, each of which is ruled by a dominant *Manu*, or "teacher." Each *manvantara* is followed by a great flood that destroys all living things, except those saved to repopulate the earth. During these floods, the continents are rearranged.

237

The Day of Brahma may also be divided into 1,000 *yugas* with each consisting of the Four Ages, discussed earlier. Four *yugas* together last 4,320,000 years—the first, 1,728,000; the second, 1,296,000; the third, 864,000; and the last *yuga*, 432,000. The year 1993 was the 5,093rd of the Kali *yuga*. This is ominous as Kali is believed by some to be the destroyer of the world.

By the time the last *yuga* has come and gone, the earth is completely exhausted of its resources. This is the point in the cycle of history where the universe is eradicated and prepared for re-creation. The god Vishnu now takes the form of Rudra the storm god, the destroyer of all things. First comes a horrible drought that lasts for 100 years, by which all life on earth is decimated if not extinguished.

Rudra then enters the sun, and all the water on earth—the seas, oceans, lakes, and rivers, as well as the water beneath the earth—dries up. All of the water is drawn off the earth into the sky. The ancient teachers called this "the sucking of the waters by Rudra," for it is as if all of the moisture on earth has been sucked up by a straw. What is left of the earth is then burned and cleansed by the power of the superheated sun, so that all things are purged on earth and then throughout the universe.

Then Rudra breathes out great clouds filled with the moisture drawn from the earth. He begins sending thunderbolts out of heaven, the harbinger of a rain in sheets that lasts for 1,000 years, extinguishing the fires. The water rises and rises until it reaches the realm of the seven sages, far above the surface of the earth.

Then Brahma sends a wind that drinks up much of the water, establishing clouds in heaven. The world is now a watery chaos, the primordial state from which a new world can be created. ◆

THE PERSIAN APOCALYPTIC MYTH

The Believer of the True Faith:

> O Ormazd, I ask you concerning the present and future
> How shall the righteous be dealt with,
> And how shall the wicked be dealt with,
> At the last judgment?
> I ask you O Ahura [Lord], what will be the punishments
>   of them that serve the Evil One—
> Of them who cannot make their living except by doing
>   violence to cattle and herdsmen?
> O Ormazd, I ask you whether the well-disposed, the one
>   who strives to improve the houses, villages, clans
>   and provinces through justice—
> Can he become like you?
> And when?
> By what deeds?
> Tell me, O Lord, that I may no longer be deluded;
> Be my instructor of Good Disposition!

Ormazd the Wise Lord answers:

> O well-disposed believer
> Don't listen to the followers of the Evil One,
> For they seek to destroy houses, villages, clans and
>   provinces.
> They can only cause disaster and death.
> Fight them with all your might!
> The righteous alone shall be saved from destruction and
>   darkness;
> From foul food and the worst curses at the time of the
>   end of days.
> But wicked ones—beware!
> For you will be delivered all these foul things because
>   of your evil spirit.
> He that serves the Wise Lord in mind and deed
> To him shall be granted the joy of divine fellowship, and

the fulness of health, immortality, justice and
power and the Good Disposition!

There will be three saviors sent to earth by the Wise Lord before the
final, inevitable battle that will result in the ultimate triumph of good
over evil, the Last Judgment, and the resurrection of the dead. First will
come a period called the Period of Iron, in which demons will attack
the earth relentlessly, sparing no one. They will be more interested in
causing the faithful to suffer than in killing them. The darkness will be
so pervasive that the light of even the sun and moon will be dimmed.
At that time a shower of stars will occur to herald the birth of the first
savior, the champion of the faithful, named Anshedar.

A virgin, fifteen years old, will bathe in a sacred lake in Iran that
has been miraculously impregnated with the sperm of the prophet
Zoroaster; the virgin will then conceive the child Anshedar. When
Anshedar reaches the age of thirty, the sun will be motionless in the
sky in the noonday position for ten days. After the appearance of this
heavenly portent, Anshedar will meet with the angels and return to
earth to preach the teachings of righteousness—exhorting all humankind to resist evil. When Anshedar leaves the earth, it will be better
than when he found it. However, evil will only be temporarily subdued. At the end of this time of Anshedar, people will no longer die
of disease, which is now inflicted by demons; they will only expire
as the result of advanced age, accidents, or homicide.

A thousand years later, evil will again be ascendant and humankind will experience a hardship that had been long forgotten. Out of
nowhere, suffering, disease, war, and hunger will appear. Again, a
fifteen-year-old virgin will bathe in the sacred lake, become pregnant, and give birth to the second savior, Aushedarmah. Once more,
when Aushedarmah reaches the age of thirty, the sun will remain in
the noonday position, only this time for six days. Evil will again be
subdued, but not entirely conquered. At the end of this period, no
one will eat meat anymore and, as vegetarians, the people will be
less aggressive.

But while Aushedarmah is on earth, the evil dragon Azhidahaka
will awaken from his sleep in a cave and terrorize the earth, killing

one third of all humans and animals. However, the ancient hero of the Persians, Keresaspa, will be resurrected by the Lord and slay this beast. Good will again be temporarily ascendant over evil.

The third and last savior, Saoshyant, will appear one thousand years after that; it is he who will herald the final judgment of the living and the dead, as well as the unchallenged rule of the Wise Lord over all things. He too will be born of a virgin in the same manner as the first two saviors. All the world will know him as the great champion of good on earth. A great flood of molten metal will sweep over the earth, killing the wicked in great pain; for the righteous, it will seem like a refreshing warm bath.

After this purge of the earth, the bodies and souls of all who have ever lived will be rejoined in the resurrection. After this will come the Final Judgment. The Wise Lord will appear out of the heavens, attended by angels. His light will be reflected in all those who follow good; the righteous will shine like the sun. The evil, on the other hand, will be seen for all the filth that they are.

It is Saoshyant who will preside over the last judgment. The wicked humans and Ahriman, the Evil One, will be consigned to hell forever, even as the Wise Lord rules uncontested over the universe. All death, disease, and suffering shall cease forever. The earth will be re-created and the blessed will enjoy immortality in a new Paradise.

Take heart, O righteous ones, and live in hope! ♦

THE ISLAMIC APOCALYPTIC MYTH

NOTE: For Muslims the Koran (or Qu'ran) is not myth, nor is it even the word of God revealed and written by man. Rather, Muslims believe their Scripture to be the actual words of God dictated to the prophet Muhammad.

In the name of Allah, the Compassionate, the Merciful. When that which is coming comes—and no soul shall then deny its coming—some shall be abased and others exalted.

When the earth shakes and quivers and the mountains crumble away and scatter into fine dust, you shall be divided into three multitudes: those on the right (blessed shall be those on the right!); those on the left (damned shall be those on the left!); and those to the fore (foremost shall be those!). Such are they that shall be brought near to their Lord in the gardens of delight: a whole multitude from the men of old, but only a few from the later generations.

They shall recline on jewelled couches face to face, and there shall wait upon them immortal youths with bowls and ewers and a cup of purest wine (that will neither pain their heads nor take away their reason); with fruits of their own choice and flesh of fowls that they relish. And theirs shall be the dark-eyed houris,* chaste as hidden pearls; a guerdon for their deeds.

There they shall hear no idle talk, no sinful speech, but only the greeting, "Peace, peace."

Those on the right hand—happy shall those be on the right hand! They shall recline on couches raised on high in the shade of thornless sidrahs and clusters of [bananas]; amidst gushing waters and abundant fruits, unforbidden, never-ending.

We created the houris and made them virgins, loving companions for those on the right hand: a multitude from the men of old, and a multitude from the later generations.

As for those on the left hand (wretched shall be those on the left hand!) they shall dwell amidst scorching winds and seething water; in the shade of pitch black smoke, neither cool nor refreshing. For they have lived in comfort and persisted in the heinous sin [of idolatry] saying: "When we are once dead and turned to dust and bones, shall we, with all our forefathers, be raised to life?" [from Sura 56].

The day shall surely come when you shall see the true believers, men and women, with their light shining before them and on their right hands, and a voice saying to them: "Rejoice this day. You shall enter gardens watered by running streams in which you shall abide forever." That is the supreme triumph.

On that day the hypocrites, both men and women, will say to the true believers: "Wait for us that we may borrow some of your

---

*The houris are perfect and beautiful women for the pleasure of the righteous in the Islamic Paradise.

light." But they will answer: "Go back and seek some other light!"

A wall with a gate shall be set between them. Inside there shall be mercy, and out, to the fore, the scourge of hell. They will call out to them saying, "Were we not on your side?" "Yes," they will reply, "but you tempted yourselves, you wavered and you doubted, and were deceived by your own desires until Allah's will was one and the Dissembler tricked you about Allah. Today no ransom shall be accepted from you or the unbelievers. Hell shall be your home: you have justly earned it, a dismal end" [from Sura 57]. ♦

The Hadith

NOTE: The Hadith is to Islam what, roughly, the Talmud is to Judaism. The Hadith is not part of the Koran, but rather a collection of oral traditions attributed to the Prophet Muhammad and his companions.

The companion of the holy prophet Muhammad asked him what the signs would be of the end of the world.

The prophet told him of this terrible time, about which much is written in the Holy Koran: People will no longer study the Koran but will spend all of their time seeking material wealth, pleasure, and worldly power. There will be an epidemic in Jedda, a famine in Medina, and a plague in the holy city of Mecca. There will be earthquakes, unlike any ever seen before, throughout the entire Maghreb [North Africa]; lethal thunderstorms will strike throughout Turkey and Iran; Iraq will be the domain of murderous bandits. The peoples of the Far East will be wiped out through a succession of floods. The morality that binds societies together will be completely loosened—it will be every man for himself. At that time, the Dajjal—the Antichrist—will appear, riding on a donkey and subjecting all the peoples of the earth to his rule.

Dajjal will rule but forty days through terror and force. Then God will send Jesus from heaven on a white horse, with a lance in his hand, to subdue Dajjal. The remnant of faithful believers will form a powerful army of God to assist Jesus in the defeat of the Dajjal. Dajjal will be defeated but not killed, until God causes the feet of Dajjal to be fixed firmly to the earth; then Jesus will administer the fatal blow.

A throne will come down from heaven and Jesus will reign over the earth for forty years of perfect peace and justice. Each of these forty years will be twenty-six months in length, rather than the usual twelve—so they will actually be like eighty-seven of our present years.

At the end of his reign, Jesus will go to Jerusalem and pray at the Mosque of the Dome of the Rock, where God will take Jesus into heaven. Seven days after the arrival of the soul of Jesus in heaven, the monstrous Gog and Magog, monsters who had been imprisoned by Alexander [Iskandar] the Great, will break free, ruining civilization.

At this point God will call two angels into service. The first of these is Azrail, the angel of death. For believers, Azrail will appear as a beautiful star that calls them to their rest in a sweet, gentle voice. To the wicked, in contrast, Azrail will appear as a monster that rips their souls out of their bodies.

Another angel, Israfil, has the duty of blowing the trumpet of the last day. As all of the righteous will have been killed by the wicked at this point, all those left on earth will deserve the doom that begins with this trumpet call. Tired of the wickedness, God will tell Israfil to blow the horn and the mountains will crumble into dust. At the end of this destruction, forty years of terrible earthquakes and storms, the trumpet will sound again. At this sound, the souls of the faithful dead will search for their bodies to be reunited for the resurrection. Then, when souls and bodies are joined, the faithful will spend forty years praising Allah.

At the third blast of the trumpet, the holy prophet Muhammad will return to earth on his horse, Burak, led by a rope held by the angel Gabriel. All will then see the great scales of judgment descend from heaven. The throne of God will then be visible to all. There will be no secrets: The secret sins of everyone, believer and unbeliever, will be known to all. These secret sins will be weighed on the left side of the scale, and all good deeds, no matter how small, will be weighed on the right. If the right outweighs the left, then the soul is saved; if the opposite is true, the soul will be damned.

But what of those whose good deeds and evil deeds balance equally? These souls may be saved on that terrible day by crying out to God for mercy. If the soul cries in sincerity, honestly sorry for its sins, a note written in God's own hand will fall onto the right side of the scale and paradise will be opened for that soul.

The Judgment will last only one hour.

Then the righteous and wicked alike will cross the bridge into Paradise, which is as thin as a hair. The righteous will cross it with ease, even as the wicked fall down into the chasm of hell. Some will be able, with much difficulty and a heart of sincere repentence, to crawl up out of hell. These and all faithful ones will drink of the sweet waters of Muhammad's lake and never know sorrow, thirst, hunger, or any suffering. ◆

MAITREYA
(Tibet, Korea, Mongolia)

In a future time there will be great changes in the world. The ocean will dry up partially, causing the Indian subcontinent to be larger and flatter at present. People will thus have an easier time traveling around Asia, and the subcontinent will be large enough to hold all of the world's people. The world will suddenly be filled with abundant food. Human beings who were hostile one day will suddenly be kind to one another. There will be only three problems among human beings—hunger, elimination of waste, and growing old—sickness and war will be obsolete. But people will live to be very old indeed, not even marrying until they are 150, and living to be about 500.

There will be one ruler over all the world. Named Shankha, he will spread the Dharma of the Buddha as law throughout the world. During his reign, the future Buddha, Maitreya, will be born. His mother will be pregnant with him for ten months and he will emerge from the womb completely clean. At his birth he will announce that this is his last birth—only Nirvana (the supreme enlightenment) awaits him. As did the first great Buddha, the Buddha Shakyamuni, or Gautama Buddha, before him, Maitreya will contemplate the nature of things and see the illusory aspect of mortal life. He will then have eighty-four thousand people following him, attending him at all times. At that time, Brahma, the Eternal God, will announce the truth of the Dharma out of heaven in his own voice.

This period will witness the end of all selfishness and illusion. Possessions will mean nothing at all. No one will be concerned about anything but achieving enlightenment. People will no longer live according to their passions, but lead a life of perfect chastity, such as monks do now. For there will be no need to produce children anymore, given the long life span. In fact, Maitreya himself will preach for over sixty thousand years in this environment of perfect harmony, after which he will leave the earth to go to his Nirvana, absolute union with God. The eternal law, the Dharma, will be in force for an additional ten thousand years, and all humans will achieve Nirvana.

All persons will be freed of every suffering and pain; all obstacles to human understanding of the Dharma will be removed. At the end of the ten thousand years, Brahma himself will teach the universal truth directly to humankind, revealing things concealed even from the Buddhas. ◆

RAGNAROK: THE TWILIGHT OF THE GODS
(*Norse*)

Ever since Odin bartered his eye for a drink from Mimir's well of wisdom, he had known of the inevitable destruction of the universe, including himself and all the gods. The beginning of the end will be marked by signs in nature. Watch the animals carefully—one year, they will begin gathering food for the winter beginning in early spring—for they know what is coming before humans do. Winter will come that year and last for three seasons—from the autumn of one year to the beginning of the next autumn. These will be the coldest winters ever known. There will be three such winters, punctuated only by three months of thawing, before the Twilight of the Gods. Then the earth will begin to quake as never before. Earthquakes will strike in places that have never known them, causing the sea to rise up and flood the land. These earthquakes will be caused by Loki, the Evil One, breaking loose.

Loki, as you may remember, is the evil giant who is responsible for the death of Odin's son, Baldur. As punishment, the gods chained him to a rock. As the chains grow rusty and weak, Loki will churn about to break free, causing these horrible earthquakes. For centuries, he has been seething with thoughts of revenge against the gods. When he breaks free, he will join all other enemies of the gods to invade their home, Asgard.

On earth, human beings will die by the multitudes from hunger, the cold, flooding, earthquakes, and other calamities. But, unlike before, Odin will be unable to help them.

For Odin will have to fight for his own survival. Heimdall, the sentinel of the gods, will sound blasts on his battle horn announcing the invasion of Asgard by Loki and the other foes. All creatures will hear these trumpet blasts and shake with terror.

Fenris the wolf, who had been subdued by the gods during the earliest times, will break free. The great serpent of the sea will rise up. Loki and the sons of Muspelheim, the dwarves, will ride over the rainbow and attack the gods, leaving a wake of fire that will destroy the earth. Thor the thunder god will kill the great sea serpent; in the last moments, the serpent will spit venom that slays Thor. Surtur, leader of the armies against the gods, will throw great blasts of fire on the earth that will devour anything that remains alive. The sun will no longer shine, and the stars will fall from heaven.

Odin himself will be slain, as will all the gods. Not one of their enemies will survive either. This final war will be a war without victors or vanquished, with all combatants perishing.

But with the destruction of the world completed, Alfadur ("All Father"), the great and only eternal God, the God behind the gods, will be the only one left. With his own hands he will fashion a new earth, new creatures, and a man and a woman to start the human race anew. ◆

NORTH AMERICAN APOCALYPTIC MYTHS

Pawnee

Tirawa Atius is the lord of all things and it is he alone who determines fate. At the beginning of the world, he set a large bull buffalo in the sky to the far northwest. With the passage of each year, the bull loses one hair; when all these hairs are gone, the world will end. As that hair falls, there will be widespread meteor showers, and the sun and moon will become dim.

In the beginning, Tirawa Atius appointed the North Star and the South Star to control fate. The North Star once spoke directly to the Pawnee and told them that the South Star moved just a little bit to the north with each passing year. When the South Star catches up with the North Star, then the world will end.

The command for the final destruction of the world is in the hands of the four gods of the directions. The West will issue the command that the world be destroyed and the East will obey. Then the stars in heaven will fall to the new earth and become people. The people left in this world at the time of destruction will fly high into the sky and become stars themselves. ◆

Cherokee

The earth floats like a great island on the waters and is held up by rawhide at the four points of the compass. This rawhide is attached to a ceiling of rock crystal in the heavens. Sooner or later, the rawhide will grow old and crack, and when it breaks, the earth will plunge back under the waters and all life will end. Then, as happened the last time, the Creator will pull the earth back out of the water and re-create the world. ♦

THE OLD TESTAMENT
(*Daniel 11:40–12:13*)

When the time comes for the End, the king of the South will try conclusions with him [the Great Persecutor]; but the king of the North will come storming down on him with chariots, cavalry, and a large fleet. He will invade countries, overrun them and drive on. He will invade the Land of Splendor and many will fall, but Edom, Moav and what remains of the sons of Ammon will escape him.

He will reach out to attack countries: the land of Egypt will not escape him. The gold and silver treasuries and all the valuables of Egypt will lie in his power. Libyans and Cushites will be at his feet: but reports coming from the East and the North will worry him, and in great fury he will set out to bring ruin and complete destruction to many. He will pitch the tents of his royal headquarters between the sea and the mountains of the Holy Splendor. Yet he will come to his end—there will be no help for him.

At that time Michael [the archangel] will stand up, the great prince who mounts guard over your people. There is going to be a time of great distress, unparalleled since nations first came into existence. When the time comes, your own people will be spared, all those whose names are found written in the book. Of those who lie sleeping in the dust of the earth, many will awake, some to everlasting life, some to shame and everlasting disgrace. The learned shall shine as brightly as the vault of heaven, and those who have instructed many in virtue, as stars for all eternity.

But you, Daniel, must keep these words secret and the book sealed until the time of the End. Many will wander this way and that, and wickedness will go on increasing. ♦

THE NEW TESTAMENT

NOTE: Christian theologians refer to the discussion of the End as the "eschaton."

Excerpts from the Gospel of Mark

The Eschatological Discourse (Mark 13:1–4)

As he [Jesus] was leaving the Temple one of his disciples said to him, "Look at the size of those stones, Master! Look at the size of those buildings." And Jesus said to him, "You see these great buildings? Not a single stone will be left on another: everything will be destroyed."

And while he was sitting facing the Temple, on the Mount of Olives, Peter, James, John and Andrew questioned him privately, "Tell us when is this going to happen and what sign will there be that all this is about to be fulfilled?"

The Beginning of Sorrows (Mark 13:5–32)

Then Jesus began to tell them, "Take care that no one deceives you. Many will come using my name and saying, 'I am he,' and they will deceive many. When you hear of wars and rumors of wars, do not be alarmed, this is something that must happen, but the end will not be yet. For nation will fight against nation, and kingdom against kingdom. There will be earthquakes here and there; there will be famines. This is the beginning of the birth pangs.

"Be on your guard: they will hand you over to sanhedrins;* you will be beaten in synagogues; and you will stand before governors and kings for my sake, to bear witness before them, since the Good News must be proclaimed to all the nations.

"And when they lead you away to hand you over, do not worry beforehand about what to say; no, say whatever is given you when the time comes, because it is not you who will be speaking: it will be the Holy Spirit. Brother will betray brother to death, and the father his child; children will rise against their parents and have them put to death. You will be hated by all men on account of my name; but the man who stands firm to the end will be saved.

"When you see the disastrous abomination set up where it ought not to be ... then those in Judaea must escape to the mountains; if a man is on the housetop, he must not come down to go into the house to collect any of his belongings; if a man is in the fields, he must not turn back to fetch his cloak. Alas for those with child, or with babies at the breast, when those days come! Pray that this may not be in winter. For in those days there will be such distress as, until now, there has not been equalled since the beginning when God created the world, nor will there ever be again. And if the Lord had not shortened that time, no one would have survived; but he did shorten the time, for the sake of the elect whom he chose.

"And if anyone says to you then, 'Look, here is the Christ,' or, 'Look he is there,' do not believe it, for false Christs and false prophets will arise and produce signs and portents to deceive the elect, if that were possible. You therefore must be on your guard. I have forewarned you of everything.

"But in those days, after that time of distress, the sun will be darkened, the moon will lose its brightness, the stars will come falling and the powers in the heavens will be shaken. And then they shall see the Son of Man coming in the clouds with great power and glory, then too he will send the angels to gather the chosen from the four winds, from the ends of the world to the ends of heaven.

*Sanhedrins were the Jewish ecclesiastical courts.

"Take the fig tree as a parable; as soon as its twigs grow supple and its leaves come out, you will know that summer is near. So with you when you see these things happening; know that he is near, at the very gates. I tell you solemnly, before this generation has passed away all these things will have taken place. Heaven and earth will pass away, but my words will not pass away.

"But as for that day or hour, nobody knows it, neither the angels of heaven, nor the Son; no one but the Father."

Excerpts from the Apocalypse (The Revelation to John)

The Beast 666 (Revelation 13:15–18)

It was allowed to breathe life into this statue so that the statue of the beast was able to speak, and to have anyone who refused to worship the statue of the beast put to death. He compelled everyone—small and great, rich and poor, slave and citizen—to be branded on the right hand or on the forehead, and made it illegal for anyone to buy or sell anything unless he had been branded with the name of the beast or with the number of its name.

There is need for shrewdness here: if anyone is clever enough he may interpret the number of the beast: it is the number of a man, the number 666.

The Final Battle of the End (Revelation 19:11–22)

And now I saw heaven open, and a white horse appear; its rider was called Faithful and True; he is a judge with integrity, a warrior for justice. His eyes were the flames of fire, and his head was crowned with many coronets; the name written on him was known only to himself, his cloak was soaked in blood. He is known by the name, The Word of God. Behind him, dressed in linen of dazzling white rode the armies of heaven on white horses. From his mouth came a sharp sword to strike the pagans with; he is the one who will rule them with an iron scepter, and tread out the wine of Almighty God's fierce anger. On his cloak and on his thigh there was a name written: The King of Kings and the Lord of Lords.

I saw an angel standing in the sun, and he shouted aloud to all the birds that were flying high overhead in the sky, "Come here. Gather together at the great feast that God is giving. There will be the flesh of kings for you, and the flesh of great generals and heroes, the flesh of horses and their riders and of all kinds of men, citizens and slaves, small and great."

The Judgment (Revelation 20:11–15)

Then I saw a great white throne and the One who was sitting on it. In his presence, earth and sky vanished, leaving no trace. I saw the dead, both great and small, standing in front of his throne, while the book of life was opened, and other books opened, which were the record of what they had done in their lives, by which the dead were judged.

The sea gave up all the dead that were in it; Death and Hades were emptied of all the dead that were in them; and every one was judged according to the way in which he had lived. Then Death and Hades were thrown into the burning lake. This burning lake is the second death; and anybody whose name could not be found written in the book of life was thrown into the burning lake.

The Heavenly Jerusalem (Revelation 21:1–8)

Then I saw a new heaven and a new earth, the first heaven and the first earth had disappeared now, and there was no longer any sea. I saw the holy city, and the new Jerusalem, coming down from God out of heaven, as beautiful as a bride all dressed for her husband. Then I heard a loud voice call from the throne, "You see this city? Here God lives among men. He will make his home among them; they shall be his people and He will be their God; his name is God-With-Them. He shall wipe away all tears from their eyes; there will be no more death, and no more mourning or sadness. The world of the past has gone."

Then the One sitting on the throne spoke: "Now I am making the whole of creation new," he said. "Write this: that what I am saying is sure and will come true." And then he said, "It is already done. I am the Alpha and the Omega, the Beginning and the End. I will give water from the well of life free to anybody who is thirsty; it is the rightful inheritance of the one who proves victorious; and I will be his God and he is a son to me. But the legacy for cowards, for those who break their word, or worship obscenities, for murderers and fornicators, and for fortunetellers, idolaters, or any other sort of liars, is the second death in the burning lake of sulphur."

Excerpt from the Second Letter of Paul to the Thessalonians (2 Thessalonians 2:1–12)

To turn now brothers to the coming of our Lord Jesus Christ and how we shall all be gathered around him: please do not get excited too soon or alarmed by any prediction or rumor or any letter claiming to come from us, implying that the day of the Lord has already arrived. Never let anyone deceive you in that way.

It cannot happen until the Great Revolt has taken place and the Rebel, the Lost One, has appeared. This is the Enemy, the one who claims to be so much greater than all that men call "god," so much greater than anything that is worshipped, that he enthrones himself in God's sanctuary and claims that he is God. Surely you remember me telling you about this when I was with you? And you know, too, what is still holding him back from appearing before his appointed time. Rebellion is at work already, but in secret, and the one who is holding it back has first to be removed before the Rebel appears openly. The Lord will kill him with the breath of his mouth and will annihilate him with this glorious appearance at his coming.

But when the Rebel comes, Satan will set to work: there will be all kinds of miracles and a deceptive show of signs and portents, and everything evil that can deceive those who are bound for destruction because they would not grasp the love of the truth which could have saved them. The reason why God is sending a power to delude them and make them believe what is untrue is to condemn all who refuse to believe in the truth and chose wickedness instead.

PART THREE

THE MODERN READINGS OF MYTH

I use the concept "myth" in the sense in which it is customarily used in the science of history and of religion. Myth is the report of an occurrence or an event in which supernatural, superhuman forces or persons are at work (which explains why it is often defined simply as history of the gods). Mythical thinking is the opposite of scientific thinking. It refers certain phenomena and events to supernatural, "divine" powers, whether these are thought of dynamistically or are represented as personal spirits or gods. It thus separates off certain phenomena and events as well as certain domains from things and occurrences of the world that are familiar and can be grasped and controlled. Scientific thinking, by contrast, is preformed in the "work thinking" that also reckons with a closed continuum of cause and effect; in fact, scientific thinking is basically the radical development of such work thinking and presupposes both the unity of the world and the lawfully regulated order of things and occurrences in the world.

—Rudolf Bultmann, German theologian and Bible critic,
New Testament and Mythology & Other Basic Writings,
selected, edited, and translated by Schubert M. Ogden

12. Views of Myth and Meaning

Jeremiah Curtin (1835–1906)

Nineteenth-century Irish scholar of myth.

> The reason is of ancient date why myths have come, in vulgar
> estimation, to be synonymous with lies; though true myths—and
> there are many such—are the most comprehensive and splendid
> statements of truth known to man. A myth, even when it contains
> a universal principle, expresses it in a particular form, using
> with its peculiar personages the language and accessories of a
> particular people, with the connected accidents of time and
> place, are familiar and dear, receive the highest enjoyment from
> the myth, and the truth goes with it as the soul with the body.

Sigmund Freud (1856–1939)

Austrian father of psychoanalysis.

> I believe that a large portion of the mythological conception of
> the world which reaches far into the most modern religions, is
> nothing but psychology projected to the outer world.

Ananda Coomaraswamy (1877–1947)

Twentieth-century Indian philosopher.

Myth embodies the nearest approach to absolute truth that can be expressed in words.

Nikolay Berdyayev (1874–1948)

Russian-born Christian existentialist philosopher.

I am therefore inclined to believe that the mysteries of the divine as well as of the human and world life, with all their complexity of historical destiny, admit of solution only through concrete mythology. The knowledge of the divine life is not attainable by means of abstract philosophical thought based on the principles of formalist or rationalist logic, but only by means of a concrete myth which conceives the divine life as a passionate destiny of concrete and active persons. . .

Carl Gustav Jung (1875–1961)

Swiss pioneer of psychoanalysis.

Myth is the natural and indispensable intermediate stage between unconscious and conscious cognition.

. . . it struck me what it means to live with a myth, and what it means to live without one. "Myth," writes a Church Father, "is what is believed always, everywhere by everybody; hence the man who thinks he can live without myth or outside it, is an exception. He is like one uprooted, having no true link with either the past, or the ancestral life within him, or yet with contemporary society.

George Santayana (1863–1952)

Spanish-born American philosopher.

The primitive habit of thought survives in mythology, which is an observation of things encumbered with all they suggest to a dramatic fancy. It is neither conscious poetry nor valid science, but the common root and raw material of both.

Alan Watts (1915–1973)

Twentieth-century British writer and expositor of Zen Buddhism to the West.

> Every positive statement about ultimate things must be made in the suggestive form of myth, of poetry. For in this realm the direct and indicative form of speech can only say "Neti, neti" (Sanskrit for "No, no"), since what can be described and categorized must always belong to the conventional realm.
>
> Myth is a symbolic story which demonstrates the inner meaning of the universe and of human life.

Thomas Mann (1875–1955)

German novelist, winner of the 1929 Nobel Prize in Literature.

> It makes clear that the typical is actually the mythical, and that one may as well say "lived myth" as "lived life".... The mythical interest is as native to psychoanalysis as the psychological interest is to all creative writing. Its penetration into the childhood of the individual soul is at the same time a penetration into the childhood of mankind, into the primitive and mythical.... For myth is the foundation of life; it is the timeless schema, the pious formula into which life flows when it reproduces its traits out of the unconscious.... What is gained is an insight into the higher truth contained in the actual; a smiling knowledge of the eternal, the ever-being and authentic; a knowledge of the schema in which and according to which the supposed individual lives, unaware, in his naive belief in himself as unique in space and time, of the extent to which his life is but formula and repetition and his path marked out for him by those who trod it before him.

Friedrich von Schlegel (1772–1829)

German romanticist critic and philosopher.

> Mythology is such a poem of nature. In its fabric the supreme values are actually shaped by art; all is connection and transformation, related and translated, and this relation and translation constitutes its peculiar procedure, its inner life, its method.

F. Max Müller (1823–1900)

German-born British linguist, scholar of myth, and translator of the Hindu scriptures.

> Mythology is inevitable, it is natural, it is an inherent necessity of language, if we recognize in language the outer form and manifestation of thought; it is in fact the dark shadow that language throws upon thought, and which can never disappear until language becomes entirely commensurate with thought, which it never will. Mythology, no doubt, breaks out more fiercely during the early periods of the history of human thought, but it never disappears altogether. Depend upon it, there is mythology now as there was in the time of Homer, only we do not perceive it, and because we ourselves live in the very shadow of it, and because we all shrink from the full meridian light of truth . . . Mythology, in the highest sense, is the power exercised by language on thought in every possible sphere of mental activity.

Bruno Bettelheim (1903–1990)

German-born American psychiatrist and interpreter of fairy tales.

> Plato—who may have understood better what forms the mind of men than do some of our contemporaries who want their children exposed only to "real" people and everyday events—knew what intellectual experiences make for true humanity. He suggested that the future citizens of his ideal republic begin their literary education with the telling of myths, rather than with mere facts

or so-called rational teachings. Even Aristotle, master of pure reason, said: "The friend of wisdom is also a friend of myth."

Modern thinkers who have studied myths and fairy tales from a philosophical or psychological viewpoint arrive at the same conclusion, regardless of their original persuasion. Mircea Eliade, for one, describes the stories as models for human behavior [that] by that very fact give meaning and value to life.

Robert Graves (1895–1985)

British poet, author, and scholar of myth with Raphael Patai, Israeli scholar.

Myths are dramatic stories that form a sacred charter either authorizing the continuance of ancient institutions, customs, rites and beliefs in the area where they are current, or approving alterations.

Bronislaw Malinowski (1884–1942)

Polish-born British anthropologist.

I maintain that there exists a special class of stories, regarded as sacred, embodied in rituals, morals, and social organization, and which form an integral and active part of primitive culture. These stories live not by idle interest, not as fictitious or even as true narrative, but are to the natives a statement of a primeval, greater and more relevant reality, by which the present life, fates, and activities of mankind are determined, the knowledge of which supplies man with the motive for ritual and moral actions, as well as indications of how to perform them.

Studied alive, myth . . . is not symbolic, but a direct expression of the subject matter; it is not an explanation in satisfaction of a scientific interest, but a narrative resurrection of primeval reality, told in satisfaction of deep religious wants, moral cravings, social submissions, assertions, even practical requirements. Myth fulfills in primitive culture an indispensable function: it expresses, enhances and codifies belief; it safeguards and enforces morality; it vouches for the efficiency of ritual and contains practical rules for the guidance of man. Myth is thus a vital ingredient of human civilization; it is not an idle tale, but a hard worked active force; it is not an intellectual explanation or artistic imagery, but a pragmatic charter of primitive faith and moral wisdom.

Claude Lévi-Strauss (1908–)

French anthropologist and founder of Structuralism.

We are able, through scientific thinking, to achieve mastery over nature ... myth is unsuccessful in giving man more material power over the environment. However, it gives man, very importantly, the illusion that he can understand the universe and that he does understand the universe.

Joseph Campbell (1904–1987)

American scholar of myth.

Throughout the inhabited world, in all times and under every circumstance, the myths of man have flourished, and have been the living inspiration of whatever else appeared out of the human body and mind. It would not be too much to say that myth is the secret opening through which the inexhaustible energies of the cosmos pour into human cultural manifestation. Religions, philosophies, arts, the social form of primitive and historic man, prime discoveries of science and technology, the very dreams that blister sleep, boil up from the basic, magic ring of myth.

Hans Küng (1928–)

Contemporary Roman Catholic theologian.

... myth, legend, images and symbols may not be criticized because they are myths, legends, images and symbols. ... Thus, even when the mythical element is simply eliminated [from Christianity]—as becomes evident in the theology of the Enlightenment and liberalism—it is at the expense of the Christian message, which is thrown out together with the myth.

Carlos Fuentes (1928–)

Contemporary Mexican author and essayist.

Myth is a past with a future, exercising itself in the present.

Louis-Auguste Sabatier (1839–1901)

French Protestant theologian.

> Creer un mythe, c'est a dire entrevoit derriére la réalité sensible une realité supérieure, est le signe le plus manifeste de la grandeur de l'âme humaine et la preuve de sa faculté de croissance et de developpement infinis.

> To create a myth, that is to say, to venture behind the reality of the sense to find a superior reality, is the most manifest sign of the greatness of the human soul and the proof of its capacity for infinite growth and development.

Rudolf Bultmann (1884–1976)

German theologian and "Form Critic" of the Bible.

> The real point of myth is not to give an objective world picture; what is expressed in it, rather, is how we human beings understand ourselves in our world. Thus, myth does not want to be interpreted in cosmological terms but in anthropological terms—or, better, in existentialist* terms. Myth talks about the power or the powers that we think we experience as the ground and limit of our world and of our own action and passion. It talks about these powers in such a way, to be sure, as to bring them within the circle of the familiar world, its things and forces, and within the circle of human life, its affections, motives and possibilities. This is the case, say, when it talks about a world egg or a world tree in order to portray the ground and source of the

---

*This refers to the philosophy of the meaning of human existence. In this context, one might also say "in terms of human feeling and experience."

world in a graphic way or when it talks about the wars of the gods from which the arrangements and circumstances of the familiar world have all arisen. Myth talks about the unworldly as worldly, the gods as human.

What is expressed in myth is the faith that the familiar and disposable world in which we live does not have its ground and aim in itself but that its ground and limit lie beyond all that is familiar and disposable and that this is all constantly threatened and controlled by the uncanny powers that are its ground and limit. In unity with this myth also gives expression to the knowledge that we are not lords of ourselves, that we are not only dependent within the familiar world but that we are especially dependent on the powers that hold sway beyond all that is familiar, and that it is precisely in dependence on them that we can become free from familiar powers.

. . . Myth talks about gods as human beings, and about their actions as human actions, with the difference that the gods are represented as endowed with superhuman power and their action as unpredictable and able to break through the natural run of things. Myth thus makes the gods (or God) into human beings with superior power, and it does this even when it speaks of God's omnipotence and omniscience, because it does not distinguish these qualitatively from human power and knowledge but only quantitatively.

In short, myth objectifies the transcendent into the immanent, and thus also into the disposable, as becomes evident when cult* more and more becomes action calculated to influence the deity by averting its wrath and winning its favor.

Reinhold Niebuhr (1892–1971)

American Protestant theologian.

A vision of the whole is possible only if it is assumed that human history has meaning; and modern empiricism is afraid of that assumption. Meaning can be attributed to history only by a mythology.

—*Reflections on the End of an Era*

---

*The word *cult* is used here to mean a system of practice or worship. This is not the same, necessarily, as the popular use of the word.

Myth alone is capable of picturing the world as a realm of coherence and meaning without defying the facts of incoherence. Its world is coherent because all facts in it are related to some central source of meaning; but it is not rationally coherent because the myth is not under the abortive necessity of relating all things to each other in terms of immediate rational unity.

—An Interpretation of Christian Ethics

The essential truth in a great religious myth cannot be gauged by the immediate occasion which prompted it; nor apprehended in its more obvious intent. The story of the Tower of Babel may have been prompted by the fact that an unfinished temple of Marduk in Babylon excited the imagination of the surrounding desert people, who beheld its arrested majesty, to speculate on the reason for its unfinished state. Its immediate purpose may have been to give a mythical account of the origin of the world's multiplicity of languages and cultures. Neither its doubtful origin nor the fantastic character of its purported history will obscure its essential message to those who are wise enough to discern the permanently valid insights in primitive imagination.

—Beyond Tragedy

Paul Tillich (1886–1965)

German-born American Protestant theologian.

Mythological language seems to be equally old, combining the technical grasp of objects with the religious experience of a quality of the encountered that has highest significance even for daily life, but transcends it in such a way that it demands another language, that of the religious symbols and their combination, the myth. Religious language is symbolic-mythological, even when it interprets facts and events which belong to the realm of the ordinary technical encounter with reality. The contemporary confusion of these two kinds of language is the cause of one of the most serious inhibitions for the understanding of religion, as it was in the prescientific period for the understanding of the ordinarily encountered reality, the object of technical use.

The language of myth, as well as the language of the ordinary technical encounter with reality, can be translated into other kinds of language, the poetic and the scientific. Like religious language, poetic language lives in symbols, but poetic symbols express another quality of man's encounter with reality than religious symbols.

13. Parallel Myths and Ways of Interpreting Them

THE DISCOVERY OF PARALLEL MYTHS

The great historical encounters between Europeans and the various peoples of Africa, Asia, and the Americas had many wide-reaching consequences. Perhaps the most interesting—and, to the early explorers, astounding—result was the recognition that cultures vastly separated from them by time and geography had religious practices and myths strikingly similar to their own.

When the Spaniards first arrived in the New World, for example, they were amazed by the many parallels that existed between the indigenous religions and Roman Catholicism. In comparing the faith of Spain with that of the Aztecs of Mexico, the nineteenth-century American historian William Prescott wrote in his book *The Conquest of Mexico*:

> A more extraordinary coincidence may be traced with Christian rites, in the ceremony of naming their children. The lips and bosom of the infant was [*sic*] sprinkled with water and "The Lord was implored to permit the holy drops to wash away the sin that was given to it before the foundations of the world; so that . the child might be born anew." We are reminded of Christian morals in more than one of their prayers, in which they used

267

regular forms. "Wilt thou blot us out O Lord forever? Is this
punishment intended not for our reformation but for our destruction?" Again, "Impart to us, out of thy great mercy, thy gifts
which we are not worthy to receive through our own merits."

... The secrets of the confessional were held inviolate, and
penances were imposed of much the same kind as those en-
joined in the Roman Catholic Church.

The conquistadores found many parallels to Catholicism among the
people of the Inca empire of Peru and Bolivia. This account is from
Gerald L. Berry's *Religions of the World*:

Rites of baptism and confession were practiced. Infant sacrifice
was replaced by a ritual in which blood was drawn but the life
spared (a practice which should be compared to that of circumcision of males). There is a trace in the story of Abraham and
Isaac in the Old Testament of the Inca custom of offering a son
for the sins of the father. The Incas had a Holy Communion ritual, using a sacred bread called the "sancu" sprinkled with the
blood of a sacrificial sheep [Author's note: the "sheep" was
probably a llama].

On the Great Plains of North America, nineteenth-century American
artist and traveler George Catlin lived among a number of different
tribes, and he found that the rituals of these tribes resembled those
of the Jews as given in the Old Testament. The following is from Catlin's *Letters and Notes on the Manners, Customs and Conditions of the
North American Indians*:

I am deduced to believe thus from the very many customs which
I have witnessed amongst them, that appear to be decidedly
Jewish; and many of them so peculiarly so, that it would not be
impossible, or at all events, exceedingly improbable that two
people in a state of nature should have hit upon them, and practiced them exactly alike.

... The first and most striking fact amongst the North American Indians that refers us to the Jews, is that of worshipping in
all parts, the Great Spirit, or Jehovah, as the Hebrews were ordered to do by divine precept. Instead of a plurality of gods, as
ancient pagans and heathens did—and their idols of their own

formation. The North American Indians are nowheres idolaters—they appeal at once to the Great Spirit, or Jehovah, and know of no mediator, either personal or symbolical.

The Indian tribes are everywhere divided into bands, with chiefs, symbols, badges, etc., and many of their modes of worship I have found exceedingly like those of the Mosaic institution. The Jews had their sanctum sanctorum [the "holy of holies"], and so it may be said that the Indians have, in their council or medicine houses, which are always held as sacred places. Amongst the Indians as amongst the ancient Hebrews, the women are not allowed to worship with the men—and in all cases also, they eat separately.

In their bathing and ablutions, at all seasons of the year, as a part of their religious observances—having separate places for the men and women to perform these immersions, they resemble again [the Jews]. And the custom amongst the women, of absenting themselves during the lunar influences [menstruation] is exactly consonant to Mosaic law. . . . After this season of separation, purification in running water, and anointing, precisely in accordance with the Jewish command, is requisite before she can enter the family lodge. Such is one of the extraordinary observances amongst these people in their wild state. . . .

In their feasts, fastings and sacrifices, they are exceedingly like those ancient people. Many of them have a feast closely resembling the Jewish Passover; and amongst others an occasion much like the Israelitish feast of the Tabernacles, which lasted eight days (when history tells us they carried willow boughs, and fasted several days and nights) making sacrifices of the first fruits and best of everything, closely resembling the sin-offerings and peace-offerings of the Hebrews.

Catlin was careful to point out that he did not necessarily accept the then-popular theory, which is embodied in the Mormon religion today, that the Indians were descendants of the ten lost tribes of Israel, who vanished after the fall of the northern kingdom of Israel; nor did he propose any theory of contact with the ancient Jewish people. But, writing long before the advent of psychiatry or modern anthropology, he did express his astonishment at the similarities between the two.

The German existentialist philosopher Karl Jaspers, as part of his theory of the "axial period" of history (which will be discussed in depth later in this chapter), made note of the amazement of the first Jesuit missionaries in Japan at finding a Japanese Buddhist sect that seemed remarkably like European Lutheranism. This sect, which we now know as "Pure Land" Buddhism, explicitly states its belief in "salvation by grace through faith," in this case, in Amida Buddha. The sinner, in the doctrine of the "Pure Land" sect, is absolutely helpless and has no chance of salvation through his or her own merits, but must trust in the grace of Amida Buddha to be "reborn in the Pure Land," analogous to the Protestant "salvation by grace through faith in Christ."

The European colonists and missionaries developed some curious, even bizarre, theories to explain this phenomenon of parallel beliefs. One common view, especially among the Spanish missionaries in Mexico, was that non-European religions were "satanic" imitations of the "true faith." Another theory, which is not all that far from the psychological theories we are about to consider, is that these beliefs are mainifestations of a once universally received and understood Divine revelation that had become corrupted over time. My personal favorite explanation offered for the similarities between Roman Catholicism and the Peruvian religion was the view that Saint Thomas traveled to Peru via India during the first century A.D.* The nearly identical practices between the Old World and the New became a public obsession during the 19th century, the heyday of the "Lost Tribes of Israel" theory, which was taken very seriously right up until the American Civil War.

By the year 1900, however, serious scholarship had been applied to comparative religion and mythology. This led to two basic approaches to the parallels between the myths of vastly separated cultures. The first approach is that of *diffusion*, which held that the

---

*Garcilaso de la Vega, a Spanish priest, was fascinated by the Peruvian legend of Thunpa, a wise and revered teacher who erected something resembling a cross. De la Vega identified Thunpa as Saint Thomas, who was reputed to have traveled to India during the missionary expansion of the early Christian church. De la Vega believed that Saint Thomas had traveled from India across the Pacific to Peru, where he preached the gospel.

myths were produced in a few myth-creating areas, such as India, and thence passed through contact between cultures during the earliest times. The second is a *psychological* view, whereby the core elements of myth are products of the human psyche and thus universal to all human beings. Today both points of view, as well as a mixture of the two, vie for acceptance.

MYTH AS A HISTORY OF PREHISTORY: THE MATRIARCHAL THEORY

It is generally agreed that myth is largely the product of oral history, passed down from generation to generation. As myth begins with the creation of the world, it is truly "a history of prehistory." Two scholars on the subject, nineteenth-century Swiss classicist Johann Jakob Bachofen and twentieth-century British writer Robert Graves, found within many Greek myths a record—at times thickly veiled, at other times obvious—of a prehistorical battle between a matriarchy (society ruled by women) and the emerging patriarchy (society ruled by men) that supplanted it. For Bachofen and Graves, this is the record of one of the pivotal moments in ancient European history.

As one reads the myths today, one is often struck by both lofty philosophical content and a brutally cruel attitude toward women within the text.

Johann Jakob Bachofen (1815–1887)

Bachofen, a native of Basel, Switzerland, studied law but pursued a career in archaeology and was a scholar of the Greek classics. He was fascinated by mythology, and tried to sift through it for clues to the earliest history of Europe. Bachofen came to the conclusion that there were three clear stages in early European culture. The first was a barbaric stage; this was followed by a matriarchy that, in turn, was supplanted by patriarchy.

In his view, the history of this struggle, subsequent relapses into

the earlier phases of development, and the eventual victory of patriarchy, are all fairly clearly chronicled in many of the myths.

Bachofen called the barbaric stage "hetairism," from the Greek
hetero, meaning "both." In this earliest stage, neither males nor females were dominant in society. This was a period of widespread sexual promiscuity when children did not know their fathers, women
were defenseless, rape took the place of marriage, and family life was
virtually nonexistent. The characteristic goddess in Greek mythology
during this period, according to Bachofen, was Aphrodite, the goddess of love, with no aspect of order or morality.

Next, women banded together for their own defense, leading to the
development of a matriarchal society that replaced the chaos of hetairism. This phase saw the first blossom of civilization, laws, agriculture, and the arts. Love of the mother and worship of a mother
goddess were characteristic of this age, which was symbolized for
Bachofen by Demeter, the goddess of the crops. In an important
Greek myth, Demeter's daughter Kore (or Persephone) is seized by
force from her mother by Hades, the lord of the Underworld. According to Bachofen, the Greek myths of fierce female warriors, the Amazons, are an ancestral memory of women banding together for
protection.

He interpreted the myth of Oedipus as the depiction of the three
phases of this struggle. Oedipus kills the Sphinx, symbol of the old
hetairistic age (the Sphinx was hermaphroditic, having both male and
female genitalia). Oedipus then marries his own mother, who is the
ruler of Thebes. The tragic events describing her downfall were interpreted thus as a thinly veiled account of the transition from matriarchy to patriarchy.

Bachofen, as we shall see, was an influence on Sigmund Freud's
development of the Oedipal theory. Bachofen also may have influenced another psychoanalytic pioneer, the Austrian-American Alfred
Adler. Adler believed that the oppression of women by men as adults
was an overcompensation for the dependence felt by male children
toward their mothers. Graves and Bachofen would have said that this
was a conscious persistence of an unconscious ancestral memory of
a time when adult men were ruled by adult women.

It is interesting to note that in our own time, during the fight for the ratification of the U.S. Equal Rights Amendment, opponents of the bill warned of a type of hetairism (although they never used the word) that would result from the equality of the sexes.

Robert Graves

Robert Graves was, by any standard, a most prolific and varied writer: a classical scholar, critic, novelist, and poet. Son of an Irish writer and his German-born wife, Graves was a gifted linguist, a co-translator of the *Rubaiyat* of Omar Khayyam, and was eulogized in the *London Times* as "the greatest love poet in English since [John] Donne." He is best known today in the United States and Canada for his historical novels about ancient Rome, *I, Claudius* and *Claudius the God*, on which a successful BBC-TV drama series was based.

In his studies of Greek, Germanic, Celtic, and Semitic myths, he concluded that European mythology may only be properly understood in light of a primeval matriarchal period when "the white goddess" (also the title of one of his books) was the universal Earth Mother deity throughout Europe.

Graves felt that the myths that told about the male chief of the Greek gods, Zeus, overthrowing an earlier pantheon of gods, as well as other myths, were the surviving records of the triumph of patriarchy over the matriarchy. Graves was certain of this as a historical fact in ancient Europe, but felt that it might or might not have been the case in other cultures. In the introduction to his celebrated book *The Greek Myths*, he wrote:

> Ancient Europe had no gods. The Great Goddess was regarded as immortal, changeless and omnipotent; and the concept of fatherhood had not been introduced into religious thought. She took lovers, but for pleasure, not to provide her children with a father. Men feared, adored and obeyed the matriarch: the hearth which she tended in a cave or hut being their earliest social centre, and motherhood their prime mystery. . . . There is however, no evidence that, even when women were sovereign in religious matters, men were denied fields in which they might act

without female supervision, though it may well be thought that they adopted many of the "weaker-sex" characteristics hitherto thought to be entrusted to man. They could be trusted to hunt, fish, gather certain foods, mind flocks and herds, and help defend the tribal territory against intruders, so long as they did not transgress matriarchal law.

Graves, like Bachofen, saw the moon as an important religious symbol during the time of matriarchy. The goddess Artemis (Diana in Latin), goddess of the hunt, was also identified with the moon, even as her brother Apollo was identified with the sun in addition to being a patron of arts and culture. The hunt was considered by the Greeks to be a decidedly unfeminine pursuit and her role may well be interpreted as a remnant of earlier matriarchic thinking. Graves considered this indicative of the roles of women in matriarchal Europe as hunters and warriors, before men became mercenaries under the control of the matriarch.

Consistent with the example of the moon goddess Artemis and with Bachofen's theories, Graves contended that time during the matriarchal era was measured by the moon, reflective of the menstrual cycle of women. The change from the lunar-based religion to worship of a sun-god, as well as the switch for measuring time from increments of lunar years to those of solar years, are all illustrations of the transition from matriarchy to patriarchy.

Nor was the end of matriarchy entirely sudden and final; the struggles between the matriarchy and patriarchy still have influences on our culture today. The modern women's movement was seen by Graves as a reaction to the tyranny of the patriarchy that has dominated society since preclassical times.

Graves was mainly a believer in the diffusion theory of explaining parallel myths. This is only natural, as Graves was chiefly concerned with Europe, and saw certain myth-producing centers in the ancient Near East and among the Indo-European invaders of Europe. The Greek myths are the result of "syncretism," a blending of traditions from these two sources of myth.

TRANSITIONAL THINKING IN THE INTERPRETATION OF MYTH

Adolf Bastian (1826–1905)

Bastian, a Berliner, was trained as a physician, but he soon lost interest in the practice of medicine and devoted himself to his real love: ethnology, the study of cultures. He was largely self-educated in this discipline and traveled throughout Asia, Africa, and South America, impressed by the parallels between myths of widely distant cultures. Bastian was one of the first to express this phenomenon as something common to all human beings in all cultures and all periods of history.

Bastian's observations are reflected today in both the modern structural and the psychological schools of myth. Bastian advanced the theory of two components of myth: the Elementary Thought (a series of basic mythic patterns common to all human beings and possibly centered in the brain) and the People's Thought (the specific "coloration" of the Elementary Thought by a given ethnic group at a given time).

As has been pointed out by both the Hindu scholar Ananda Coomaraswamy and the American Joseph Campbell, Bastian's approach is similar to a traditional Hindu view of the parallel myths. There is the *marga*—the universal path, the elements of myth common to all human beings; this is Bastian's Elementary Thought. There is also the *deshi-marga*,* the specific form taken by *marga* in a given place and time.

Leo Frobenius (1873–1938)

Frobenius was an amateur scholar of myth, working by day in an export firm in Bremen, Germany, and studying Greek, anthropology,

---

Deshi is Sanskrit for "of the country." NOTE: *Bangladesh* means "country [desh] of the Bengali people [*Bangla*]."

and mythology by night. During his lifetime, Frobenius was hailed as the world's foremost authority on prehistoric art.

In 1898, Frobenius announced the then-radical theory called "Kulturkreislehre" (the study of "cultural circles"). He believed that there was a central myth-producing region that stretched from West Africa to India, thence through Indonesia and Oceania to the Americas. In other words, Frobenius was the first radical diffusionist.

Frobenius noted many common myths and cultural relationships in this area and believed that parallel myths were the result of cultural exchanges between ancient peoples on a scale beyond that which most scholars had considered possible. For example, it was the nature of the ancient Polynesians to travel vast distances by sea as they populated islands as distant from one another as New Zealand, Tahiti, Easter Island (off the coast of Chile), and Hawaii. It wouldn't be reasonable, thought Frobenius, to assume that the early Polynesians would have turned back after reaching as far as Easter Island; it was only natural that they had gone on, to make contact with Peru, also located on the coast of South America. Likewise, there were currents that could have carried the Hawaiians to the northwestern coast of the United States.

Following the theories of Frobenius, the Norwegian explorer Thor Heyerdahl, in his epic 1947 journey, recounted in *Kon Tiki*, traveled by a South American balsa-wood boat from Peru to Polynesia in an attempt to prove contact between the two cultures was possible. *Kon Tiki* is a term common to the mythologies of Peru, where Con Tiqui is the name of a Creator god, and *tiki* is Polynesian for the image of a god.

Lucien Lévy-Bruhl (1857–1939)

The celebrated French anthropologist Lévy-Bruhl concentrated his studies on the thought processes of "primitive" or "traditional" peoples. He concluded that the "traditional" cultures make no distinction between the natural (or objective) world and myth, nor between myth and history. For the people in such cultures, myth is the only history.

Lévy-Bruhl advanced an influential theory of parallel myths, believing that there were "motifs" or "representations collectives"—shared plots and characters—of myths that were common to all human beings.

Émile Durkheim (1858–1917)

> ... There is something eternal in religion, namely the faith and the cult.
>
> To adore the gods of antiquity was to provide for their material life with the aid of offerings and sacrifices, because the life of this world depended on their life.
>
> Even the most rational and secularized religions cannot and never will dispense with a very particular form of speculation that cannot be scientific.

In the course of this book, we have already encountered several quotes by Émile Durkheim, the great French sociologist who focused on the power of myth to bind societies together. A key function of the myth, according to Durkheim, was to conform the behavior of the individual to the group.

Originally planning to be a rabbi, Durkheim was keenly interested in the impact of myth and religion on culture. He was particularly impressed with the concept of the "civic myth," on which states are founded, as well as with the power of myth as an agent of morality.

Durkheim explained the striking similarities between the myths of diverse historically and geographically distant cultures by a theory he called the "collective conscious." He believed that the basic ingredients of myth, the plots and characters, were the products of a neurologically based function of the human brain, and thus they were common to all human beings. These universal mythic patterns were the "molds" from which myth came, and the specific cultures "poured" their own elements into these molds. In *The Elementary Forms of the Religious Life* Durkheim wrote:

The collective conscious is the highest form of the psychic* life, since it is the consciousness of the consciousness. Being placed outside and above all individual and local contingencies, it sees things in their permanent and essential aspect, which it crystallizes into communicable ideas . . . it alone can furnish the mind with the molds which are applicable to the totality of things and which make it possible to think of them.

With the idea that myth is a product of the collective conscious, a shared "pool" of ancestral memories and images common to all human beings, Durkheim is a direct contributor to the psychological interpretations of myth given by Carl Jung (and expanded by Joseph Campbell), as well as to the "structuralist" school of the interpretation of myth founded by Claude Lévi-Strauss.

Durkheim's own life was marked by great tragedy. A frail, nervous, and sensitive man, he was devastated by World War I. He had been attacked as a "professor of German origin" who taught the "foreign" study of sociology, which was considered an import from the hated Germans. And perhaps there was an anti-Semitic element to these attacks as well. His son, a soldier in the French army, was killed in battle in 1916, and Durkheim died the following year—at only fifty-nine years of age.

As we shall see, Durkheim's contributions to the interpretation of myth were enormous.

Bronislaw Malinowski

Myth as it exists in a savage community, that is, in its primitive form, is not merely a story told but a reality lived. It is not of the nature of fiction, believed to have once happened in primeval times, and continuing ever since to influence the world and human destinies. This myth is to the savage what, to a fully believing Christian, is the Biblical story of Creation, of the Fall, of the Redemption by Christ's Sacrifice on the cross. As our sacred

---

*Durkheim, and later Jung, use the term *psychic* to mean "of the mind," recalling the Greek word *psyche* for "soul." It is not used in the popular sense of the word to mean "paranormal" or "supernatural."

story lives in our ritual, as it governs our faith and controls our conduct, even so does his myth for the savage.

Bronislaw Malinowski was a Polish-born British anthropologist who studied the power of myth in primitive cultures, especially his own field work in the Trobriand Islands of the Pacific. Malinowski saw that "primitive" peoples view myth as the only history that matters, believing all objective life lived today is merely a replay of the events described in the myths.

Malinowski stressed that myth is central to every culture, not merely to traditional cultures. Myth, in his view, is the source of ritual, moral conduct, and social relationships, and is the key element in the worldview of a people.

Malinowski followed the view of Durkheim, but his explanations of parallel myth were strongly influenced by Frobenius; thus Malinowski felt that mythic themes were diffused from a few mythic centers.

PSYCHOLOGICAL THEORIES OF PARALLELISM IN MYTH

Pierre Janet (1859–1947)

We are not to suppose that religion ever could have persisted if the gods had not spoken.

By the year 1900, four different functions of the unconscious mind had been identified and generally accepted by the psychological and medical community:

1. The conservative function: the recording of personal memories.
2. The dissolutive function: things that were once conscious became unconscious (for example, habits) or repressed.
3. The creative function.
4. The "mythopoetic function." This was a term coined by the English literary critic and amateur psychologist Frederick Myers, who was possibly the first to say that mythic and epic stories were a permanent part of the human mental structure, and that

they were constantly composed and played out in the unconscious of the individual.

It is at this time that Sigmund Freud, Pierre Janet, and Carl Jung began or were in the early stages of their careers. In 1900, Sigmund
Freud, then forty-four, published his landmark book *The Interpretation of Dreams*. This was also the year in which speculations were
first advanced that myths were an expression of images in the unconscious mind. Pierre Janet was forty-one in 1900; Jung was a twenty-
five-year-old medical student.

Janet, French psychiatrist and philosopher, was a friend of the
American psychologist and philosopher William James and of the
French philosopher Henri Bergson, who was born in the same year
as Janet. Bergson, in particular, had an impact on Janet, and vice
versa. Janet, like his friend James (author of the celebrated *The Va-
rieties of Religious Experience*), considered religion and mythology vital keys to understanding the human psyche. Although Janet was one
of the most celebrated and respected men of his time, he is all but
forgotten today, overshadowed by such contemporaries as Freud,
Jung, and Adler. Freud never acknowledged any debt to Janet, who
was even angrily denounced by a key Freud disciple and biographer,
Ernest Jones.

Janet, like Jung after him, felt that the key to understanding many
forms of human behavior was to understand the spiritual nature of
human beings. Janet believed that spirituality was an essential part
of being human and not merely a phase in human cultural development to be "outgrown" and supplanted by "scientific thinking." This
latter view was held by Freud. Janet began by studying spiritualist
mediums and, later in life, with the cooperation of the Catholic authorities, he studied "Madeleine," a woman who was seized by flights
of religious ecstasy. "Madeleine" even had the stigmata, actual physical wounds in the form of the imprints of the nails on Christ's hands,
as was said to have happened to many saints throughout history. He
diagnosed such flights of religious ecstasy as a very unique form of
hysteria, but saw this as a possible key to the mythic functions of the
mind.

(Janet, raised in the Roman Catholic faith, was reticent about his own religious ideas and was variously reported to be agnostic and a practicing Catholic. He was, however, deeply impressed by his experiences with "Madeleine." He made certain that his own children were raised in the Protestant faith, though he himself was to be buried in the Catholic faith.)

Janet viewed the functions of the mind as "economies." In other words, he viewed the mind as working to allocate mental resources in the most efficient manner possible in a healthy individual. For example, a person who was coldly logical at the expense of his or her emotions was not well; the converse, in a person whose emotions were dominant, was also true. He believed in a function of mind that he called the *Fonction fabulatrice*, an identifiable thinking process through which myth and fables were composed.

Janet had definite views on the development of myth and religion. Human beings, at the most primitive level, perform rites, which are, in his words, "complicated conducts in which the least details are rigidly fixed." These rites may be "transactional" in nature (for example, sacrifices to a rain god to ensure rain), and after the rites are performed for a time, then myths are composed to justify them and ensure that they are continued. This is a point of view also expressed by Robert Graves. In this stage of religious thinking, animism, the practice of investing natural features such as rocks, lakes, and so forth with a soul, or personifying them, is characteristic. Janet wrote: "Animism springs up spontaneously the moment you first learn the necessity of distinguishing between the man who talks and acts as if he were a friend, and the invisible, inaudible enemy who lurks behind him."

According to Janet, societies need religion and myth in order to function. All societies everywhere have had alliances or "covenants" with God or the gods, in his words, "out of fear, the need for morality, or a need for direction and love." In a society, priests and shamans are a necessity to "make the god speak." When the god fails to speak, the society abandons the myth. Examples of this can be found in a number of societies, most notably the Greeks and Romans. When the Olympian gods ceased to "speak" to the needs of their societies, the people sought out Eastern mystery religions, such as the cult of Isis, or Mithraism, until finally the old religion was completely supplanted by these faiths and, ultimately, by Christianity.

The gods speak in many ways. One is through prayer, which Janet believed to be an internal dialogue between the individual and one's spirit, or between the individual and a neurologically based "god." Human beings, according to Janet, inherently believe that they have a "spiritual double," the soul. Likewise, Janet believed that demoniac possession is the reverse of prayer: The spiritual double becomes evil because evil is transferred onto the double to the exclusion of the conscious personality.

Janet also felt that ritual precedes the myth, then myth is exposed to abstract philosophical speculation and becomes religion, which is a systematic dialogue between the individual and the soul, with fixed forms shared by a society.

Sigmund Freud (1856–1939)

Sigmund Freud was born in Freiburg, Moravia, in 1856, and he spent nearly all of his life in the city of Vienna. Considered the father of modern psychoanalysis, Freud believed that the study of dreams was the essential element to understanding the human unconscious psyche. Myth, for Freud, was a collective projection of the processes taking place in the unconscious mind, a sort of "shared dream." Unlike Bastian and Jung, however, Freud felt that these images were the products of repressed individual childhood memories played out in conscious language; they were the products of the individual unconsciousness alone and not the products of any universal myth-producing area of the unconscious universal to all human beings. Freud's explanation of the parallels in myth was that everyone in the world had a mother and father, and thus the images of the personal unconscious would be similar across cultures.

Freud himself was a devoted student of the myths. In describing the Oedipus complex, Freud's theory of the infantile erotic love felt by a male child toward his mother, he reached into Greek myth:

Oedipus is a tragic figure who kills his father and marries his mother (see page 285). Freud reached again into the Greek myths when he needed a term to describe excessive self-love; thus we have the now-common word *narcissism* (from the story of Narcissus).

Freud even used allusions to myth in his personal life. As the promulgator of the Oedipal complex, he referred to his own daughter and professional protégé, Anna Freud, as his "Antigone" (Antigone was Oedipus's daughter by his own mother, Queen Jocasta). Thus, Freud meant to imply that Anna was closer to him than merely a daughter.

Freud considered myth as a transitional phase toward an "inevitable" scientific worldview. Although raised in Orthodox Judaism (and possibly strongly influenced by Catholic nannies in his childhood), Freud wrote that he was "totally alienated from the religion of his fathers—as from every other." In his writings, he considered himself an "atheist." In *A History of the Psychoanalytical Movement*, he wrote:

> In my four essays on "Totem and Taboo," I made the attempt to discuss the problem of race psychology by means of analysis. This should lead us directly to the origins of the interdictions of incest and of conscience.
>
> If we accept the evolution of man's conceptions of the universe . . . according to which the ANIMISTIC phase is succeeded by the RELIGIOUS, and this in turn by the SCIENTIFIC, we have no difficulty in following the fortunes of the "omnipotence of thought" through all three phases. In the animistic stage, man ascribes omnipotence to himself; in the religious he has ceded it to the gods, but without seriously giving it up, for he reserves to himself the right to control the gods by influencing them in some way or another in the interest of his wishes. In the scientific attitude toward life there is no longer any room for man's omnipotence; he has acknowledged his smallness and has submitted to death as to all other necessities in a spirit of resignation. Nevertheless, in our reliance upon the power of the human spirit which copes with the laws of reality, there still lives a fragment of this primitive belief in the omnipotence of thought.

Although Freud did not see the elements of myth as a universal element in every unconscious, nor as an inborn feature of the unconscious, a projection of collective inner images of the unconscious mind of our entire species, he did consider the myths to be an outward projection of the unconscious, albeit the individual unconscious, and he also knew the commonality between the images in dreams and in myths. In so doing, he set the stage for his erstwhile "heir" and later opponent, Carl Jung.

In his history of the psychoanalytic movement, *The Discovery of the Unconscious*, Henri F. Ellenberger suggests a strong connection between the matriarchal theories of Bachofen and the psychological theories of Freud. The connections between mythology and the psychology of the individual were perceived even by Bachofen, and the parallels between Bachofen's theory on the development of early European culture and the Freudian view of human development are striking.

Bachofen	Freud
Hetairistic period of primitive sexual promiscuity	Infantile sexuality, "polymorphous perversion"
Matriarchy: domination of society by the "mothers"	The pre-Oedipal period of strong attachment and complete dependence of the child on his or her mother
Dionysian period: a reversion to the orgiastic cults, a "backsliding" into hetairism	The "phallic" stage: the male child becomes aware of his penis and "maleness"
The myth of Oedipus: evidence of a shift from matriarchy to patriarchy. The "social stress" of the transition.	The male child experiences the "Oedipal stage," sexual attachment to the mother, jealousy of the father, and suffers stress
Patriarchy: rule by the "fathers"	The genital adult stage: male children now identify with Father, female children with Mother

Repression of the matriarchy and hetairism, now available only in the myth	Infantile "amnesia," where the childhood memories are repressed

In order to understand the connection between the myth of Oedipus and Freud's theory of infantile sexuality, it is helpful to read this myth.

THE MYTH OF OEDIPUS

Laius, the king of Thebes, was married to Jocasta [Iocaste], but the marriage remained childless. Desperate for an heir to his throne, Laius went to the oracle of the god Apollo at Delphi for advice. What the oracle told him was horrifying: It was for the best that Laius remained childless. For it had been ordained that any child of Laius and Jocasta would grow up to murder his father and marry his mother. Terrified by the prophecy, Laius ordered the confinement of Jocasta to a small room in his palace; she was under strict orders never to sleep with him again.

However, Jocasta was hurt by this and wanted a child; she now plotted how to have intercourse with him. So, with the complicity of their servants, Jocasta saw to it that Laius drank large quantities of wine. The Greeks usually mixed their wine with water to cut its potency. But the servants gave Laius undiluted wine in an effort to intoxicate him. This accomplished, Jocasta seduced her drunken husband and conceived a son.

Remembering the prophecy, Laius took the baby boy, pierced a hole in each foot with a nail, bound the feet together, and left the child to die on a mountain, exposed to the elements.

But the gods had ordained that Laius's son would live a long life. A shepherd passing by heard the boy's cries and took the baby home to raise him himself. Looking at the child's pierced feet, the shepherd named the child Oedipus, meaning "swollen foot." Later the shepherd took the foundling back to the city of Corinth and presented

Oedipus to King Polybus's servants. The child appeared to be of royal birth, and it happened that Polybus and his wife, Periboea, childless, needed an heir to the throne. Polybus adopted Oedipus as his own son.

In another version of the story, Laius pierced the boy's feet, bound them together, and placed the child in a wooden chest that was cast out to sea. When the chest washed up on shore, it was recovered by Queen Periboea. In order to produce an heir to the throne, Periboea took the baby into the bushes and made cries as if she were in childbirth. Her servants heard these cries and soon the word went throughout the kingdom that Periboea had at last produced an heir to the throne. In any case, Polybus and Periboea loved Oedipus and raised him as a pampered prince.

However, while Oedipus was growing up, it was clear from his looks that he could not be the natural child of Polybus and Periboea. Children teased him about this; there was a great deal of gossip about who his real parents might be.

Seeking advice, Oedipus himself went to the oracle to learn who his true parents were. The oracle told him that he was destined to kill his own father and marry his mother. The Pythoness, the voice of the oracle, told Oedipus, "Get away from this sacred place, you horrible wretch—you monster! Get out and do not defile this holy place!"

Shocked by the oracle's words, and still believing that Polybus and Periboea were his real parents, Oedipus resolved to leave their court at Corinth.

On the road out of the city, Oedipus encountered the entourage of King Laius of Thebes, his true father. Laius called to the boy to get out of the way and let royalty pass. Oedipus answered Laius that he himself was a royal prince and had no betters. Laius ordered his charioteer to advance. Livid, Oedipus threw his spear at the charioteer, killing him. The horses reared up, throwing Laius from the chariot, killing him instantly. The prophecy was fulfilled; Oedipus had murdered his own natural father.

It happened that Laius was on the way to consult the oracle at Delphi on how to rid his kingdom of the Sphinx. This creature had the head of a woman, the tail of a serpent, the body of a lion, and wings like an eagle, not to mention both male and female genitalia. She stopped every traveler on the road to Thebes and asked a riddle. When the hapless traveler was unable to solve the riddle, the Sphinx killed and ate him. This was ruining trade and depleting the royal treasury of Thebes.

Oedipus, nearing Thebes, encountered the Sphinx, who asked him the riddle: "What has four legs in the morning, two legs at noon, and three legs in the evening?" No traveler had yet successfully answered this question. Oedipus, however, replied without hesitating, "The human being." For, as an infant, the human crawls on all fours; as an adult, it walks on two legs; and as an old man or woman with a cane, it goes about on three legs. The Sphinx was completely undone by Oedipus's statement and plunged to its death down a gorge.

The Thebans rejoiced to be freed of the Sphinx; their city was once again the most prosperous in Greece and they acclaimed Oedipus as their king. With Laius dead, Jocasta gladly married the young hero. She had no way of knowing that Oedipus was, in fact, her own son. The prophecy was now complete.

Such a violation of the basic laws of the gods could not go unpunished, and Thebes was stricken with a horrible plague. Oedipus sent a Theban envoy to the oracle to learn how to end this plague. The Pythoness responded, "Get rid of the murderer of King Laius and the plague will end." Oedipus obediently issued an edict pronouncing a curse on Laius's killer and ordered the culprit's exile. The investigation began.

After months had passed without finding the criminal, Oedipus despaired of ever reversing the plague. At this time, the blind seer Teiresias, the best-known in all Greece, demanded an audience with him.

Teiresias himself had an interesting life history. It is said that he had once seen two serpents engaging in the sexual act, which was always bad luck. When the serpents struck at him, Teiresias killed the female with his staff. According to Greek tradition, killing a female serpent turns a male into a homosexual, or even into a woman. In Teiresias's case, he became a lascivious female prostitute. The situation was made right when Teiresias went back and killed the male serpent, thereby regaining his manhood.

Another tale relates that he once, by chance, spied the virgin goddess Athena naked in her bath. For this he was blinded. However, his mother went to Athena to explain that it was only by accident that Teiresias had seen her bathing, not by design. Athena left him blind, but stationed a pet serpent to lick the boy's ears, enabling him to understand the prophetic language of the birds and making him the greatest seer in all Greece.

In an alternate version of this story, he was blinded by Hera. Hera and Zeus were engaged in one of their frequent marital arguments as a result of Zeus's unfaithfulness. Zeus defended himself by saying that females receive more pleasure than males from sex. Hera disagreed and called Teiresias, who had been both male and female, to settle the argument.

Teiresias answered the question in rhyme: "If the elements of sexual pleasure are ten, three times three parts are the women's and but one part to men!" Zeus laughed heartily at the verse that supported his opinion; Hera was furious and struck the seer blind. As a reward for his service, however, Teiresias was given an extraordinarily long life. Thus this seer appears in hundreds of myths at very distant points in epic history.

With all of these stories of Teiresias's general knowledge, it was very common for kings to ask the blind seer to settle disputes, solve crimes, and answer difficult questions. So Oedipus gladly accepted Teiresias's offer to help. Teiresias responded that the murderer of Laius was a descendant of the children of the Hydra's teeth. If this descendant were killed, the plague would end.

The Hydra was a monster that had been slain; when its teeth were sown as seeds, adult human beings sprang from the ground. One of these descendants of the Hydra's teeth was old Menoeceus, the father of Jocasta and unwitting grandfather of Oedipus. When Teiresias spoke, Menoeceus knew that he had few years left anyway and threw himself from the city wall. The plague then ended.

However, it was not Menoeceus that Teiresias had had in mind; it was Oedipus, who, as Menoeceus's grandson, was also a descendant of the Hydra's teeth. When Teiresias told all of the court of Thebes that the old man's grandson needed to die, Jocasta replied that Menoeceus had no grandchildren. The seer then revealed to all that Oedipus was Menoeceus's grandson, Laius's son, and Jocasta's son and husband: Oedipus had killed his own father and married his mother. Even more horrifying, Oedipus and Jocasta had had a daughter, Antigone, through their incestuous union.

At first, this news was too shocking to be believed. But Oedipus wanted the whole matter settled once and for all. So he contacted Periboea and asked her to tell of his origins—was he the son of Periboea and Polybus or was he not? Periboea responded by letter.

In the passing years, her husband had told her the oracle's shocking prophecy about Oedipus. Her letter described this prophecy, and told of how the child was found and raised. She further reported that Oedipus was in the area where Laius was killed at the time of the murder. This damning evidence, confirming the allegations of Teiresias, was too much to bear.

Queen Jocasta hanged herself. Oedipus, seized with remorse and disgust, gouged out his own eyes. He was led away by Antigone, who was both his sister and his daughter.

It is said that Oedipus wandered the earth for many years thereafter, later encountering the hero Theseus. There are conflicting tales that he died bravely in battle or was hounded to death by the vengeance of the Furies at Colonus. ♦

The fact is that no logical explanation of the many kinds of suffering is possible. But in certain experiences, and in the contemplation of certain events, we can on occasion grasp, momentarily and elusively, a shadowy outskirt of the truth. We can grasp it as we contemplate the Crucifixion—considered as at once the voluntary and necessary suffering of God himself. And we can grasp it as we read certain myths, such as that of the death of the blind Oedipus, who had suffered so atrociously and unjustly. But the reconciliation implied in this myth must be understood, not with reference to a future life, but as existing in eternal reality.
　　　—Victor Gollancz (1893–1967),
　　　　British publisher and writer, *From Darkness to Light*

Carl Gustav Jung

> Myth is the natural and indispensable intermediate stage between unconscious and conscious cognition.
>
> The need for mythic statements is satisfied when we frame a view of the world which adequately explains the meaning of human existence in the cosmos, a view which springs from our psychic wholeness, from the cooperation between conscious and unconscious. Meaninglessness inhibits fulness of life and is therefore equivalent to illness. Meaning makes a great many things endurable—perhaps everything. No science will ever replace myth, and a myth cannot be made out of any science. For it is not that "God" is a myth, but that myth is the revelation of a divine life in man. It is not we who invent myth, rather it speaks to us as a word of God.

Carl Gustav Jung was the son of a Protestant minister of the German-speaking canton of Basel; he spent all of his life in Switzerland, between the cities of Basel and Zurich. Interestingly, Johann Jakob Bachofen was a friend and colleague of Jung's paternal grandfather, also named Carl Gustav, and the elderly Bachofen was a familiar sight on the streets of Basel during the boyhood of the pioneer psychiatrist. Trained as a physician and neurologist, Jung became a disciple of Sigmund Freud, who for a time referred to Jung as "my dear son" and as his "heir" to the leadership of the international psychiatric movement.

By 1912, however, the two had parted company, and not on the best of terms. Jung freely acknowledged the contributions of Janet and others to Freud's thinking; Freud was loathe to concede this. Jung questioned Freud's "sacred" Oedipal theory of infantile sexuality; Jung thought it ridiculous to suppose that a male child was sexually attracted to his mother and jealous of the father. Jung also acknowledged the contributions of the anthropologists and sociologists Bastian, Lévy-Bruhl, and Durkheim, incorporating them into his psychological theory. Most important, however, he continued to believe, following Freud, that the images in our dreams and our myths are definitely related. However, Jung did not feel that they were the products of individual memories.

Jung noted the connection between the symbols of dreams and those found in myth early in his career:

> As early as 1909 I realized that I could not treat latent psychoses if I did not understand their symbolism. It was then that I began to study mythology.

Jung was critical of Freud's dismissal of myth and religion as mere projections of the personal unconscious. For Jung, these images were universal, shared by all human beings. These theories were popularized during the 1970s and 1980s by Joseph Campbell, who wrote:

> An altogether different approach [to myth] is represented by Carl G. Jung, in whose view the imageries of mythology and religion serve positive, life-furthering ends. According to his way of thinking, all the organs of our bodies—not only those of sex and aggression—have their purposes and motives, some being subject to conscious control, others, however, not. Our outward-oriented consciousness, addressed to the demands of the day, may lose touch with these inward forces; and the myths, states Jung, when correctly read, are the means to bring us back in touch. They are telling us in picture language of powers of the psyche to be recognized and integrated in our lives, powers that have been common to the human spirit forever, and which represent the wisdom of the species by which man has weathered the millenniums [sic]. Thus they have not been, and can never be, displaced by the findings of science,* which relate rather to the outside world than to the depths that we enter in sleep. Through a dialogue conducted with these inward forces through our dreams and through a study of myths, we can learn to know and come to terms with the greater horizon of our own deeper and wiser, inward self. And analogously, the society that cherishes and keeps its myth alive will be nourished from the soundest, richest strata of the human spirit.

Following the "Elementary Thought" advanced by Bastian, the "conscious collective" of Durkheim, and the "representations collectives" of Lévy-Bruhl, Jung believed in the "collective unconscious," that

---

*You will recall that Freud viewed myths as projections of the personal unconscious only, and that mythic thinking would inevitably be superceded by "scientific" thinking.

every human being carries an inborn, neurologically based element of the unconscious that is manifested in dreams and myth.

The scripts of our dreams and our myths are contained in the collective unconscious; the characters are called "archetypes" by Jung. For example, Jung and Campbell identify "the hero" as an archetype common to all parallel heroic myths. Likewise, "the trickster" appears in similar myths as a recurring archetype.

Of the collective unconscious, Jung wrote:

> A more or less superficial layer of the unconscious is undoubtedly personal. I call it the "personal unconscious." But this personal unconscious rests upon a deeper layer, which does not derive from personal experience and is not a personal acquisition but is inborn. This deeper layer I call the "collective unconscious." I have chosen the term "collective" because this part of the unconscious is not individual but universal; in contrast to the personal psyche, it has contents that are more or less the same everywhere and in all individuals. It is, in other words, identical in all men and thus constitutes a common psychic substrate of a suprapersonal nature which is present in every one of us.
>
> My thesis, then, is as follows: In addition to our immediate consciousness, which is of a thoroughly personal nature, and which we believe to be the only empirical psyche (even if we tack on the personal unconscious as an appendix), there exists a second psychic system of a collective, universal and impersonal nature which is identical in all individuals. This collective unconscious does not develop individually, but is inherited. It consists of preexisting forms, the archetypes, which can only become conscious secondarily and which give definite forms to certain psychic elements.

Jung wrote of the archetypes:

> The concept of the archetype, which is an indispensable correlate of the idea of the collective unconscious, indicates definite forms in the psyche which seem to be present always and everywhere. Mythological research calls them "motifs." In the psychology of the primitive they correspond to Lévy-Bruhl's concept of "representations collectives," and in the field of comparative

religion they have been defined by Hubert and Mauss* as "categories of the imagination." Adolf Bastian long ago called them "elementary" or "primordial" thoughts. From these references it should be clear that my idea of the archetype—literally a pre-existent form—does not stand alone but is something that is recognized and named in other fields of study.

What the word "archetype" means in the nominal sense is clear enough, then, from its relations with myth, esoteric teaching and fairy tales. . . . So far mythologists have always had recourse to solar, lunar, meteorological, vegetal and various other ideas of this kind. The fact that myths are first and foremost psychic [i.e., of the psyche, or "mind"] phenomena that reveal the nature of the soul is something that they have absolutely refused to see until now. Primitive man is not much interested in objective explanations of the obvious, but he has an imperative need . . . an irresistible urge to assimilate all outer experiences to inner, psychic events. . . . All the mythological processes of nature, such as summer and winter, the phases of the moon, the rainy seasons, and so forth, are in no sense allegories of these objective experiences; rather they are symbolic expressions of the inner, unconscious drama of the psyche which becomes accessible to man's consciousness by way of projections.

Note the similarities between Jung's concept of the archetype and Victor Hugo's description of the "types" that recur in literature (from *The Modern Tradition*, edited by Richard Ellmann and Charles Feidelson, Jr.).

. . . the type lives. Were it but an abstraction, men would not recognize it, and would allow this shadow to go its own way. The tragedy termed "classic" makes phantoms; the drama creates living types. A lesson which is a man; a myth with a human face so plastic that it looks at you in the mirror; a parable that nudges you. . . . Types are cases foreseen of God; genius realizes them. It seems that God prefers to teach a lesson through man, in order to inspire confidence. The poet walks the street with living men; he has their ear. Hence the efficacy of types. Man

---

*Marcel Mauss was Durkheim's nephew.

is a premise, the type a conclusion; God creates the phenomenon, genius gives it a name.

Types go and come on a common level in Art and in Nature; they are the ideal realized. The good and the evil of man are in these figures. From each of them springs, in the eye of the thinker, a humanity.

Jung saw that myth gives meaning to human life. An example of this was found during his visit to the Pueblo people of New Mexico. Jung was keenly interested in their myths and religious views, yet he found the Pueblos reluctant to discuss these matters with an outsider. Finally an old chief told him, "The sun is God. Everyone can see that." He then told Jung that the ceremonial dances of the Pueblos were necessary to keep the sun shining and on its proper course. The Pueblos did not do this for themselves alone, but for all humankind. Moreover, the old man despaired of what would happen if these dances were forgotten.

Jung's theory of the collective unconscious led him into extensive study of esoteric religions, Gnosticism, alchemy, and mythology. Throughout his studies of all of these, he saw a consistent pattern of more or less identical archetypes at work.

Jung himself was reticent about giving any precise definition of his own religious views. Joseph Campbell describes him as a "polytheist" who saw in the archetypes "gods" that were manifestations of a single "God," much as the Hindus consider all the many "gods" to be mere manifestations of Brahman. Jung had a very critical view of his own pastor father; he felt that the elder Jung had experienced a crisis of faith but was too weak to deal with it or even to admit it. Yet Jung often spoke of God in terms that are reminiscent of the Protestantism of his boyhood. Considering the unconscious nature of the archetypes and their presence in every human psyche, he may be spoken of as a "panentheist," or one who believes that God is inside of everything. But one thing is certain, Jung did not consider the elements of spiritual life "unreal," nor did he dismiss them as mere "projections," as did Freud. My conjecture is that Jung believed in a transcendent-other God who was made available, or "revealed," to human experience through the archetypes.

Even thirty years after his death, Jung remains controversial. His presidency of a Nazi-sponsored German psychiatric society has led to loose charges of Nazi sympathies. Jung angrily denounced such charges, pointing out that his leadership of the society enabled him to help many German Jews. Many of Jung's closest circle of disciples were Jews. Moreover, although he published some articles in the 1930s that may be construed as sympathetic to Nazism, his writings after 1940 are uniformly pro-Ally.

On the one hand, the Jungian approach to myth and religion has been viewed by Christians as a valuable tool for understanding man's innate spiritual behavior, and viewing religion as a permanent part of humanity—not as a phase to be "outgrown." He is quoted by the American Protestant theologian H. Richard Niebuhr, and his writings have been used by Protestant, Roman Catholic, and Eastern Orthodox theologians. Jung's speculation that "sonship" and the role of the Holy Spirit would be revitalizing to the Christian faith presaged the widespread charismatic movements within the Church.*

Juxtaposed to this, one finds the Jungian archetypes have also been adapted by New Age religion as a justification for a new polytheism and a reduction of religion to esoteric symbols. Here, Jung is given as a psychological rationale for a new Gnosticism, a form of Christianity based not on faith but on "secret" knowledge imparted to an elite.

In any case, the Protestant pastor officiating at Jung's funeral eulogized him as having restored the dignity and intellectual standing of the religious life after its rejection by Freud and other twentieth-century thinkers.

Nevertheless, the Jungian approach to the interpretation of myth provides an intriguing psychological explanation for parallelism, blending psychiatry with sociology, anthropology, and literary criticism.

---

*See *Carl Jung and Christian Spirituality*, edited by Robert L. Moore (New York and Mahwah, N.J.: Paulist Press, 1988).

A MODERN NONPSYCHOLOGICAL APPROACH: STRUCTURALISM

Claude Lévi-Strauss

> Probably there is something deep in my own mind which makes it likely that I was always what is now being called a structuralist. My mother told me that, when I was about two years old and still unable to read, of course, I claimed that I was actually able to read. And when I was asked why, I said that when I looked at the signboards on shops ... "boulanger" [French for "baker"] or "boucher" [French for "butcher"]—I was able to read something because what was obviously similar, from a graphic point of view, in the writing could not mean anything but "bou," the same first syllable of "boucher" and "boulanger." Probably, there is nothing more than that to the structuralist approach; it is the quest for the invariant, or for the invariant elements among superficial differences.

The earlier modern interpretations of myth, those of Frobenius, Bastian, Lévy-Bruhl, and Durkheim, were based on cultural history and the social relationships within cultures. The psychological approach of Janet, Freud, and Jung (and thus Campbell) viewed myth as something different from cultural history, with an internal psychological source. Yet another approach can be found in the Structural anthropology of Claude Lévi-Strauss.

During the 1960s, an announcement by Lévi-Strauss stirred great excitement in the scientific and anthropological communities. He claimed that if one were only able to unravel the invariant structures of human thinking, then laws of human behavior could be formulated that were as certain and precise as the law of gravity.

Claude Lévi-Strauss was born to Jewish parents in Brussels, but grew up in France and spent most of his life there. This is fitting, as he is, to some degree, the heir to Lucien Lévy-Bruhl and Émile Durkheim. Durkheim, you will recall, believed that the parallel myths could be explained by a neurologically based set of "molds" of myths common to all human beings. As Marvin Harris writes in his book *Cultural Materialism*:

> Structuralists follow Durkheim in believing that the mind has "molds" that make it possible to think of the totality of things. These molds are the structuralist's structures. In their most elementary form they are present in all human minds and are ultimately part of the neurophysiology of the human brain. However, each culture fills the "molds" with its own distinctive content— its own ideas.

Lévi-Strauss is careful to avoid using the term *primitive* to describe "traditional" cultures, pointing out that the allegedly primitive man has the same brain structure as you or I. The "primitive" person is physically capable of understanding the same things that we do, but our term *primitive* carries the connotation of being "childish." In fact, our so-called modern way of thinking is as much the result of "primitive" thinking or mythology as it is the product of science and technology. And our thinking, according to Lévi-Strauss, operates in the same "infrastructure" as does that of the tribesman.

At times Lévi-Strauss appears to be the hardest to read of all contemporary interpreters of myth. His works are full of abstract, complex, and graphic interrelations between structures, as they are supposedly demonstrated in the myths. However, any overview of structuralism includes the following characteristics:

1. A structure is not a collection of social relationships, nor is it a theme or trend in cultural history. Unlike Durkheim's and earlier anthropologists' view of myth as a collective cultural function, the structure is a "playing out" of the basic human thinking mechanism. Lévi-Strauss says that a structure "is a system of which the members of a society being studied are unaware."

2. All human beings have the same basic neurologically based "hardware" for thinking. The fact that this basic brain "infrastructure" is common to all human beings explains parallel myths. Lévi-Strauss calls Durkheim's "molds" "elemental cells." Myths are similar because all people have the same "el-

emental cells" that are filled with the "software" of a particular culture.

3. Human beings think in dialectical terms, that is to say, we tend to think in pairs of opposites such as god/demon, light/dark, bad/good, and so forth. This dualism means that sometimes one finds a theme in a myth of one culture that does not make sense until it is matched, like a puzzle piece, with the myth of another culture.

Needless to say, many themes can appear in any one given myth. Thus, in matching them with opposites, structural analysis can be very complex and confusing.

Some of the most interesting observations of Lévi-Strauss are on his comparison between the structure of myth and the structure of music. Lévi-Strauss believes that both myth and music are specific forms of language in which a meaning can be found only by taking them in their totality. The following is taken from Lévi-Strauss's *Myth and Meaning*.

> ... My main point was that, exactly as in a musical score, it is impossible to understand a myth as a continuous sequence. This is why we should be aware that if we try to read a myth as we read a novel or from left to right, we don't understand the myth, because we have to apprehend it as a totality and discover that the basic meaning of the myth is not conveyed by the sequence of events ... but ... by bundles of events even though these events appear at different moments in the story. Therefore we have to read the myth more or less as we would read an orchestral score.... And it is only by treating the myth as if it were an orchestral score, written stave after stave, that we can understand it as a totality, that we can extract meaning out of the myth.

Structuralism has been very controversial for a number of reasons. First, its method seems to rob myth of its "truth," or an application to life. It can be a very sterile and lifeless treatment of a subject that has given meaning to human life for thousands of years.

With its complex and abstract charts of interrelationships between myths, critics say that structural analysis unnecessarily complicates the study of myth and puts it into the hands of an "initiated" elite. Another criticism of this method is that if one is looking for structures, one will find them.

Structuralism rejects the psychological approaches of Jung and Freud; the "elemental cells" are part of the structure of the brain and not an element in the human subconscious that is manifested in dreams and myth. It is thus irreconcilably opposed to the theories of Jung and Campbell, as well as to those of the other interpreters of myth we shall look at.

The most damning criticism of structuralism, however, is that it is dehumanizing. Existentialists and literary critics feel that if structuralism is true—and there are, in fact, basic structures that govern human thinking—then we are really biological "cybernetic" thinking machines. This is in sharp contrast to the human faculties of "feeling" and "belief." Structuralism is seen as a coldly scientific approach to myth, the most human of functions.

During the 1970s, structuralism was a potent source in many of the social sciences, especially in Europe and Latin America. However, Lévi-Strauss has yet to formulate laws of human thinking that are as precise and certain as the law of gravity.

PHILOSOPHICAL PERSPECTIVES ON MYTH

Paul Ricoeur (1913–)

Diametrically opposed to his countryman Claude Lévi-Strauss is French Christian philosopher Paul Ricoeur, who is very interested indeed in the human function of "feeling."

Heavily influenced by existentialist philosophy, which stresses the importance of a sense of meaning in human life, Ricoeur sees human beings as "fragile" and "fallible," "suspended between two poles of existence, finitude and the infinite." Myth, according to Ricoeur, is the cry of "pathos," an anguished attempt to reconcile the objective, finite world with the infinite. Ricoeur believes that man has always been open to the idea of a transcendent God to reconcile these two poles, and in the Christian idea of the incarnation of God as Jesus Christ, these poles are reconciled.

Ricoeur is interested in the transition from *mythos* to *logos*. *Mythos* is a Greek word from which we derive our English word *myth*. It originally carried the connotation of being certain and final, not open to debate, generally accepted.* *Logos*, in contrast, was the usual Greek word for "word," and was something that could be debated, or discussed. The passage from *mythos* to *logos*, then, is the passage from a worldview based on a universally accepted myth to philosophical speculation about the human place in the universe.

As *mythos* became *logos*, the certainty was gone and with it the sense of meaning. Without the necessary sense of a certain place in the universe, human beings became fragile.

To compensate for the sense of security that myth once provided, human beings now rely on the faculty of "feeling" to give them the necessary sense of meaning.

Ricoeur's theories are interesting because they are a point of intersection between existentialist philosophy and the interpretation of myth. Myth is a "reality" because it is felt.

Karl Jaspers (1883–1969)

Karl Jaspers, a native of Oldenburg, Germany, began his working life in neuropathology and the emerging discipline of psychiatry. These led him to his now-famous career as a philosopher, one of the important existentialist thinkers of this century along with such men as Jean-Paul Sartre and Martin Heidegger.

A professor at both Heidelberg and Basel, Jaspers was fascinated by the independent and parallel development of the world's great religions over a comparatively short period in history, roughly five hundred years, during which prophets emerged independently of one another in China, India, Iran, and Palestine.

Jaspers noted that this was the first great shift from *mythos* to *logos*, or from a mythical view of the world to a philosophical speculation, and

---

*See the *Encyclopaedia Britannica* entry on "Myth."

religion in our present sense of the word. During the "mythological era" of thinking, relationships with the gods were transactional, based on appeasement or rewards with sacrifices and offerings. The "gods" now gave way to God. In Greece, philosophers abandoned the polytheism of their ancestors and began to speak of "God" as a unified force for the first time. Jaspers speculated on why this happened at one time in so many places independent of each other.

Jaspers called this period the "axial period." He chose the word *axial* because, for Christians, the "axis" of their history is the life and ministry of Christ. However, Christianity is only one of several world religions, and the "axis" seemed to extend throughout other cultures in Europe and Asia.

> The most extraordinary events are concentrated in this period. Confucius and Lao-Tse were living in China, all the schools of Chinese philosophy came into being, including those of Mo-ti, Chuang-Tse, Lieh-Tsu and a host of others; India introduced the Upanishads [scriptures] and Buddha and, like China, ran the whole gamut of philosophical speculation down to scepticism, to materialism, sophism and nihilism; in Palestine the prophets made their appearance, from Elijah, by way of Jeremiah to Deutero-Isaiah; Greece witnessed the appearance of Homer, of the philosophers—Parmenides, Herclitus, and Plato—of the tragedies—Thucydides and Archimedes. Everything implied by these names developed during these few centuries almost simultaneously in China, India and the West, without any one of these regions knowing of the others.

According to Jaspers, what had taken place was a wholesale advancement in human spiritual thinking, an "evolution" of thought from objective, transactional deities in a polytheistic and ritual-bound world to the concept of a universal God. This necessitated a transformation of the function of myth.

> The mythical age with its tranquility and self-evidence was at an end. The Greek, Indian and Chinese philosophers were unmythical in their decisive instincts, as were the prophets in their ideas of God. Rationality and rationally clarified experience launched a struggle against the myth; a further struggle

developed for the transcendence of the one God against non-existent demons, and finally an ethical rebellion took place against the unreal figures of the gods. Religion was rendered ethical, and the majesty of the Deity thereby increased.

Do you remember that Pierre Janet wrote that a society abandoned its gods when the gods failed to speak? This is a basic description of what appeared to happen during the axial period.

The myth, on the other hand, became the material of a language which expressed by it something very different from what it originally signified; it was turned into parable. Myths were remoulded, were understood at a new depth during this transition, which was myth-creating after a new fashion.

The myth persisted, but it had matured into a vehicle for truth, not an unquestioned truth in itself.

Jaspers felt that humanity was on the verge of a new axial period, the first period in history where the globe was united by telecommunications. This too could prove a critical juncture in the spiritual development of mankind.

Jaspers saw science as the modern myth, but an incomplete myth. Certainly science, like so many of the earlier myths, appears to explain the natural world around us. But science can only answer *how* things happen; it is unable to tell us *why*.

THE "HISTORY OF RELIGIONS" SCHOOL OF MYTH

Mircea Eliade (1907–1986)

[Myth and] religion are not phases in human consciousness, but a part of human consciousness itself.

Mircea Eliade was born in Romania, but spent most of his life in France and the United States. He was probably the world's foremost scholar of myth as "sacred history," and of the distinction between the "sacred" and the "profane." For Eliade, myth was the record of the breakthrough of "the transcendent into our world."

A professing Christian, Eliade believed that myth and religion are permanent parts of human consciousness and that it is truly human to think in terms of things that are transcendent or infinite. Eliade was careful to distance himself from the psychological schools of myth, stressing, for example, that when he used the word *archetypes* it did not mean the same thing that Jung meant by the term. Eliade was most concerned by the reduction of "man's innate religious" function to a mere psychological projection, and he even spoke of the psychological theories of the interpretation of myth as "a second Fall from grace," a modern version of the Fall that took place in Eden.

Eliade felt that no society could be understood without an understanding of its sacred history; all of the institutions, morality, and culture of any given society were vitally dependent upon a shared sacred history of the "breakthroughs of the transcendent."

In explaining parallel myths, Eliade was a diffusionist; he was particularly indebted to Frobenius's theory of the myth-producing cultural centers.

As to answers to the question of meaning, Eliade felt that the Christian religion offered a complete set of mythic images that satisfied an innate human need. Rather than abandon Christianity as a societal myth, Eliade argued that the Christian faith must be reexamined in light of our modern society.

14. Myth—Yours, Mine, and Ours

But time and again it is seen: for us the Deity, if it exists, is only as it appears to us in the world, as it speaks to us in the language of man and the world. It exists for us only in the way in which it assumes concrete shape, which by human measure and thought always serves to hide it at the same time. Only in ways that man can grasp does the Deity appear.

Thus it is seen that it is wrong to play off against each other the question about man and the question about the Deity. Although in the world only man is reality for us does not preclude that precisely the quest for man leads to transcendence. That the Deity alone is reality does not preclude that this reality is accessible to us only in the world; as it were, as an image in the mirror of man, because something of the Deity must be in him for him to be able to respond to the Deity. Thus the theme of philosophy is oriented in polar alternation, in two directions: *deum et animam scire cupio.* [Latin: "I desire knowledge of God and the soul."]

—Karl Jaspers

MODERN QUESTIONS OF FAITH

Christian Myth

The word "myth" is used in the title of this volume in a specific and definite sense. A myth is a symbolic story which demonstrates, in Alan Watts's words, "the inner meaning of the universe and of human life." To say that Jesus is a myth is not to say that he is a legend but that his life and message are an attempt to demonstrate the "inner meaning of the universe and of human life." As Charles Long puts it, a myth points to the definite manner in which the world is available for man: "the word and content of myth are revelations of power." Or as A. K. Coomaraswamy observes, "Myth embodies the nearest approach to absolute truth that can be stated in words."

Many Christians have objected to my use of this word even when I define it specifically. They are terrified by a word which may even have a slight suggestion of fantasy. However, my usage is the one that is common among historians of religion, literary critics, and social scientists. It is a valuable and helpful usage; there is no other word which conveys what these scholarly traditions mean when they refer to myth. The Christian would be well advised to get over his fear of the word and appreciate how important a tool it can be for understanding the content of his faith.

—Father Andrew Greeley, *Myths of Religion*

Myth, whether Christian or other, is an exposition of truth in the form of a story. The meaning given to "myth" in the 19th century—i.e., that myth is fiction—continues to exert a pervasive influence in popular and journalistic literature. It is this 19th-century view of myth as fiction that has caused many Christians to reject the notion that Christianity contains within its Scriptures, theology, and practices various mythological elements. Mythological themes taken over from the Greeks and the Jews . . . have been transformed by Christian concepts of history and the development of Christian doctrine.

. . . The function of Christian myth is to express in imaginative and often dramatic terms answers to the most significant questions asked by man: Who am I? Where am I going? Though these questions are universal, in Western Civilization they have been answered, for the most part, by those cognitive and imaginative elements influenced by Christian myth. Concerned with the nature, origin and destiny of man, his society and the world, Christian myth seeks to elucidate and describe the truth of the human condition (for those affected by Western Civilization) in a manner that goes beyond the mere apprehension and comprehension of facts that can be empirically verified—i.e., substantiated by the senses.

Employing the imagination to communicate concepts, Christian myth is concerned with the realm of the spirit—i.e., the sphere of meaning and value. That area—involving man's understanding of himself and his relationship to his society and his world and to the sacred or holy . . .

>   —*Encyclopaedia Britannica*, 15th ed., entry on "Christian Myth and Legend"

Jewish Myth

A distinction must be made, of course, between myth and legend. In common parlance, a myth is a story about gods or otherwordly beings. Judaism, however, is a rigorously monotheistic religion; hence, in this narrower sense, there can be no original Jewish myths. . . . If, however, the term is interpreted in a larger sense, to mean the portrayal of continuous, transtemporal [beyond time] concerns in the context of particular and punctual events, myth is indeed one of the essential vehicles by which Judaism conveys its message; for it is only when historical happenings are translated into this wider dimension that they cease to be mere antiquarian data and acquire continuing relevance. In Judaism, for example, the Exodus in Egypt is projected mythically from something that happened at a particular time into something that is continually happening, and it thus comes to exemplify the situation and experience of all men everywhere—their emergence from the bondage of obscurantism [i.e., "the state of being obscure or causing to be obscure or unknown"], their individual revelations at their individual Sinais, their trek through a figurative wilderness, even their death in it so that their children or children's children may eventually reach the figurative "promised land." By the same token, the historical destruction of the Temple of Jerusalem is transformed by myth into a paradigm of the continuing mutual estrangement of God and man, their exile from one another.

>   Legend, on the other hand, implies no more than a fanciful embroidering of purportedly historical fact. Unlike myth, it does not transcend the punctual and local.

>   —*Encyclopaedia Britannica*, 15th ed., entry on "Jewish Myth and Legend"

This chapter is a necessary one: The study of mythology naturally raises questions for the believing Jew, Christian, and Muslim, the heirs of the religion of One God, revealed. Myth has much to say in helping us understand the concept of our faith and the faiths of others. However, the "stuff" of myth consists of stories of pagan gods and goddesses—"false gods," according to our tradition.

My goal here is not to proselytize, but rather to demonstrate that there is myth —if *myth* is correctly defined—in our faiths. Still, the fact that there is myth in our faiths hardly makes them false or fictional.

The use of the terms *Christian myth* or *Jewish myth* immediately elicit a negative, defensive, even hostile response from those accustomed to the popular definition of *myth* as "fable," "fiction," or "a widely believed falsehood." The use of *Christian* and *myth* in the same sentence would appear, to the average person, to be a denunciation of the truth or validity of that faith. Indeed, in the nineteenth century, all that might be termed "supernatural" or "transcendent" was deemed as fiction, or myth.

In our own times, the incorrect definition of *myth* is constantly reinforced by headlines such as TEN MYTHS ABOUT AIDS, THE MYTH OF A MIDDLE-CLASS TAX CUT, THE MYTH OF INVINCIBLE JAPAN, and many others. In each case, these headlines appear over stories that are intended to dispel a widely believed misconception.

But let's return to the definition of *myth* by a historian of religion (and a professing Christian), Mircea Eliade. Eliade said that myth was a "sacred history" of breakthroughs of the sacred or supernatural into our world. Certainly Christianity, Judaism, and Islam fall under this definition. In this context, use of the word *myth* is hardly a judgment of falsehood passed on our faiths.

If we correctly look at what myth is and how it functions, the use of the word is no longer threatening or offensive, but rather a validation or affirmation of what we believe. Do Christianity, Islam, and Judaism myths provide meaning to our lives? Do they provide us with a "sacred history" of God acting in the affairs of human beings? Do they provide a code of morality? Of course they do. We live by these myths, and many people have given their lives for them. Were such myths a fiction, a falsehood, or even a mere psychological projection, it is unlikely that they would have endured and have persisted as a crucial force throughout human history.

The study of myth certainly gives the believer something to think about. The parallels between the myths of our traditions and those of vastly different cultures offer parallel myths of the Fall, virgin births, resurrections, and so on—often strikingly similar to our own cherished sacred stories. This may lead one to wonder whether our tradition is merely one of many valid choices on a cosmic menu of the transcendent. It may even "dent" our faith to think that "primitive" or "pagan" peoples have such stories in common with us. The following experience demonstrates the two opposite reactions of Christians, in particular, to the study of myth.

Some years ago, I attended a Christian conference and had occasion to speak to two women with dramatically different reactions to their experience in the study of myth.

The first woman had nothing whatsoever good to say about myth or mythology. The subject matter, she pointed out, exalted false gods. For her, the study of myth was merely a "tool of the devil" in the hands of "secular humanists" in a wholesale effort to devalue Christianity and excise its influence from society. The study of myth caused her to doubt her own faith. She did not want her children to study mythology in the public schools.* She had even gone so far as to throw out her books on the subject in order to make certain that her home, her children's minds, and her own mind would never be contaminated by them.

The second woman drew the opposite conclusion from her studies. Lest you think that she was a "liberal" Christian, a New Age adherent, or anything but orthodox in her beliefs, think again. She was from Alabama, the heart of the American Bible Belt, and described herself as "born again" and "spirit-filled."† She could not even remotely be construed as a "secular humanist." She had just completed the third of three classes in comparative religion at her local university and was enthusiastic about the effects on her religious life. The parallels between the myths of distant cultures and the stories in

---

*The author pointed out that he had first heard the Greek myths in a parochial school!

†"Charismatic" or "pentacostal" Christians of many denominations stress the experience of baptism of the Holy Spirit, evidenced by supernatural phenomena such as speaking in tongues, healings, and so on.

the Bible intrigued her and led her to see her faith as the satisfaction of universal human needs. She was fascinated, not threatened, by parallel virgin births and resurrections. For her, these motifs persisted in myth—and were expressed in Christianity—because they are true.

The Christian, Jew, and Muslim, and their nonbelieving cultural heirs, share a profound tradition of the value of the individual human being that is originally rooted in a humanism based on the belief that man was created in the image of God. Animals do not make myths; we have no indication that they have any sense of the transcendent or supernatural. The core elements of myth are a demonstration of the uniqueness of the human consciousness with regard to things beyond the reality of the senses. Only a human being has the innate need to figure out his or her place in the universe. As Joseph Campbell writes of myth: "The way to become truly human is to learn to recognize the lineaments of God in all the wonderful modulations in the face of man."

It is not only modern anthropology, history of religions, and psychology that recognize the constancy and power of myth. Rather, these are things that have been recognized since ancient times. The early Christian church fathers wrote that man is indelibly marked by the *Imago Dei*, the "image of God," present in every human being, believer and unbeliever. In their thinking, the human being innately knows that there is a God; this is a fundamental part of human consciousness. As Saint Paul wrote in his Epistle to the Romans: "For since the creation of the world, God's eternal power and his divine nature have been clearly seen, being understood from what has been made, so that men are without excuse." Of course, Paul then went on to say that this knowledge led humans to make idols, and he delineated the difference between their idolatry and the Christian proclamation.

Jewish thinkers such as Maimonides, Catholic theologians such as Saint Augustine and Saint Thomas Aquinas, and the Protestant Martin Luther, all readily acknowledged their belief that man had some innate knowledge of God and the supernatural even before being exposed to revealed religion.

You will recall that Pierre Janet wrote that a society abandons its myths when its gods fail to speak. Any society that ignores the innate human need for myth, a myth-based system to live by, and a religion, or that attempts to concoct a myth-based system with gods that fail to speak, does so at its peril. An "artificial myth" such as the Religion of Reason of the French revolutionaries, or the Soviet myth, that does not respond to the innate human mythic demands, fails. For it is only the truly mythic that endures. Stalin might have been evil, but he was no fool—faced with an imminent German invasion, he appealed to the Tsarist civic myth of "Holy Russia" and opened the churches.

So then, if all the materials, the "truths" of revealed religion, are encoded in our genes, why then would we need revealed religion? Shouldn't the study of the myths alone be sufficient for our spiritual understanding? Many people think so; I do not. Following the knowledge that the elements of myth are within each of us, shouldn't our spiritual needs be met by a New Age vision quest for "the God within us," à la Shirley MacLaine? As Reinhold Niebuhr wrote, without the "benchmark" of revelation, our religious experience would not be communal, and would be subject to "caprice."

First, myth is the "glue" that holds societies together; thus there is the collective dimension of a need for a civic myth and a shared sense of morality. In a pluralistic society such as ours, the shared traditions of the Judeo-Christian ethic, the sense of classical Greek values and aesthetics, are the heritage shared by Christian, Jew, Muslim, agnostic, and atheist—and a "moral code" that is a point of agreement on right and wrong that is based on myth. We have a secular "sacred history" that binds us together in addition to the "sacred history" of our respective faiths.

But how does revealed religion work with the innate need for myth?

Let's use an analogy. Consider the lawnmower. If your mower doesn't start, chances are that it either isn't getting a "spark" from the spark plug to ignite the gases in the engine, or else it isn't getting enough fuel to feed the engine. Nine times out of ten, if you solve either problem, the grass gets cut.

So it is with the relationship between myth and revealed religions. Myth, by Eliade's definition, is the breakthrough of the sacred into our world—a "revelation." We all share the rich, possibly psychological or neurologically based "spark" of the collective unconscious or of "cells" of common mythic symbols and images. But it is our revealed religions that provide the fuel that makes our faiths work.

As the Spanish-American philosopher George Santayana wrote nearly ninety years ago, "How should the gospel bring glad tidings, save by announcing that which is native to the heart?" Santayana continues, speaking of the time of Christ, "Feeling was ripe for a mythology loaded with pathos. The humble life, the sufferings of Jesus would be felt in all their incomparable beauty all the more when the tenderness and tragedy of them, otherwise too poignant, were relieved by the story of his miraculous birth, his glorious resurrection, and his restored divinity."

Remembering Pierre Janet, our modern society was forged by the fact that the gods of Greece and Rome no longer spoke. Greece and Rome then turned to the Christian God, built upon the Jewish Scriptures. When the astrological idols of Arabia failed to speak, the revelation of Muhammad swept through the Near East and North Africa, from Spain to the Philippines. These faiths in One God spoke to the innate mythic structure of human consciousness.

The images of our faiths are the images of myth—they are truly "native to the heart." Revelation has little value if it is not in mythic terms. If revelation is truth conveyed in the form of a story, then it is myth.

Is there myth in Christianity, Judaism, and Islam? Most certainly. If myth is the truth conveyed by stories, and it is a "sacred history" of the breakthrough of the supernatural into our world, then it is no contradiction to say that the revelation to Moses on Sinai, for example, is a myth—*and* that it was a concrete, objective event that occurred in human history and that it contains a metaphor applicable to every human being. To say that it is a myth is merely to say that it is part of "sacred history."

Saint Paul uses the Greek word *mythos*, or "myth," five times in the New Testament. As was already noted, the term *mythos* once

meant an indisputable, universally agreed-upon "word," in opposition to the other Greek word for "word," *logos*, which was open to
discussion and debate. Paul uses *mythos* in reference to the myths of
the pagans to whom he was preaching, and thus *mythos* is used as
"falsehood," to clearly delineate the Christian proclamation from the
"myths" of the Greeks and Romans.

Saint Bonaventure, writing in the thirteenth century, exhorted the
faithful to the study of the Scriptures. In his *Journey of the Mind to
God*, he wrote:

> There is in Scripture a threefold meaning or significance: the
> metaphorical, by which men are purified and led to a more up-
> right life; the allegorical, which illuminates the understanding;
> the analogical, which intoxicates the soul with deep drafts of
> wisdom.

In short, he wrote that the Scriptures convey truth in the form of a
story as metaphor, allegory, and analogy.

The contemporary Swiss-German Roman Catholic theologian Hans
Küng writes in *On Being a Christian*:

> The Gospels were in fact written for people thinking mytholog-
> ically at a time of mythological thinking, although in fact—as a
> result of its monotheistic faith being confronted with the pagan
> and polytheistic faith—the process of demythologizing and his-
> toricizing is further enhanced in the New Testament than in the
> Old. We cannot examine here the immense influence of myths—
> whether those of India, or those of Homer, those of ancient
> Rome, of the Middle Ages, or even the substitute myths of
> modern times—on the evolution of mankind and of individual
> nations. The comparative study of religions, anthropology, psy-
> chology and sociology have revealed in a variety of ways the
> power of myth to establish meaning and effect social integration:
> not only its function in a religious interpretation of the world in
> cult,* but also man's individual and social development as a
> whole.
>
> Certainly at that time, when the redaction of the gospels was
> completed, a vivid, narrative form of proclamation, making use of

---

*The word *cult* is used here in the sense of "ritual."

myths, legends and symbols, was absolutely necessary. . . . Even today, in the age of rational-causal and functional-technical thinking, might not a vivid, narrative form of proclamation still be necessary and certain ancient formulas—mythological in the widest sense—still be useful?

. . . Can there be any doubt about man's persistent need? Does not even modern man (and his mass media) live not only by arguments but also by stories, not only by concepts, but also by images—often very primitive images—and does he not always need valid images and stories that can be retold?

The Swiss Protestant theologian Emil Brunner defined myth in a way consistent with both Orthodox Christianity and the definitions given in this book. The following is taken from *The Evangelical Dictionary of Theology*, edited by Walter A. Elwell.

There is one further definition of myth to which attention must be drawn, one which in effect equates it with symbolism and relates it to the inherent inability of human language to express adequately the things of God. Thus [Emil] Brunner maintains that "the Christian kerygma [Greek for "proclamation"] cannot be separated from myth" since the Christian statement is necessarily anthropomorphic* in the sense that it does, and must do what Bultmann† conceives to be characteristic of the mythical—"it speaks of God in a human way." And in the same connection Bultmann explains that "mythology is the use of imagery to express the otherworldly in terms of this world and the divine in terms of human life, the other side would mean that it would become impossible for man to say anything about God, or for God to say anything to man, for we have no other medium of expression than in terms of this world.

Finally, it is interesting to see what Karl Barth, a Swiss Protestant considered the most important Orothodox Christian theologian of this century, had to say. Barth wrote that it is "the relationship of this God with this man; the relationship of this man with this God—this is

---

*In Christianity, Christ is believed to be God in human form.

†The German existentialist theologian Rudolf Bultmann is discussed at length later in this chapter.

the only theme of the Bible and of philosophy." In Barth's view, the Bible and philosophy are concerned with the breakthrough of the sacred into the world of a given "man"—by definition, a mythic event.

Having stated that there is myth in our faiths, and that this is not a judgment as to their validity, it is hoped that a proper understanding of the word *myth* is established. But just how did *myth* come to be a four-letter word that is taken as offensive when applied to our faiths?

THE DEMYTHOLOGIZATION OF JUDEO-CHRISTIAN CULTURE

Causative and Purposive Thinking

The history of rationalism is equally instructive. The endeavor to understand all processes as the effects of known causes has led to the development of modern science and has gradually expanded over ever-widening fields. The rigid application of the [scientific] method demands the reduction of every phenomenon to its cause. A purpose, a teleological viewpoint, and accident are excluded. It was probably one of the greatest attractions of the Darwinian theory of natural selection that it substituted for a purposive explanation of the origin of life a purely causal one.

. . . it would be an error to assume that the universal application of rationalism is the final form of thought, the ultimate result which our organism is destined to reach. Opposition to its negation of purpose or its transformation of purpose into cause and to its disregard of accident as influencing the individual phenomenon, is struggling for recognition.

—Franz Boas, German-American pioneer anthropologist, *Anthropology and Modern Life*

In our reading of the myths we have seen that they functioned as the science, history, religion, philosophy, and literature of traditional cultures. In today's world, however, we have carefully separated science and myth, even placing them in opposition to each other. But science and myth—or, by extension, science and religion—are two very different things directed toward two very different questions.

Science tells us *how* things happen; myth (and religion) tells us *why* they happen. Science relies on objective observation to show us the *causes* of things. Myth and religion rely on things beyond our senses, our faculty of "feeling," in order to show us a *purpose*.

In traditional cultures, human beings had a sense of purpose in life. However, to our way of thinking, they needlessly suffered from diseases and hardship due to the lack of technology and science. While science has created dramatic improvements in the quality of human life, individuals now suffer from a lack of meaning. In our most advanced cultures we see illnesses and social problems relating to this deficiency: suicide, alcoholism, mental disorders, and other problems that are associated with a modern, rather than a traditional, society.

Contemporary culture has tenuously tried to reconcile science and religion, at times even trying to eliminate the mythic element of religion altogether. This rationalist attitude is called "secular humanism" by religious fundamentalists. Although the term is widely ridiculed, there is some validity to it. The modern worldview is "secular" in that it rejects the operation of the supernatural in the world. However, it is not "humanistic" in the classical sense of the word. Humanism originally stood for understanding the human condition, the idea that "the proper study of man is man," and stressed the value of the individual. Industrialized society, and post-industrial society, in contrast, has made many of us feel as if we are mere "units" or "numbers." This is the result of a loss of meaning that myth traditionally provided. "Secular humanism" is, essentially, "life without myth."*

If science and myth are two very different things directed toward two very different questions, why then do we perceive them to be mortal enemies, their validity seen by some as mutually exclusive?

One of the by-products of the scientific revolution is causative thinking: the reduction of every phenomenon to its cause through observation with the five senses ("empirically"), and then the formulation of laws to predict future behavior.

Myth and religion, in contrast, are not causative—they do not rely on empirical observation but on the human faculties of "feeling" and

---

*Or perhaps the substitution of a new, incomplete myth.

"belief." They attempt to explain for us things that are beyond the range of our senses: the human place in the universe, the place of the individual in the world, and so forth.

The difference between causative and purposive thinking can be best illustrated by using the analogy of a wristwatch. You may take the wristwatch apart, spring by spring, gear by gear, and with any luck you can observe what causes it to work. (I have mastered taking it apart; putting it back together still eludes me!) However, knowing how the watch works tells you nothing of *why* you need to know what time it is, how to tell time, or why we consider punctuality to be important— the purposes of the watch. Knowing how your watch works is of little comfort to you—or your boss—if you are late for work.

There is much good to be said about causative thinking. However, as Franz Boas wrote, it is not the final form of human thought. Particularly in the nineteenth century, there were people who thought just that, and they nearly rejected purposive thinking altogether. If causative thinking is taken to its extreme, then the validity of anything that cannot be observed empirically is in doubt. If a phenomenon cannot be reduced to an identifiable cause, then it is taken, in this way of thinking, as not "real."

Because modern people have come to think in largely causative terms, this perspective has been a major factor in our culture. The materialist viewpoint rejects the existence of the "supernatural" or of "God," calling it "unreal." That is how *myth* came to mean "fiction."

There has been a serious effort to reconcile the "myth" in Christianity and Judaism using causative thinking; that is, to "demythologize" them. As Hans Küng writes, the message was thrown out with the myth.

The definition of *myth* as "falsehood" has deep roots, which point to the German philosopher Georg Wilhelm Friedrich Hegel.

Georg Wilhelm Friedrich Hegel (1770–1831)

We all too often read of philosophers and philosophy in boring, wooden terms. But Hegel is an important source of our "modern" way of thinking about the "quality of life."

A graduate of the University of Tübingen, he wrote to his friend Schelling for advice on a good place to live in Germany, where there were many good history books available and even *ein gutes Bier* ("a good local beer"). Because Hegel had inherited a pretty sizable sum of money, he was free to live and teach virtually anywhere he wished. But Schelling advised him to go to Jena, where there was good beer, many books, and the philosphy of history was discussed and debated. After reading a great deal on the history of Greece and Rome (and perhaps after a few beers), Hegel announced that history worked along certain observable lines.

All history is an irresistible advancement of humankind, a technological, philosophical, and even moral progression with each new stage of history more enlightened than the last. This view of history, like that of Christianity and Judaism, is linear, moving in a straight line toward a utopian end. Hegel's speculations are interesting and have been used as arguments both to support Christianity and to demonstrate that it is "outmoded," "unscientific," and "irrational."

Hegel believed that history operates as an observable process with identifiable laws and "causes" that work continuously to produce human progress. History is not merely a collection of random events arranged in chronological order but a true process that represents a "spirit" at work.

The process of history is presided over by a "dominant" people. In the earliest phases of civilized history, a period Hegel called the "Semitic" phase, the Jews and other Near Eastern peoples were the dominant "guardians of civilization." Next, in the "Classical" phase, the Greeks and Romans were in charge. Hegel felt that his own times were the "Germanic" phase, in which the Germans, English, and other northern Europeans were the "dominant" force in propelling history forward. Hegel's philosophy thus became a root of modern democratic liberalism, Nazism, and communism.

Compare Hegel's view of history with that held by traditional societies, in which human history, per se, was of little value, only a replay of the events portrayed in the myths.

Hegel maintained that history progresses through "dialectics." Using dialectics, one statement, the *thesis*, is contrasted with its opposite, or *antithesis*, to produce a new idea, the *synthesis*. Marx's theory of communism, for instance, held that class struggle between the workers (thesis) and capital, or industry owners (antithesis), would produce socialism (synthesis); all history would thus be propelled toward the utopia of pure communism. Marxism is an excellent example of Hegel's concept of linear history at work.

Hegel wrote that the most primitive stage of religious development is the "nature religion" or "sorcery" stage. From that level humankind progresses to monotheism—in his words, the recognition of "the spiritual individuality of God." At this stage God is no longer an anthropomorphic projection speaking through history but a transcendent spirit that is perceived to act in history.

Hegel believed that the great work of God in history was in the mission of Jesus Christ to reconcile God and mankind. As a result of the death of Christ, the union between God and man ceases to be a "fact" but is rather a "vital idea" that directs people's lives, giving them a purpose.

The New Hegelians

The New Hegelians were *not* a British punk rock band; they were, rather, a major force in the "demythologization" of Western culture.

After Hegel's death one group of his followers, the "Old" Hegelians, used his philosophical system to defend Christianity from another group of his followers, the "New" Hegelians. The New Hegelians were strongly influenced by the Scottish philosopher David Hume, who felt that anything that could not be demonstrated empirically (by observation of the five senses) or that was logically self-evident, was invalid.

The New Hegelians felt that the forward progression of history called for a rational examination of Christianity, which was perceived as "outmoded"; the progression of history required a new religious view that could stand the test of empirical study. As rationalists and empiricists, they believed that myth and the supernatural elements of religion were outside the realm of objective proof and were "fiction." They were skeptical of all revealed religions because they were based on "irrational" faith experience. They doubted whether any myth-based religious system would survive in the "scientific" nineteenth century.

David Friedrich Strauss of Germany (1808–1874) was the most influential of the New Hegelians. Strauss felt that Christianity needed to be studied from a historical perspective, following Hegel's framework. Strauss wrote a then-controversial book that portrayed Jesus Christ as an ordinary historical character, the natural son of Mary and Joseph. He rejected the supernatural elements of the Gospels.

In France as well, Ernest Renan (1823–1892), influenced by Hegel and Strauss, outraged the French public with a "demythologized" biography of Jesus that omitted any reference to the supernatural. He called it a "historicized" gospel. For Renan, as for Strauss, the "new" religion of the West would have to be a rational, demythologized view of a historical Jesus with an emphasis on ethical teaching.

Another New Hegelian was Bruno Bauer (1809–1882), an associate of Strauss and an erstwhile collaborator of Karl Marx. Bauer wrote that the Gospels were complete fabrications, unable to stand the tests of Hegelian historical proof, and he went so far as to question the historical existence of Jesus Christ.

Again recall Janet's statement that a society abandons its myth when the gods fail to speak. By the middle of the nineteenth century, the "gods" appeared to have very little to say.

German Form Criticism of the Bible

A group of German biblical scholars and theologians decided to undertake a critical historical analysis of the Bible that proved an invaluable contribution to both biblical scholarship and the demythologization of culture.

The best known of these was Ferdinand Christian Baur (1792–1860), who studied the New Testament, especially the writings of Saint Paul, in light of the historical circumstances—or *Sitz im Leben* (German for "setting in life")—in which they were written. Baur was particularly interested in the conflicts in the early Christian churches.

Baur was succeeded by Adolf von Harnack (1851–1930), who

studied the development of the creeds in the early Christian church and determined that the conflict between the Church and the Gnostic heresy led to the development of the creeds. Harnack believed that the mythical or supernatural trappings of Scripture that were contained in the creeds were the product of this tension. Harnack's writing influenced both Karl Barth, the twentieth-century defender of traditional Christianity, and Rudolf Bultmann, the often controversial biblical scholar who endeavored to identify the "mythic" elements in Scripture.

Another influence that must be mentioned is Albert Schweitzer (1875–1965), now remembered as a humanitarian, medical missionary, and concert organist. Schweitzer wrote a book called *The Quest for the Historical Jesus*, which stripped the Bible narrative of its supernatural trappings to show a Jesus who was a typical Jewish preacher with one message—the imminent coming of the Kingdom of God. When no apocalypse appeared, Schweitzer maintained, Jesus died an embittered man. His followers wrote the Gospels, adding supernatural elements, in an effort to make sense of the life and ministry of Christ.

Finally, there was the controversial Rudolf Bultmann of Germany (1884–1976), who viewed the New Testament texts as essentially mythical and attempted to separate the mythic from the historic in the accounts of Jesus' life.*

Positivism and Logical Positivism

A major philosophical assault on the validity of the supernatural was positivism, the philosophy of August Comte (1798–1857) of France. It is in his philosophy that modern materialism, and the interpretations of myth offered by both Freud and Lévi-Strauss, have their antecedent.

He believed that the scientific method could be applied to the study of any phenomenon and certainly to human behavior, making

---

*But remember that Bultmann defined *myth* as "a breakthrough of the sacred into history" (see page 263).

Comte the founder of sociology and the other social sciences. Anything that could not be observed scientifically, in his view, did not exist.

Not at all a modest man, Comte asserted that his positivism was the third and last of three successive phases in the history of humankind. In the first, or "theological" stage, religion and myth were needed to explain all phenomena. The second, the "metaphysical," stage was based on philosophical speculations about "ideals" or "absolutes." In the stage of "positivism," scientific observation alone would suffice. For Comte, causative thinking was the final form of thought.

Comte believed that religious beliefs based on the supernatural would soon be abandoned. So he founded his own "religion of humanity," borrowing heavily on the ritual of Roman Catholicism. Comte instituted elaborate rites, complete with robes, incense, and liturgies. This religion was described by his contemporaries as "Catholicism without Christianity." Comte "demythologized" the calendar by providing months named "Gutenberg" and "Shakespeare."

Like any good eccentric, Comte had some very entertaining inconsistencies. Although he largely lived off his wife's income—he was married to a prostitute who shocked him by offering to "entertain" wealthy clients—Comte kept a ledger of every penny, including the change in his pants pockets. He was fond of wearing the robes and vestments of his new "religion."

His direct philosophical descendants were the twentieth-century Logical Positivists, including Ludwig Wittgenstein. The Logical Positivists believed that any statement that could not be empirically proved should be rejected. Logical Positivism relied on minute examinations of the use of language, and has not proved durable.

Die Wissenschaft des Judentums: The "Science" of Judaism

The demythologization process that profoundly affected Christianity had its parallel in Judaism. For a nineteenth-century German intellectual, whether Protestant, Catholic, or Jewish, there was no greater compliment than to be called *wissenschaftlich*, or "scientific."

Prior to the European Enlightenment of the eighteenth century and its Jewish parallel, the Haskalah (Hebrew for "enlightenment"), there was but one sect in European Jewry, the Orthodox. There were differences, to be sure, between the Sephardic and Ashkenazic* rites, but in all cases, Judaism was a thoroughly orthodox and thoroughly "mythic" worldview, although the "mythological" in Judaism, as a monotheistic, revealed religion, was less advanced than in other world religions, and the nature of biblical and Talmudic Judaism was highly conservative.

Yet, the forces of empiricism were at work among European Jews, especially in Germany. The great Jewish Enlightenment thinker Moses Mendelssohn (1729–1786)† mirrored the thoughts of many of his contemporaries.

> It is true: I recognize no eternal truths, other than those which can not only be comprehended by human reason, but also demonstrated and verified by the human faculties.

The forces of "demythologization" and assimilation produced profound changes in European Judaism, characterized by the Reform movement in Germany. These forces were accelerated by the "emancipation" of the Jews—their guarantee of full civil and political rights—during the Napoleonic period. Soon, many German Jews began to think of Judaism as one of several "German" religions, destined to take its place beside Protestantism and Catholicism in "modern" Germany.

Reform Judaism was the expression of both assimilation and demythologization. German, rather than Hebrew, was to be the language of public worship; all prayers describing the Jews as a "nation" were abandoned. In fact, the first Reform services, held in a "temple"

---

*Ashkenazic Jews are the German- and Yiddish-speaking Jews of Germany, Central Europe, and Russia; *Ashkenaz* is Hebrew for "Germany." Sephardic Jews are the descendants of the Jews of Spain (the Hebrew word is *Sefarad*), who later settled in the Netherlands, North Africa, Turkey, and Greece after being expelled by Ferdinand and Isabella in 1492.

†Moses Mendelssohn was the grandfather of the composer Felix Mendelssohn-Bartholdy, who converted to Lutheranism and composed a "Reformation Symphony" based on Luther's hymn, "A Mighty Fortress Is Our God."

rather than a synagogue, very closely resembled services held by their Lutheran neighbors. A follower of Moses Mendelssohn named David Friedlaender (1756–1834) was the "father" of Reform Judaism, even going so far as to ask the Lutheran authorities in Berlin to admit him as a Lutheran, provided that he and his followers were not required to accept the divinity of Jesus. They were refused.

In 1810, Israel Jacobson established the first Reform Jewish temple in the German state of Braunschweig—complete with German-language sermons and hymns, as well as organ music—previously unknown in Jewish worship. In 1849 Samuel Holdheim of the Berlin temple went so far as to hold services on Sundays.

Contemporary with these innovations, Abraham Geiger (1810–1874) exhorted Reform Jews to review the Scriptures from a "scientific and historical" point of view, in short, a demythologized approach, which emphasized the ethical teachings of Judaism while rejecting many traditional practices, including dietary laws, circumcision, and the divine origins of the Torah.

In Germany, an effort to demythologize Judaism (as the New Hegelians were doing to Protestant Christianity) focused on Leopold Zunz (1794–1886), who founded a movement called Die Wissenschaft des Judentums, or "The Science of Judaism." It was his goal to establish a systematic and scientific study of the Jews and their history (conducted in German, of course) that emphasized the communal, rather than the religious, aspects of Judaism.

Reform Judaism was carried to the United States by immigrants, where it flourished beyond the highest hopes of its German founders. The basic statement of a demythologized Reform Judaism can be found in the Pittsburgh Platform of 1885:

> We hold that the modern discoveries of scientific researches in the domains of nature and history are not antagonistic to the doctrines of Judaism, the Bible reflecting the primitive idea of its own age and at times clothing its conception of divine providence and justice dealing with man in miraculous narratives.
> ... We hold that all such Mosaic and Rabbinical laws as regulate diet, priestly purity and dress originated in ages and under the influence of ideas altogether foreign to our present mental

and spiritual state. They fail to impress the modern Jew with a spirit of priestly holiness; their observance in our days is apt rather to obstruct than to further modern spiritual elevation.

New Hegelian thinking colored much of the intellectual life of German Jews during the nineteenth century, and "form criticism" of the Bible was even more directed at the Old Testament than the New. The term *positivism* was even applied to the study of Judaism by Zechariah Frankel's (1801–1875) "positive-historical" school of Judaism.

A reaction to the demythologized Judaism resulted in Conservative Judaism, championed by the brilliant Solomon Schechter (1850–1915) of Great Britain, who felt that there need not be a conflict between reason and traditional Judaism, nor did the communal history of the Jews need to be divorced from religious practice. Schechter spoke directly to the "form critics":

> Some years ago when the waves of Higher Criticism of the Old Testament reached the shores of this country, and such questions as the heterogeneous composition of the Pentateuch [the Torah, or "five books of Moses"], the comparatively late date of the Levitical Legislation, and the post-exilic origin of certain prophecies as well as the Psalms began to be freely discussed by the press and even in the pulpit, the invidious remark was often made: What will now become of Judaism when its last stronghold, the Law, is being shaken to its very foundations?
> ... There is hardly any metaphysical system, old or new, which has not in the course of time been adapted by able dialecticians to the creed which they happened to hold. In our own times we have seen the glorious, though not entirely novel, spectacle of Agnosticism itself becoming the rightful handmaid of Queen Theology. The real danger lies in "nature" (Natural Science) with its stern demand of law and regularity in all phenomena, and in the "simple meaning" (or Philology) with its inconsiderate insistence on truth.

Schecter's words apply to the forces of positivism and New Hegelianism dominant in the late nineteenth and early twentieth centuries; they might have been addressed to his Protestant theological colleagues as well as to European culture at large. A *wissenschaftlich* worldview, unlike a mythic worldview, answered the "how," but not the "why."

THE LEGITIMACY OF THE SUPERNATURAL

God Is Dead—Nietzsche
Neitzsche Is Dead—God
—1980s T-shirt

Friedrich Nietzsche (1844–1900), the son of a Lutheran pastor, declared "God is dead" as early as the 1880s. Again, in the 1960s, after the "demythologization" of the Christian religion, Thomas Altizer—a theologian, and not a scientist—made the statement "God is dead," launching a worldwide debate.

A contemporary German feminist theologian, Dorothee Sölle, looking back on the then-radical statement, considers it one of the great "nonstatements" of history: Those who believed in God were in no way affected by the statement, and those who did not believe in God were also not affected.

By the end of the 1960s, there was a sense that there was no longer any place left for the supernatural in our lives, the product of one hundred and fifty years of Hegelian "historical" thinking and the inheritance of positivism. It was also in the 1960s that widespread interest in Eastern religion, fantasy literature, and new forms of Christianity began to flower.

Myth now meant "falsehood" in the popular vocabulary. At the same time, the scholars of myth fought hard to demonstrate that myth did not mean falsehood, but was rather a vehicle by which truth was conveyed.

In the 1970s and 1980s, there was a large-scale interest once again in religion, and particularly in the supernatural. The period after the declaration "God is dead" was characterized by a rise in Christian fundamentalism, interest in Eastern religions, the New Age movement with all its emphasis on the paranormal, the Charismatic renewal in the Christian churches, and a rising interest in the traditional practice of Judaism. As Paul Johnson wrote in his book *Modern Times*, there were probably fewer atheists in 1980 than in 1880.

In short, the mythic worldview is alive and well and making a comeback. To be human is to have myths. The mythic worldview cannot be eliminated.

Notes

Most sources are given in the text. The edition of the Bible quoted in this book is The Jerusalem Bible. The Greek, Roman, Indian, and Norse myths are composites of sources found in the Bibliography (unless otherwise noted).

Chapter One

THE MYTH OF HUNDUN: Anthony Christie, *Chinese Mythology*, p. 57.
TIME AND MYTH: Sir James G. Frazer, *The Golden Bough*, pp. 477–78.
Martin Heidegger: quoted by Hannah Arendt in *The Life of the Mind*, p. 47.
HISTORY AND MYTH: Nikolay Berdyayev: source given in text.
Lévi-Strauss, *Myth and Meaning*, p. 42
Eliade, *Patterns in Comparative Religion*, pp. 396–98.
THE CIVIC MYTH: Durkheim, quoted by Ernest F. Wallwork in *Durkheim: Morality and Milieu*, pp. 59–60.
MORALITY AND MYTH: Ibid.

Chapter Two

All sources given in text.

Chapter Three

CREATION MYTHS OF INDIA: There Was Nothing: *Textual Sources for the Study of Hinduism*, edited by Wendy Doniger O'Flaherty, p. 33.

The Thoughts of Brahma: Ibid., p. 65.

Brahma Is Lonely: *The Upanishads*, edited and translated by F. Max Müller, vol. II, p. 33.

THE CREATION MYTH OF IRAN: Jon Hinnels, *Persian Mythology*, pp. 21–22.

CREATION MYTHS OF AFRICA: The Yoruba: Geoffrey Parrinder, *African Mythology*, pp. 21–22.

Madagascar: Ibid., pp. 45–46.

CREATION MYTHS OF EGYPT: The Watery Abyss: Adolf Erman, *Life in Ancient Egypt*; Memphite Theology of Creation, source given in text.

Pritchard, James B., Editor, *The Ancient Near East, Vol. I.* Princeton: Princeton University Press, 1958.

The Creation Myth of Japan: Joseph Campbell, *The Masks of God: Oriental Mythology*, pp. 466–73.

THE BABYLONIAN CREATION MYTH: James B. Pritchard, ed. *The Ancient Near East, Vol. I: An Anthology of Texts and Pictures*, the translation of this portion by S.N. Kramer, pp 28–37.

THE POLYNESIAN CREATION MYTHS: Padraic Colum, *Orpheus: Myths of the World*, pp. 253–55; Roslyn Poignant, *Oceanic Mythology*, pp. 88–91; Martha Beckwith, *Hawaiian Mythology*, pp. 64–68.

CREATION MYTHS OF THE AMERICAS: Sioux: Given in Text.

Pawnee: Natalie Curtis, *The Indians Book*, pp. 99–102; Cottie A. Burland, *North American Indian Mythology*, p. 85.

Arikara: Burland, p. 77.

Iroquois: Burland, p. 66.

Yuma: Curtis, p. 562–68

Zuni: Lewis Spence, *The Myths of the North American Indians*, p. 106.

The Playanos of Southern California: Ibid.

Maya: Colum, pp. 285–89; Irene Nicholson, *Mexican and Central American Mythology*, pp. 76–77.

Inca: Harold Osborne, *South American Mythology*, pp. 76–79, 105.

THE BABYLONIAN CREATION MYTH: *The Ancient Near East*, edited by James B. Pritchard, vol. I, pp. 31–34.

"The Creation"; James Weldon Johnson, *God's Trombones*, in Victor Gollancz, *From Darkness to Light*, pp. 229–31.

Carl Sagan, *The Dragons of Eden*, pp. 92–93

THE SERPENT: Campbell, *The Masks of Gold: Occidental Mythology*, pp. 9–13.

Carl Sagan, *The Dragons of Eden*, pp. 140–41.

Man and His Symbols, edited by C.G. Jung, pp. 153–55.

THE TREE: Sagan, pp. 92–93.

Jung, Ibid.

Campbell, Ibid.

Sagan, p. 140.

Chapter Four

A MODERN THEOLOGIAN'S INTERPRETATION OF THE FALL: Paul Tillich, *Systematic Theology*, vol. II, pp. 31, 37.

THE TALMUDIC FALL: Robert Graves and Raphael Patai, *Hebrew Myths*, pp. 76–78.

THE STORY OF POIA: Spence, pp. 200–205.

THE FOUR AGES OF MAN: *Textual Sources for the Study of Hinduism*, edited and translated by Wendy Doniger O'Flaherty, pp. 68–71.

THE FIVE SUNS: Nicholson, pp. 53–54.

THE FIVE WORLDS: Burland, pp. 92–96.

Kloskurbeh The Teacher: Curtis, pp. 1–6.

THREE STORIES OF MAUI THE TRICKSTER: Colum, pp. 254–60; Poignant, pp. 61–63.

THE ORIGIN OF MEDICINE: Spence, pp. 249–50.

MURILÉ AND THE MOONCHIEF: Parrinder, p. 73.

THE HUMAN RACE IS SAVED: Spence, pp. 257–60.

Chapter Five

TATA AND NENA: *Mitos Mexicanos*, edited by Octavio Mejia, pp. 139–41.

Creek-Natchez: Burland, p. 115.

Mojave-Apache: Curtis, pp. 330–31.

Cree: Burland, p. 57.

Algonquin: Spence, pp. 107–108.

Inca: Osborne, p. 98.

Egypt: Erman, *Life in Ancient Egypt*, pp. 267–69.

Chapter Six

TWO PERUVIAN LOVE STORIES: Garcia Morales, J. and Villareal, A., *Literatura Suramericana*, pp. 236–240; Osborne, pp. 98–102.

ANGUS OG: T. W. Rolleston, *Celtic Myths and Legends*, pp. 121–23.

ALGON AND THE SKY-GIRL: Spence, pp. 152–56.

Chapter Seven

MORALITY TALES FROM MAHABHARATA: Ananda Coomaraswamy and Sister Nivedita, *Myths of the Hindus and Buddhists*, pp. 367–74.

ANANSI THE SPIDER: Parrinder, pp. 134–40.

Chapter Eight

THE STORY OF TWO BROTHERS: *The Ancient Near East*, edited by James B. Pritchard, vol. I, pp. 12–16.

Nopatsis: Spence, pp. 184–87

Chapter Nine

All sources given in text.

Chapter Ten

PARE AND HUTU: Poignant, p. 66.

SAYADIO IN THE LAND OF THE DEAD: Spence, pp. 260–62.

Chapter Eleven

PARE AND HUTU: Poignant, p. 66.

SAYADIO IN THE LAND OF THE DEAD: Spence, pp. 260–262.

Chapter Twelve

Jeremiah Curtin: Colum, p. 5.

Sigmund Freud: *Totem and Taboo*, IV, *The Basic Writings of Sigmund Freud*, A. A. Brill, ed. pp. 875–876

Ananda Coomaraswamy: Father Andrew M. Greeley, *Myths of Religion*, p. 13.

Nikolay Berdyayev: *The Modern Tradition*, edited by Richard Ellmann and Charles Feidelson, Jr., p. 674.

Carl Gustav Jung: Jung, *Memories, Dreams and Reflections*, p. 311.

George Santayana: Santayana, *Reason in Religion*, p. 49.

Alan Watts: Greeley, Ibid.

Thomas Mann: *The Modern Tradition*, p. 675.

Friedrich von Schlegel: Ibid., p. 662.

F. Max Müller: Ernst Cassirer, *Language and Myth*, p. 5.

Bruno Bettelheim: Bettelheim, *The Uses of Enchantment*, p. 35.

Robert Graves: Graves and Patai, *Hebrew Myths*, p. 11.

Bronislaw Malinowski: Colum, p. 5; *The Modern Tradition*, p. 633.

Claude Lévi-Strauss: Lévi-Strauss, *Myth and Meaning*, p. 17.

Joseph Campbell: Campbell, *The Hero with a Thousand Faces*, p. 3.

Hans Küng: Küng, *On Being a Christian*, pp. 414–5.

Carlos Fuentes: Wendy Faris, *Carlos Fuentes*, p. 18.

A. Sabatier: Coomaraswamy, *Myths of the Hindus and Buddhists*, p. viii.

Rudolf Bultmann: Bultmann, *New Testament and Mythology & Other Basic Writings*, pp. 9–10, 97–99.

Reinhold Niebuhr: given in text.

Paul Tillich: Tillich, *Systematic Theology*, vol. 3., pp. 59–60.

Chapter Thirteen

Johann Jakob Bachofen: The source for all material on Bachofen is Henri F. Ellenberger, *The Discovery of the Unconscious*, pp. 218–23.

Robert Graves: Graves, *The Greek Myths*, vol. I, p. 13.

Émile Durkheim, quoted by Wallwork, *Durkheim: Morality and Milieu*, p. 140.

Émile Durkheim: Marvin Harris, *Cultural Materialism*, p. 167.

Pierre Janet: The source for all material on Janet is Ellenberger, pp. 331–409.

Sigmund Freud: Peter Gay, *Freud: A Life For Our Time*; Ellenberger; Ernest Jones, *The Life and Work of Sigmund Freud; The Basic Writings of Sigmund Freud*; Carl Gustav Jung: C. G. Jung, *Memories, Dreams and Reflections*, p. 131; Campbell, *Myths to Live By*, p. 83; "Archetypes of the Collective Unconscious," from *The Basic Works of C. G. Jung*, edited by Violet de Laszlo, p. 287; "The Collective Unconscious," *The Pocket Jung*, edited by Joseph Campbell, p. 60; H. Richard Niebuhr, *Christ and Culture*, p. 44n; Lévi-Strauss, *Myth and Meaning*, pp. 8, 44; Harris, *Cultural Materialism*, pp. 167–68; Aiken and Barrett, *Twentieth Century Western Philosophers*, pp. 647–50.

Chapter Fourteen

All sources given in text.

Bibliography

Aiken, Henry, and Barrett, E., eds. *Twentieth Century Western Philosophers.* 4 vols. New York: Random House, 1962.

Alexander, Phillip S., ed. and trans. *Textual Sources for the Study of Judaism.* Totowa, N.J.: Barnes and Noble, 1984.

Arendt, Hannah. *The Life of the Mind.* 1971. Reprint. New York and San Diego: Harcourt, Brace, Jovanovich, 1978.

Assman, Hugo, and Mate, Reyes. *Sobre la Religión—II.* Salamanca: Sigueme, 1975.

Attenborough, David. *Life on Earth: A Natural History.* Boston: Little, Brown and Co., 1979.

Beckwith, Martha. *Hawaiian Mythology.* New Haven: Yale University Press, 1940.

Berdyayev, Nikolay. *Christian Existentialism.* Translated by D. A. Lowrie. New York: Harper, 1965.

Berry, Gerald L. *Religions of the World.* New York: Barnes and Noble, 1956.

Bettelheim, Bruno. *The Uses of Enchantment.* New York: Vintage Books, 1977.

Boas, Franz. *Anthropology and Modern Life.* New York: Dover, 1986.

Brill, A. A., ed. *The Basic Writings of Sigmund Freud.* New York: Modern Library, 1966. 1938. Reprint.

Bultmann, Rudolf. *New Testament and Mythology & Other Basic Writings.* Selected, edited, and translated by Schubert M. Ogden. Philadelphia: Fortress Press, 1984.

Burland, Cottie A. *North American Indian Mythology.* New York: Peter Bedrick Books, 1985.

Campbell, Joseph. *The Hero with a Thousand Faces.* Princeton, N.J.: Princeton University Press, 1949.

————. *The Masks of God: Creative Mythology.* London and New York: Penguin, 1969.

————. *The Masks of God: Occidental Mythology.* London and New York: Penguin, 1964.

————. *The Masks of God: Oriental Mythology.* London and New York: Penguin, 1962.

————. *The Masks of God: Primitive Mythology.* London and New York: Penguin, 1959.

————. *Myths to Live By.* New York: Viking Press, 1972.

————, ed. *The Pocket Jung.* New York: Viking Press, 1971.

Camus, Albert. *The Myth of Sisyphus.* Translated by Justin O'Brien. New York: Alfred Knopf, 1955.

Cassirer, Ernst. *Language and Myth.* 1954. Reprint. New York: Dover, 1971.

Catlin, George. *Letters and Notes on the Manners, Customs and Conditions of the North American Indians.* 2 vols. New York: Dover, 1973.

Christie, Anthony. *Chinese Mythology.* New York: Peter Bedrick, 1985.

Colum, Padraic. *Orpheus: Myths of the World.* New York: Macmillan, 1930.

Conze, Edward, ed. and trans. *Buddhist Scriptures.* London and New York: Penguin, 1960.

Coomaraswamy, Ananda, and Sister Nivedita. *Myths of the Hindus and Buddhists.* New York: Dover, 1967.

Copeland, Lewis, ed. *The World's Great Speeches.* New York: Dover, 1958.

Curtis, Natalie. *The Indians Book.* New York: Dover, 1968.

Dawood, N. J., trans. *The Koran.* 1956. Reprint. London and New York: Penguin, 1971.

de Laszlo, Violet, ed. *The Basic Works of C. G. Jung.* New York: Modern Library, 1959.

de Unamuno, Miguel. *Mi Religion Y Otros Ensayos Breves.* Madrid: Espasa Calpe, S.A., 1978.

————. *Tragic Sense of Life.* New York: Dover, 1954.

Eliade, Mircea. *A History of Religious Ideas.* 2 vols. 1972. Reprint. Chicago: University of Chicago Press, 1978.

————. *The Myth of the Eternal Return.* Translated by Willard R. Trask. Princeton: Bollingen/Princeton University Press, 1971.

————. *Patterns in Comparative Religion.* Translated by Rosemary Sheed. New York: New American Library, 1958.

Ellenberger, Henri F. *The Discovery of the Unconscious: The History and Evolution of Dynamic Psychiatry.* New York: Basic Books, 1970.

Ellmann, Richard, and Feidelson, Charles, Jr., eds. *The Modern Tradition.* New York: Oxford University Press, 1965.

Elwell, Walter, ed. *The Dictionary of Evangelical Theology.* Grand Rapids, Mich.: Baker Books, 1984.

Erdoes, Richard, and Ortiz, Alfonso. *American Indian Myths and Legends.* New York: Pantheon, 1984.

Erman, Adolf. *Life in Ancient Egypt.* Translated by H. M. Tirard. New York: Dover, 1971.

Faris, Wendy. *Carlos Fuentes.* New York: F. Ungar, 1983.

Frazer, Sir James G. *The Golden Bough.* 1923. Reprint. London: Macmillan, 1971.

Fuentes, Carlos. *La Region Mas Transparente.* Madrid: Ediciones Catedra S.A., 1982.

Garcia Morales, J., and Villareal, A. *Literatura Suramericana.* Madrid: Ediciones Sol, n.d.

Gay, Peter, *Freud: A Life for Our Time*, New York: W.W. Norton, 1988.

Gollancz, Victor, ed. *From Darkness to Light.* New York: Harper Brothers, 1955.

Grant, Michael. *Roman Myths.* New York: Charles Scribner's Sons, 1971.

Graves, Robert. *The Greek Myths.* 2 vols. London and New York: Penguin, 1970.

————. *The White Goddess.* New York: Farrar, Straus and Giroux, 1948.

———— and Patai, Raphael. *Hebrew Myths.* New York: Anchor Books, 1964.

Gray, John. *Near Eastern Mythology.* London: Hamlyn, 1969.

Greeley, [Father] Andrew M. *Myths of Religion.* New York: Warner Books, 1989.

Guthrie, W. K. C. *Orpheus and Greek Religion.* New York: W. W. Norton, 1966.

Hamilton, Edith. *Mythology.* New York: New American Library, 1969.

Harrington, Michael. *The Politics at God's Funeral.* New York: Holt, Rinehart and Winston, 1983.

Harris, Marvin. *Cultural Materialism.* New York: Vintage Books, 1980.

Hinnels, Jon. *Persian Mythology.* New York: Peter Bedrick Books, 1985.

Izard, Michel, and Smith, Pierre. *Between Belief and Transgression: Structuralist Essays in Religion, History and Myth.* Translated by John Leavitt. Chicago: University of Chicago Press, 1982.

Jaspers, Karl. "The Axial Age." In *Twentieth Century Western Philosophers*, edited by Henry Aiken and E. Barrett. New York: Random House, 1962.

Johnson, Paul. *Modern Times: The World From the Twenties to the Eighties.* New York: Vintage Books, 1965.

Jones, Ernest. *The Life and Work of Sigmund Freud.* New York: Basic Books, 1961.

Jung, C. G. *Memories, Dreams and Reflections.* Edited by Aniela Jaffe. Translated by Richard and Clara Winston. New York: Vintage Books, 1965.

————, ed. *Man and His Symbols.* New York: Dell, 1968.

———— and Kerenyi, C. *Essays on a Science of Mythology.* 1959. Reprint. Princeton: Bollingen/Princeton University Press, 1973.

Küng, Hans. *On Being a Christian.* Translated by Edward Quinn. Garden City, N.Y.: Doubleday, 1976.

Lévi-Strauss, Claude. *Myth and Meaning.* New York: Schocken Books, 1979.

————. *The Savage Mind.* Chicago: University of Chicago Press, 1966.

————. *Structural Anthropology.* New York: Doubleday, 1963.

MacCana, Proinsias. *Celtic Mythology.* London: Hamlyn, 1970.

Mejia, Octavio, *Mitos Mexicanos,* Mexico City: Prensa Universidad, 1958.

Müller, F. Max, trans. *The Upanishads.* 2 vols. New York: Dover, 1962.

Nicholson, Irene. *Mexican and Central American Mythology.* New York: Peter Bedrick Books, 1985.

Niebuhr, H. Richard. *Christ and Culture.* New York: Harper and Row, 1971.

Niebuhr, Reinhold. *An Interpretation of Christian Ethics.* New York: Harper and Brothers, 1935.

————. *Beyond Tragedy: Essays on the Christian Interpretation of History.* New York: Charles Scribner's Sons, 1937.

————. *Reflections on the End of an Era.* New York: Charles Scribner's Sons, 1934.

O'Flaherty, Wendy Doniger, ed. *Textual Sources for the Study of Hinduism.* Totowa, N.J.: Barnes and Noble, 1988.

Osborne, Harold, *South American Mythology,* New York, Peter Bedrick Books, 1984.

Parrinder, Geoffrey. *African Mythology.* New York: Peter Bedrick Books, 1985.

Poignant, Roslyn. *Oceanic Mythology.* London: Hamlyn, 1967.

Prescott, William H. *History of the Conquest of Mexico and History of the Conquest of Peru* (in one volume) New York: Modern Library, N.D.

Pritchard, James B., ed. *The Ancient Near East.* 2 vols. Princeton: Princeton University Press, 1958.

Ricoeur, Paul. *Fallible Man.* Chicago: Henry Regnery, 1965.

———. *The Symbolism of Evil.* Boston: Beacon, 1967.

Rippin, Andrew, and Knappert, Jan. eds. and trans. *Textual Sources for the Study of Islam.* Totawa. N.J.: Barnes and Noble, 1987.

Rolleston, T. W. *Celtic Myths and Legends.* New York: Dover, 1970.

Sadeh, Pinhas. *Jewish Folklore.* Translated by Hillel Halkin. New York: Anchor Books, 1989.

Sagan, Carl. *The Dragons of Eden.* New York: Random House, 1977.

Santayana, George. *Reason in Religion.* New York: Dover, 1982.

Spence, Lewis. *The Myths of the North American Indians.* New York: Dover, 1989.

Tillich Paul. *Systematic Theology.* 3 vols. Chicago: University of Chicago Press, 1967.

Wallwork, Ernest F. *Durkheim: Morality and Milieu.* Cambridge, Mass. Harvard University Press, 1972.

Watts, Alan. *The Way of Zen.* 1959. Reprint. New York: Vintage Books, 1989.

Zoll, Donald Atwell. *Twentieth Century Political Philosophy.* Englewood Cliffs, N.J.: Prentice-Hall, 1974.

Grateful acknowledgment is made to the following for permission to reprint previously published material:

Augsburg Fortress: Excerpts from *New Testament and Mythology and Other Basic Writings* by Rudolf Bultmann, translated by S.M. Ogden. Copyright © 1984 by Fortress Press. Reprinted by permission of Augsburg Fortress.

Doubleday and Darton Longman & Todd Ltd.: Excerpts from *The Jerusalem Bible* edited by Alexander Jones. Copyright © 1966, 1967, 1968 by Darton Longman & Todd Ltd. and Doubleday, a division of Bantam Doubleday Dell Publishing Group, Inc. Reprinted by permission of Doubleday, a division of Bantam Doubleday Dell Publishing Group, Inc., and Darton Longman & Todd Ltd.

Doubleday: Excerpts from *On Being a Christian* by Hans Kung. Copyright © 1976 by Doubleday, a division of Bantam Doubleday Dell Publishing Group, Inc. Reprinted by permission of Doubleday, a division of Bantam Doubleday Dell Publishing Group, Inc.

Dover Publications, Inc.: Excerpt from *The World's Greatest Speeches* edited by Lewis Copeland.

J.G. Ferguson Publishing Company: Excerpts from *Man and His Symbols* edited by Carl Jung, J.G. Ferguson Publishing Company, 1964.

Alfred A. Knopf, Inc.: Excerpts from *The Myth of Sisyphus and Other Essays* by Albert Camus, translated by Justin O'Brien. Copyright © 1955 by Alfred A. Knopf, Inc. Reprinted by permission of the publisher.

Oxford University Press: Excerpt from *The Idea of the Holy* Second Edition by Rudolf Otto, translated by John W. Harvey, 1950. Reprinted by permission of Oxford University Press.

Penguin Books Ltd.: Suras 56, 57 (pp. 378–379) from *The Koran* translated by N.J. Dawood, Penguin Classics 1956, Fifth Revised Edition 1990. Copyright © 1956, 1959, 1966, 1968, 1974, 1990 by N.J. Dawood. Reprinted by permission of Penguin Books Ltd.

Princeton University Press: Excerpts from *The Ancient Near East* Volume I edited by James B. Pritchard. Copyright © 1958 by Princeton University Press. Copyright renewed 1986. Reprinted by permission of Princeton University Press.

Dr. Carl Sagan: Excerpts from *The Dragons of Eden* by Dr. Carl Sagan. Copyright © 1977 by Carl Sagan.

The University of Chicago Press: Excerpts from *Systemic Theology* Volumes I and II by Paul Tillich. Volume I copyright © 1951 by the University of Chicago. Volume II copyright © 1957 by The University of Chicago. All rights reserved.

Viking Penguin: "The Creation" from *God's Trombones* by James Weldon Johnson. Copyright © 1927 by The Viking Press, Inc., renewed © 1955 by Grace Nail Johnson. Reprinted by permission of Viking Penguin, a division of Penguin Books USA Inc.

Yale University Press: Excerpt from *Hawaiian Mythology* by Martha Beckwith. Copyright © 1940 by Yale University Press. Reprinted by permission of Yale University Press.

Index

Abanakis, emergence myth of, 109–10
Adam:
Creation story and, 77–78
Fall and, 92–96
Adler, Alfred, 272, 280
Aegeus, King of Athens, 186–89
Aegina, 194–96
"Aeneas in the Underworld," 222–23
Africa:
Creation myths of, 48–50
West, see West Africans and West
African myths
agricultural myths:
Babylonian, 200, 202–3
Egyptian, 213, 215
Ahriman, 10
apocalyptic myth and, 241
Creation myth and, 41–44
Akaiyan, 171–73
"Algon and the Sky–Girl," 153–54
Algonquins, 109, 191, 193, 231
Creation myth of, 45–46, 61–62
flood myth of, 133
love myth of, 153–54
Underworld myth of, 211–12
Amazons, 190, 272
"Anansi and the Chameleon,"
162–63
"Anansi and the Ear of Corn,"
159–61
Anansi the Spider, 159–65

Angus Og, love myth and, 151–52
anthropomorphism, 4, 8–9
Antigone, 198, 283, 289
Anubis, 173–74, 216
"Ao and Po," 56–57
Apaches, 108–9, 131–32
Aphrodite, 25, 27, 47
heroic myth and, 190–91
love myths and, 137, 139–42, 145
matriarchal theory and, 272
and "Prometheus and
Epimetheus," 115
Apocalypse and apocalyptic myths,
237–54
Christian, 250–54
Indian, 237–38
Muslim, 241–45
Native American, 248–49
Norse, 246–48
Old Testament on, 249–50
Persian, 239–41
Tibetan, Korean, and Mongolian,
245–46
Apollo, 8, 26, 28, 48
love myths and, 137, 146–47
matriarchal theory and, 274
morality myth and, 168
Oedipus and, 285
Underworld myth and, 221
"Apollo and Daphne," 146–47
Arachne, 166–67

339

About the Author

J. F. Bierlein is the author of *The Book of Ages,* and is currently writing his next book. Mr. Bierlein served as Director of Research at the Democratic National Committee from 1983 to 1986, after which he served as a congressional legislative assistant. Most recently, he worked as International Programs Coordinator for Northwood University in Midland, Michigan, and is now an adjunct professor in the Washington Semester Program at American University in Washington, D.C.

Multilingual, he is deeply interested in theology, existentialism, Latin American art, the study of classical Greek and Hebrew, as well as other languages. He is also active in counseling and jail ministry.

Mr. Bierlein and his wife, Heather Diehl, live in Virginia.